P9-CQF-530

Gravelight

Gravelight

MARION ZIMMER BRADLEY

A TOM DOHERTY ASSOCIATES BOOK

NEW YORK

This is a work of fiction. All the characters and events portrayed in this
novel are either fictitious or are used fictitiously.

GRAVELIGHT

A Tor Book
Published by Tom Doherty Associates, Inc.
175 Fifth Avenue
New York, NY 10010

ISBN 0-312-86503-1 (hardcover)

Printed in the United States of America

Gravelight

MORTON'S FORK,
AUGUST 14TH, 1917

This grave shall have a living monument.
—WILLIAM SHAKESPEARE

THE POWER OF THE WELLSPRING SURGED AROUND HER, even through the thick stone walls that kept her from it. The hour was late, and the mountain would have been robed in moonlight save for the summer storm boiling up through Watchman's Gap.

Attie swore under her breath as she shook the sanatorium's locked doors. How could Quentin dare to try the Wellspring and think she would not know? She could forgive him much, but she could not forgive him this. The Wellspring was hers—he'd stolen her land with his flat-lander lawyers and her brother's weakness, but he could not steal this. It was in her blood, in her mother's blood, back to the Bright Beginning. But he'd balked her at every turn, binding her with chains of law and wealth and making her powerless in his search for power.

"Quentin!" Attie's voice cracked like a whip. She slammed the heavy glass-and-oak door with the flat of her hand, knowing that wherever he was he heard her, that he must have expected her to come. Expected her to join him.

But he was wrong.

"Quentin!" Attie shouted again. The storm was through the Gap now, and the first fat drops of rain made fat dark stars on the fancy flagstone terrace.

She abandoned the front door and turned, running to the back of the building, where the kitchen door was. As she ran, she felt in the pocket of her nurse's uniform for the ring of keys. Quentin had been so pleased to have her come work for him at his fancy hospital—as if she'd had any choice, her with a daughter to feed and no man's help to command as if by right. Briefly she thought of her young daughter at home asleep in her bed. Little Melly, whose charge the Wellspring would one day be—or would have been. Already she thought it might be too late; Quentin Blackburn had flung open the sacred path to the Bright Lords with no thought for the consequences—there was no escape now, for either of them.

A bright blue-white flash of lightning illuminated the pale stone wall beside her, and, as if this were a signal, water fell from the heavens like the spill from a broached dam. The icy drench took Attie's breath away, shocking her consciousness back into the material realm, but its effect lasted only a moment. The Wellspring was roused, and the power of it made the natural world around her seem like something in a conjure-man's shew-glass—unreal. Attie moved forward as if she were underwater, and in her mind she was already within, in the vault above the Wellspring with Quentin and his loathsome congregation. Their words echoed in her inner ears:

"We call upon the Goat to command thee! Come, thou elemental prince, Undine, creature of water: Thou who was before the world was made—bornless, uncreated, exile from the elemental City! As death calls to death, as slave to master, we call thee—"

Attie shook her head, trying to drive the chanting from her mind, and as she did the fear returned, stronger than before. For a hundred generations, the Dellon women and those who'd come before them had approached this hidden Wellspring in dread and lamentation. Even now she would have begged mercy for her lover from the powers that he had so rashly awakened, but the Bright Lords were as implacable as the stony earth itself.

She reached the back door. Her stolen key opened the lock.

The darkened kitchen reverberated like a drum with the sound of rain.

The matches trembled in her hand, and she broke three before she coaxed one to light. Once the kerosene lamp was lit, the hulking shapes of the black iron stove and purring kerosene refrigerator cast shifting, looming shadows upon the whitewashed plaster walls. The hanging pots swung faintly, as if disturbed by the power in the air. Attie clutched the lamp tighter.

Carrying the fragile lantern carefully, Attie hurried through the kitchen into the dining room beyond. Lightning flared through the tall glass windows and the tables, already set for breakfast, glowed with white damask and silver plate.

Where was the entrance to his temple? *Where?* He had been so secretive. What if she could not find it?

"Quentin . . ." Attie moaned, and this time her voice held a note of defeat.

One hundred feet below the surface of the earth the liturgy approached its peak in the temple Quentin Blackburn had made. The stone of its building had once comprised the walls of a convent's chapel in France, infused with centuries of the prayers of holy virgins. The altar upon which the sacrifice lay was a thing of an even older magic; from its Egyptian temple the worn black basalt had seen the rise and fall of Imperial Rome herself.

Surrounded by the members of his black coven, Quentin Blackburn, Magister Magus of The Church of the Antique Rite, loomed over the naked woman upon the altar, the goat-horn crown upon his head, his robes open to reveal his own painted nakedness. The red-hilted knife of sacrifice was in his hand, and the consecrated blade seemed to quiver with eagerness to be about its bloody work. He had told Sarita that tonight would bring her immortality—but he had not told her how.

Around the walls, the torches that were the room's only light leapt and guttered, painting the walls with dancing shadows as his congregation whipped themselves with chant and dance to new orgiastic heights, but it was Sarita's blood that would bind the power of this Gate Between the Worlds to him . . . if the Gate accepted the sacrifice of one not of the Bloodline.

He could have had this power months ago, if the little Dellon girl had cooperated. How dare she set her foolish backwoods superstitions against the illumination of the full power of twentieth-century Occult Science?

Couldn't she see how the old world was changing? Even now, the war that was the earthly manifestation of the conflict on the Inner Planes was raging across the map of Europe, sweeping away the old order in the name of the evolution of the Superman to whom all the races of the Earth would someday bow. Once the power was his, Attie Dellon would bow down to him as well—or she would be his next gift to the Gate.

The frenzy reached its peak. Quentin raised the dagger over his head, not caring now if Sarita saw it.

"Stop!" The cry cut across the nimbus of power like a flash of cold lightning. The rhythm of the ceremony faltered; the momentum of the worshippers was lost. Quentin Blackburn raised his head and met Attie Dellon's eyes. On the altar, Sarita sat up abruptly. She pulled her ritual robe around her and stared, whimpering, at the knife in Quentin's hand.

There were two loci for the power now, and it swirled between them, pulling the man and the woman together, binding them into one great event. Silence spread out from Attie Dellon like the ripples from a stone dropped into a pool. She was dressed in white—her nursing uniform—and held a burning kerosene lantern in her hand.

"So you've come to join us, Athanais Dellon?" Quentin said, forcing a confidence into his voice that he was far from feeling.

"No." Her voice was as hard and as harsh as stone. "I've come to stop you, Quentin Blackburn."

Her body was haloed in a golden haze; it took Quentin a few moments to realize that he was seeing that halo through temporal, not spiritual, eyes. It was the light of the lantern in her hand reflecting from the smoke in the air that surrounded her.

"I warned you from the first not to trifle with the Wellspring," Attie said. "You've stolen everything else from my family, Quentin Blackburn, but you won't steal this. I warned you," she said again, and now, at last, over the perfume of the incense, Quentin could smell the smoke.

Quentin began—slowly, oh so slowly—to move toward her. In the center of the elaborately decorated temple the members of his coven milled, frightened and disorganized, turning toward the entrance that Attie blocked.

"Stand aside, woman!" Quentin barked, summoning up the power that had let him raise an encampment of The Church of the Antique Rite in this place. And Attie did move, but the mantle of a greater Power was about her now, and she curtseyed in mocking silence as she stepped away from the passage.

Half a dozen worshippers rushed into the stairwell in that instant, their elaborate ritual robes an impediment now rather than a manifestation of the occult forces at their command. A moment afterward the first screams came, as someone opened the door at the top of the stairs and a wall of oily black smoke began rolling down into the passage. Distantly, above the screams, Quentin could hear the iron tocsin of the sanatorium's fire alarm.

Wildwood Sanatorium was burning.

He ran to the door—the other door, the one whose steps led down, not up—and dragged futilely at it. It was locked, and, thinking himself clever to be so on guard, he had not brought the key down with him tonight. Tonight there was only one exit from the temple.

There was a crash behind him. Quentin whirled, searching for Attie and finding her standing before the altar, laughing madly as the spilled fuel from the lamp she'd flung ignited the altar's draperies. The roar of the flames eradicated any other sound—the storm, the shouting, the raging cthonic waters over which they stood.

"Why?" His demand was a roar of disappointment and rage.

"I warned you." He saw her lips move in soundless reproach, saw the fire that licked among her skirts, feeding on anything it could catch.

He could see the tears that coursed down her cheeks in the moment before the surviving members of the coven surged around him, pushing the two of them apart as they pleaded with him to save them where there was no deliverance possible. For one betraying instant the man broke through the mask of the Magus; in despair he shouted out his lover's name.

"Athanais!"

And then there was nothing but the fire.

ONE

A GRAVE AND PRIVATE PLACE

A traveller from the cradle to the grave
Through the dim night of this immortal day.
— PERCY BYSSHE SHELLEY

MORE THAN THREE CENTURIES AGO THE FIRST EUROPEANS had penetrated these mountains; people driven by the need to see what lay beyond the horizon of the strange new land they had come to. In the wake of these trailblazers followed those whose purpose it was to take this land and hold it; it was they who had named the place of their settlement Morton's Fork, after a churchman's judgment whose unfairness still rankled after generations.

Through the 1700s and into the nineteenth century the town flourished after its fashion, until coal was found in the West Virginia hills, coal enough to fuel a young nation's expansion—if only it could be harvested from the bones of the mountains in which it lay. And so the mining companies moved into the West Virginia mountains, bringing wealth and despotism, poverty and hope, and changing the landscape and the people forever. The corporations that owned the coal did not care how lavishly it spent men, or at what cost to the future the coal was harvested.

Morton's Fork was strangely unaffected by the wildcat growth of company towns and mine-heads that transformed and destroyed other communities; what coal the mountains of Lyonesse County held was too poor and scant to attract the attention of the Eastern robber barons. Those men who worked the mines traveled miles to do it: Morton's Fork itself slumbered on. And when the time of coal was past, the big corporations left nothing in their wake but a desolation and blight greater than their presence had caused, but Morton's Fork remained unchanged.

Four great wars did little more than the mines had to change the lives of the people who lived in those hills; in 1914, on the eve of America's entrance into the European War, there was a sanatorium built in the hills above Morton's Fork, and more than a decade later a WPA road-building project left behind a cluster of cabins that imposed a false uniformity upon the wild Appalachians. Then the world moved on, and in its wake the isolated hamlet of Morton's Fork slid back into its decades-long sleep, willing to dream the rest of the twentieth century away as it had slumbered through the nineteenth, and the eighteenth.

Neither radio nor television disturbed these sheltering hills with their rambling cover of pine and birch and laurel. The nearest library was twelve miles away, the nearest supermarket, twenty. There was no FedEx nor MTV to interrupt the even tenor of the passing days.

It was a good place to hide.

He had been driving all night, and now, several hours past dawn, the view through the convertible's windshield alternated between sharp-cut valleys still filled with July-morning mist and the abrupt darkness of pine-covered mountainsides; coal country, as beautiful and uncharitable as a rich man's daughter. Each time the car swung to follow the road, the assortment of bottles lying on their sides in the passenger footwell clanged together with a high sweet sound, and he found himself hoping one of them would break and spill. As a parched man dreams of water in the desert, he wanted to smell the liquor. It was the only constant in his life, and it had taken everything he had so eagerly given it.

Despite the craving, he hadn't opened any of the bottles yet. Perhaps he would. Perhaps a drink or two—or three—would make the highway beneath his wheels more challenging.

His name was Wycherly Ridenow Musgrave, and at the moment he had only the faintest idea where he was. Somewhere west of New York, he knew that much, but the days he'd spent behind the wheel of the little foreign car had blurred into a mosaic of road signs seen by moonlight and sunrises that revealed odd and unfamiliar landscapes. He was not lost. To be lost required a destination, and Wycherly Musgrave had none.

The dawn chill windstream pulled his coppery hair—too long; it made his father furious to see it—straight back from his forehead, and inside his expensive leather coat he shivered, but Wycherly was unwilling to stop driving even long enough to put up the Ferrari's top. If he were not driving he would have to do something else, and he didn't want to do something else. He wanted the road to be everything, to blot out thought, to destroy time.

There was an unmarked turnoff ahead. He jerked the wheel left to take it, fighting the wheel as the car slewed back and forth across the narrow road. The low-slung car responded gallantly, its racing engine skirling in protest as Wycherly downshifted and gunned it. The road was barely wide enough for it; Wycherly wondered briefly what he'd do if he met another vehicle, but it never occurred to him to slow down. He took a certain satisfaction from his easy mastery of the fast car on the difficult road; a symbol of competence in a life that normally had none. The car swerved. The bottles clanged. One of them would have to break soon.

Broken. All broken. Nothing left. The thought gave Wycherly perverse pleasure. Everything was broken now, and it was Winter who had broken it. Winter Musgrave, his perfect trophy sister, who had launched the blow that set the Musgrave family spinning like a burst piñata. The golden girl had failed, and as if her failure were a magic dagger, the web of family and privilege and *not getting caught* that the Winters and the Musgraves and the Ridenows had spun round themselves for more than a century was rent asunder, and everything began to unravel.

For a moment the Ferrari drifted slyly to the right; the wheel—as Wycherly yanked it in the opposite direction—turning with frightening freedom beneath his hands. Then the wheels found the road surface again, and bit, and held. The car snapped back along the curve of the narrow road as if it were a greyhound after a rabbit, and Wycherly's mind drifted free of the present once more.

He didn't understand most of what had happened to the Musgrave family in the last year, but he did know that last fall Kenneth Jr.—petted, pampered, perfect Kenny—had finally committed some banker's crime that the authorities had taken notice of. Now the young prince—

the aging, bloated, deteriorating prince, Wycherly emended viciously—had lost his Wall Street throne and his Wall Street salary. He and his perfect Patricia had been forced to give up all their expensive privileges and move home to Wychwood, living off his parents' charity, and the legal bills yet to come would put even more of a strain on the family finances.

At the same time—as if money had been his lifeblood in truth—the Musgrave patriarch, Kenneth Sr., had fallen gravely ill, a series of strokes knocking him from his Jovian throne and forcing him to retreat to Wychwood as a wounded animal would seek the shelter of its cave. Now the Musgrave patriarch was a ruined colossus, his remaining lifespan a thing to be measured in months.

Father was dying.

And Wycherly had fled. Because he needed—Because he needed—

He needed to know if he was supposed to die, too, and no one at Wychwood would tell him that. In the Musgrave family, facts were often a matter of opinion, and all the Musgraves were good at keeping secrets.

Echoes of fear and anger made him press harder on the accelerator, and the convertible was going much too fast for the road when it shot over the crest of the hill. For a moment it hung weightless and tractionless upon the air. Wycherly, not understanding had happened, ground the pedal harder into the floor: When the car struck the ground again, the forward thrust caught him by surprise, and in that fatal moment of inattention the car slewed right instead of left—away from the road entirely.

There wasn't even a guardrail.

Wycherly felt the car's wheels leave the pavement again, and instead of the brief hang time, this time the sensation went on and on. In the brief moment of weightless fall there came a menacing sense of peace, and then the implacable reality of thrust and gravity.

Impact came an instant before he expected it, swift and vicious as the executioner's blade.

In the days when Morton's Fork had been a flourishing community, this building had been a schoolhouse, and even now its red brick walls preserved something of that past. But now the building possessed both electricity and running water instead of a wood stove and outhouse; expensive modern furniture mingled with the charming country antiques that had replaced the blackboard and the rows of desks, and the spacious great room that had been created within the shell of the one-room schoolhouse was encircled on three sides by a living loft. Antique stained glass replaced all the ground-floor windows, as if the person who had made this place had a more than ordinary need for privacy, even in this enchanted, isolated place.

Her name was Melusine Dellon—Sinah to her friends, "Melly" to those who wanted to pretend to know her well. The first group had never been large, but the second was growing bigger every day.

At this exact moment, Sinah was "almost famous," meaning that while she was already more well-known than most people became over the course of their lives, so far it was only to a small group of people— Broadway producers, theater critics, casting agents. This December that select circle would widen to every person in the world who could turn on, download, or read the news, when Castle Rock Films released *Zero Sum Game*, the film adaptation of Ellis Gardner's successful Broadway play. On December 18, Sinah Dellon would make the jump from moderately-well-known Broadway actress to certified Hollywood star.

And instead of being on the Coast, working her career, she was here.

Sinah looked around the room. If she were a proper movie star, Sinah supposed, she would be traveling with an entourage, and have a personal assistant to see to the business of unearthing experts and persuading them to explain things to her. But the Hollywood fast track seemed so . . . overblown, in comparison with its opposite number back East. Or, as *Variety* still referred to it, "*Legitimate* theater."

But Hollywood, once taken up, was not so easily dropped. There was a magic in being in front of the camera, in filtering out everyone else's emotions to concentrate on the director, taking from him, feeding him, searching for that addictive moment of transcendence.

She wondered if that was such a healthy thing to want, really. But if it wasn't, Sinah didn't know what other kind of life to wish for. The thought of turning back to the beginning and starting over again as a stockbroker or a marine biologist was something she couldn't even imagine. She was what she was.

A freak. Who had turned her freakish, unnatural empathy into a fast track in the dramatic arts, and now, like the lady who went for a ride on a tiger, she wasn't quite sure how to get out of the situation.

With a sigh, Sinah flung down the copy of *Variety* she'd been pretending to read and rubbed her temples, at last acknowledging the headache she'd been fighting all day. All around her, the home she had made mocked her with the memories of the haven she'd thought it would be. From the moment she'd come to Morton's Fork, everything had gone wrong—as if now, at last, it was time to pay for all the undeserved good fortune that had followed her for all her twenty-eight years of life.

God help her, she'd thought becoming an actress would solve her problems, not make them worse—and it had been so easy . . .

On her eighteenth birthday she'd boarded the bus for New York. Unlike so many other hopefuls, her time waiting tables was mercifully brief. Within six months Sinah was working steadily, though it would be another five years before her first starring role. Then she'd been cast in *Zero Sum Game,* which had run for almost two years before it had been sold to Hollywood, and Jason Kennedy—its star—had been part of the package, signed to recreate his role for the movie. Jason had possessed clout enough to specify that Sinah was a part of the deal, too.

Everyone had told her it was a stroke of luck, but she'd known it would happen from the moment the negotiations began. Melusine Dellon had been the very best at what she did for so long that praise had become another form of abuse—because the praise wasn't for *her,* or for anything she did, but for a simple freak of nature. She *was* Adrienne, just as she'd been Juliet, Maggie the Cat, Antigone, Hedda Gabler. Sinah was always perfect for the role.

Each role. Every role. Any role. Except, it seemed, the one of daughter.

On August 14, 1969, Athanais Dellon, of Morton's Fork, West Virginia, had given birth to Melusine Dellon, father unknown, and died. Sinah had the documents; she'd trusted the information implicitly. But when at long last she'd come home to reclaim her history, everyone here in Morton's Fork said Athanais Dellon had never existed.

It really didn't matter if her expectations of being welcomed had been unrealistic. When she'd arrived to take possession of her rebuilt schoolhouse, Sinah had felt as if she'd walked into an episode of *The Twilight Zone.* There were no Dellons in Morton's Fork, people said. No one named Athanais Dellon had ever lived here. It would have been easy to write the whole thing off to stiff-necked rural pride, except that there was more to it than that. They were lying. Lying to her, hating her, trying to drive her down into madness and darkness; Sinah Dellon knew that better than she knew her own—reclaimed—name.

If she'd been smart she would have let matters slide right then, maybe even gone away again. But Sinah had always been a fighter—she'd announced herself to be Athanais' daughter and dared them to go on with their lies.

So they'd shut her out, and left her to her lonely splendor here in this wild beautiful place. Just as her foster parents had. Just as everyone who knew the truth about her did.

She didn't want to think about that, but what else was there to think about? Losing her mind? Dying? The taint in her blood—the monstrous gift that her dead mother must have shared, else how could the local people hate her so?

The carefully crafted social mask that Sinah wore even while alone crumbled, and she groped for a tissue to blot away the sudden, aching tears. *Tainted blood.* It sounded like the title of a cheap thriller, but it was the truth she'd fought against acknowledging all these years. Normal people couldn't do what Sinah Dellon could.

Normal people couldn't read minds.

She'd never known a time when she couldn't do it: the baby in the crib, absorbing its foster mother's thoughts and feelings with her touch; the schoolgirl with the answer to every test, who knew all her classmates' secrets—and told them, before she'd learned better. The word for what she was existed only in books, not in the real world.

Telepath. Mind reader. *Filthy prying snooping freak no daughter of mine monster—* Sinah choked back a sob. She'd prayed for the gift to leave her, but it had only gotten stronger as she'd gotten older, until she didn't need to touch someone to read his or her mind, though touch brought the sharpest images. With her gift, she could be anyone's dream girl, a perfect mirror. It had brought her success on Broadway, in Hollywood. . . .

But when she wasn't being a perfect reflection, who *was* Sinah Dellon? Here in her dream house she could be only herself, but she felt strangely empty, restless. As if, without someone else's emotions to mirror, she was nothing at all.

No. That can't be true.

But she thought it might be. That the tiny spark of individuality that called itself "Sinah" had already been ground away to nothing by the imprint of other minds, and that soon even the consciousness of that fact would be extinguished forever.

No. That isn't true. I won't let it be true. There must be others like her here—others of her bloodline who had also inherited her gift.

Unless they were all dead of the same "gift" that tormented her. Dead and gone and she was the last.

Wycherly's shout of primitive terror ripped him from his twilight dream and returned him to a world where the sun struck like a hammer, making the world dissolve into a red-lit kaleidoscope of pain. But he did not fear the pain as much as he feared whatever lay below the surface of consciousness, and so he forced his eyes to open, feeling the shock of the pain as a thousand burning pulses through his body.

When he sucked a deep lungful of air, he felt the sullen ache of blossoming bruises over his chest and ribs and the warning pressure of the dashboard against his thighs. The edges of the footwell were folded almost tenderly around his extended legs; there was a thick reek of liquor—the bottles had broken at last—mingled with the sharp, dangerous scent of spilled gasoline. With infinite care, Wycherly turned his head—and was stopped.

His cheek came to rest upon the rough bark of a tree trunk that plunged through the center of the windshield. All around him the crumbled safety glass lay like thrown rice at a wedding, and the chrome and steel frame of the windshield was twisted into a mere decorative ribbon. The headrest at the back of his seat had been torn away by the forward thrust of the trunk; the tree had passed just above his shoulder, a few inches away from his right ear, a raw splintered spike of wood as thick as Wycherly's thigh.

It could have killed him.

For a moment his consciousness of every other pain vanished as Wycherly realized it had only missed his head by inches.

I could be dead. For the first time in his life, the thought repelled him. Dead—here, now, with all his promises unkept and decisions unmade. He looked down the hill. The sun was just rising above the trees, but the summer heat was already beginning to build. Below, the valley was still in deep shadow, its floor was shrouded by mist, suggesting that water lay somewhere below. The alcohol, the waking dream, and seventy-two hours without sleep coalesced into a conviction that Camilla was waiting for him across the river of death, and that he must make his peace with her or face worse than death when the time came.

The bizarre fantasy faded almost at once, leaving behind the odd, urgent feeling that there really was something he must do before he could safely die. Slowly, Wycherly began the painful process of prying himself out of the car. He found that he didn't seem to be badly hurt—a bruise over his left eye, a gash along his leg from something that had sliced open his Dockers. It had bled freely but didn't even seem to ache at the moment.

The driver's-side door was jammed shut, and it took him several painful minutes to pull himself backward across the trunk before he could slither free, only at the last minute remembering to grab his leather shoulder bag. Its surface was dark with spilled liquor.

He rested his hands on the driver's-side door while he looked around. The nose of the little car was pointed down the slope; the convertible was wedged securely between a large rock and a small stand of pines. The rock and several of the trees were smeared with the bright scarlet of the Ferrari's paint. It must have ricocheted off them before settling. The angle it was at now suggested it had still been airborne when it hit.

Gasoline and oil spread beneath the car in a glistening puddle oddly reminiscent of blood, and the bottom of the hill was a very long way down. Gingerly, Wycherly reached out and touched the splintered tree trunk, every muscle protesting the movement. He could see now that the bark was weathered and peeling; a fallen tree, wedged among the others at the precise angle to skewer him like a butterfly on an entomologist's pin.

Well, that's totaled. I wonder if I have any insurance?

Wycherly patted himself down automatically, finding his wallet but failing to turn up either a driver's license or an insurance card. Experience told him that he probably didn't have either one—hadn't his license been revoked a few months ago after the latest DWI conviction? Wycherly suspected it had, which would account for the lack of insurance. He looked back at the Ferrari again, wondering with a certain pleased and distant malice if it was even his car. Perhaps it was Kenny's. Perhaps he had stolen it.

He was lucky to have hit the pines and not gone all the way to the bottom. He was lucky the car hadn't rolled.

He'd been lucky. Wycherly contemplated the unfamiliar concept. Lucky.

He wondered where on earth he was.

He wanted a drink.

Wycherly shuddered and turned away, starting his climb back up the hill to safety and the road.

* * *

Half a day's drive north of New York City, along the eastern bank of the Hudson River, lies Amsterdam County, home of Taghkanic College. The college's nearest neighbors are the town of Glastonbury and a small artist's colony that seeks anonymity for its residents. The college was founded in 1714 and lies between the railroad tracks and the river, a location easy to miss unless one knows the area well. Taghkanic is a liberal arts college of the sort that once flourished in this country before a college diploma became only the overture to and preparation for a job. It exists to this day on the terms of its original charter, and has never accepted one penny of government support to cover its operating costs, choosing to remain independent first from Crown and Royal Governor and later from the representatives of the fledgling United States.

But a changing economic climate has forced the closure and assimilation of most of the private colleges in the United States, until only a handful of such privileged and expensive relics remain. Taghkanic does not owe its survival to the generosity of its alumni or the foresight of its trustees but to its affiliation with a most peculiar institution: the Margaret Beresford Bidney Memorial Psychic Science Research Laboratory, founded in 1921 by a bequest from the estate of Margaret Beresford Bidney, class of 1868.

Like so many of those who sought their loved ones amid the ghosts of the aftermath of the Insurrection of the Southern States, Margaret Bidney was a Spiritualist, a follower of the Fox Sisters of Hydeville, New York. In later life, Miss Bidney's interests broadened to include the Cayce work and Theosophy, and eventually, as a disciple of William Seabrook, the whole broad field of parapsychology and the Unseen World. She never married, and when she died, her entire fortune went to fund research into the psychic sciences—including a prize of one million dollars to the individual who conclusively provided proof of paranormal abilities. The prize has never been claimed.

From its inception, the Laboratory—or, as it came informally to be known, the Bidney Institute—was funded independently of the College, though offering courses in psychology and parapsychology to the Taghkanic students and working with the college to provide one of the country's few degree programs in parapsychology. Nevertheless, the Taghkanic trustees had been attempting to claim the entire Bidney bequest on behalf of Taghkanic College for more than fifty years and were on the verge of success when Colin MacLaren accepted an appointment as director of the Institute in the early seventies.

When Dr. MacLaren came to the Institute, it was on the verge of closing. Though the height of the anti-occult backlash was still twenty years in the future, occultism as science had received one of its not-infrequent death blows, and parapsychology was not far behind. The dark side of the Age of Aquarius had become more evident in recent years, and less than five years previously Thorne Blackburn, Magick's most notorious advocate, had vanished in a lurid ritual that left one woman dead, Blackburn gone, and a number of unanswered questions.

Colin MacLaren changed all that. Publisher, lecturer, parapsychologist, he held the opinion that Magick and Science were both fruitful fields of study, and that Mankind could not be understood without the use both of Science and of Science's dark twin: the Occult. MacLaren maintained that there should be no distinction made between occultism and parapsychology when studying the paranormal—that if anything, the occultists should have the edge since they had been studying the Unseen World for centuries and attempting to distill a scientific method of dealing with its effects.

Pragmatist and born administrator, MacLaren hurled himself wholeheartedly into the work of winnowing the deadwood at the Institute and turning its focus toward documentation and standardization. Under his guidance the Bidney Institute became an international clearing house for research into the irrational truths of human perception. As the Age of Aquarius reinvented itself to become simply The New Age, MacLaren's steady guidance kept the Institute from following popular culture into a frenzy of crystal points and channeling. By the time MacLaren left the Institute at the end of the eighties the specter of its discontinuation had vanished like expended ectoplasm, and it became clear to the disappointed trustees of Taghkanic College that their rich but unwanted foster child would be around until the time Hell froze over—an event that the staff of the Bidney Institute intended, in any event, to measure.

The beautiful Federalist campus drowsed in the muggy heat of a Hudson Valley summer. Pollen and humidity gave the air a glistening shimmer and the rows of apple trees which covered and surrounded the campus were in radiant summer leaf. Although it was June, a month in which most private colleges—which closed early and opened late—would be easily likened to ghost towns, there was still a great deal of activity on the campus: The Institute operated year-round. Its non-faculty staff enjoyed the quiet of a campus without students, and its associated faculty—technically members of Taghkanic's Psychology Department—used the time to generate the "publish or perish" projects common to academia and Science both.

Dylan Palmer was typical of the "new breed" of faculty who had come up under Colin MacLaren. A 1982 graduate of Taghkanic College, he had gone on to pursue the College's doctoral program in parapsychology, and then returned to the Institute to teach. He was a professor in the Indiana Jones mold, being tall, blond, handsome, easygoing, and occasionally heroic. A researcher by profession and a ghost-hunter by avocation, Dylan's primary field of interest was personality transfers and survivals—or, in more mundane parlance, hauntings.

Dylan taught the undergraduate Introduction to Occult Psychology course that Professor MacLaren had pioneered, as well as handling his share of the usual influx of inquiries and requests that occupied the Institute's working year.

But he saved his summers for ghosts.

"Here it is," Dylan announced, spreading the West Virginia map out on his hastily cleared desk.

Dylan's office, like its occupant, possessed a rumpled and friendly informality. There was a *Ghostbusters* movie poster on the back of the door, and another one over the desk.

"Morton's Fork, Lyonesse County, West Virginia."

His glasses and the gold ring in his ear glinted in the overhead lights as Dylan bent over the map. In his rugby jersey and baggy jeans, he looked more like one of the students than one of the teachers.

His companion peered at the map over his shoulder. She presented a far more professional appearance than Dylan did, even garbed in a simple blouse and tailored slacks—and a cardigan worn against the Institute's over-enthusiastic summer air conditioning.

Truth Jourdemayne was not a teacher at Taghkanic College; she worked exclusively for the Institute as a statistical parapsychologist, the person ultimately responsible for rendering the findings of all the others into graphs and charts and dry tables of comparisons. Until recently, the most exciting thing in her life had been the chance to design an experiment to compile a statistical baseline for incidents of clairsentient perception. That had changed on the day that Truth had finally acknowledged that she was Thorne Blackburn's daughter.

Black-haired and grey-eyed, Truth Jourdemayne did not much physically resemble her golden-haired—and infamous—father, Thorne Blackburn. Blackburn had been at the forefront of the previous generation's Occult Revival, and had claimed to be a *hero* in the Greek sense; a half-divine son of the Shining Ones, the Celtic Old Gods. When her mother had died in an accident during a magickal ritual at Thorne's Shadow's Gate estate in the Hudson Valley and Thorne had vanished, it had taken Truth almost a quarter of a century to come to terms with the bereavement.

It had taken even longer for her to accept that Thorne's boasts were no more than the literal truth, and that Truth herself was not quite human. *Sidhe* magic and Earth magic made an uneasy alliance in Thorne Blackburn's daughter; each time she reached out for her inheritance, it seemed that she must choose afresh which horse to ride. Decide whether to be human, or . . . not.

Through the years, Truth had managed to accept everything else about her Blackburn heritage but that. It was the one thing she had never discussed with Dylan: that Thorne's claims of *sidhe* blood were not claim, but fact. That its ever-present inhumanity lived in her very bones, the mocking ghost of a bloodline that saw humanity as clever and incomprehensible children, barely worthy of notice—that thought of human emotions as toys, and manipulation of human lives as sport. Even diluted as the blood ran in her veins, it still lured Truth with the promise of power if she embraced its path.

But there was no more haven for her among her distant kindred than she had found among humans. She was an outsider. She always had been. To pretend that things would ever be any different was to open a gateway to endless grief.

Automatically, Truth pushed the intrusive thought away. It didn't help to dwell upon it. There wasn't anything she could do to change things, after all—no one had ever yet figured out a way for children to choose their parents. And she had to admit that she probably wouldn't change parents if she could, though it did make things difficult sometimes.

"Stony Bottom? Clover Lick?" Truth frowned at the map.

"No. Look here where I'm pointing, between Pocahontas and Randolph Counties. There's Lyonesse," Dylan said.

Truth peered intently at his finger. "Astolat River, Big Heller, Little Heller Creek. . . ." The names were tiny type on an area that seemed to be mostly composed of national parks and wilderness areas.

"That's it," Dylan said encouragingly.

Truth straightened up. "Do we have permission to go there?" she asked dubiously.

"We don't need it," Dylan said, "but as a matter of fact I've written to a number of folks—the mayor of Pharaoh, the Lyonesse County Executive Director, the President of the Historic Arts Preservation Trust—and none of them have any objection to our paying Morton's Fork a visit in a few weeks, once I've cleaned up my end-of-year paperwork."

"Whether the natives like it is another matter," Truth commented almost to herself. "People tend to have an inbred aversion to being treated like goldfish, Dylan."

The tall blond man accepted her rebuke in good humor. "And members of isolated mountain communities in particular. We'll just have to see what happens, but if we get any cooperation at all, the results could be fascinating. Once I started charting what I was able to get from published sources onto this big survey map—" Dylan motioned toward the wall of office, where a foam-mounted map of Central Lyonesse County studded with small colored pins hung, "As you can see, Morton's Fork is the center of unexplained activity for a fifty-mile radius. There's got to be a lot more going on there than they've reported."

"Maybe even ghosts," Truth teased. Dylan grinned at her.

Truth glanced back at the map. The blue pins were for hauntings. Since the first Europeans arrived in those mountains in the seventeenth century, the area that would later be known as Lyonesse County had possessed the reputation of being haunted. Headless horsemen, spectral soldiers, Indians, ghostly maidens, and more, were a staple commodity in Morton's Fork, along with their attendant murders.

Red—that was poltergeists. When Nicholas Taverner came to Morton's Fork in the 1920s to gather material for his book on Appalachian folklore, *Ha'ants, Spooks, and Fetchmen,* he noted that the place seemed to be populated by whole families of poltergeists. Poltergeist activity—more usually these days called RSPK phenomena, for Recurrent Spontaneous Psychokinesis—usually centered on a person, not a place, and usually ended when its locus matured, as the usual loci for poltergeist activity were girls just entering puberty.

Green stood for UFO sightings. While many argued for a purely mechanical, science-based explanation of UFO phenomena, the stories the self-defined contactees related belonged far more to the continuum of "fairy abductions" and the lore of the Wild Hunt than they did to some rational, reasonable *Star Trek* future. The fact of the matter was that UFOs and parapsychological phenomena seemed to go hand in hand.

In all, the map seemed to hold plenty of material for investigation by any number of parapsychologists.

"Which of the students are we taking?" Truth asked.

"Rowan and Ninian. You remember them."

Truth nodded. Only the fact that slots in the graduate parapsych program were so hotly contested explained Rowan Moorcock and Ninian Blake's continued toleration of one another—both were aware that a prima donna attitude could get either of them relegated to less desirable positions in the sixteen-place program, or dismissed from it entirely.

"That should make for an interesting six weeks," Truth commented. "I remember I spent an hour and a half explaining to Rowan about statistical averages and why I didn't want her participating in my study—where would I get if I included known strong psychics?—last year and she still threw a fit. Ninian's sweet, though."

"Ah, do I have a rival?" Dylan said jokingly.

Truth looked down at the emerald-and-pearl ring on her left hand. She and Dylan had set a December wedding date—this was June, and the closer December came, the more uncertain she felt.

When she'd first met Dylan Palmer, Truth had been young, confused, and rigidly obsessed with maintaining the distinctions between magick and science. Anything that seemed likely to cross over the boundary— like Dylan's ghost-hunting, or his interest in the esoteric borderlands of parapsychology, Truth had dealt with through harsh intolerance. But with her acceptance of her father's legacy, Truth had become a citizen of those realms that Dylan only mapped. Magick had invaded her life— now Dylan, with his insistence on cause preceding effect and a rational explanation for every event, seemed to be the rationalistic, hidebound one.

One of us has to change. And I know I won't. Not again. How could she, when her beliefs were not only the evidence of her own eyes, but the result of accepting a sacred trust to walk the boundaries between Light and Dark, down a path grey as mist? And how could Dylan commit himself to something that strange and magnificent, with no more assurance of its reality than her own bare word and the evidence of his unreliable human senses?

Our relationship is doomed, Truth thought gloomily.

"Truth?" Dylan said. She looked up, and met his summer-blue eyes.

"No," Truth said. "No rival."

Dylan frowned. "I know it doesn't make for much of a pre-wedding honeymoon—six weeks in an RV in Appalachia, measuring spooks. Would you rather stay on campus? You could ask your sister to come and visit; use my place. . . ."

"Light's with Michael."

Light Winwood was Truth's half-sister, another of Thorne Blackburn's children. For Light, there *was* no barrier between this world and the next, and her uncontrolled psychic powers had been a harrowing burden to her for most of her life. But now Light had found safe harbor with Michael Archangel. He helped Light to build walls around her gift and shut it out, and although Truth respected Michael Archangel, their ethical positions inevitably ensured that the two of them would clash. To Truth's regret, she had never really gotten to know her half-sister; she and Light grew farther apart as time passed—and Truth could see no way to bridge that gap.

"You could invite her to visit by herself," Dylan said patiently, and Truth shook her head.

"My place is with you, *kemosabe.* Besides, there's something odd about this pattern . . ."

Truth walked over to the survey map on the wall. With the aid of long practice—Dylan had been planning this expedition for well over a year—she deciphered the shaded green surface with its nests of contour lines, and the rainbow of push-pins that studded its center. Blue for hauntings, green for UFOs . . .

Truth peered at the arc of red pins that straggled down the side of the mountain away from Watchman's Gap. She knew—because she had helped Dylan mark the map—that the events the red pins represented were spread over most of a century. It looked, in defiance of conventional wisdom, that this time RSPK activity focused on a place, using the people who lived there like so many unwitting lightning rods.

And then there were the black pins. They were the fewest of all, marking as they did the disappearances recorded in the newspapers that did not come with any aura of mundane foul play or spectral intervention. Just people who . . . vanished. There was a small red X inked at the center of the ragged circle of pins.

"Dylan, what's this mark?" Truth pointed.

Dylan came over and stood behind her, looking over her shoulder at the map. "Wildwood Sanatorium. I marked it because Taverner gives it an entire chapter in his book—according to his informants, two wizards had a duel up in Watchman's Gap, drawing the attention of the Almighty, who struck them both down and burned the sanatorium to the ground. The sanatorium, incidentally, burned in 1917."

"A little late for wizards," Truth mused. "But your missing persons seem to center right around the place. What did Taverner say about that?"

"Only that a dragon lives in Watchman's Gap." Dylan shrugged, dismissing personal investment in the belief. "He was a folklorist, not a scientist—and unfortunately, he died in the sixties, so there's no way of going back to him and seeing if he remembers more about Morton's Fork than he put in his book—which is all too likely."

"Pity," Truth said. She looked back at the map. "Does it strike you that this place is a little too good to be true—from an investigator's point of view, I mean?"

Dylan put his arms around Truth and turned her to face him.

"Well, if it turns out to be some sort of locals-pulling-a-fast-one-on-the-strangers sort of thing, proof of that would be worth writing up as well—and then we can give Rowan and Ninian a quarter to go to the movies, and . . ."

Truth tilted her face up so that Dylan could kiss her, trying to share his lighthearted mood. She did not fear the Unseen World, and she could certainly handle anything Morton's Fork could throw at her, from "noisy ghosts" to little green men.

No, it was the so-called real world that she feared. She loved Dylan, but she could see nothing ahead for the two of them but pain.

TWO

SECRETS OF THE GRAVE

O me, why have they not buried me deep enough?
Is it kind to have made me a grave so rough,
Me, that was never a quiet sleeper?
— ALFRED, LORD TENNYSON

THE BATTERED AND ANCIENT FORD TRUCK MIGHT—BY some stretch of charity and the imagination—be called red, but there its kinship with the sleek Italian machine Wycherly had just ruined ended. It shuddered and bounced and wheezed along the narrow mountain road at a brisk thirty-five miles per hour, and its flat bed and wooden slat sides were something out of a fifty-year-old photo.

Wycherly sat carefully upright on the battered, blanket-covered bench-seat, his bag balanced on his knees. He tried to shut out his present situation, but the attempt wasn't working very well.

It wasn't that the situation was out of control. He trusted that—it was what he lived with. But the situation had passed into the control of others, and that Wycherly couldn't bear.

At least he'd gotten away from what was left of the Ferrari.

The Ford had been the first thing that had come by once Wycherly had reached the road above the wreck. He'd accepted the driver's offer of a lift to the nearest telephone without a second thought. The ninety-minute trip gave Wycherly's headache time to fully establish itself, and was enough time for the first faint intimations of a hangover to appear on his horizon. He almost wished he'd stayed with the wreck.

Almost.

Occupied with his misery, Wycherly hardly noticed when the truck came to a stop. He'd seen no sign that they were approaching a city, only the slow unfolding of the wild landscape.

"Here you are, mister. This is Morton's Fork," his rescuer said at last.

Roused from his thoughts, Wycherly looked around.

No. He has to be joking.

Morton's Fork looked like something out of an old photograph. The place seemed to consist in its entirety of a dispirited straggle of wood-framed buildings that clung to the side of the hill as if disputing with the pinewood for possession of the land. The one exception was the combination gas station and garage across the road from the other buildings. Wycherly glanced at it briefly—the area was filled with junked cars, none readily identifiable as having been built more recently than 1963—and turned his attention back to the other structures.

There was a general store—the signs in the window said PELTS BOUGHT and FAX—with an almost-archetypal collection of sitting locals grouped upon its porch, a narrow post office with American flag, and two or three other buildings whose purpose did not seem immediately definable. The sign above the post office door said MORTON'S FORK, WEST VIRGINIA.

West Virginia. Appalachia: a world of poverty light-years away from the universe of debutante balls and sporting gentry that made up Wycherly's previous exposure to the South.

It didn't seem far enough away, somehow, for all the driving he'd done—and in another way, there was no place on Earth he could have gone that would be farther from Wychwood on the North Shore of Long Island, New York. *Poor white trash.* The label came easily to his mind. That was what the people here were.

And what was he? Rich white trash?

"Mister?" the driver said again, as if perhaps Wycherly hadn't heard him.

"Yes," Wycherly said shortly.

The driver—they might have been introduced, but Wycherly hadn't bothered to remember his name—looked at him, and Wycherly reached into his bag and pulled out his wallet, extracting the first bill his fingers touched. The man accepted it and peered at the fifty for a moment as if he'd never seen one before.

Gritting his teeth, Wycherly forced the door open, ignoring the protests of abused muscles. The stiffness was only going to get worse. The ground seemed a long way down.

Once he was on his feet, pain crawled like electric snakes up his legs, into his back. He glanced to the side and saw that a few feet beyond the last building even the crumbling paving ended, and the road became the rutted pale dirt of the hills.

The driver was still looking at him.

"For your trouble," Wycherly said, indicating the bill. Didn't the people here have even the rudiments of civilization? His head hurt and he wanted a drink. At least he'd be able to buy liquor at the store.

"This'n's too much for just bringing you up here. H'ain't you got nothing smaller?" the driver said, holding it back out to him.

Enlightenment dawned. The driver didn't trust the money. *Probably thinks it's counterfeit,* Wycherly decided, taking it back. It wasn't worth arguing about; and the man *had* stopped for him in the first place. Wycherly looked through his wallet again, passing over the tens and pulling out a twenty. "Will this do?"

The local looked at it dubiously, as if this note, too, were not acceptable.

"I still need somebody to haul my car to the nearest garage," Wycherly snapped, losing patience. "I don't suppose I can hire you to do that?"

The man grinned, exposing large yellow teeth and shoving the money into his pocket as though Wycherly's question had settled some lingering doubt in his mind.

"Well, you *could* call to Buckhannon for the wrecker, but I don't know that she's going to get you'm up that grade whether she comes or not. Might be you need to see if Caleb's a mind to bring his team out." There was secret delight in the local's voice.

If he'd had the energy, Wycherly would have flayed the man verbally for amusing himself at his expense, but he was tired, in pain, and far from home. Most of all, Wycherly didn't want his family to know where he was, even as he suspected that when the police—of whatever stripe— came to inspect that crash, their actions would put him beyond Kenneth Musgrave's power to save.

Arrest. Jail this time, even though no one had been hurt.

This time.

The memory of Camilla Redford rose up instantly before his mind's eye like all of the Furies; Wycherly shuddered, stepping back from the truck.

He needed a drink. Enough playing around. He *really* needed a drink.

"Francis?"

The new voice seemed to come out of nowhere; the shock of hearing it told Wycherly he was more badly hurt than he'd thought. Carefully he turned toward the speaker; it was one of the locals who'd been gathered in front of the general store.

The newcomer, like Francis, had the faintly malnourished, inbred look of West Virginia's coal-mining country, a pocket of poverty in the midst of Rustbelt affluence. Pale blue eyes and skin as light as Wycherly's own proclaimed kinship with the Celtic forbears who had settled this unforgiving land in the eighteenth century, but there the resemblance ended. Wycherly Musgrave was the end product of money: expensive health care, expensive nutrition. He looked younger than his thirty-two years; the body he abused so casually had the resilience to endure what he did to it. He suspected the stranger was near to his own age, and the thought gave Wycherly an odd, uncomfortable feeling that might almost have been pity.

The newcomer's remark had been addressed to the weathered truck driver. Francis. *His mother probably named him after the talking mule he so resembles,* Wycherly thought pettishly.

"Smacked up his fancy furriner car on the overlook to Frenchy's Hollow," Francis said. "I expect he'll be needing the loan of Caleb's team to get her out." As if satisfied that Wycherly was now someone else's problem, Francis drove off, leaving Wycherly and the stranger standing alone in the street.

Wycherly glared at the other man balefully, somehow at a loss for words. The man stared back at him with equal suspicion, and Wycherly realized with a sudden shrewdness how he must look: bruised and bloody from the crash, pale and disheveled and possibly not quite sane.

He couldn't afford to seem out of control. The stakes were too high. If his family should somehow find him . . .

"I have to say I'd be grateful for Mr., ah, Caleb's help. If, um, Francis hadn't come along, I'd still be sitting on the edge of the road. I'd hate just to leave my car there." *Especially if there's something in it that ties it to me.* "So I really need to get my car . . ." *Towed to some place it can be worked on? Or just hidden before the highway patrol finds it?* Wycherly forced what he hoped was a friendly smile. "And I'd really be awfully grateful for any assistance you could give me." His words faltered to a stop, and still the other man said nothing.

Wycherly hated to make these false conciliating speeches; he always had. They were an admission of powerlessness, and more than many things, Wycherly craved the power he knew he was too weak to grasp. Wycherly ran a hand through his hair distractedly, wincing when his fingers encountered a tender spot. More than anything just now he wanted oblivion, and he wasn't particular about how he got it.

"I need it towed here, I guess," he repeated. "If someone can do that."

At last, as if having wound his way through some complex process of decision, the man smiled and held out his hand.

"Looks like you need more than that. I'm Evan Starking." He pronounced the name as if it were two separate words: Star King. "My pa owns the general store."

Wycherly nodded. There didn't seem much to say about that.

"Why don't you come inside and set, and I'll send my sister Luned over to Caleb." Evan hesitated. "It's going to take most of the day to get your car up the hill with Caleb's ox team, mister, so if you're in a hurry . . ."

"No," Wycherly said, taking Evan's hand. The palm was harsh and callused against his own. "I haven't got anywhere else to go." He followed Evan, past the waiting loiterers, inside the general store.

For all its external shabbiness, the inside of the general store was neatly stocked; dark and cool, its shelves were crammed with merchandise whose modern labels looked garish and out of place in their antiquated surroundings.

Evan sent Luned off in search of Caleb—Wycherly got a jumbled impression of a young street urchin, blonde and none too clean—and once she was gone, Evan reached beneath the counter and pulled out a blue spatterware cup and a familiarly shaped bottle. The battered condition of its label suggested it did not contain its original contents, and it was half-filled with a liquid about the color of gasoline.

"There's a washroom in the back if you want to get cleaned up, mister, but you look like you could use a little stiffener first." Evan uncorked the bottle. The raw scent of alcohol was potent on the morning air. Moonshine.

He half filled the cup. Wycherly took the bottle away from him and filled it to the brim, then picked up the cup. The main ingredient of shine was usually cane sugar—sometimes with the addition of arsenic or lead—and Wycherly could smell a candy-like sweetness hovering on the surface of the liquor smell.

He felt every cell in his body contract with the craving, and his hand shook slightly as he raised the cup to his lips, drinking down the caustic, overproof spirit as though it were water.

The panicky clutch of deprivation receded as the seductive, toxic warmth of the drink spread through him. The shine seared his mouth and throat, as if it were in fact the gasoline it so resembled, and its arrival in his stomach masked any hunger pangs Wycherly might have felt with a sullen hurting burn. When he was sure it would stay down, Wycherly drew a deep breath. Evan was regarding him with some respect.

"Last time a flatlander tried that, he fell over backwards and we had to sweep him out with the sawdust," Evan said.

Wycherly smiled faintly.

"I'm Wycherly Musgrave," he said, as if that were some sort of explanation. One cup of whiskey was far from enough to get him drunk—to make him drunker, he scrupulously amended—but it had taken the edge off the demons. "And I'd like to buy a bottle of whatever that is, if you've got any to sell."

Evan looked thoughtful. "I guess you'd have to talk to Mal Tanner about that. All we sell here in the store is beer."

"I'll take a couple of six-packs then." Wycherly laid a ten on the counter. "Thanks for the drink. And now I guess I'd better wash up."

An hour or so later Wycherly was sitting on the front porch of the general store gazing out at downtown Morton's Fork.

The morning's loiterers had vanished, and no one had come to replace them. No policeman came, either, and Wycherly began to believe that none would come. He'd escaped his well-deserved punishment—from the laws of Man as well as the laws of physics—one more time.

Wycherly felt like an actor playing a part. He was wearing a painfully-new pair of work pants bought in the store to replace his shredded and bloody pair and was working his way slowly through the six-pack of beer. He was nicely insulated now, in momentary charity with the world. His aches and pains were a distant thing, as long as he didn't move too much.

There was no blinding revelation, no sudden stroke of insight, but it slowly occurred to Wycherly that as he looked at Morton's Fork he was looking at his last chance.

He glanced down at the beer in his hand, then at his wristwatch. It was a little after ten o'clock in the morning. He'd totaled his car and then drunk six ounces of moonshine and five cans of Rolling Rock, and now he was probably going to drink five more. And he knew just as he knew that the sun would eventually set and rise again that he'd go on drinking—and driving, too, if he could get his hands on another car.

And it would kill him. If not next time, then the time after that.

Wycherly resented that. He resented it as much as if it were something someone else was making him do. Automatically, he drained the can in his hand, and then looked at it as if he'd never seen it before. Beer, the breakfast of champions.

Could he stop? He'd never thought seriously about it before. Wycherly had been dried out by experts at expensive clinics in three countries. He'd *been* stopped a dozen times—but could he stop himself? He could phone home and—

The image of his parents' reactions was sudden and immediate, and Wycherly shuddered—at his father's easy contempt and his mother's crippling pity. No. If he did this thing, he would do it here, alone, telling no one. There would be no audience for his attempt—and failure.

Here—or nowhere. This time—or never.

It was odd the way the battle lines were suddenly so clear, as if this were actually something important that he and he alone could do. As if the condition of his liver actually mattered.

Which it didn't—not even to him.

But he'd do this thing anyway.

How? He turned his mind to practical matters, away from the disturbing world of ideals. Money was the first thing he'd need. Although Wycherly doubted either his AmEx or Visa would be of any use to him here, the thousand in cash he was carrying would probably go a long way toward buying him a place to hide.

To hide. He'd named the truth to himself without realizing it. That was what he'd been looking for on the road; that was what he wanted here. A place to hide.

Suddenly the sleepless hours he'd spent dragged at him, and the need for sleep pulled at his body with its promise of oblivion. The wet July heat was like a hand pushing him down, and he ached persistently in his legs, his neck, his back. . . . Wycherly got carefully to his feet. Feeling more than a little light-headed, he walked with extra care back into the general store.

Luned Starking was back, leaning against the old-fashioned soda cooler with a Coke in one hand and a glossy magazine in the other. This time Wycherly got a better look at her. Evan's sister was a washed-out blonde girl who looked ten and was probably fourteen and had the big-eyed elfin look of long privation. Her attention was riveted on the page, her lips moving slightly as she read.

Evan glanced up, surprised, when Wycherly entered. "You ready for some more beer, mister?"

"I need someplace to stay," Wycherly said. "Is there someplace around here that I could rent—someplace quiet?" As if his screams wouldn't be noise enough, once he started drying out. *If* he started drying out. The certainty of purpose he'd felt only moments before was fading.

The request seemed to take both Evan and Luned by surprise. They stared at Wycherly, mouths slightly open.

"I—I'm sure old Bart'll have your car running again just as soon as Caleb hauls it back here," Evan said.

Wycherly's emotional radar, fine-tuned by years of Musgrave disasters, picked up the sense of worry, almost of desperation, in Evan's voice. As if he were afraid of Wycherly? Why?

"I don't think anybody can get that car working again, and actually, I don't care. I just need a place to stay. Surely somebody has a place here they can rent?" Wycherly said again.

"You want to *stay* here?" Evan ran his hand through his sandy, light brown hair, now looking baffled as much as wary. "Mister, *nobody* stays in Morton's Fork if they've got any way of getting out, except—" He broke off suddenly. "Nobody."

At the moment Wycherly was too tired to pursue the other exception to the rule. "But there *is* someplace?" he demanded.

"There's this old cabin up on the mountain. It doesn't exactly belong

to anybody. . . . There isn't any electricity, and you'd have to pump all
your own water. And could be some folks say there's ha'ants around the
place, on account of a woman died there. . . ."

If Evan was trying to make the place sound unattractive, he wasn't doing a very good job. Wycherly didn't believe in ghosts, and that kind of
isolation sounded as if it were made to order for what he had in mind.

"I just want someplace with a roof and a bed and I'll pay for it,"
Wycherly snarled. "Which part of the preceding sentence don't you understand?"

"Well, there isn't really anyone to collect the rent. . . ."

Wycherly took out his wallet and laid six fifty-dollar bills on the
counter.

"I expect this will take care of everything. All I want is a bed."

Evan shrugged, not meeting Wycherly's eyes as he slid the money off
the counter.

Wycherly felt a black self-loathing well up inside him like bitter water from an underground spring. This was the way to get things done, his
father said: Ignore all opposition. Crush it. But even on the occasions—
such as now—that it worked for him, Wycherly drew no pleasure from
it. It always seemed to him somehow like cheating, as if he'd stolen
something that would have been freely given if only he had asked.

"And perhaps you could have someone show me where it is?"
Wycherly added. It wasn't an apology, but he wasn't very good at those.
They'd have to take what they got.

"Luned!" Evan's voice was sharp. "You show Mister Wycherly up to
Old Lady Rahab's old place and get it cleaned up."

"But it's *ha'anted*—" Despite her washed-out appearance, Luned
Starking had spirit—enough spirit to sass her brother, anyway.

"You just shut your biscuit-trap, little miss," Evan said. "Nobody's
asking you to sleep there, are they? And Mister Wycherly don't give a fig
for ha'ants. Now you take a broom and scoot on up there."

Rahab, Wycherly thought. The name sounded Biblical—or gothic—
and depressing. His head had started to hurt again, and he desperately
wanted unconsciousness, one way or the other. He wondered what the
cabin would be like.

It was easily a two-mile hike, and by the end of it Wycherly cared about
nothing other than stopping. He hadn't counted on having to walk there,

and although Luned took him by what she called "the easiest way," and carried the three six-packs besides—he couldn't go cold turkey, of course, and tomorrow would be soon enough to really assess the situation. When Luned pushed open the door he shoved past her, looking for the bedroom. He had a vague impression of a brass bed and a bare mattress before he collapsed full-length upon it, ignoring his bruises.

And he was asleep.

The spacious kitchen was like something out of an *Architectural Digest* spread: terra-cotta tile floor, exposed brick walls and silvery paneling from a salvaged barn. Sinah had designed it herself; it was her perfect place, the one she'd fashioned through a decade of lonely daydreams in a succession of shabby New York apartments, waiting for that big break. There was a copper double sink and an institutional refrigerator and stove, their starkness warmed by the brick and wood. The center food prep island had a single burner surrounded by more red tile, and a working surface that was half marble, half butcher's block oak. Well-used copper cookware—brought from Sinah's L.A. apartment—hung on the walls.

With the deft, economical movements of one used to working in confined spaces, she set out her tools and measured out flour, soda, yeast, and salt into an enormous stoneware bowl, added milk and eggs from her refrigerator, and began to blend the dough. Making bread was good for the soul, and she didn't need some fancy automated machine to do it.

She frowned, seeing how little flour was left in the sack. The contractor who'd rebuilt the schoolhouse had run in good heavy power lines for a big chest freezer, but with the best pantry in the world, people did still run out of things. Unless she wanted to risk getting thrown out of the Morton's Fork general store again, she'd have to get out her keys and drive twenty miles to the IGA in Pharaoh.

Why? What could her family have done to these people—even *with* the power to read minds?

Somewhere in these hills there must be others like her, others who had learned to tame their unwanted gift. It was why she stayed here, among people who hated her, who denied her to her face and thought her mother was a child of hell.

Please, let there be others like me. Please . . .

* * *

In a timeless place, awareness hovered just out of reach like a waiting shark. Camilla was here somewhere—but Camilla was dead. Wycherly Musgrave knew that for sure; he'd visited her grave once and seen the headstone: January 16, 1966–August 14, 1984.

His nineteenth birthday . . .

Night. The air was hot and wet, and adrenaline had combined with the alcohol in his blood to create a surreal state of false consciousness in which logic played no part. It took him several minutes to realize that he was wet, and longer to understand that he was standing in the river shallows, staring back toward the middle of the river in idiot fascination at the submerged headlights of his car.

This is a dream. The understanding did nothing to assuage the guilt or the fear. He tried to stop, to wake, but it was no good. He always came back to this night—the night that had revealed him to himself for what he was.

He turned back to the car, and when he touched the door it opened. Camilla's lifeless, moon-pale body floated serenely from the car, slithering boneless like a white eel through the black glass of the river water, reaching out her white arms to coil about him, dragging him down to share the death he'd forced on her. . . .

Wycherly sat up with a strangled shout.

For a moment he wasn't sure where he was, then he remembered. The crash—the town—the cabin. Someplace called Morton's Fork.

He looked around. He'd slept most of the day away; the light coming in through the window was the pale deceptive illumination of July's long twilights.

The room was dominated by a wide brass bed with an ornate marble-topped table beside it; the bed was stripped down to its mattress and box spring, the exposed brand labels bringing a weirdly modern note to a room that in so many other ways resembled a museum piece. There was a window, a cedar wardrobe chest, and a braided rug on the floor. The pressed-glass lamp on the table beside the bed, though covered with dust, was still half-full of lamp oil.

What the hell? Those kids said this place was deserted.

No. They'd said it was haunted, and that it didn't belong to anybody. Wycherly got gingerly to his feet. The pain was a little less, but still no picnic. Never mind: There was codeine in his bag, and considering what part of the country he was in, he could probably get a drink. Besides,

Luned had brought beer, hadn't she? There wasn't any running water, and he had to drink *something*.

Hadn't he been going to stop? an inner voice gibed. *Well, yes,* Wycherly temporized, *but not all at once. Nobody could expect that.*

He hauled himself off the bed, ignoring the mocking silence inside his head. Every muscle protested. He looked around for something to distract him, and settled on the wardrobe.

Monumental in the style of an earlier day, it towered over the other contents of the room. Wycherly regarded himself in the greenish, mottled mirror.

Reflexively, he pushed his hair out of his eyes—wincing as he encountered the bruise—and inspected himself critically.

He was still wearing his leather jacket; it was spattered with blood, and the shirt beneath it was grimy, torn, and bloody. His eyes were red; bloodshot and pouched, their pale-brown color looked positively inhuman by contrast. His pale skin—the redhead's curse—showed every scrape and bruise and crust of blood. His hair brushed his shoulders, dirty and uncombed; he was several days late for a shave, and rubbed his chin reflexively, wondering what he was going to do about it. If anything.

You look just . . . wonderful, Wycherly told himself. He wondered if there was any place to wash up. A creek?

He opened the door of the wardrobe.

There were dresses inside—plain cotton housedresses of the sort that could be ordered from a catalog, their timeless unfashionability nearly unchanged in thirty years. The drawer at the bottom of the wardrobe proved to contain women's underwear; Wycherly retreated hastily.

When he straightened up he was dizzy, and the room spun giddily around him. He backed up, holding on to the brass bed for support. What was all this stuff still doing here? Even if Evan's "Miss Rahab" had had no heirs, in Wycherly's experience, anyone would steal—and what could be easier than stealing from the dead?

This is weird, Wycherly thought with the serenity of drink and lingering exhaustion. But he didn't actually care much.

And that, Wycherly thought to himself, clutching the bed frame for support, was the bottom line, as Kenny Jr. was so fond of saying. Wycherly didn't care what was going on, how many women had died here, or if they'd all been murdered by Charles Manson. Kenny'd said he was selfish. His father'd said he was weak. They could both be right for once, and he hoped it would make them happy: The only person Wycherly was interested in was Wycherly Musgrave, and Wycherly Musgrave needed a place to hide.

And a drink.

He pushed open the door to the main room.

Someone had been busy, though no one was here now. The front door to the rustic cabin was open, and Wycherly moved reflexively to shut it, although the only trespassers he was likely to get would be squirrels. But squirrels—or even raccoons—could not be responsible for the condition of the cabin as it was now. The table was covered with a clean, bright red and white cloth with a wooden bowl of wildflowers and four gleaming hurricane lamps on it. He smelled the scents of white vinegar and pine soap. Little trace remained of the dust and eerie abandonment that still filled the bedroom.

Coals and kindling heaped beside the iron stove, pots and pans on the wall, canned goods on the shelves. Two wooden settles flanked the wood stove, a table and chairs in the middle of the room, cups and plates filled with grey dust still upon it . . . A flash of recollection appeared and was gone. Someone had cleaned here while he slept. Was it that mountain girl, Luned?

The notion disturbed him deeply, though Wycherly had lived his entire life against a backdrop of invisible service. From buying the groceries, to preparing the food and a thousand other tasks, there had always been unseen hands to take care of it. Wycherly had never been called upon to perform any of the common chores of daily living, yet having someone else do it bothered him deeply.

Hunger made its presence faintly known. A drink would take care of that.

Wycherly walked over to the battered white refrigerator on the far wall. But when he opened it, all that greeted him was room-temperature air and a faint smell of bleach. Where was the beer? He'd brought at least two six-packs up with him. He looked all through the refrigerator, but found nothing other than dry cleanliness.

His attention was momentarily distracted by the calendar on the wall beside the sink. It was curled and faded, a promotional calendar from some supplier of bottled gas. The date was 1969, the month was August. A bad omen. August, his birthday—the anniversary of Camilla's death—was always a bad time.

He turned away, and saw a yellowed newspaper on top of the pot-bellied cast-iron stove in the other corner. Wycherly picked it up. It was yellowed and crumbling, but he could clearly see the masthead: THE PHARAOH CALL AND RECORD, PUBLISHED WEEKLY FOR LYONESSE COUNTY, INCLUDING THE TOWNSHIPS OF PHARAOH, MORTON'S FORK, LA GOULOUE, BISHOPVILLE, AND MASKELYNE; AUGUST 4, 1969.

No one had been here, even to steal, for nearly three decades. For a moment, Wycherly was distracted from his search for the missing beer; despite his professed disinterest, he felt the hackles on the back of his neck begin to rise.

The door banged open.

"Oh, *there* you are, Mister Wych!" Luned said.

She strode through the door, a filled bucket in one hand, a six-pack in the other. Wycherly hurried over and took the beer from her. It was icy cold.

"Been settin' in the crick," Luned said, setting the bucket down beside the stove with a sigh of relief.

Wycherly pulled off the top of the can, sitting down in one of the wooden chairs to pour the beer down his throat in one long swallow. The need to have it available was almost stronger than his craving for it; he drank the next one more slowly.

"I'm sorry about the pump, Mister Wych, I truly am," Luned said. "I 'spect I can get it to run, but I didn't like to wake you or anything. Leastways now you can wash up and all." She looked anxious. "And there's a backhouse up the hill a-ways; you can see it from the window here."

Thanks, but no.

"Never mind. I imagine, ah, 'crick-water' will be just fine," Wycherly said. He wasn't sure he'd be willing to drink it, no matter how clear it looked, but then water hadn't been his preferred beverage for a very long time.

"Icebox works on white gas," Luned went on. "The tank's empty, and there won't be any more along until Monday. You'll need kerosene for your lamps, and I guess Mal Tanner'll bring that too, along with what else you might think to ask for."

Mr. Tanner, Wycherly remembered, was the local bootlegger. Evan had told him. He hesitated. Beer was one thing. Moonshine was something else again.

"What day is this?" he asked instead, shoving the rest of the six-pack aside.

"Thursday. It's about six. Dinnertime," Luned added, as if Wycherly were ignorant of the most basic facts of life.

Wycherly said nothing, nursing his second beer. He wasn't entirely sure of what was going on here, and he wanted to know. For all her talk of ghosts back in the general store, Luned seemed to have had no hesitation in scrubbing the cabin from top to bottom. And the sun was starting to set, and she was still here.

Why?

As he stared broodingly at her, Luned moved to the cabinets over the sink and began taking down cans. They were new, obviously stock from the general store. Wycherly glanced around the room. Several cardboard boxes—some filled with bulging rusted cans, some with shining modern ones—were tucked into corners.

"Evan sent up a load of groceries," Luned said, catching his look. "He says there's everything here you'll need. Bread comes in on Wednesday, milk on Monday, big store's in Pharaoh and you could maybe pay Francis Wheeler to run you down there or borrow Bart Asking's pickup."

The speech had the air of something planned beforehand and carefully rehearsed. Wycherly wondered who else Luned'd had the chance to say it to; from the way Evan Starking had acted, Morton's Fork wasn't exactly on the tourist-trade map.

"And my car?" Wycherly asked, remembering it with an effort. The crash that must have been only this morning seemed an episode from another lifetime already.

"Jachin and Boaz pulled it right up the hill and it's down to Asking Garage right now. Mister Asking says he says he doesn't think it's any kind of an American car."

Boaz and Jachin, Wycherly deduced, must be the oxen owned by Caleb. He felt a faint spasm of relief at knowing that the car was safely out of sight.

"It isn't. It's Italian."

"Well! Fancy that—and it uses American gasoline and everything?" Luned asked.

Wycherly stared at her, not sure whether she was serious or pulling a joke. After a moment, Luned turned away and went back to opening cans.

Silence.

"I thought you said no one lived here?" he said, just to break the silence. *So why are there still clothes in the closet?*

Luned turned and stared at him.

"Old Miss Rahab did, thirty year gone, but it ain't good luck to talk about people that clears out, Mister Wych, 'specially for a fella with red hair like yours," Luned said.

"Clears out"? Not "dies"? Wycherly grinned sourly to himself, finally understanding why he'd gotten the reception he had at Morton's Fork. Once upon a time people had believed that red hair was unlucky, and apparently that superstition still held in this backward place.

"All right—Luned, is it?—we won't talk about the missing Miss Rahab. Just as long as you're sure she won't be back."

"Don't you worry yourself. They don't never come back, Mister Wych," Luned said seriously.

I wouldn't, if I lived here.

"Well, that's fine then," Wycherly said, a shade too heartily. He felt awkward talking to this skinny, painfully-ignorant girl-child; to treat her as his equal when she would never have the resources that had been available to him seemed cruel, but to patronize her seemed worse.

He'd much rather not talk to her at all, but considering the amount of cleaning she'd done, he certainly owed her a little polite conversation. As polite as he ever got, anyway.

"Now if you'll just get that fire going, Mister Wych, I can get your dinner ready and give your bedroom a lick and a promise while the vittles heats, and besides, you'll be wanting to heat up some good hot water for your shaving and all," Luned said, apparently addressing her remarks to the silent refrigerator.

A shave. A wash. And little Luned to clean up for me. Wycherly shook his head in bemusement. He had, he realized, entered a simpler world, one where men built fires and women cleaned house. It held no particular appeal for him. In Wycherly's universe, men and women both idled, and paid laborers ordered by his parents took care of the mechanics of living. He wasn't sure he wanted to think of Luned as a servant.

"Are you sure you want to do that?" Wycherly said, making no move toward the stove. "I mean, it was very kind of you to show me up here, and everything. . . ." *Go away so I can get drunk in peace.*

"And what'd you give Evan three hundred dollars for, cep'n so I could clean this place up for you and lay you in a nice mess of fixin's?" Luned answered inarguably. "I'll get my share out of him, Mister City Man, don't you worry your head none about that. So if you'd be so kind as to see to that fire, if it wasn't no trouble?"

She placed her hands on her hips and stared at him, and Wycherly really didn't have any choice. Fortunately the expensive summer camps where he'd had been warehoused as a child—as well as a number of the more innovative detox programs he'd attended—had stressed wilderness survival as the pathway to self-improvement; once Wycherly managed to unlatch the front door of the stove and make sure that the inside was reasonably empty, he had no difficulty in laying down a pattern of logs to light.

The antique newspaper made excellent starter, and he still had a box of matches in his jacket pocket from whatever New York restaurant he'd been thrown out of last. The well-aged wood caught quickly, and Wycherly shut the door, pausing only to wonder if the draw pipe still worked after all these years.

Apparently it did, because the fire burned cleanly, its flames visible in orange flashes through the glass of the stove's front door.

"Take that a while to heat," Luned commented, struggling toward the stove carrying an enormous cast-iron pot filled with what looked like soup or stew. Wycherly rushed to take it from her. Every muscle he'd strained in the crash complained, and he nearly dropped it himself.

Once it was settled, Luned carried a second, smaller pot to the stove and ladled water from the bucket into it.

"There." She inspected him critically. "H'ain't you got no other clothes, Mister City Man?"

"My name's Wycherly, I'm not a 'Mister,' and no I don't." He looked down at the crisp grey work pants. *Couture courtesy of the Morton's Fork general store.*

"Well-l-l, I reckon I'll just have to stitch up a shirt for you, Mister City Man," Luned said slyly, turning away and sashaying—there was no other word for it—into the bedroom. "Mind you stir that soup now, or it'll burn."

* * *

Wycherly stared at the pot. He'd be damned if he'd stir soup.

He needed a wash, and probably to find that backhouse. Country plumbing—an outdoor privy, probably full of spiders and wasp nests if nothing worse. Wycherly shuddered. He looked at the cans on the table, beaded with condensation and creek water. He'd could wash up there, as he'd first planned. Abruptly the thought of going near the water made him shudder.

Don't be feeble-minded, Musgrave. Camilla Redford is safely in her grave and has been since 1984. You saw the gravesite, remember?

Only the dead never stay dead. That's the only real problem with them. In the Musgrave family, there was no such thing as a dead issue.

He got to his feet and knocked back the rest of the second can. Removing his jacket was a struggle, but he managed, laying it carefully over the back of the chair. He looked back at the beer. One for the road.

But no. Not right now. The two beers he'd already had were nothing more than a cushion, fuzzing the edges but not really intoxicating him. He meant to stop, he really did. He'd been dried out before, and he knew the drill. This time Wycherly had been drinking heavily for several months—heavily for him, which meant a considerable amount of alcohol every day. When a man reached that point, the trick was to sober up slowly—no d.t.'s as the alcohol slowly worked its way out of his system. After he'd reached technical sobriety, he could start drying out. And then he could see if he could stay sober.

He already knew the answer to that.

But he'd pretend he didn't, just for a giggle.

Wycherly turned away from the cans on the table and went to the door. By now it was late enough that the last rays of the setting sun webbed the clearing in horizontal bars of yellow gold. He walked out into the open air and turned back to look at his new home. The brass fittings of the door had oxidized to a blackish green, and the door of the cabin hung slightly open, despite his best efforts to shut it.

Old Miss Rahab's cabin was a large split-log building. Flowering vines grew up over the stone chimney and spread over the roof; where volunteers had sprouted, young trees grew close to the cabin, and land that might have been clear-cut in its former owner's day now sported a dense, second-growth forest. It gave the isolated cabin the look of something out of a fairy tale; an enchanted cottage set in the middle of an impenetrable wood. If the exterior had ever known paint it was a thing of the past, and time had weathered the wood to a soft, uniform grey that made it blend in seamlessly with the aspens and rowans that grew near it. Though the structure had been built less than a hundred years ago, it bore a strong family resemblance to the cabins that had dotted the rolling woodland of the Western Expansion. There was nothing in sight to tie it to the twentieth century, as if to cross its threshold was to lose one's grip on the present, and tumble helplessly down the corridors of the past. A steady pillar of smoke came from the cabin's chimney. All the windows were open, and several yards away he saw a tall narrow shed.

From the backhouse Wycherly moved reluctantly toward the creek. It was downhill, about six hundred yards from his cabin, running narrow and deep beneath a canopy of rambling rose.

Wycherly knelt painfully beside it and leaned over. The sight of a white face looking up at him out of the water made him cry out and lose his balance, until he realized it was nothing more than his reflection staring back up at him from the creek's dark surface.

He could not escape the feeling that Camilla was somewhere in that black water, waiting for her vengeance. And when he least expected, she'd reach up with those white, white arms and drag him screaming down into Hell.

Stupid, Musgrave. Have we already gotten as far as hallucinations? Doesn't bode well for the future, I'd say.

With trembling fingers, Wycherly unbuttoned his shirt. He was not going to let her win this time.

The T-shirt beneath was also stained with dried blood. Wycherly peeled it away from his skin gingerly, and then crumpled it up in both hands and plunged it into the creek. The water was icy, despite the July heat. When the shirt was as clean as plain water could make it, he used it as a rude washcloth to scrub his face, his neck, and as much of his torso as he could reach.

It hurt to move. Crusted scrapes reopened, staining the shirt a delicate pink. He blotted at his head with the sopping rag until his hair was soaked and hung down his bare back in dark copper tendrils. Last of all he simply held the T-shirt over his eyes, savoring its coldness and trying to compel his headache to go away. A drink—or several—would make it go away. He knew that from experience.

But he wasn't going to take them. Beer didn't count.

Yeah, Wycherly jeered at himself. *That's right. You're going to quit.* He could almost always manage the first month fairly easily. And then what?

Wycherly didn't know. He'd been dragged that far toward sobriety on his father's whim so many times that he'd come to look upon drying out as a short vacation, an intermission to remind him of why he drank and how pleasant it was. Like Columbus, Wycherly Musgrave wasn't really certain there was anything on the other side of the ocean.

What if there wasn't?

All at once a crushing sense of panic descended over him. Nauseated, he leaned forward and rested his head on his knees, clutching the wet T-shirt to his face. Why go through all of this just to take control of his own life? What would it be *for* once he had? He'd spent thirty years learning to be an embarrassing liability—did he think he could turn that around on a whim?

The pointlessness of everything appalled him. Wouldn't it be much better just to die?

No. Three decades of not conforming to other people's hopes aided him now with a spasm of reflexive stubbornness. He wouldn't die just because it was probably the most rational course of action.

But if he lived, what would it be for?

He didn't know.

Wycherly faced that head-on, sitting beside the creek and letting the terror roar through him. *This* was what he'd foolishly vowed to face without the soothing peace of alcohol—a beast that wasn't even black, because blackness at least would be something, a positive attribute, and the beast was nothing at all; the abyss, the void.

And it was coming for him.

He did not fight. Wycherly had never fought back. He'd only run, and now he was here, and there was no further place to run to.

Like it or not, this was his last stand.

THREE

GRAVE MATTERS

I have no relish for the country; it is a kind of healthy grave.
—THE REVEREND SYDNEY SMITH

MAKING BREAD HAD DONE NOTHING TO RELIEVE SINAH'S feelings—her heart still fluttered panickily, as if at any moment the scattered inhabitants of Morton's Fork would appear outside her door with torches and pitchforks, baying demands that they be given the witch to kill. . . .

I won't think like that! She needed to get away from this place—go to Pharaoh for supplies, that was it. Get out among people, where every casual closeness—sitting on a bus, standing in an elevator—brought her their life histories and secret desires, their angers and their griefs. But it was better than staying here to let her empty mind collapse inward upon itself. Down in Pharaoh, they'd never heard of Athanais Dellon or her daughter, and furthermore, they didn't care. She could shop, maybe even have dinner in the Pharaoh diner.

With brisk determination, Sinah changed her flour-spattered jeans and T-shirt for a sundress and denim jacket more suitable for a grocery shopping expedition. Even the mutter of the storm approaching through Watchman's Gap wasn't enough to deter her—she could wait it out in town and come back afterward.

She opened the door and stepped out, mildly surprised to see that the evening was clear. The storm must still be on the other side of the Gap, then; well, it could stay there for all she cared. Holding her keys in her hand, she stepped toward her Jeep Cherokee, her lifeline to the outside world, her means of escape.

That was when she smelled the smoke.

Something was burning.

She looked wildly in all directions, but there was nothing in sight. Only the soft summer twilight slanting through the white stands of birch trees, and the purling of a creek somewhere in the middle distance.

And the smell of smoke.

Why couldn't she see anything? The smell of smoke was so strong, the fire must be close by. The dappled sunlight burned on her skin like falling embers; the sky was darkening fast and suddenly she couldn't breathe. . . .

The smoke was choking her. Sinah stared in horror. Fire made bright walls around her; the heat of it tightened her skin. She stared into the flames, unconsciously searching for the gas jets that would tell her this was all a fake, a movie set.

But this was no set, no stage. There were no cameras, no audience. This was real.

Sinah stood in the middle of a burning room, one that she'd never seen before, not even in pictures. There were brightly colored banners edged in fire, and tall candlesticks whose melting candle wax trickled down like water. Around her she could hear screaming, as though a hundred people suffered here just beyond her sight.

"Hello!" Sinah cried, and almost immediately began to choke on the acrid smoke.

Fire climbed the walls. Now the bright silk banners were all aflame. Soon the flames would reach her. Choking on her own panic, Sinah took a tentative step backward, away from the worst of the fire.

There was a door beneath her hands, its handle already blisteringly hot. With a sense of trapped unreasoning horror she flung it open—there was darkness on the other side, and blessed quiet. Sinah rushed through the door and slammed it. She held it closed for several seconds before she dared look around.

She'd thought this place was dark. And it was, but somehow she could see her surroundings, as if she knew them so well that her memory was something she could trust. Stairs. Old and worn and shallow, leading down into the body of the earth, to where the crushing weight of rock became a separate living intelligence, waiting to crush her. Sinah put her foot forward and felt the edge of the first step.

The wood of the door behind her grew warm against her back, reminding her that there was no retreat. She must go forward, down into where something waited—waited for her specifically, for Sinah Dellon. This was the past she'd so recklessly conjured; this was her heritage.

It was waiting for her.

This is a dream! Sinah thought wildly. She was—

She could not remember where she'd been a moment before. All she could remember was the fire. Fear, and grief—and a wild sense of failure and despair.

She had failed—herself, and the Line. And that which she had failed was here, waiting for her. In the dark.

She could hear the sound of underground water, its plashing bizarrely magnified by the staircase beneath the earth. It was that insane adherence to the laws of physics that frightened her most; as if the reality of the small details of this vision were the most damning proof of her madness. What she'd called her gift was next to madness, after all. Perhaps this was only some logical evolution.

The thought was unbearable. *It's a dream—it's a dream—it's a dream—* Caught between the soft seduction of the darkness and the fire's roaring destruction, Sinah flung open the door and ran back out into the fire.

No, no, NO—

First heat, then pain. Unbearable brightness that seemed to penetrate her flesh and her perceptions. She died in flames.

And was reborn.

Sinah opened her eyes. She was rolling on the ground, covered with the flecks of last year's leaves, weeping with the terror and the pain of being burned alive. It took a long time for her battered mind to comprehend that those things were not real. That she was here, and safe. There wasn't even the smell of smoke in the air.

The memory of the vision began to fade even as she grasped at it, until all the images were shadowy, as inchoate as any nightmare.

What . . . happened? Slowly Sinah got to her feet. The fear of madness—never far from her—returned afresh. What had happened had not been a secondhand experience stolen from another's mind. It had been something else—*she'd* been someone else. And instead of remembering what she'd taken from that other mind, she'd been drowned in it and discarded.

As though she hadn't quite fit.

"You let it burn!"

Luned's accusation was the first thing Wycherly heard as he came through the door. His undershirt was balled up in his hand, and his tattered shirt was draped across his shoulders, still damp from the sluicing he'd given it.

He glanced around. The room was oven-warm from the fire in the wood stove, and the iron pot was still sitting on top of the stove, steaming gently. The table was set with napkins, bowls, and spoons, and there was a tin box of crackers placed prominently on the table. Beside each plate there was a tin cup filled with tawny liquid. Luned was sitting in one of the chairs waiting for him. Her hands were in her lap and her whole demeanor was one of painful dignity.

"I'm not the cook." Wycherly went to the table and picked up the cup at the unoccupied place. He sniffed at it suspiciously.

"It's hard cider," Luned said, relenting. "Don't they have that where you come from?"

"I doubt Mother would let it cross the threshold," Wycherly said absently.

Luned got up and picked up one of the bowls, moving toward the stove; Wycherly walked past her into the bedroom.

The bed had been made up with fresh sheets and blankets, topped with a patchwork quilt. The white window curtains, which looked to have been at least shaken out, if not washed, swirled gently at the window. Most of the obvious dust was gone; the room looked like one in some over-quaint bed-and-breakfast.

What in the name of all that was reasonable was he doing here?

"Do you guess you'll want dinner now?" Luned asked from the doorway. She sounded uncertain. She wiped her hands down the apron she had tied around her waist.

I'd rather have a drink. Wycherly pushed the automatic thought aside out of some reflexive perversity. "You don't have to wait on me," he said instead.

"I don't mind," Luned said shyly. "I'm sorry I rowed at you before; I was just scairt, is all. Looks like you're going to need someone to do for you, cooking and cleaning . . . and like that."

"I'll manage," Wycherly said shortly. Shouldn't this girl be in school somewhere, or off playing with dolls? An odd suspicion made him ask: "Look, exactly how old are you anyway, Luned?"

"I'll be seventeen next birthday," the girl replied. "And I guess I could take care of you right well, Mister Wych."

Oh, Lord. Not a backward twelve as he'd vaguely imagined, but sixteen. Old enough to think of herself as an adult, with what could be disastrous results.

"No," Wycherly said carefully, "I don't really think you could. I'll be happy to have you come here and clean for me, and bring me things from the store, Luned. I'll pay you for that. You see, I'm going to be . . . sick for a while. I won't really need someone to, ah, 'do' for me."

"Was it the church bells?" the girl asked eagerly. "Ev an' me, we figured it'd be something like that, with them ringing the bells down to Maskelyne for that Prentiss boy that drowned—"

Drowned. It was silly, but Wycherly felt real fear. As if the possibility of drowning were a tangible and concrete thing, that could rise from a riverbed and seek him out as surely as a silver bullet. As if the waters could give up all the dead they had swallowed, and Camilla Redford could come back for him.

"Drowned? Where is there around here that anyone could drown?" he asked sharply.

"In the river," Luned said, as if this were something everybody ought to know. "The crick out back's the Little Heller; she runs right into the Astolat, and the Astolat runs pretty fast just below the dam. The funeral was this morning, and Reverend Betterton was going to ring a long peal at sunup, so we figured the church bells must be what made you crash. . . ."

Wycherly stared at her, wondering if Luned were a violent maniac or just delusional. What in God's name could *church bells* have to do with his accident this morning, or whether he was going to dry out?

"Did I say something wrong?" Luned asked anxiously.

"Just who is it—precisely—that you think I am?" Wycherly said slowly. "And don't lie," he added, "because I'll know." He took a menacing step toward the doorway.

Luned Starking turned pale enough for her faint freckles to show plainly, proof enough that she took the threat seriously.

"You're a conjureman, Mister Wych. Wouldn't nobody else be coming to Morton's Fork to live in old Miss Rahab's cabin. And you've got red hair—that's the mark of Judas—and you drank down Gamaliel Tanner's best shine like it was well water. Couldn't any mortal man do that." Her confidence seemed to return as she enumerated the reasons for Wycherly to be a "conjureman."

"And you said you'd know if I lied," Luned added seriously, "so that proves it."

Hearsay, innuendo, and half-truths. If this was some elaborate rural practical joke, Wycherly intended to see that its perpetrator got no joy from it.

"This is medieval," he said bluntly. "Do you know what year this is? It's practically the year 2000, and you're going on with this—nonsense. Who do I look like to you, the Flying Nun? There's no such thing as a 'conjureman'—and if there were, I wouldn't be one."

His angry speech did not have the effect he intended. Luned's eyes filled with tears, and she fixed her eyes on her feet. "Then you cain't help me?" she said in a low voice. "I thought maybe you could."

Ghoulish apprehension kept Wycherly from speaking for a moment, while his fancy made him imagine every sort of terminal illness beyond the help of medical science. The vigor with which Luned had polished and cooked now took on the luster of a desperate act—a bid for aid from a fantastic creature summoned up from her own imagination.

"Tell me," Wycherly said harshly.

Luned launched into a rambling explanation so filled with euphemism and dialect that Wycherly couldn't really understand it. "Haven't you seen a doctor?" he demanded, cutting through her words.

"Doctors just want to put you into the hospital," Luned said scornfully. "Doctor Standish comes around four times a year from the County so the babies can get their shots for school and all, but he won't *do* nothing. There's the sanatorium up the hill a ways—if you go on up the ridge you can probably see it, if you go in daylight—but it don't do folks around here much good."

"Why not?" A sanatorium implied a medical staff of some sort, and the doctors there should at least be willing to refer local emergencies—though if Luned's assessment of the County Medical Service's Dr. Standish was any indication, the inhabitants of Morton's Fork would do anything rather than be sent out of the area to the hospital.

"Wildwood Sanatorium burned down eighty year ago next month. Ain't nothing there now but ha'ants and brambles," Luned explained simply.

They don't go because it isn't there.

Feeling as if he'd been played for a fool, Wycherly snarled, "So what do you expect *me* to do for you?" He was hungry, and he wanted a hot bath that it didn't look as if he was going to get, and he felt an uneasy sense of responsibility that he didn't like, as if merely by virtue of coming from a privileged background he had some responsibility to those who had less.

Luned stared at the floor, biting her lower lip to keep from crying, something that irritated Wycherly even more.

"I thought . . . maybe . . . if you were a conjureman like old Miss Rahab . . . you could maybe fix me up a tonic so's I didn't feel so poorly all the time," she finally said.

That's ALL? Wycherly nearly said. But there was no "all" to it; that *something* was wrong with Luned was clear, from her pallid complexion to the fact that it had been so easy to mistake her for a child half a dozen years younger. He could tell her to eat better food, to rest more, but was there any way for her to follow such orders, living as she did?

"I better go," Luned said.

"No." Though Wycherly hated the thought of getting entangled with some ignorant mountain girl, still less did he like the thought of being a man just like his father: someone who used people and then threw them aside when they were no longer useful.

And ignored them until they were.

"Sit down. Eat your soup. I may be able to do something for you. And quit sniveling," he snapped.

Though Luned had said the soup had burned, there was more than enough for dinner. Even though most of the ingredients had come out of cans, it was surprisingly good, enough to awaken even Wycherly's flagging appetite. As they ate, Luned pattered on about her housekeeping skills, demanding that he give her his shirt so she could clean and mend it for him.

"—and I'm a powerful good seamstress, Mister Wych—you'll see."

He supposed that he would, like it or not. But at least he had a solution for some of her problems.

"Wait here," Wycherly said, when dinner was over.

He got up from the table and went back into the other room, not waiting to see if she obeyed. His shoulder bag was right where he'd left it, on the floor beneath the window. She hadn't touched it when she'd cleaned—at least, he hoped she hadn't. He slung it onto the bed and opened it.

In it were all the necessities of a wastrel's life: his shaving kit with its rechargeable electric razor, a bottle of "1903" cologne. An address book, containing the telephone numbers of enough doctors and lawyers to keep the police away from him for at least a little while, if the need came. A cellular phone he wasn't going to use, a roadmap leading nowhere. A shirt and underwear he didn't remember packing. Reading glasses he never used. Tylenol-3. A bottle of sleeping pills, the prescription carefully doled out to him in non-fatal amounts—as if that would slow him down when the time came. A pint of Scotch.

Wycherly held it up to the light: It glowed like amber, like fire, like everything good and precious in his world. Its loving warmth seemed to radiate through the glass into his hands. He knew that if he was serious about drying out, he had to get rid of it.

But he couldn't bear to do that just now. He set it carefully on the pile with the other things, as gently as if it were alive.

And here, down at the bottom, the thing he was looking for.

The prescription bottle was the size of a small jar of instant coffee and made of white plastic to protect its contents from the light. The bottle held 150 pills—no one cared how many he had of these.

Vitamins. Strong ones. A contribution to his therapy from the psychiatrist he was—in theory—currently seeing, who felt she should preserve his health while not interfering with his drinking. Alcoholics, she'd said, usually suffered health problems exacerbated by malnutrition; either because they preferred drinking to eating or because chronic drinking stripped the body of essential nutrients. These were supposed to make up for that. He supposed they'd work equally well for someone whose body had been stripped of essential nutrients by something else.

But Luned was expecting magic from a red-headed conjureman who flew through the air in a sorcerous automobile. He unscrewed the cap. God knew why he was humoring the simpleminded wench. She had all the sexual appeal of a backward ten year old, and Wycherly was no Humbert Humbert.

The foil seal was still in place, which meant the bottle was full. About five months' supply. But how to get her to take them?

He looked around the room.

There was a small, hinged silver box on top of the dresser, about the size of two packs of filter cigarettes taped together. He picked it up, wondering why Luned had left it behind when she'd cleaned out everything else. Because it looked valuable, probably. He turned it over, looking for a hallmark, but all he saw were some odd square imprints, the designs too muddled to make out.

Possibly this was an antique snuffbox, but even if it was, Wycherly felt no qualms about using it—old and ornate, it was just the right size to hold the contents of the pill bottle, and Wycherly dumped the contents into it and closed the lid. Hefting the box in his hand, he walked back out into the other room.

Luned was still sitting at the table, just as he'd left her. In that moment, the whole situation took on a surreal clarity that Wycherly associated only with being very drunk indeed. What was he doing meddling in the life of a stranger on whom he could have no hope of having a permanent effect? And meddling just for fun; Wycherly could imagine no other reason. What was Luned to him? Nothing. So why should he help her?

He walked over to the table.

"These are pills," Wycherly said. "I want you to take one of them each day. Don't take more. Don't skip any days. Don't share them with anybody. Don't let anyone know you have them." He felt suddenly, eerily, mature. Had that covered all the possibilities for misuse? "I'll know if you do," he finished, hoping that would cover all the rest.

Luned looked at the box, her eyes wide. Before he could stop her she'd opened it and poured the caplets out on the table. "These look just like plain old ordinary store-pills," she said in a disappointed voice.

"But they aren't," Wycherly said, possessed of a mad urge to bend her to his will. "They're magic. But magic never looks like what it really is— it wouldn't be magic then, do you see?"

And you're the village idiot, trying this Dr. Strange routine on this feeble-minded, credulous, backwoods Lolita.

Only was it so very credulous, a part of Wycherly's mind wondered, for someone to believe with such matter-of-factness in things they'd actually seen? Perhaps Luned expected him to be the new warlock on the block because such things were common here.

Angrily, Wycherly clamped down on such a dangerous fantasy. Soon enough he'd have the opportunity to see any number of things that weren't there; there was no point in making what was to come worse for himself by making up ghoulies and ghaesties with his conscious mind.

"If you don't want them, fine. You asked me for them, remember?" he pointed out.

"I'll take them," Luned said quickly. The silver box disappeared into her pocket.

"Fine. Come back to me when they're gone."

An hour later true dark had fallen, and Wycherly was alone in his new home. It was starting to cool down now, as the fire in the wood stove died. Luned had warned him that the night would be cold, and he'd want heat even in summer, but he could always light it again later.

She'd promised to come back tomorrow and bring all the beer that two twenty-dollar bills could buy. He'd have to be more careful with his money from now on. The general store didn't take AmEx, and he doubted that there was an ATM anywhere within walking distance of Morton's Fork—and to use either was to risk having his family find him.

But he could manage. He'd managed in worse situations.

Wycherly looked around the cabin. Two of the kerosene lamps burned brightly in the main room; one on the table, one on a shelf above the stove. Pale moths fluttered around both of them, making the shadows leap and flicker.

Wycherly studied the absence of alcohol on the table, trying not to think about the bottle of Scotch in the bedroom. Did he really want to do this? *Could* he do this? And if he could, why do it here, in a place that already reminded him of a cross between Green Acres and the Twilight Zone?

He wasn't completely sure, even now. But deep within him, a faint smothered voice said that whatever he did he must do here, and now. That there was no other safe place, and that to delay at all would be to delay until it was too late.

So be it. But it was an odd feeling to be responding to the prompting of an inner instinct that urged him to save himself. Wycherly had much more experience with self-destruction.

She was losing her mind, having low-rent visions like a straight-to-video Joan of Arc. Sinah Dellon sat in the darkened great room, huddled in her big terrycloth robe, trying to put her world back into order. Maybe starting the search for her roots ten years earlier would have made a difference. She'd never been adopted; her records had never been sealed. From the moment she'd realized she had a real mother somewhere, she'd dreamed of meeting her with a longing that bordered on pain. If she'd come here the moment she'd turned eighteen, would it have helped?

No. It was too late even then.

She ran a hand through her hair distractedly. It had hurt to give up the long-cherished fantasy of meeting her birth mother. Athanais Dellon was dead, had been dead for all the long years her daughter had dreamed of their reunion while dwelling in the house of strangers. And now she needed her bloodline's help more than ever. Now she was having visions.

She ought to be running through the woods screaming her head off. Or at least driving for the nearest coast as fast as she could.

Sinah got up from the couch and wandered through the renovated schoolhouse. It was too fantastic—there was no place to begin to think about something so far removed from reality. She glared at her dream house with real anger; the longer she stayed here, the more it seemed like a prison, not a refuge. As if instead of bringing her home, this house was insulating her from it.

Don't be ridiculous, darling. There isn't any "home" here. They don't want you. And now you're going nuts.

Sinah knew her behavior was right up there with that of heroines in

gothic novels who, when confronted with all manner of ghastly appari-
tions, stayed right where they were (in the moldering isolated mansion)
and waited to be murdered by the Byronic young master. But Sinah was
looking for the truth about her family; without it, she couldn't go forward and she couldn't go back.

She went over to the window that looked out beside her front door.
The Jeep still sat there, a guaranteed magic carpet that would take her
away at the turn of an ignition key. A sensible woman would go—and
check herself into the nearest psychiatric hospital. Just because she didn't
feel crazy didn't mean she wasn't—after all, didn't she think she could
read minds?

And see visions.

Fire. There'd been something burning; that was all Sinah remembered
of her vision by now. Fire, pain, and terror. It must mean something—
but what? If only the people here would *talk* to her; tell her what it was
that Athanais Dellon had done to them that made them shun her daughter nearly three decades later. Had Athanais had powers like Sinah's?

Were they what had killed her?

Wycherly didn't feel even slightly drunk, and, in an experimental spirit,
decided to see if he could get to sleep without drugs as well. But once he
lay there in the darkness, sleep seemed to retreat until it was a thousand
miles away.

And in the darkness, he heard voices. Murmuring just at the threshold of audibility, low purling chuckling cozening voices. . . .

The black beast was coming for him, coming out of season, as if it had
heard that Wycherly meant to free himself from it and was punishing
him for even the thought of escape. And Wycherly realized that the
sounds he heard were not voices, but something worse: water, the sound
of running water somewhere near, outside the window, out in the dark. . . .

*Pulling at him. Lapping around his legs, pulling him under, cold and im-
placable. He was hurt, bleeding—he could not remember what he was doing here,
standing in a river in the middle of the night, but a reflexive automatic sense of
guilt made him look around sharply, and that was when he saw it. A car—his
car?—submerged beneath the water, the beams of its dying headlights shining
dimming, golden beacons beneath the water. The warm blood eddied about his legs;
he fell to his knees in the river, and the icy water reached his chest, making his*

heart clutch with its coldness. How could the water be so cold? Even the air seemed frigid now, as if all warmth, like love, was gone from his surroundings.

The river pulled at him, trying to drag him under, pulling him with it in its journey to the sea. Behind him he could see the lights of the car submerged beneath the surface of the water, its weakening beams like the eyes of an angry dragon, and Wycherly knew it was too late. He started toward it, only to feel the slippery surface of the riverbed dissolve beneath his feet, carrying him under.

He tried to climb out and the water dragged at him, growing deeper and colder the more he struggled toward the shore. On the distant shore he could see the faint blue and red sparks that were the lights of rescue vehicles, but it was as though they belonged to a different world, a world that no amount of struggle would let him reach. He was going to die now.

In that irrevocable moment Wycherly realized that his death was not a private thing affecting only him. If he died here he would die with promises unkept, die without completing the task that he had been sent into the world to perform.

Suddenly the need to live was sweet and urgent, and that was the moment when Wycherly saw the white shape moving toward him beneath the water. Its teeth were white and sharp and its staring vacant eyes were dark with blood.

It was coming for him.

Wycherly struggled to awaken, groping for a light switch that wasn't there. His face was wet, and he sobbed aloud in terror until he realized that it was raining, that rain blowing in through the open window was what had triggered the dream as well as forcing him awake.

He swung his legs over the side of the bed, and winced at the pain of still-sore muscles as he rubbed his eyes. He wasn't quite awake, but he was far from being asleep. The dry sandy flatness of insomnia made every nerve ache, and he knew that for the rest of the night he could only buy sleep through alcohol or drugs.

Cursing, Wycherly got up and dragged down the window, shutting out the bursts of cold wet air. The worst thing was that even over the rain he could still hear the mocking babble of the water. It was no hallucination, just the Little Heller Creek going about its mundane business. But fantasy or reality, the black beast was coming for him, no matter how he fled. There was a rendezvous he must keep—with the night, the river, a sunken car, and a murdered girl. . . .

Camilla!

But he should not call on her, Wycherly realized tardily. She didn't love him any more—she hated him, and when he called her, she would come. He shook his head stubbornly. Light, he needed light.

Several fumbling attempts to light the lamp at his bedside at last produced success, and he lowered the glass chimney into place with a real feeling of accomplishment.

With illumination, the room looked more normal, and the night terrors receded. Inside himself, Wycherly despaired. If it was this bad already without the blunting effect of liquor, how was he ever going to last another day—let alone a year?

Who knows? Who cares? Not me.

Turning away from the window, Wycherly went prowling through his new domain. He opened the refrigerator by automatic reflex, and inside were the plastic jug of cider and four cans of beer, as well as the remains of suppertime's soup. He hesitated, then reached for the cider.

It was pleasant; alcoholic, but not enough to have much of an intoxicating effect. He wandered around with the jug in his hand, closing the window over the sink and poking at the embers of the fire. He felt keyed-up, restless: stage one of detox right on schedule. Next would come depression, inertia, wild craving, and the black beast, after which he would be—at least technically—clean and sober.

Wycherly thought about taking a sleeping pill or two—they gave a pleasant buzz—but decided against it. Here, tonight, even his insomnia would be his own. He sat in the rocker with his jug balanced upon his knee, and after an hour or so found himself nodding off again. Might as well try the bed one more time.

The next time Wycherly woke it was morning. He saw the sunlight streaming in through the bedroom window and smelled the linen-and-lavender scent of the sheets.

He felt as though he'd died sometime last week.

He reached for the bottle on the bedside table before he remembered that there wouldn't be one. But it was too late; he was awake. Attempts to go back to sleep were useless now; the room was too bright for that. He felt heavy and dull, and wanted nothing more than to roll over and shut the world out again, but at least he'd slept most of the night without any more dreams.

As Wycherly lay there, regretting the fact that he was conscious, he could hear movement out in the other room. Luned? He supposed he should at least get up and see if she'd done what he told her. He hoped she'd remember whatever that was, because he didn't.

Wycherly threw back the covers reluctantly and swung out of bed. He felt achy and fuddled, with the faint beginnings—once again—of a hangover. It didn't improve his mood, a familiar one that he hesitated to inflict on anyone he wasn't trying to make acutely miserable. And though that list was very short, for some reason Luned was on it.

He dressed quickly in the clothing he'd worn last night, wincing in anticipation of the rudimentary sanitary arrangements to be found in the backhouse, but there was no help for it. He grabbed his jacket and tucked the Tylenol-3 into a pocket. Better safe than sorry, he thought confusedly; he was going to need those later.

Before he went out, a native fastidiousness made Wycherly use the mirror on the wardrobe to shave. The electric razor still held a charge, and it didn't matter how much his hands shook, so long as he was persistent. Maybe he could find someplace today to recharge the thing. *Someone* in this backward hamlet must have electricity.

Rubbing his now-bare chin, Wycherly walked out into the other room. The door and the window were open again—as he'd suspected, Luned was already there, happily discovering new things to scrub down.

And to his shameful relief, there were four six-packs of beer on the table.

"Good morning, Mister Wych. Evan says he'll be bringing the rest of your supplies up later in the cart. It's a pretty day to do washing," she added hopefully. "And I mended your shirt." She indicated it, crisp and ironed and folded neatly on the table.

Wycherly glanced out the door. He could not assess the "prettiness" of the day—all he knew was that the sun was out and its brightness made his eyes ache. He wondered where his sunglasses were. Probably lost in the crash. He'd have to make the best of things, then. He slung his jacket over his shoulder and walked outside without speaking, as reluctant as a cat stepping into a puddle.

When he came back, there was a smell of pancakes in the air—Luned was cooking on a soapstone griddle balanced on top of the wood stove—and Wycherly's stomach rebelled.

"No," he said. A sudden riptide of nausea tugged at him, treacherous and unexpected. He barely reached a chair before his knees gave way. He stared at the six-packs on the table in front of him, and then reached out and pulled one of them toward him. Luned glanced over her shoulder at him to see what he was doing.

"Thank you," Wycherly said with venomous precision, "but I find I do not care for pancakes today." Sweat trickled down his face; his mouth filled with bile.

Luned stared at him as if he were speaking Greek.

Wycherly pulled back the tab on the can in his hand. The warm beer frothed out through the opening; he drank it off anyway, wiping the foam from his mouth when he was done.

He reached for another.

"I don't want breakfast. I don't want pancakes. I don't want—" But he wasn't sure what he *did* want—or didn't—so he stopped talking.

He stared sullenly at Luned, to see if she was going to argue, but she only shrugged, and turned away to get a plate to scrape the griddle's leavings onto.

Wycherly finished a second beer and opened a third. He was dissatisfied with his own behavior, but couldn't quite see himself behaving any other way.

"I just don't like sweet things," he said reluctantly. He tried to remember what he usually ate for breakfast, and couldn't.

"I could heat you up a can of stew, maybe," Luned said doubtfully. "Or some of the soup."

His head was spinning now—not from the beer, but in a demand for stronger poison that he didn't intend to give it.

"Just—I'm going out."

The image of the sanatorium came back to him from last night's conversation. It would make as good a destination as any, and keep him away from Luned and people. Wycherly got to his feet with difficulty, trying not to see the look of hurt disappointment on Luned's face. He set the now-empty can down on the table next to its brothers.

"I'm going for a walk. I think it would probably be better if you didn't come up here for a few days after today. Until I'm settled in."

He'd probably be better later today. In fact, he could be quite charming at the point that just preceded his getting incapably drunk.

"I don't dislike you," he said reluctantly—and she, poor girl, would never realize how rare even that mild compliment was—"but I think it would be better for you if you weren't here."

"You have to eat something," Luned said stubbornly. "If you think I haven't seen a man drink himself stone blind before, Mister Wych, you're wrong. But you've got to have something in you for the drink to bite on. You just wait right there."

So he didn't even have shock value going for him. Wycherly sat back down at the table and reached for another beer. Number four. He was starting to feel quite waterlogged, but far from drunk. That was the trouble with beer. It wasn't efficient.

Hadn't Luned said Mr. Tanner might come by today? He wondered if there was time to get a message to him about bringing some moonshine when he did.

No. Wycherly concentrated on sitting in the chair, sipping restrainedly at his fourth beer. He was too stubborn to turn and watch what Luned was doing behind his back.

A few minutes later Luned set before him a cup of black coffee so strong there was an iridescent blue sheen on its surface, and a thick slab of cornbread, toasted dark and crisp.

"Where did this come from?" Wycherly asked, poking at the cornbread.

"I brought it for my lunch, but it looks like I'm going to have pancakes," Luned said without regret. "Now drink up that coffee—it's black as a coal miner's heart."

Wycherly, faced with the choice of either eating or driving Luned from the cabin by some means, picked up the cornbread and bit into it. It was dry, crisp, and tasted faintly of charcoal, but he couldn't have managed much else. Between swallows of scalding coffee strong enough to make his heart race, Wycherly managed to get all of it down. Once he'd finished the bread and the coffee he felt much better. Even the headache had retreated.

"I appreciate what you're doing for me," Wycherly said unwillingly. "But you'd still better steer clear for the next few days. I mean it."

"You need somebody to look after you!" Luned protested.

"I need to look after myself," Wycherly said, trying to keep from snapping at her. "At least, to see if I can. If I get into trouble, I'll come down to the store to find you, Luned. I promise."

"I guess you're set on it," Luned said grudgingly, and Wycherly felt a small unwilling flash of triumph. He'd managed to browbeat a sixteen-year-old girl into doing what he wanted. The petty victory made him angry, and in another moment he'd lash out at her again.

"I'm going out now," Wycherly said hastily, standing and picking up the other two cans of beer. "I'll see you in a few days."

Luned handed him his jacket.

"You mind you don't get into any trouble, Mister Wych," she said seriously.

Wycherly only laughed.

The morning air was cool and green, and once Wycherly got beneath the trees the dimness of the forest canopy provided him a welcome relief from the sun's brightness. One can of beer fit snugly into each of his two jacket pockets. Wycherly promised himself that he'd just carry them, not drink them unless things got bad. A little exercise would probably help the drying-out process, as well as working out the last of the kinks from yesterday's crash. So he told himself.

While the main reason for the excursion was to get away from Luned before he added one more thing to his list of regrets, it was true that he did have a faint amount of curiosity about the sanatorium—enough to make that his destination. Luned had said it was up the hill. Wycherly took the first trail he found leading upward.

He could put names to few of the plants that surrounded him. Unfamiliar patterns of birdsong fell upon his ears, and small invisible animals scurried away through the underbrush. Once he startled a deer—nearly as much as it startled him when it exploded into motion and fled with awkward powerful leaps.

The narrow foot-trail had not quite been overgrown by the decades of abandonment, or else someone from Morton's Fork still came up here, but his first clue that he was nearing the sanatorium came when Wycherly stumbled on a strip of paved road. It was nearly overgrown, but even eighty years of snow and rain had not managed to reduce the blacktopped slabs to rubble.

He followed the road until he came to two pillars overgrown with green. The wings of a painted iron gate still hung between them. The gate hung open, twined with vines, sagging and eaten with rust. On the iron arch above, the faint gleam of gold leaf could still be seen, the ornate gilded letters spelling out WILDWOOD SANATORIUM.

The large brass plaque set into the pillar was blackened and pitted with years of corrosion. He lifted the vines away from it; you could still see the words "Wildwood Sanatorium, est. 1915" engraved on it.

He was already sweaty and gasping from the mild exercise; it hadn't occurred to him that a walk through the woods could be so exhausting. Wycherly had always counted on his body even while he was abusing it, and took this betrayal as a personal attack. His body was starting to fail him, just as legions of doctors had always insisted it would. So it wasn't only his soul that was running out of time.

A soul? You're reaching for that one, chummy. Who says you've got a soul to risk?

No answer. But he never got answers, not this soon. Soon enough he'd have a whole chorus of horrors to talk to.

Simple thirst, rather than tainted craving, made him reach for one of the cans he carried. Once he'd opened it, he got out two Tylenol and threw them back, draining the can in a few swallows. That much accomplished, he leaned back against the nearer of the two pillars.

When he touched it, the bolts that held the brass plaque in place crumbled. He turned around to look, and it fell away from the stone, narrowly missing his foot.

He bent down to pick it up, thinking vaguely that he would keep it for a souvenir. As he straightened with it in his hands, he saw that there was a shallow opening in the pillar behind the plaque, and it seemed to have something in it. Wycherly set the plaque down and reached cautiously inside, wary of spiders. He pulled the object out and shook it carefully to rid it of the worst of the accumulated grit.

It was a bag of some sort. About four inches square, made of undyed linen—which explained why it was still here and not rotted away to rags. A design was embroidered on one side in colored thread: something that looked vaguely familiar to Wycherly. It was sewn shut.

He weighed it between his fingers, debating if he should satisfy his curiosity by ripping it open immediately. It seemed to be filled with coins and beads, and a crackling between his fingers suggested leaves. He raised it to his nostrils and sniffed cautiously, but could smell nothing but decades-old dust. He shrugged and slipped it into his pocket. It would keep.

He felt steady enough to go on now, and pushed his way between the hanging, overgrown gates. The flagstone path beyond had once been wide enough for an automobile, and a trace of it remained. He walked down the center, but his shoulders and sides were still brushed by the trailing canes of wild rose that had overgrown the drive. After several minutes' walk, he caught his first glimpse of the sanatorium.

Even in ruin it was breathtaking. It had been built at the same time the last palaces of the American merchant princes had risen, and that same unconscious arrogance and celebration of wealth must have been in evidence here in its heyday. From where he stood at the foot of the drive, Wycherly could see that what remained of vaulting walls of native granite covered an amazing amount of territory—a ruined palace indeed.

With the sanatorium's remains as a focal point, Wycherly thought he could see the outlines of the grounds; a series of terraces falling away from the main house. As he stared directly toward it, Wycherly suddenly realized he was looking at a sundial on its white marble plinth. It stood in the middle of what once must have been a sweeping lawn. The grass had been choked out by weeds, which had been strangled in turn by the dense growth of vines and bushes that thrived beneath the trees.

He walked over and pulled away some of the greenery about the sundial. It had been lavishly gilded once, but the gilding had been melted and burnt away by a swift heat that had left only the brass behind. The marble base, streaked with verdigris and softened by the passing years, also showed the effects of fire.

Luned said this place burned in . . . 1917?

And it didn't look as if anyone had been back here since, even to salvage objects with resale value, like an antique sundial.

It made no sense. Haunted? People believed in ghosts until the moment they realized there was a dollar to be made. The notorious Amityville house had been bought by people well aware of its history—and who had been willing to overlook that history because of the house's low asking price. But in eighty years, Wildwood Sanatorium had neither been looted—nor rebuilt.

Wycherly tried to imagine a motivation stronger than human greed and failed. Even self-preservation barely ranked in the top ten. This unlooted place did not conform to his experience of human nature, and Wycherly considered himself something of a connoisseur of human nature. Wildwood Sanatorium represented a vast outpouring of money even in a luxurious and exhibitionistic time. Even after the fire, there must have been something worth salvaging. Why would the place simply have been abandoned?

The Depression. Wycherly's brow cleared. He'd known there must be a rational explanation, and that was it. The so-called Great Depression that had begun in 1929 had ruined fortunes vaster than this sanatorium represented. This place, and its owners' ambitious plans, would have been nothing more than another casualty of that catastrophe. And after World War II, when there might have been money to rebuild, the eastern mountains had been supplanted by the Sunbelt as the preferred destination of the ailing.

Pleased to have assigned the puzzle to its appropriate pigeonhole, Wycherly walked on up the drive. The closer he got to the sanatorium, then thinner the overgrowth became. Though drifts of fallen leaves were rotted away to dust and mounded against the ruined walls where the wind had left them, there were no brambles growing over the stones.

Wycherly scuffed at the ground with the toe of his shoe. Beneath its cover of fallen leaves, the soil was sandy and crumbling, as sterile as the vermiculite around the roots of a potted plant in a florist's window. In fact, the earth around the sanatorium—at least on this side—was as barren as if it had been poisoned.

Poison was the first thing a child of the nineties would think of. Poison, radiation, toxic waste . . . but toxic waste was a byproduct of industry, and there had never been any industry in these mountains as far as he could see. Even the nearest coal mines were twenty and thirty miles away, and their blight, while profound, was nothing like what had happened here.

For a fleeting, fantastic moment Wycherly considered radiation—had this been the site of some still-unpublicized Manhattan Project half a century ago? But Luned had said the place had burned decades before that, and it certainly seemed to have been abandoned since the fire.

He shook his head. There could be a dozen prosaic explanations for the bare earth, including an antique insecticide spill. He pushed aside his speculations, and with them any acknowledgment of potential danger. He wondered how much of the inside was left.

Wycherly circled the building, choosing his footing carefully. The curving drive had led up to a front entrance reached by a grand terraced staircase. The stairs and their balustrades were still there, although the closer he got to the top, the more the stonework showed the effects of that long-ago fire. Finally he reached the last step. The archway through which a long-ago patron would have entered remained, as did a part of the wall.

There was nothing else.

Wycherly stood on the last step and gazed down, fascinated. The floor plan of the house remained, printed on the earth, but the years and the fire had left nothing behind but the house's shell. The upper stories had caved in and burnt to ashes, and where there had been cellars, those too stood exposed, opening a chasm three stories deep beneath his feet. Below the level of the sheltering earth the outer walls were intact; he could see the decades-old bricks and mortar, and everything was laid out in such a neat regular fashion—all straight lines and right angles and cubes—that he'd only been staring at it for several minutes when the thing that didn't fit caught his eye.

It was a black stone staircase running down along the left-hand wall. It began at what had once been ground level and made a gentle curve out into the main part of the cellar, running from nowhere to nowhere. When Wycherly's eyes had adjusted fully he realized that the staircase ended below the basement level. He wondered where it led, and why.

It did not occur to him that no one knew where he was; that a fall could leave him trapped and helpless. He felt the same irresistible glee that he had always felt when he stumbled on someone else's secrets: that the secrets here belonged to long-dead strangers made no difference.

Wycherly circled the building until he reached the black stairs. They were marble, and might once have even been ornate, though they seemed to begin below the levels of the public rooms. Another oddity in a sanatorium that seemed to have been erected by eccentric plutocrats. There was a landing two-thirds of the way down the black stairs, and after that, one last short flight would take him below the sub-cellar.

Wycherly started downward. The walls of the sub-sub-basement seemed to close in on him as he descended; he looked back the way he had come, and the far-off daylight was cool and dim. He could escape easily. He was perfectly safe.

So Wycherly told himself, but it was with a certain reluctance that he stepped off the bottom step, onto the floor. It was smooth and flat and dark: a close-grained stone like basalt or even sandstone, covered with fallen leaves, ancient cinders, and blown dust. The surface made for slippery footing.

The walls were rougher than the floor, and bore the marks of the hammers and chisels that had sculpted them out of the living rock. He could still see the marks where the bolts anchoring some framing or wallcovering had been sunk, though the paneling had gone to dust and ash as if centuries, and not mere decades, had passed.

Walking gingerly across the floor, Wycherly felt a sensation of weight, of depth—though logically there was no way for him to be able to sense such things. He looked around, trying to distract himself from the sense of claustrophobic pressure that being here gave him.

The room was . . .

Wycherly frowned, peering into the gloom. To tell the truth, he couldn't tell exactly *how* big the room was, or even its shape. A phrase from an old book he'd read once came back to him: non-Euclidean geometries. Maybe the architect had been drunk when he designed the place.

As drunk as Wycherly would like to be.

He thought of the remaining can of beer in his pocket. He and the beast both knew he was going to drink it, but just to spite the beast he thought he'd see if he could hold off a little longer. What else was there down here to see? He took a few steps toward the center of the room.

That.

In the center of the room stood a vaguely loaf-shaped object. It stood about forty inches high and was the same color as the walls, and the camouflaging shadows and uncertain perspective had made it blend in with its surroundings so well that Wycherly had first taken it for part of the back wall of the cellar. At first he thought it was a coffin; it was roughly sarcophagus-shaped: eight feet long and nearly as wide as it was tall.

It was an altar.

He wasn't sure where the notion came to him from—certainly the Musgraves' visits to the smug Episcopalian temple of their expensive faith had been rare enough that Wycherly was largely unfamiliar with religious things. But the conviction remained: This was an altar.

He went closer, curious. If it was an altar, then an altar to what? He crouched down beside it, studying it closely. The sides were covered with purposeful, delicate carvings that seemed halfway between letters and pictures. He traced over one with one finger. If they were letters, they did not look like any language he knew—but he suspected he knew the sort of book that would contain them.

For most of his adult life Wycherly had moved through the shadow-world of pointless self-indulgence, where evasion of personal responsibility frequently crossed the line into all sorts of New Age manifestations: channeling, reincarnation, the worship of peculiar spirits. . . . They didn't really believe in it any more than Kenneth Musgrave truly believed in the impressive God to whom he paid sketchy homage at Christmas and Easter. The pretence of belief, of *fealty*, was just a . . . convenience.

Black Magick in West Virginia? It was unfortunately not unbelievable.

Stiff muscles quickly protested the crouch, and Wycherly got to his feet, clutching at the altar for support. The top was smooth and flat; he ran the palm of his hand over it and felt an odd sense of inadequacy hovering just below the surface of his mind.

As if someone had made him an offer he'd failed to understand.

As if he'd failed.

Wycherly wasn't sure why he was angry, only that he was. He flung himself away from the carved block of stone, but he'd gotten muddled and ended up moving away from the stairs, not toward them.

That was when he saw the doorway.

It was a carved gothic archway in the smooth stone wall of the basement. As Wycherly approached, he could see the charred remains of a wooden door blocking it.

Leave it alone. It was the clear, quiet voice of self-preservation, and Wycherly brushed it aside easily. The wood came away in his hands, and in a few moments the doorway was clear. He put his hand on the frame. It was the same stone as the walls of the basement, and when he poked his head through it, he felt a cold, wet draft of air blowing toward him from the darkness. There were steps cut into the rock leading down. He could only see the first one or two; beyond that, the wide low steps disappeared into the darkness and he could not tell where they went. They were worn and shallow, the depression in the center of each tread suggesting that they had seen the passage of hundreds—thousands—of feet.

Wycherly took a hesitant step backward, wishing for a flashlight. It was a little after noon on a hot July day; the sun was nearly overhead. But here in this black room it was cold and dim, and what light there was did not penetrate beyond the archway to whatever lay below.

Don't be an asshole, Wycherly sneered at himself. Afraid of a hole in the ground because of some carvings on an altar? There weren't any carvings.

There probably wasn't any altar. He knew the beast was already prowling, blurring the borderline between reality and delusion. All there could possibly be down there was spiders and snakes.

And Camilla.

Dark. Dark icy water climbing his body, and he could not see what lay beneath. White body, white teeth, wound-red mouth. Coming for him, to draw him beneath the surface and feed upon him forever. . . .

Wycherly struggled free of the vision. He'd been here before; this was the shadowland that the black beast lived in. His heart hammered and he was sweating; there was a taste of copper in his mouth.

More than anything in life Wycherly feared the return of the night river and its profane undine. Camilla shouldn't be coming back for him like this. It wasn't fair. It was daytime. He was awake.

In a sudden frenzy, he dragged the unopened can of beer from his coat pocket and flung it into the cave opening. He could hear it bouncing and rolling for a long time as it clattered to the bottom of the stairs. He turned and fled back to the black stairs, as though safety could be found in the sunlight.

But it was too late. As he climbed the water mounted around his legs and the light drained away.

The river was cold, so cold, and he could feel his warm blood draining away into it—

—and he fell, leaves crumbling beneath his hands, and looked down over the edge of the black staircase at a twenty-foot drop onto bare rock. A little closer to the edge and he would have been dead—if he were to fall over the side, it would be a broken leg at the very least.

Wycherly ran his tongue over dry lips and wondered if he dared get to his feet and walk the rest of the way. He looked up. Another flight of stairs to go to reach the surface. Maybe he should crawl.

But he could still hear the water. And suddenly, horribly, came the realization that he was directly above the water, that the night river was rushing along beneath his feet, and at any moment he might fall *through* the stone, into the water beneath.

But not to drown. Wycherly shook his head, trying to dislodge the image of the white shape moving beneath the surface of the river. He could live through this. Wycherly took a deep breath, trying to hold onto the objective reality before his eyes.

Climb. Get out. Get away. You can outrun this if you try.
On hands and knees he began to crawl up the stairs.

He reached the top of the stairs, and . . .

. . . *rolled onto his back. The river gravel was harsh through his shirt, and his legs were still in the water, but Wycherly didn't care. He was safe.*

Out in the water, the dragon's eyes sank slowly beneath the surface. He could hear Camilla screaming from beneath the waters as the warm blood drained out of her, leaving her pale and cold . . . and hungry.

The chill of the river seemed to cut into his hands and knees like sharp rocks as he struggled away from her. He thrashed around in the water, seeking anything like solid ground, but the bed of the river seemed to liquify as he struggled, pulling him deeper.

He was in trouble. That despairing realization was something to cling to in the moment before it vanished. In trouble. Blindsided once more by failure he could not predict, much less guard against.

The river stole his senses one by one, until, blind and helpless, he fled the white shape sliding through the water, shark-mouthed and predatory. The shore was so very far away, spangled with colored lights—they did not promise safety, but a witness to his death.

Escape. He had to escape. The cold was burning him now. He could feel his heart hammering in his throat and taste his own blood billowing through the water. He did not mind dying, but he could not bear the thought of the innocents who would suffer because his work had been left undone.

With his last reserves of strength Wycherly lunged forward, struggling as the lamia seized him—

And in a brief moment of clarity realized he was not drowning, but falling.

Falling.

FOUR

THIS SIDE OF THE GRAVE

Methought I saw my late espoused Saint
Brought to me like Alcestis from the grave.
Love, sweetness, goodness, in her person shined.
But O as to embrace me she inclined,
I waked, she fled, and day brought back my night.
— JOHN MILTON

THE HEAVILY LADEN WINNEBAGO MOTOR HOME HAD left Glastonbury, New York at dawn, its destination the small Appalachian hamlet that had seemed so easily accessible on Dylan Palmer's survey map a few weeks before. But as the hours wore on toward dark, it began to seem (as in the words of the old adage) that you couldn't get there from here.

There were four of them in the overloaded RV—Dylan and Truth and the two grad students, Ninian Blake and Rowan Moorcock, neither of whom was allowed by the Institute's insurance company to drive the Winnebago. Truth wasn't even certain that Ninian *could* drive—there were times that the boy seemed so vague and dreamy that Truth was surprised he'd made it as far as graduate school.

"Boy?" He's at least twenty-four; you aren't exactly old enough to be his mother, Truth admonished herself.

Ninian Blake was gaunt, weedy, and obsessive—more like a

slacker/hacker than an embryonic parapsychologist—and reminded Truth more than a little of herself at the same age. He was strongest in psychometry, the ability to read the traces events had left behind in inanimate objects, though his psychic ability was frustratingly erratic. Other than that, Ninian nearly matched the textbook stereotype for a nineties psychic—long black hair and bemused brown eyes, known neither for his fashion sense nor his social graces. He got along well enough with the rest of the Institute's staff—or possibly didn't really notice them—except for one person.

"Are we there yet?" Rowan asked from the back, her tone only half-joking. Holding on to the countertops for support, she made her way cautiously to the front of the vehicle and peered out. She was wearing a long-sleeved purple T-shirt with two firebreathing dragons locked in mortal combat silkscreened on it in acid colors. Cargo shorts and hiking boots completed the outfit. The bright yellow earphones for her Walkman were around her neck, their cord leading down to a bright orange fanny pack.

Rowan Moorcock was a strong psychic talent who had accompanied Dylan to a number of haunted houses in Europe and America as his trance medium. Freewheeling, easygoing, and so matter-of-fact about her abilities that it was easy to forget that a large percentage of the human race still considered them freakish, Rowan entered trance to the strains of the loudest possible rock music played through the earphones of her Walkman, and, when particularly baffled, took omens from her gaming dice to unlock her psychic gift. If Rowan were asked to define Ninian Blake in one word, it would probably be "pretentious," and Ninian would probably reciprocate by calling her "superficial."

Truth stifled a sigh, and peered at the road map spread out across her lap. "The man in Pharaoh said we had to go back to State Road 92 and pick up 28 and look for the turnoff into Morton's Fork from that. It should be marked something like 'Watchman's Gap Trace,'" Truth recited from memory.

The Winnebago heeled over alarmingly as Dylan negotiated a curve in the road—posted forty-five miles per hour—at a maidenly thirty miles per hour. Truth, looking out at a sheer right-hand drop, could only applaud his conservative attitude. The area was beautiful but wild, and she didn't relish attempting to explain to the Institute's director what had happened to two fee-paying students, a hundred thousand dollars' worth of temperamental recording equipment, and their extremely expensive mobile unit, should the Winnebago be in even the mildest of accidents.

"We found 92," Dylan said hopefully.

"We *always* find 92," Rowan muttered under her breath. She swung her heavy red braid back over her shoulder and assumed a spurious look of cheer.

"Look!" Truth said. "Isn't that it?"

Warily putting on his flashers—the headlights were already on, though it was still an hour and more to sunset—Dylan pulled to a halt. When the RV stopped, Ninian came up to the front and joined the others staring out through the windshield. The headlights cast their wan daylight radiance on a patched narrow turnoff that angled sharply up and back.

"Is that Route 28?" Ninian asked doubtfully.

In contrast to Rowan's party-girl informality, Ninian was almost painfully formal, wearing a collarless long-sleeved black shirt, baggy pleated pants with sneakers, and a photojournalist's vest with brimming pockets. His hair was long, but it was pulled back into a excruciatingly neat tail of hair.

"I don't know whether it is or not, but it's the only turnoff I've seen anywhere along this road," Dylan responded. "If we're going to be lost, let's be lost somewhere new."

Half an hour later, no one in the van had the heart to remind Dylan of his bold words. The vehicle inched up the narrow road at a stately fifteen miles per hour, but no one complained; the road's potholed surface was treacherous, but it was too narrow for Dylan to be able turn the Winnebago around and go back. And the sun was sinking rapidly; despite July's promise of long summer twilights, the illumination that remained once the sun had sunk below the crest of the mountains was more harm than help.

Truth suspected that they actually were heading in the right direction to reach their destination—the turnoff was the only possible route. If only the crumbling road weren't so narrow. The feeble attempt at a guardrail someone had put up on the outer curve of the turns only served to underscore the sheerness of the drop-off beyond. She only hoped they didn't meet a car going the other way.

"Hey—look at that!"

Rowan pointed over Truth's shoulder, and a moment later Truth saw what Rowan was pointing at: a place where the greying, white-painted wood was freshly broken. Something *had* gone over the side and into the valley below—and not that long ago.

"Somebody didn't have a nice day," Rowan said, and Truth could only agree. The drop-off there was not as steep as it was elsewhere along the road, and both women could see the scars of the tires on the earth, the battered tree trunks, and the glass surrounding the base of the boulder where the crashing car had obviously come to rest.

"At least it means there's some traffic along this road," Dylan said lightly. Truth bit her lip. She wanted to tell him to be careful, but it certainly wasn't Dylan Palmer's driving that worried her—if she could say that anything was truly worrying her.

You're just edgy. And you've been edgy all spring. Since, in fact, they'd really set the date for the wedding. Truth twisted her emerald-and-pearl engagement ring around her finger, fidgeting. She turned on the radio, hitting the AUTO-SEEK button to allow the antenna to search for the strongest signal. Maybe some music would distract her.

But all that the machine could pull in was a mushy hash of static, through which only an indistinct mutter of voices could be heard.

"Great!" Dylan said happily. "I should have thought of that for myself. Morton's Fork is a radio dead area. If we can't pull in anything, maybe we're getting closer."

"Or the radio's broken," Ninian pointed out.

"How can *this* be radio dead?" Rowan demanded, gesturing at the mountain panorama spread out before every window. "We're on top of a mountain—what could be interfering with a signal?"

"Any number of things—natural magnetism or radiation, placement of transmitters, distance," Dylan said in his best professorial voice.

As he drove, he began to lecture his two students upon the importance of being familiar enough with the laws of physics to keep from assigning a supernatural explanation when a natural one would do. Students who came to the Bidney Institute intending to take its degree program in parapsychology were often surprised that one of the freshman offerings was a course on famous frauds and debunking methodologies, but the Institute had no more interest in being defrauded than any private person did—and a real stake in being able to separate the true paranormal manifestations from the work of the con men, frauds, and hoaxers that the psychic sciences invariably attracted.

Truth let Dylan's words wash over her—she had heard this lecture many times, in one form or another, and agreed with its sentiments as well as he did. But was that enough to build a shared life upon? She didn't think it was. And there was more—so much more—that they disagreed upon.

At the heart of the matter was that Dylan preferred to watch, to study, to record the situation in full without altering it. And Truth felt she ought to intervene, even if she didn't completely understand what was happening, in order to make things come out the way they should.

"Be sure you're right, then go ahead." But the words usually attributed to one of America's most beloved presidents failed to comfort her. It was so hard to know when you were right.

Another twenty-four hours brought Sinah no more clarity. She had walked the floor all night, drank endless cups of tea, but found no real answers.

Still, the fiery vision seemed to mark a turning point of a sort—as if, though no one in the village would speak to her, there was something in Morton's Fork that would. Something hovering just out of reach. Something that could help.

Or maybe she was just going mad. *You pays yer money and you takes yer choice,* Sinah told herself mockingly.

She smelled smoke several times several times through the night, but each time as the flames rose she could not keep herself from struggling, and each time the vision had faded before it had really begun. *I'll never get anywhere at this rate.*

By the time dawn came she was able to force herself to lie down on her bed and sleep for a few hours, but when she awoke again the rest of the day—and the night to come—stretched before her like a jail term with no end. She had to do something more than wait passively to fill the empty hours. *A walk. That's what I need. Clear my head, tire me out.*

The day was sunny but cloudy—why did no one ever say a day was partially sunny, instead of partially cloudy?—so Sinah threw a waterproof poncho into her backpack before starting off. She chose her destination on impulse: the burnt-out sanatorium that lay in the direction of Watchman's Gap. Her vision had possessed such a sense of reality, as though it were a replay of something that had truly happened. And the ruins had burned. She knew that much. *Fire in fact to counter fire in fantasy? Well, it's worth a try.*

But when she had locked her front door behind her she hesitated, as if she weren't sure whether she wanted to see what came next or not. With an angry shrug, Sinah finally forced herself to move. There was nothing on earth that she was afraid of except herself, and she knew just where *she* was, didn't she?

Yes. In trouble.

As she walked, she kept a wary eye on the sky. Unlike California, where the residents expected 360 cloudless days a year, an Appalachian summer was changeable, capable of raining and shining at the same time. And storms here were quick and violent.

She'd just come in sight of Wildwood Sanatorium when a storm of another sort hit. Formless, intangible, but intensely real, the force of the borrowed emotion threw Sinah to her knees and wiped away the summer day.

Terror. Black, intense, and final; emotional and physical agony powerful enough to make her weep. It was there and gone, fading like a cry for help that had taken the caller's last strength. *But there's no one here to touch—no one in sight—where did it come from?* Sinah was on her feet again and running in the direction the psychic cry had come from before she had quite collected her wits; running toward the ruin.

He isn't dead. Her first really coherent thought since hearing the mental shout came as Sinah knelt beside the man lying on the ground. He was lying on the bank of Little Heller Creek, one of the many tributaries of the Astolat. The creek might be only a few inches deep, but it could drown an unconscious man who fell face-down into it. He'd been lucky.

He was no one she knew, and not from around here: He showed none of the marks of malnutrition and inbreeding that distinguished the native-born of Lyonesse County from their more fortunate flatlander cousins. Sinah hesitated only a moment before touching him, then reached out and rolled him onto his back. The surface of his mind was still with unconsciousness; he was blank, as were those she touched who were lost in dreamless sleep.

His skin was paler than hers: the skin of a convict or a computer hacker—some sort of social subspecies who never saw the sun. There was a strawberry blush beginning to dawn across the cheekbones and nose; he was a real redhead, hair a shade between copper and strawberry blond, with the pale copper lashes and brows that went with such dramatic coloring. A young man, somewhere close to her own age, but there was an odd graininess to his skin that suggested illness or drink to Sinah's trained eye. She wondered how long he'd been out here.

Having spent her life trying to shut others out, Sinah lacked the skills to probe further, and told herself she would not have chosen to in any case. Still, she wished there was someone here to tell her who he was and how he'd gotten here—both to Morton's Fork and into his current trouble.

And just what are you going to do with him now? an inward voice asked her. Though he wasn't musclebound, he still weighed more than she did, and she couldn't carry him anywhere—nor could she get someone to come and move him for her; the natives of Morton's Fork were barely on speaking terms with her.

"Hey? You?" Sinah said tentatively. She dipped her hand in the icy water and flicked some drops at his face.

The effect was immediate and electrifying. With a rush, all the architecture of his mind woke to life again, dragging itself up through the veils of unconsciousness. Sinah tasted a faint, grudging anger—confusion, and fear, but most of all a strange blankness, as if the hot immediacy of his real feelings had been somehow siphoned off.

He opened his eyes. They were a startling pale brown, almost light enough to be called amber. Sinah removed her hand from his face; her sense of him receded slightly, but she could still sense his emotions swirling through each other in a shifting, changing panorama that only she could perceive.

Fear spiked and then receded as he got a good look at her.

"*. . . pretty eyes—too thin—looks like a normal girl—blackout? Haven't had a real drink in three days at least; not long enough; it isn't fair—*" Fragments of his internal monologue came to her like scraps of a conversation being held in the next room. His inner voice jumbled into unintelligibility when he spoke.

"Hello? I don't suppose you've seen a St. Bernard with a cask of Benedictine around its neck?" His voice was educated, cultured, with a sort of flat drawl that placed him squarely on Long Island, New York to Sinah's theater-trained ear.

"I think they only send them out for skiers."

Sinah sat back on her haunches to put as much distance between them as she could, but there was no real way to shut out the chaotic spill of his thoughts and feelings when she was this close. She'd need to be at least thirty feet away, and no one could spend their entire life staying thirty feet away from every other human being.

Wary approval. Assessment, its measuring of factors flashing by faster than verbalization could keep up. She had a sense that he was surprised to be here—as if he had evaded some danger—but whatever peril occupied his thoughts, it was not concrete enough to come to the surface of his mind.

"Well, I'll just have to manage on my own, then," the man said. She almost had his name, but it flitted from her mental grasp like a recalcitrant goldfish.

"I'll do what I can. My name's Sinah. What's yours?"

Musgrave-failure-son. "I'm Wycherly Musgrave. Call me Wych."

A cascade of powerful images accompanied his words—all unpleasant. Sinah never got the option of learning about people slowly, or of discovering the mitigating circumstance. She had it all, and all at once: the North Shore and its Green Mile, hereditary wealth and unmet expectation. Alcoholism. Violence.

Vicious spoiled drunken rich boy said Wycherly's mind.

"Let's get you up, then," Sinah said evenly.

It looked like it was going to be easy—or at least possible—until the moment Wycherly tried to put weight on his left foot. The pain made him lose his balance; his feet slid out from under him and he fell back to the ground, jarring the bad ankle painfully.

"I can't stand up." His voice sounded bewildered and childish, even to him. Wycherly gritted his teeth angrily. It wasn't so much that he wanted to impress her, as that he didn't think his response would be entirely rational if she laughed at him. He tried to get to his feet again with even less success. All the muscles still hurt from the crash yesterday, and overriding all those aches was the bright, hot pain in his left ankle.

"I think it's sprained," he said evenly.

To distract himself he took a closer look at his rescuer. Not a local. She looked . . . expensive. Wide grey eyes and shoulder length pale brown hair—no, light brown was too ordinary a description; it was actually a ruddier color than that, with streaks of red and gold in it, like an autumn forest. She was dressed in a softly stonewashed denim shirt embroidered with Indian patterns, a pair of white cotton jeans, and Mephisto trekking boots. Small white stones glittered in her double-pierced ears. The whole look was one of more sophistication and money than Wycherly had seen in all the rest of Morton's Fork.

"It looks like it," the woman—Sinah?—said in a neutral voice. "I think you'd better get that shoe off before someone has to cut it off."

Wycherly studied her warily, wondering if he knew her, if she'd been sent to bring him back. But no. She was someone he would like to know, certainly—at least if she wouldn't nag him—but not anyone he knew. Although there was something very familiar about her face. . . .

"Do I know you?" he asked suddenly.

Her fingers were cool on his ankle, pushing up his pant leg and pulling at his shoe.

"Ouch!"

"I'm sorry—does that hurt?" she asked.

"Of course it hurts!" Wycherly snarled, instantly out of patience. "The damned thing's broken!"

"I don't think so," she said. "It would be a lot more swollen if it were."

How the hell do you know? "Do you want to debate it?" Wycherly snapped, losing his hold on his better self. His head hurt, and he felt nauseated by the dank, rotting smell of the river.

Sinah pulled his leather deck shoe free, and Wycherly unwarily wiggled his toes. It was a mistake. He gritted his teeth. He wanted a drink—or two—or *ten*—and though he knew it was ridiculous, he could not keep himself from watching the surface of the river to make sure nothing came up out of it. Nothing white, and sinuous, with huge dark eyes and pointed teeth—

"—all right?" she said. "Wycherly?"

"I'm fine," he grunted. A blackout—a small one. He had to get away from this woman before the beast came back.

Sinah ran a hand over her forehead, brushing her hair back. Sunlight sparkled off a sudden dew of perspiration on her skin.

"I don't think it's broken," she said. Repeated? "But you can't very well walk out on it—or stay here until it mends."

Wycherly darted a wary glance at the river. It was stupid to be afraid of a little water, but he couldn't shake the irrational conviction that it was *after* him somehow, impossible as that was.

Or was it? What if Camilla climbed out of it while Sinah was here? That was something to think about. No, better not.

His head hurt.

"What is it you suggest that I do?" he asked, enunciating with venomous clarity. "Or do you just go wandering through the woods addressing oblivious homilies to helpless strangers?"

"I *could* just leave—and let you try to find your way out of this by yourself," Sinah shot back tartly.

"Go ahead," Wycherly suggested, glaring at her coldly.

There was a long pause while the two of them locked gazes. Wycherly tried to shift to a more comfortable position, and was rewarded with a new jab of pain. A flicker of distaste crossed Sinah's features. She looked away.

"I believe you think I would," she said after a pause.

"Why not? I'm sure you know that what makes most people behave according to the dictates of society is the fear that they're being watched."

I'm being watched.

"Aren't we?" Sinah asked, looking around.

Coming for him, sliding up out of the dark water— She was cruel, cruel to tease him this way. Wycherly firmly shut visions of undines out of his mind. "No. And if you can't think of anything else to do, why don't you be a good girl and go down to the general store and—"

He stopped. She wasn't listening to him. She was looking back over his shoulder, up the mountain, and on her face was the purest expression of terror that Wycherly had ever seen.

"Smoke." Her voice was high with strain, flattening out from her carefully educated vowels into an Appalachian drawl. "Don't you smell the smoke? Something's burning."

"Nothing's burning."

Sinah heard the words only faintly, but his hands on her wrists were like an anchor, his pain and anger keeping her from being drawn in as swiftly as she had been the first time. This time, the flames receded, and Sinah was outside the walls of an enormous yet strangely familiar building, seeking to gain entrance. She felt dread and a need to hurry. There was a stored wealth of information cached tantalizingly out of reach, if she could only merge with it she could gain all of the answers she sought, but her hands were chained with fetters of red-hot iron—

"Sinah!"

She felt herself being shaken, felt her mind fill with the selfish fear of being abandoned here, injured and sick, unable to get away to hide before the shakes began and the need for a drink—

The impact of the slap knocked her sprawling, wiping the traces of that strange possession from her mind. Her cheek stung; she put her hand to it as she backed away on hands and knees.

"Nothing's burning," Wycherly said hoarsely.

Sinah got to her feet and looked at him. He was kneeling awkwardly, clutching at a bush for support. She could feel the suffering that radiated from him in waves, but somehow it was distant, as impersonal as a news report.

"Don't ever hit me again," she said evenly.

He stared at her, frustration and guilt written so plainly on his face that it didn't take a mind reader to see it. She was far close enough to him to hear his undervoice plainly: *What else was I supposed to do?*

What had she done to provoke that reaction from him? Had he seen the fire, too?

"Sorry," Wycherly said briefly.

He collapsed to a sitting position again with a groan of effort, and closed both hands over his injured ankle, squeezing it as if he could crush away the damage and make it do what he wanted. It showed a streak of ruthlessness that seemed oddly inconsistent with the whipped-dog flinching and snarling of his surface personality. But the surface of most people's minds were a lie they told themselves. That was the first thing someone, who was cursed the way Sinah was, learned.

The fiery vision was fading, sliding off into her unconscious mind again. Each time it came it was less frightening and seemed to give her more room to manipulate it. But once she had control of this new manifestation . . . what then?

What would be next—and would it kill her?

"The first thing we need to do is get you back to civilization," Sinah said, standing up.

No! He'll tell— "Doctor . . . ?" Wycherly groaned. *Pills—drugs—make it all go away—*

"Well, the nearest one's probably in Pharaoh," Sinah said, trying to ignore his conflicting emotions. "I've got a car. I'll be happy to drive you there—but I've got to get you down the mountain first. Wait right here."

Wycherly's sudden flash of murderous rage was enough to make Sinah step backward hastily. A moment later she'd taken to her heels and was fleeing down the mountain.

There were old trails leading from the Little Heller to practically everywhere on this side of the mountain, and after living shunned here for a month Sinah knew them all. It was an easy matter for her to grab some emergency medical supplies, throw them into the back of the Cherokee, and head back up the hill.

"This is stupid," Wycherly said when she reached him. He eyed the Jeep parked a few yards away.

"Would you like to walk?" Sinah answered. "Take the pills."

Wycherly looked at the bottle of over-the-counter Tylenol she'd handed him with the bottle of spring water. He flung it into the river in eloquent silence, and began rummaging through his jacket.

He produced a brown pharmacy bottle at last and shook several pills into his hand. As Sinah watched—calmly, because her gift told her exactly what they were and his tolerance for them—he tossed them back and followed them with a few reluctant swallows of water.

Without waiting for further permission, Sinah got out the Ace bandage she'd brought with her and began wrapping his swelling ankle tightly. The important thing, whether Mr. North Shore Redhead realized it or not, was to get him out of the sun before it finished cooking him. She didn't think the ankle was badly sprained, and he'd probably be able to walk on it after a day or so if he was careful. And somehow, after the reaction to her offer to drive him into Pharaoh, she didn't think he was going to be any too keen on seeing a doctor.

"Okay, you're as ready as you'll ever be. Think you can make it to the car?"

She felt the swirl of his thoughts as he assessed the possibility. He thought he could.

"No," Wycherly said.

Sinah gritted her teeth. "March or die, my friend," she said with a wholly spurious cheerfulness. "C'mon, now. You can lean on me."

With no resistance—but no particular help, either—Sinah got Wycherly to his feet. She pulled his arm around her neck, and slowly they made their hobbling progress toward the car.

His body pressed against hers filled Sinah's mind with Wycherly's sensations, emotions, and scattered thoughts, until she was living his life and could not be certain which of them was running away. She had never wanted a drink so badly in her life.

Sinah had never been even a social drinker. She didn't like the taste, and feared the loss of control—and the premature aging it brought to skin and face was something no actress could afford. But now she found herself longing for the scouring bite of straight whiskey, the burn and the half-nauseated exhilaration of slugging it back as if it were water, the insulation it would put between her and daily life. All her problems would vanish, any new ones that appeared she could outrun with enough liquor. . . .

Only long practice—a distrust of every feeling that seemed to be hers—enabled her to deny the craving. *You are truly messed up, my friend,* Sinah thought, and was not sure which of them she meant.

Axe-murderer or saint, though, there was very little Wycherly could do hampered by a bad ankle—and Sinah knew exactly how much pain he was in. She thought she could trust him.

Conditionally.

The ride was bumpy, but Wycherly braced himself in his corner of the front seat and endured it silently. The sun was angling westward, and automatically he glanced at his watch. Two o'clock. A hell of a way to spend an afternoon.

The Jeep stopped.

"We're here," Sinah said unnecessarily. "Now, do you want to come inside, or do you want me to drive you on down to Pharaoh?"

She reminded him of his sister, Wycherly thought to himself: his bossy, arrogant, take-charge sister Winter, who had to be perfect at everything she did, even being imperfect—like all the people who had perfectly planned lives with all the accessories. And this slumming silver-spoon bimbo seemed to be struck from the same die.

His head hurt. His foot hurt. He wanted desperately to be unconscious. There was a bottle in his cabin that would be enough for tonight at the very least, and if he was lucky, tomorrow would never come.

"Never mind. Thanks for all your help. I'm going home," he said, as civilly as he could manage.

"I don't think I want to drive you all the way to Long Island," Sinah answered.

Wycherly's head snapped up. She did know him! He knew he'd seen her before—she must be one of Mother's candidates, paraded before him like mares in heat in the hope he'd take the plunge into suitable matrimony. Which would, so his father said, make a man out of him, though it didn't seem to have done as much for Kenny Jr.

She seemed to recoil under the impact of his baleful glare.

"It's . . . I mean, it's in your voice. The Island accent," she faltered. "It's in your voice. I know about regional accents. I have to be able to mimic them. I'm an actress."

"An actress," Wycherly echoed derisively.

Maybe not one of Mother's candidates. Mother only approved of older male actors, possibly with a Tony or Oscar to their credit. But the woman was so familiar. . . .

"Come inside," she said pleadingly. "We can discuss it there, okay?"

"No. Take me home. I'll show you the way," Wycherly said brusquely. He felt awful, and knew he looked worse—sweaty, shaking, and greenish. More than anything, he wanted to be alone—the beast had its claws into him now, and things were only going to get worse. He thought longingly of oblivion—he wanted oblivion, and the liquor kindly gave it to him: Things got fuzzy, then disappeared entirely, long before he passed out.

He recanted his decision to dry out. Fervently. Only now the blackouts were invading what he thought of as his nondrinking life. It had to stop. Wycherly rubbed his jaw—the skin felt stiff and tender—and thought of the bottle in his cabin.

"Are you sure?" Sinah said.

My God, woman, do you want me throwing up on your rug? "Yes. Please. If you would be so kind," Wycherly said.

Old Miss Rahab's cottage stood amidst its guardian trees in the afternoon sun. No smoke came from the chimney, and Wycherly hoped that Luned had already gone home. The presence of the woman beside him was growing intolerable, and Luned's proprietary sunniness would be the final straw.

The Jeep Cherokee was parked as close as Sinah could get it to Wycherly's ramshackle rented cottage, but the young saplings made it impossible to get very close. Had he left here only this morning on his ill-considered ramble? That had been one of his worst ideas in a lifetime that contained no good ones.

"Are you sure? I could—"

"I don't need—"

"—a woman's help?" Sinah finished for him angrily. She turned to look at him. Wycherly thought she looked like safety, sanity, and hope. None of which were for him; not for Wycherly Musgrave.

"A *person's* help. Any person," Wycherly said. He shoved open the passenger-side door. It banged into a tree, but he didn't care; it opened far enough for him to swing his right leg out, and gingerly lift the left one after it. He stood, hanging onto the door.

"You are the stubbornest man I ever met," Sinah exclaimed, glaring at him in half-amused exasperation.

"You should get out more," Wycherly told her with a death's-head grin. Clinging to the door for support, he groped for one of the tree trunks and clung to it in a death grip. "I'm fine. Go away."

"I'll check on you tomorrow," Sinah said. She reached across the passenger seat of the Jeep Cherokee and pulled the door shut.

"Go to the devil," Wycherly invited her. He made the mistake of testing his bad ankle to see if it would support him.

Sinah winced empathically at the bright flare of pain. But there was no sound or outcry that she could legitimately use as an excuse to ask if he was all right, and she already knew Wycherly Musgrave well enough to know that he wasn't the sort of man who accepted help gracefully. As she watched helplessly, he dragged himself from tree to tree and finally through the door of the cabin. She saw him hesitate upon the threshold as he searched for another handhold, and then the door swung closed behind him.

Sinah leaned forward, resting her forehead on the Jeep's steering wheel for a moment. Let him go. Selfishness was the first law of self-preservation for something like her—but how much longer could she bear to purchase her own survival at that high a price?

"Oh, Wycherly," Sinah said softly. "Everybody needs help sometime."

The question was, where could a person get it whose problems were more than human ones?

Wycherly clung to the back of the chair, listening to the sound of the engine fading in the distance. He'd half expected Luned still to be here, waiting for him just the way Camilla did, but the cabin seemed to be deserted. His ankle ached like a broken tooth. Sinah had suggested that he pack it in ice to ease the pain; he hadn't told her that his cabin had no electricity.

At least there was still daylight.

Dragging the chair with him like a bulky, recalcitrant crutch, Wycherly groped his way over to the sink. He was thirsty; so thirsty that he didn't care whether what he drank was alcoholic or not. In the background, the sound of the Jeep's engine persisted.

No, that wasn't it.

He glanced at the dirty, chipped door of the refrigerator suspiciously. Unbelievably, it was running; from the sound of it, it might take off or explode at any moment.

Clutching at the sink for support, Wycherly pulled open the refrigerator door. The handle vibrated beneath his fingers, and the air inside was perceptibly cooler than that in the cabin.

The refrigerator was filled with six-packs of beer in half a dozen brands; last night's soup had been removed to make room for them.

Wycherly let out a sob of relief. He dragged the chair around and sat down in front of the open door, yanking the nearest six-pack toward him. Hastily, as though it were life-giving medicine, he popped the tab on the first can and chugged the still-warm foamy liquid down, gulping and dribbling in his haste. A second can followed the first, then another. He felt bloated, and not in the least drunk, but it had taken the edge off. . . .

His addiction.

He winced. He might have suffered less if he could deny it, but unfortunately, he'd never lied to himself. He'd driven Sinah away because he'd wanted to be alone with a six-pack of cheap beer and a bottle of Scotch. Driven her off so she wouldn't see him—though a part of him knew that he wouldn't have cared, so long as he could feed the beast. Nothing mattered except feeding the beast, so that it would grant him oblivion and keep Camilla away.

An odd, uncomfortable feeling pressed outward on his chest. It was a little like fear, a little like anger. It made him restless, uncomfortable. It grew stronger, and cautiously, disbelievingly, he identified it.

It was shame.

He was ashamed of what he did. He was ashamed of what he was.

Wycherly looked down at the can in his hands and laughed. Why should his own contempt be harder to bear than the humiliation he'd caused everyone he'd ever known? It would do as little to stop him as the contempt of others.

But I am stopping. I am. I won't open the Scotch. I'll stick to beer.

That wouldn't help. It was possible to be a toxic alcoholic on beer, wine coolers, or even cough syrup. Alcoholism was a thing of the spirit. It was a matter of intention.

Did he intend to stop? Was he using the beer to blunt the jagged edges of detox? Or was he using it to get drunk?

If you go on drinking you will die. The inner voice was as unequivocal as a judge's sentence. Wycherly didn't even bother to argue with the truth of that; he knew it in a level below rationality. The only trouble was, he wasn't strong enough to stop, and he was damned if he was calling upon some smug sanctimonious Higher Power.

Even to save your life? the inner voice asked, and some cold ophidian part of Wycherly's mind answered: *Yes.*

Deliberately—defying even himself—Wycherly opened a fourth can of beer. That made nine today plus the codeine, and he planned on more beer, more codeine, and maybe a sleeping pill later. Not bad for his first day's march toward sobriety, he supposed.

It's the thought that really counts, Wycherly reflected mockingly. He finished the beer and threw the can on the floor to join its fellows; a petty rebellion against Luned's housekeeping. He stared into the refrigerator broodingly.

It was because of Luned that the refrigerator worked. He could not imagine what fire she'd lit under Tanner to command this kind of service, and this evidence of her devotion angered him. He didn't want Luned—or Sinah, for that matter. He wasn't sure what he wanted, but when he got his hands on it, everyone was going to be sorry, by God. Wycherly took a long pull on the fresh beer, lowering the level to the point where he'd probably be able to carry it without spilling it.

Far from drunk—but filled with that soothing hyper-clarity that was the seductive reward of his drinking—Wycherly pulled himself to his feet. He gingerly tested his weight on the damaged ankle. It hurt profoundly but didn't give way; if he used the chair for a crutch he thought he could get as far as the bedroom.

And there was whiskey in the bedroom.

But you promised. . . .

Luned had been busy in here as well, and Wycherly experienced a moment of blind, murderous fury at that fact before locating his shoulder bag neatly placed beside the washbasin. He slung it onto the bed, then flung himself down beside it, scrabbling around until he was lying more or less straight on the bedclothes. He kicked off his remaining shoe and began to loosen the bandage—all he needed on top of everything else was gangrene.

The flesh over the wrenched joint was deeply indented: swollen above and below the bandage, mottled green and violet beneath it. Wycherly shucked off his pants and his torn and muddy shirt; he was grimy and sweaty and his skin burned rawly, and he wished furiously for the comforts of civilization. At least the codeine he'd taken before getting into the Jeep was finally beginning to kick in. Without even thinking about what he was doing, Wycherly pulled his shoulder bag over to him and dug through it until his fingers touched the smooth coolness of the bottle.

This was what he wanted.

It was all right—he'd still quit—but tomorrow, when things weren't so bad. . . .

Wycherly stared at the sealed bottle, hearing his own thoughts with brutal clarity. Things would always be worse tomorrow. That was just the way it was.

There was no good time to stop.

He rolled on his side and shied the bottle out through the open bedroom window. He heard it clink as it hit the ground, but he didn't know if it broke. He didn't care, Wycherly told himself angrily. Everything stopped here: no Scotch, no shine, no vodka. Beer only until he finished what was in the cabin.

Then, nothing. Nothing, nothing, *nothing.*

He reached into his bag again and found the bottle of Seconal, but the pills were too big to swallow dry. That meant he had to retrieve his unfinished beer from the washstand, and as soon as Wycherly touched his bad foot to the ground it sent a lightning flash of pain up his leg. Maybe he should have left the bandage alone. He gritted his teeth. Sweat beaded his forehead and ran down his face. The foot throbbed like a beating heart.

But finally he grabbed the half-empty can and settled back on the bed. He opened the bottle and gazed at the capsules hungrily, but only removed one. If one of these and codeine and beer wouldn't put him to sleep, he'd lie awake and comfort himself with the knowledge that his family probably thought he was dead.

Wycherly tossed the pill to the back of his throat and drained the beer can, flinging the empty out the window to join the bottle. He'd have to start being more careful after this; he had no intention of ending his life with a bottle of pills—or surviving an overdose as a drooling, brain-damaged vegetable warehoused in the critical care wing of some nursing home. No, Wycherly intended to annoy as many people as possible for as long as he could—and then go out in a brief, bright, flare of glory.

The thought was oddly alien in a number of ways, as if it was something he'd never thought before. Somehow the image made his thoughts turn toward the overgrown grounds of Wildwood Sanatorium again.

He finally remembered what the place had reminded him of: Sleeping Beauty's castle, silent and deserted. Where everyone inside was enchanted and lay sleeping, dreaming. . . .

Or dead.

FIVE

GRAVEN IMAGES

Make less thy body hence, and more thy grace;
Leave gormandizing; know the grave doth gape
For thee thrice wider than for other men.
— WILLIAM SHAKESPEARE

"I THINK WE'RE HERE," DYLAN ANNOUNCED.

The twists in the road had made it difficult to spot, but a while ago the travelers from Taghkanic had reached the crest of the peak and begun working their way down into the hollow. Dylan's announcement had been a trifle premature, but the four of them were seeing signs that they were nearing civilization—if civilization could be defined as discarded Coke cans and rotting automobile tires.

A rusted road sign Truth had spotted along the way was bent so far out of true that it could not be read from the Winnebago, but Rowan had disembarked with a flashlight and brought back the information that this was Watchman's Gap Trace, sometimes known as State Road 113.

"And wasn't that the one that was supposed to branch off 28 and lead right down into Morton's Fork?" Rowan asked.

"We must have taken the last turn without realizing it," Truth said, relieved.

"Now all we have to do is get there," Dylan said.

There was a noncommittal grunt from Ninian.

After all the dead ends and wrong turns, arrival in Morton's Fork itself was almost anticlimactic. The road gradually leveled off—though becoming, if possible, narrower—and, as the dusk deepened, it brought them to the town itself—and the end of the paving.

"This is it?" Ninian said blankly.

"This," Dylan confirmed, "is Morton's Fork—the center of paranormal activity for the entire fifty-mile area surrounding it."

He turned off the engine; in the sudden silence they could hear the twilight calls of crickets and frogs, and, somewhere nearby, the sound of running water.

The town of Morton's Fork did not look as if it were the center of any activity whatever. The windows were dark, but a lone light bulb burned outside the general store, and in the illumination from it the travelers could see signs which offered fax service, cold beer, and pelt-purchase, a weird commingling of centuries that made Truth smile. Across the street from the store was a gas station, and that seemed to be it for the Morton's Fork commercial strip.

Lights came on inside the general store again, and by the illumination the party could see a man moving from the back of the store to the front. Dylan climbed out of the driver's seat. Truth felt the camper rock as Rowan went out the back door.

"Are you all right, Ms. Jourdemayne?" Ninian asked.

His face was grave as he studied her, and Truth wondered what he saw. She wondered what anyone saw who really had the eyes to see beyond the accepted and conventional limits of twentieth-century Man's devising.

"I'm just tired, Ninian. It's been a long day. And I hope nothing else goes wrong—Dylan wasn't completely sure of our reception here, despite all his groundwork he'd laid."

Voices outside the camper pulled her attention back to the present.

"We're not lost," Dylan was saying. "We're researchers from the Margaret Beresford Bidney Institute."

"Oh, *you're* them," the local said, in a voice of discovery. "I'm Evan Starking—you wrote to my pa; he sort of runs things around here." The tall redhead with the pockmarked skin held out his hand. "You're lucky you come in when you did. It's almost dark; I was just about to shut up for the night and then you'd of been out of luck until morning. But welcome to Morton's Fork anyway."

"Thanks." Truth saw Dylan shake the proffered hand. He gestured back at the camper. "Is there some place here we can park and set up our campsite? We might want to move later, depending on what we find, but right now we'd just like to settle in."

"Sure," Evan said.

As the two men were speaking, Truth and Ninian climbed out of the camper as well. It was good, Truth reflected, to have solid nonmoving ground under her feet after the day's long drive, and Evan Starking didn't seem to share any of the region's inhabitants' legendary suspicion of strangers—or if he did, he had excellent manners.

"Will you be needing anything from the store? Milk, eggs, that sort of thing? I could stay open for a few minutes," he suggested.

"That'd be great," Dylan said, and Truth, thinking of the chance of a cold drink, heartily agreed.

The general store was almost a cliché. Shelves extended all the way to the high, pressed-tin ceiling, filled with the daily needs of a lifestyle that Truth found unimaginably remote. What on earth was Fels-Naptha, and why did they sell it in bricks?

"This isn't whole grain," Rowan said, looking at a loaf of Whole Wheat Wonder Bread. She shrugged, and added it to the pile of purchases on the counter.

"No, ma'am," Evan said. "Folks up here mostly bakes their own—and if they don't, they aren't wanting bread that fights back. But we get another delivery on Thursday, and I could have Harry put a couple of loaves on the truck for you."

"Can he get twelve-grain? Or sprouted wheat?" Rowan asked, moving back toward the counter. Truth smiled to herself, continuing toward the back of the store. Evan's willingness to accommodate the visitors wasn't hard to ascribe a reason to. Rowan was pretty, friendly, and outgoing—and how many strangers did someone like Evan Starking see from one year to the next?

Unless he's leading a secret life, Truth thought. It wasn't out of the question. With an automobile, the twentieth century was only an hour's drive from here.

She perused the shelves. Mason jars and shotgun shells. Flypaper and mosquito netting. Citronella, pectin, wooden clothespins, coarse salt, cola syrup—and beside them, boxes of Twinkies and Hefty bags, like emissaries from the mainstream consumer culture. Absently Truth picked up a jar of peanut butter and a box of Twinkies. She knew that Dylan was taking care of important matters like milk and eggs. They hadn't brought many supplies with them because they'd expected to be able to buy their groceries here—or, at most, drive out to Pharaoh for them. But having driven the Watchman's Gap Road once in the Winnebago, Truth wasn't sure she ever cared to do it again.

Well, they'd think of something.

Arms full, she carried her purchases up to the counter, and piled them beside the others'. As Evan toted everything up on an old-fashioned mechanical adding machine, Truth browsed through a revolving book rack standing in front of the counter. The rack's contents said a good deal about the clientele the Morton's Fork general store entertained. There were road maps, guides to fishing and hunting, foil-embossed romance novels, first-aid manuals, and medal-bedecked military adventure books. Among the other books, the white cover of what was obviously a small-press volume stood out.

A History of Lyonesse County, West Virginia by E. A. Ringrose. The cover was printed with what looked to be an early map of the area.

Worth a look, Truth thought. The books she'd brought with her as leisure-time reading suddenly didn't look appetizing, and neither did any of the other offerings here in the book rack. Unless she wanted to read the latest issue of *The Pharaoh Call and Record, Published Weekly for Lyonesse County, including the townships of Pharaoh, Morton's Fork, La Gouloue, Bishopville, and Maskelyne,* a newspaper fully eight pages thick. On impulse, she picked up a copy of that, too—it was only a quarter—and when Dylan had finished paying for the other purchases and Evan had packed them into several cardboard boxes, Truth stepped forward with her acquisitions.

"Looks like you're interested in local history," Evan said, as he carefully added up her total.

Truth smiled distantly. Local history was really the only kind there was, and most people were blind and deaf to the wonders and terrors that happened in their own backyards.

"I guess so," she admitted. "Maybe this book will give me some idea of what to see around here." The other three might be on a field trip, but this was her vacation—unless they had some statistics for her to collate.

"Maybe," Evan said doubtfully, "but there's a lot of stuff you'd better stay away from. Dangerous things."

The jail cell smelled of fear, urine, and rats. The cold sea air of the Bristol coast wafted in through the open window, and the woman sitting at the table beneath it shivered.

Her name was Marie Athanais Jocasta de Courcy de Lyon, Lady Belchamber, and she was to have been a queen. Forget Jamie's whey-faced Scottish countess— she could have been set aside easily enough once Jamie had taken the throne from his canting Catholic uncle.

Set aside—or killed.

Only the usurper had not cooperated by losing to her lover's troops. Jamie had raised his standard—the standard of the true king, rightful son of Charles Stuart and Lucy Waters—but the English, the war-torn forties still clear in their minds, had not followed him.

Now her Jamie was dead, and the false king's revenge began. Those of Monmouth's supporters who were not transported to the King's New World Maryland colony were to be hanged.

SHE was to be hanged.

They were building the gallows already, but her rank ensured she would spend her last days with more comforts than those wretches in the general population beyond her door. They were to be transported on the morning tide, to a world populated by savages and monsters.

And cities of gold.

Athanais opened the casket that lay on the table before her. A costly French toy of silver and enamel work, it bespoke her status, that of a great lady with royal blood in her veins—though now they called her traitor, murderess, whore, and worse.

Witch.

The accusation—flung at her in hissed whispers, and not in open court—made Athanais smile as she lingered among the small glass vials of the casket like a woman choosing among sweetmeats. If it was witchcraft to damn God and set Man on the highest throne of the heavens, so be it. And she cared not what compact she had to make with any being, celestial or infernal, to ensure she got her own way.

But her servants had failed her one by one, and now she was reduced to this last mad gamble. They had been weak, but she would not be.

Athanais poured the contents of the vial into one of the costly glass goblets upon the table, closed the casket, then topped up both cups from the pitcher of wine upon the table. She pulled the untainted cup safely to her and left the other beside the decanter. Everything was ready.

"I need a woman to help me undress: you." Athanais stood in the doorway of her room and pointed at the young woman sitting huddled in the corner of the prison's great room, one of those who were to be transported on the morrow. The woman looked up, meeting Athanais' steely grey gaze, and slowly got to her feet.

"What's your name, girl?" Athanais asked, turning her back so that the other could attend her. She and Athanais were much of a size, which was why Athanais had chosen her from among the transportees.

"Jane, ma'am. Jane Darrow." Jane followed Athanais docilely back into her private quarters and closed the door to the outer room before hurrying over to unlace Athanais' elaborate dress.

"And shall you like living in the New World, among heathens and slaves?" Athanais asked. Silence greeted her, and the stifled sound of tears held back. She smiled as she heard it. She'd made the right choice, then.

"Peace, child. Dry your tears. Even Hanging Jeffries is not immune to bribery—and I promise you for this night's work enough gold to soften even a Puritan heart."

"Truly, ma'am? My Charlie and me—"

Athanais closed her ears to the girl's grateful babble, and concentrated on instructing her on just how to undress her and take down her hair. When her hair— how Jamie had praised it, calling it perfumed honey—hung loose and she stood dressed only in her shift, Athanais reached for a shawl to wrap herself in and turned to her conscript maid.

" 'Swounds, it is cold in here." She forced a shiver she did not feel. "Let us take wine to warm us." Athanais picked up her goblet, and handed the tainted one to her companion.

The girl was flattered by the illusion of equality. She drank off the contents of the cup as if it were cider, and, at Athanais' urging, quickly followed it with another. She was probably more used to the taste of small beer than that of vintage wine, and after a few minutes her eyelids began to droop.

"Lord," Jane said. "I feel so sleepy. . . ."

"Come and lie down for a moment and rest your eyes," Athanais invited cordially.

The girl was so far gone with the effects of the potion that she made no demur

as Athanais got her to her feet and led her toward the rude bed tucked into a corner of the room. In a few moments more Jane Darrow was sleeping soundly, and
Athanais began to strip her of her clothes.

Shoes and stockings, sturdy plain gown and country cap—in a few minutes the
sleeping girl was bare to her shift, and then Athanais began to dress her again in
the gown the girl had helped remove, a bright thing of satin and velvet and lace
that would immediately identify its wearer as Lady Belchamber. Then she
painted the girl's face with care, and placed a few of her jewels upon her.

Last of all, Athanais gave Jane Darrow quite as much gold as she had
promised . . . only Athanais doubted that it would do either Jane or the Charlie
she sighed for much good at all.

Once Jane was arranged to her satisfaction, Athanais flung the blanket over
the girl—as a further aid to concealment rather than out of any desire to make her
more comfortable—and turned to her own preparations.

The great ladies of the court painted their faces, but the common folk did not;
Athanais, shivering for real now in the cell's chill, carefully washed every last
trace of paint and perfume from her body with water from the bucket and a scrap
of scavenged cloth. With the knife that usually reposed in a sheath in her bodice,
she cut the fine point-lace from the cuffs and hem of her shift, then donned Jane
Darrow's unfashionable plain gown and flannel petticoats over it. The coarse material chafed her skin through the fine muslin, but hangman's hemp would be
harsher. In Jane's clothes, with Jane's shawl about her head, Athanais could pass
unnoticed among the others when the ship for America was loaded, and afterward
it would be too late for the captain to return. She would be on her way—to her
destiny.

Athanais swept the room with a glance, allowing herself one last pang of regret for the luxury she was leaving behind—most of all for the unavoidable loss
of her casket of irreplaceable poisons and drugs. The items in it had gained her a
high place in Monmouth's service, but all her venoms had not gained either of them
the prize. In the end, her Jamie had failed her.

But she would not be defeated. Her capture had been a setback, nothing more.
Lifting the inset trays out of the casket, Athanais tripped the latch of the secret
compartment, and pulled out a carefully folded sheet of vellum. She would have to
abandon all the rest of her clothes and most of her jewels, but she would not leave
this.

It was a large sheet, carefully scraped and bleached, of the sort astrologers liked
best for drawing horoscopes. Part of it was Athanais' own natal chart—she had
cast it herself—and she saw among the tangled aspects her rise—and, now, her

fall. The rest of the page contained a map overlain with the planetary aspects to which they corresponded. There, somewhere in the West, was the place where her stars and the very land itself conspired. There was her power, ripe for the claiming.

Her power—and her revenge. Athanais tucked the paper carefully away in a pouch beneath her skirts along with the tiny store of valuables that would be her stake in the savage land of her exile.

Everything was ready. Athanais quenched the candles and stood by the door, waiting for the moment when the others in the chamber outside would be asleep. Then she would add herself to their number and await the morning tide.

She did not spare a moment's thought for Jane Darrow's fate.

Cold stone beneath her fingers; the stifling air of the jailhouse; and somewhere like a ghost of future memory the surging deck of a ship and the sharp bite of salt air. . . .

Sinah flung herself up out of sweat-soaked sheets and stared around her, gasping wildly. The room that should have been so familiar looked alien, bizarre.

She could not remember who she was.

"My name is . . . " But even her voice was wrong, flat and countrified where it should have been . . . what?

"Dellon." The name came at last, dragged up out of some black pit, bringing a faint flicker of sanity with it. "Sinah. Melusine Dellon."

The name was a touchstone that helped her grope back to herself. At last the room looked familiar enough that Sinah could find the light switch and turn on the bedside lamp, and the illumination restored more of her sense of self.

She was in her loft bedroom, in the king-sized cherry sleigh-bed she'd chosen so happily six months before. Over the side of the railing she could see the faint glitter of her stained-glass windows, their surface rendered opaque by darkness. Everything was quiet.

And beneath the surface of her mind, Athanais de Lyon lurked like a malignant cancer, carrying with her the sensations and imperatives of a time centuries before Sinah had been born.

It was not a dream. The fearful conviction stayed with her. She got out of bed, groping for her robe and pulling it tightly around her, only then realizing how badly she was trembling. It had been so cold in that cell. . . .

A chill that had nothing to do with the body struck through her. The
cell and its occupant were a dream, nothing more. Sinah's gift was a thing
of the living world. It always had been.

Until she'd come back here.

Just a nightmare. That's all it is. A bad one, but just a nightmare. Please.
She hugged herself miserably, trying to feel safe and failing. Despite the
air-conditioning her nightgown was plastered to her body with the rank
sweat of fear.

Sinah crossed the loft and descended to the ground floor. The resonant
ghost of Wycherly's presence in her mind made her head first for the
liquor cabinet in the corner of the great room. There was a row of name-
brand bottles and a set of slightly dusty Waterford tumblers beneath its
lid; Sinah hastily wiped one of them clean on her robe, poured it half-full
of Scotch, and drank.

She gagged as she felt the burning passage of the Scotch down her
throat; the vile smoky taste of the liquor—kept only for Justin, in the
event he ever visited—set up a reassuring disassociation in her mind between herself and Wycherly. He liked the taste of Scotch: She didn't.
Therefore, she was not Wycherly.

Nor was she that other—the cold, reptilian intelligence from centuries past.

Sinah clung to that thought like a lifeline and looked around the
room, trying to take comfort from the familiar things she had gathered
all around her. Only they weren't familiar, not any more. She saw them
through the sensibilities of a Jacobean harlot.

The worst of it was, it was hard to decide whether she was more upset
by the danger Athanais had been in . . . or by Athanais herself.

I am me—I am me! Sinah told herself desperately, but she realized with
a frenzied despair that it wasn't really true. This was not like the temporary lives her gift brought her. Even though often she could not separate
herself from her borrowed lives, she always knew that the situation was a
temporary thing. But Athanais had come from nowhere . . . and she was
still here. Just as Sinah's body might at any moment be invaded by some
virus, so her mind and heart now hosted this unwelcome guest who
brought a cold, malicious insight that destroyed any comfort Sinah
might have found in once-familiar things.

She shook her head, bewildered, reaching out to pick up her half-fin-
ished Scotch and stopping at the last minute. *I don't need another drink, I*

need a cup of tea. Feeling oddly unsteady on her feet, Sinah headed toward the kitchen.

The kitchen lights glinted off copper and enamel, dazzling her eyes and giving her a headache. Sinah filled the kettle and set it to boil, her mind still churning.

A dream. She called herself Athanais—that proves it. Your mother's name— you saw it on your birth certificate. It's just old data—part from you, part from Wycherly's mind. It will all blow over by tomorrow.

But it had been so vivid . . . as vivid as the impressions she picked up with her gift.

But how could you have touched a mind centuries dead?

And in Maryland, Sinah reminded herself with a touch of gallows humor. *Don't forget that your ghost was being sent to Maryland, not West Virginia. She's hardly likely to turn up here.*

The kettle boiled; Sinah made herself a strong pot of peppermint tea, willing herself to relax as she waited for it to steep. The unremitting hostility she'd experienced ever since she'd come to Morton's Fork would have been enough to overset a steadier mind than hers had ever been. What she'd experienced was only a nightmare, a nerve-storm. Everyone had them. Making it into anything more than that was to court madness in truth.

She added honey to her tea, staring broodingly into it as she stirred. A pretty enough color, and a flavor strong enough to hide hemlock or larkspur; give a man this to drink and he'd sleep never to wake, and no magistrate the wiser. . . .

Sinah recoiled from the direction of her own thoughts, sending the cup to spin crashing to the floor. The honeyed tea made a sticky puddle on the brick floor, one that spread like blood.

I'm losing my mind. I know I am. What am I becoming?

Sinah choked back a sob. In her heart she already knew the answer to that. What was she becoming? Something crazy, something mad.

Something evil.

Evan had said that they could park the camper in the field just past Bartholomew Asking's gas station, and all of them were anxious to get settled before true night fell. Dylan drove cautiously past the welter of junked cars clustered around the front of the service station. The other three walked ahead in the twilight with flashlights to spy out potholes.

"Hey, look at that!" Ninian said, pointing off to the right with his flashlight.

The light illuminated a spot of blinding, lipstick-red paint, as out of place here as roses in a toxic waste dump. They all turned toward it.

"Anything wrong?" Dylan stopped the camper, leaning over to call out the passenger-side window.

"No . . ." Ninian didn't sound sure. "It's just a wreck. But what's a Ferrari doing *here?*"

Even Truth—who didn't have the easy facility with automobile brand names that seemed almost to be a genetic feature of masculinity—could see that the red wreck dumped casually down between two rusting hulks had once been a fancy little sports car. Now it looked like a giant had taken a sledgehammer to the hood, and the windshield frame was twisted completely out of shape.

I hope no one was killed, Truth thought automatically. But there didn't seem to be anything they could do about the car except exercise their imaginations, so Truth turned her flashlight back to the road. She'd be just as glad to be able to stop moving, all things considered.

When they reached the place Evan had indicated, the ground was clear, level, and only sparsely covered with grass. It looked as if it had once been a gravel-covered lot of some kind. Dylan stopped, turned off the ignition, and went into the back of the camper.

A few moments later the entire field was lit with hissing, blue-white light from half a dozen propane lanterns set out around the area, and Rowan and Ninian—who either had unbounded reserves of energy or were trying to impress their advisor, were unpacking chairs, tents, tables, and even a stove from the camper.

Truth, shamelessly, had commandeered one of the first chairs to be set out and a can of diet iced tea from the Winnebago's refrigerator. Now she sat and inspected E. A. Ringrose's history by lantern light as the students set up the camp and Dylan began preparing dinner.

The book was apparently an updated and expanded version of Mr. Ringrose's original 1950 work, and bore the imprint of the Lyonesse County Historical Society. *Dylan ought to be interested in this. I wonder if he's seen it?*

Reading, Truth learned that Lyonesse County had been founded in 1726 (though parts of the original grant were partitioned off and added to Randolph and Pocahontas Counties in 1793), that much of Lyonesse County now lay within the modern-day Monongahela National Forest, and that part of the county bordered on the Laurel Fork Wilderness Area.

Ought to make for a quiet life, Truth thought, absently watching Dylan across the field. *I wonder what we're all doing here, if the place is this quiet?* She turned back to her find. *Lyonesse and Commerce,* the section heading read, and Truth learned that though the county's principal river, the Astolat, was once used to ferry coal and timber to eastern markets, settlement of Lyonesse County seemed to drop off almost before it began. The opening of the mines (she read) had brought a renaissance of a sort, but Ringrose's book ended with a mournful coda—written in 1950—that mourned the flight to the cities and the increasing industrialization of America, and looked to a time when there would be nothing in Lyonesse County except ghost towns and fully-mechanized mines.

Too bad things hadn't worked out that way. Like that T-shirt she'd seen one of the students wearing: LET THE MEEK INHERIT THE EARTH— THE REST OF US WILL GO TO THE STARS, those who could had gone to the cities, and left their less-fortunate kindred behind in places like Morton's Fork. In the rush to separate the worthy and the unworthy, everyone always assumed the line would be drawn to include them among the elect. The real truth was that nobody could go to the stars if everyone couldn't—anything else created a haves versus have-nots culture that only led, inevitably, to bloodbath.

What morbid thoughts! Do you think the glorious revolution is going to start here in Morton's Fork? Truth jeered at herself.

No, she replied to that inner audience. *But it could.* And the people who were so casually ready to leave half the human race behind in search of their own comfort were the ones who'd cause it.

"I think dinner had better show up soon," Truth muttered aloud.

She'd thought the balance of the book would be bibliography and sources, but in fact it was an essay written for the 1993 edition of the book, covering the changes in the county since the early fifties, and ending on a rather surprising note.

Lyonesse County owes most of its modern fame to the ground-breaking work of Nicholas Taverner, a turn-of-the-century folklorist and preservationist who saw the country ways he had grown up with vanishing almost overnight with the increasing industrialization of the United States. The gasoline engine was beginning to replace the horse as the motive force on farms and in towns, and in the headlong rush to progress, both the country ways of doing things and the stories a dying generation had to tell were being lost.

Taverner, like many of his post–World War I generation, had an abiding interest in Spiritualism, and collected many more stories of magic and the supernatural than did his contemporaries. Despite its thinly-settled nature, a disproportionately large number of the folktales of ghosts, hauntings, and wandering spirits have their location in the hills of Lyonesse County, and eventually, the mass of material he had collected on his travels led him to publish *Ha'ants, Spooks, and Fetchmen,* where he noted the peculiarly fey nature of the area and mentioned in passing that one town—named Morton's Fork—seemed to be populated by whole families of poltergeists.

Truth checked for the name of the author of the Afterword, and found it to be the rather unlikely one of Pennyfeather Farthing. *Well, Mr. Farthing, we know in what direction YOUR interests lie,* she thought with a smile. Mr. Farthing seemed to share Dylan's interests, and might be able to give them an idea of where to start. She wondered if Evan Starking knew where the man was now.

The savory scent of roasting burgers began to waft skyward. The bubble tents that would hold Ninian, Rowan, and much of their gear were up, and now Rowan was setting the table for dinner; cups, plates, cold salads they'd bought in Pharaoh, brownies they'd brought from Bread Alone in Glastonbury. They could have been any group of friends on a social outing. The fact that tomorrow Dylan and his students would begin looking for the ghosts or other supernatural events that haunted Morton's Fork and trying to confirm each event symbolized by a colored pushpin on Dylan's map only added an air of surreality to the evening.

Oddly, the fact that the Unseen World was such a natural, accepted part of Truth's life didn't mean she was any more willing to see it as a normal part of others'.

When it's only me I don't have to think about it. I only need to react to what I see and feel. It's almost as if I can't trust other people to have similar perceptions.

And why should she? She could blame her gift on the *sidhe* legacy from her father, the nonhuman heritage that forever separated her from the human race.

That's my excuse. What's theirs?

Truth was abstracted all evening, though the others, excited by the morrow's prospects, hardly noticed. After dinner and clean up—involving a sparing use of the RV's water supply—the party separated for the night. Truth helped shift the two polybarometers around inside the Winnebago to make room for the transformation of the dinette into a double bed, and then stood in the doorway looking out at the night. She'd loaned Ninian the book on Lyonesse County, and his bubble tent glowed like a bright orange night-light from the illumination of the battery-powered lamp inside.

"It doesn't work." Rowan's voice was raised in indignant disgust. Truth saw the door flap of the blue tent unzip, and Rowan scrambled out. She came toward the Winnebago, a small portable TV/VCR in hand. "It's broken," she said to Truth in an aggrieved voice.

"Did you test it before we left? You know there's no radio or television reception here," Truth reminded her.

"It worked fine then—now it won't even play tapes," Rowan said more quietly. "Anyway, could you take it inside there with you, Truth? If it isn't going to work, I'm not going to give it tent-room."

"That should teach it a lesson," Truth said gravely, opening the screen door and taking the portable television set. It was only a little larger than a shoebox—and Rowan was right, it *had* worked just fine in Glastonbury. She stared at the TV, as though she could force it to explain itself.

"Well . . . goodnight," Rowan said, half waving. She walked back to her own tent, and a few moments later Truth could see her silhouette moving around inside the blue nylon dome again. Truth set the TV/VCR on the counter and closed the Winnebago's door.

"Trouble?" Dylan said, settling the last of the blankets into place on their bed.

"Her VCR didn't work." Truth attempted to deliver the information with the seriousness that Rowan obviously felt it deserved. She didn't quite manage.

"The batteries are probably dead. I'll plug it in here tomorrow when

I've got the motor running and see if they'll hold a charge. They might not, of course—"

Impulsively, Truth reached out and ruffled his wheat-blond hair. "I think she's got a crush on you, Dylan."

"Ah." Dylan smiled. "All women do, Truth—didn't I warn you about that?" He stepped forward and put his arms around her, and Truth snuggled into his warm solidity, glad to leave the puzzles and problems of the day behind.

She was dreaming. Blackburn's sidhe *daughter, Mistress of Shadow's Gate, rode upon the back of the white mare. The red stag bounded ahead, her guide through the Otherworld, and behind her loped the black dog and the grey wolf—tenacity and ferocity; loyalty and cunning. Surrounded by her kindred spirits, Truth searched the Otherworld.*

In the dim distance, the sparks of working Blackburn Circles burned bright, and scattered among them like brief candles were the lights of the powerful on other paths: Wiccan covens, White Lodges, the Brotherhood of the Rose. . . .

She was searching for something else.

Abruptly, the white mare was no longer running over the featureless plains of the Otherworld; the animal's legs splashed through the icy water of a running stream, and a wholly realistic forest had sprung up in what had been trackless mist. A leafy branch brushed Truth's cheek, and the red stag was nowhere to be seen.

In the Otherworld, which had no shape save that which human minds gave it, such definition was a warning sign that she was intruding into territory which some entity had made its own. At the same time Truth realized that she was not dreaming—her body might be asleep in Morton's Fork, but her spirit was roving in an equally real though intangible realm, doing what New Agers called "lucid dreaming."

Time to go.

Truth tried to turn her mount, and felt a faint thrill of disquiet when the mare did not even slow her headlong pace. The White Mare was one of the four Guardians of the Gate, servants and protectors of the Gatekeeper—an extension of her will. Her servant should not disobey her like this!

Truth struggled to leave the Otherworld by any means possible: to wake, to dismount. She could not—it was as if she were frozen in place, cut off from her Will and carried forward no matter what her wishes.

A moment later she realized why.

Once she had stood beside Thorne Blackburn upon a hill of vision, before a Gate barred by spinning sword blades, behind which sidhe *armies waited to ride forth into the world of Men. She had closed that Gate and locked it with the force of her intention in a realm where words were made real—but the Gate she had closed was not the only Gate that lay between the pleasant worlds of Men and the dread realms of the Lords of the Outer Spaces.*

There was the clash of water upon rocks. Deep in her bones Truth felt its ungoverned power—a spinning whirlpool in a turbid river that lured swimmers to their deaths—and knew that there was no keeper for this Gate. If there were, it would not stand as it did—open to any entrant, able to pass things that should remain safely locked in the world beyond.

"IT IS POWER—AND I SHALL HAVE IT."

The symbolic nature of the Otherworld turned the churning whirlpool to a silver snake, a gleaming serpent that struggled vainly in the hands of a tall man who bore the dark aura of a magus about him.

"Leave the Gate alone. It is nothing to do with you," Truth said. He was not the Gatekeeper. The Gates answered only to women; it was women's magic to open or close them.

"IT IS POWER—AND I SHALL HAVE IT," the dark man repeated. Cold flames played about his body, as though he stood on a pyre, and the coldness radiated from him as strongly as heat. Coldness—control—power—

Truth's Guardians had long since vanished, driven from her side by this man's antithetical power. Truth had no choice but to face him alone, to learn why she'd been brought here; to free the serpent, to find the Gate's Keeper if she could—

To close the Gate herself if she could not.

But first, she must put an end to this charade. Summoning all the force of her directed will, Truth sketched a glyph in the air between herself and the dark usurper. It burned as she shaped it; a tangible silver knot; fire against ice.

"I charge you to go from this place; to deliver up what you have seized; by Fire and Air, by Earth living and unliving, by Water and—"

He swept his hand down, and in it was a sword she had not seen before. Her glyph dissolved like smoke.

"Best go back to your kitchen, witch-girl; you've met your match in Quentin Blackburn! By blind Azathoth and the Black Christ: Eno, Abbadnio, Iluriel—"

Each of the Names he spoke seemed to swarm out of his mouth like clouds of insects, surrounding Truth and stinging the strength from her limbs. She hadn't rec-

ognized him for what he was, and now it was too late: If she couldn't escape this attack she'd pay the price for her bravura.

Truth summoned her power once more, and summoned, too, its animal aspects: dog and wolf, horse and stag. The magus's attention wasn't entirely focused on her: He was wrestling with the serpent he still held, trying to bend the power of the Gate into another weapon to attack her. At the moment that he was most distracted, Truth turned and ran, on foot now in the tangling forest.

She heard a crashing in the underbrush; a moment later she saw the grey wolf, pacing her as she ran. The wolf was power, but it was also danger; there was always the possibility that it could turn upon her if she were weak enough. The black dog would never turn upon her, but this more reliable servant would never act independently of her, either.

Behind her, she felt the darkness gathering for another try at her. If Quentin Blackburn—that name! —could make her a sacrifice to the Gate's insatiable appetite, he would have gained further power over it.

And she would be dead.

There was a flash of moon-whiteness through the underbrush ahead, and Truth threw herself against the body of the white mare and twined her fingers through its mane, letting the force of the spirit-animal's flight draw her up onto its back. A few moments later—if such a thing as time could be imputed to the events of the Otherworld—Truth and her Guardians had broken free of the last of the tangled undergrowth, and were running free upon the plains of the Otherworld once more. Quickly Truth dismounted, dismissing her companions, and retreated further, down the spiral stair into manifestation, into matter. . . .

Wycherly's first conscious thought was that nothing hurt. He was wise enough to know that this meant that something *ought* to hurt, and to lie very still until he woke up completely and remembered what it was.

He was lying in his bed in the cabin in Morton's Fork. The sun was up—cautiously he located his left wrist, and moved the arm enough to bring his wristwatch into view. It was the day after he'd gone to bed—he made sure of the date—and a little after noon. His face, his neck, his arms—they all felt raw and stiff. Sunburn, to add to his luck.

Where was Luned? He couldn't remember whether she was supposed to be here or not—or what he'd said to her yesterday. Probably something ghastly—if there was one virtue he could claim, it was consistency.

He risked a more athletic move, and was rewarded with pain that raced like summer lightning across his nerves. Strained muscles—from the fall yesterday, from the car crash the day before. Wycherly grinned in triumph, pleased to have remembered that much. He wasn't seriously injured, only stiff. If he was careful, he could move without causing himself too much pain. And he needed to see if the ankle—he remembered that too—would bear his weight.

He threw back the covers and looked down. His ankle was the size of a young cantaloupe and mottled with greenish bruises.

He wasn't sure he could walk on that after all.

This is just . . . jolly, Wycherly thought to himself, irritated past emotion. Alone, trapped, unable to move . . .

It might not be as bad as it looked.

He thought longingly of a bath, hot water up to his neck and fresh clean clothes. Fat chance of that here in this rural retreat. Wycherly sighed. He wasn't sure why coming to stay here had seemed like such a good idea.

Because you're drinking yourself to death. Because you just smashed up yet another car—without insurance—while your license was suspended. Because you need to know . . .

What? Wycherly shook his head. Whatever answers he thought he needed, they certainly weren't to be found here. There wasn't anything in Morton's Fork except poverty, disease, and *nothing*.

Other than the Addams Family Hotel up there on the hill.

The burnt-out shell of Wildwood Sanatorium—so like present company—was an oddity in an otherwise ordinary area, and Wycherly welcomed the thought of anything that might distract him. He felt as if someone had inserted sand beneath his skin, like the rhinoceros in Kipling's "Just So" story. Soon, if he were unlucky, it wouldn't be sand, but bugs—hallucinations of bugs in his skin, in his clothes, crawling all over the walls—

With effort, Wycherly wrenched his mind away from that unpleasant forecast. It didn't have to happen. Not if he was careful, and prudent. He could start by getting out of bed.

Carefully, wincing and snarling at every motion, Wycherly levered himself upright. He rested his good foot on the floor and then, grabbing the bedframe to steady himself, began to put weight on the bad foot.

No good. Wycherly fell back to the bed, panting. It wouldn't support him. But maybe if he strapped it back up again . . .

"Hello?"

It wasn't Luned. He leaned forward and through the open bedroom door he could see Sinah step through the unlocked front door. She was wearing shorts and a bright sleeveless blouse, and her soft brown hair was pulled back under a scarf, California-style. The round, tortoiseshell-rimmed sunglasses she wore made her look like an archetypal Hollywood actress.

No, not Hollywood . . . Broadway. Recognition was very nearly a tangible weight in his mind.

"Wycherly?" Sinah called again.

The moment she stepped over the threshold Sinah felt as though she'd slipped back in time fifty years. The only stove was a big, black, potbellied monster and the refrigerator looked like something out of an old movie. Its door was hanging open, and there didn't seem to be anything inside but beer. Automatically, Sinah walked over and closed it. The cabin interior was dim, stiflingly hot; she could feel Wycherly's presence, a faint painful turmoil.

"Here," Wycherly's voice called.

Sinah turned and walked into the bedroom, approaching Wycherly with less reluctance than she'd felt yesterday. Any distraction, however unpleasant, was better than sitting and probing her own mind for the traces of Athanais de Lyon.

The bedroom was tiny, furnished in early Sears-Roebuck. An ornate brass bed dominated the room. Wycherly was sitting on the edge of the bed, a fold of sheet thrown across his midsection. Sunburn striped his face and body in random splotches, angry and painful-looking. He stared warily. She felt a sense of failure strong enough to choke her, a paralyzing inadequacy; his reality beat against her mind insistently, drowning out the presence of Athanais de Lyon.

"I came to see how you're doing," Sinah said. Bracing herself, she walked into the proximity that would allow her to feel not only Wycherly's emotions, but his thoughts.

Anger. *stupid cow coming back here to meddle* Fear. *don't let her see me like this* Hatred. *should have expected it they always do* The only thing that would let him function effectively with another person was the one thing he was denying himself. Alcohol.

The empathy that was her curse and her gift reached out to him. Better than anyone else on earth, Sinah understood exactly how he felt.

"I'm doing just fine," Wycherly said. There was a pause; Sinah watched as he seemed to realize that something more seemed to be needed. "It wasn't as bad as I'd thought."

"I see," Sinah said, taking another step forward. "Can you stand on it?"

Wycherly glared, unwittingly providing her with the answer. He'd already tried and it hadn't worked out.

"Well, it looks like I showed up just in time," Sinah said, forcing a brightness she did not feel. "I brought some things you might need; Epsom salts, liniment—"

"Give me my clothes." Wycherly's voice was a harsh, peremptory bark. Sinah stopped.

"Do you treat all your good Samaritans this way?" she snapped back.

"It depends on what's in it for you," Wycherly said sullenly.

Sinah laughed shortly. "It must be your body, since it can't be your sweet temper. Look, let's call it a truce, okay? You need help, and I'm willing to donate a few hours to the cause. And after that, I don't care what happens to you."

"Yeah. No one does." The words came out with an edge of self-pity that she could feel he hadn't intended.

"Look. I'm sorry, okay? I'm tired and everything hurts, and besides that, it's damned inconvenient. I just wish I—" Wycherly sighed harshly. "Look, could you get me my clothes? They're on the floor somewhere."

They were, in fact, on the floor at the end of the bed. Sinah picked up the ripped and filthy items with distaste.

"These?"

"They're what there is. My luggage was delayed."

"There's a clean shirt in the other room," Sinah said, tossing him the pants. She went back out into the other room.

The shirt was right where she'd seen it—nice enough once, but now mended with careful rows of stitching. Apparently Mr. Musgrave was hard on his clothes. She went back out to the Jeep for her supplies—and his other shoe. Wycherly's mind-voice faded until it was only a faint mutter in the background, like an oncoming storm.

Her presence here this early in the morning couldn't really be chalked up to altruism. Like a bad movie playing in a constant loop just below the surface of Sinah's mind, Athanais de Lyon was *there*, and three centuries had not dimmed her avarice—or her malice. Though her enemies were long since dust in their graves, Athanais still wanted revenge.

And Sinah would be her instrument.

No . . . Sinah pressed clammy hands to her temples and closed her eyes tightly, leaning against the Jeep.

It had taken her nearly a year to recoup her fortunes once she'd reached the Maryland Colony and longer to find a spoiled priest that she could bend to her will—one who knew the local dialects and had connections to the savages in the West. . . .

A vision of these mountains—not as they were, but as they had been when only the deer and the Tutelo roamed these hills—burned behind her eyes.

"Stop it," Sinah said aloud. *I'm me! I'm* ME!

And if she wasn't, who was she?

Sinah drew a ragged breath. Was this what happened to all her kind eventually? Was it what had happened to her mother? Sinah closed her eyes tightly, fighting back tears. When you acknowledged that you needed help, help was supposed to arrive. But if she could not find help in Morton's Fork, she did not know where it could be found.

Maybe nowhere.

Meanwhile, the thought of being alone was intolerable. She needed other minds, other thoughts to drown this usurper—and like it or not, Wycherly Musgrave was the only person she could get.

SIX

CRUEL AS THE GRAVE

She is older than the rocks among which she sits; like the vampire,
she has been dead many times, and learned the secrets of the grave;
and has been a diver in deep seas, and keeps their fallen
day about her . . .

—WALTER PATER

WHEN SINAH CAME BACK INSIDE, WYCHERLY HAD HIS
pants on and had made it out to the main room, clutching at a chair.

"Well, you're stubborn, aren't you?" Sinah asked, smiling to take any
sting out of her words. His pain and craving beat at the edge of her senses
like heavy surf.

"So I've been told," Wycherly drawled. He lowered himself to a chair
and began putting on his shirt.

"I know who you are, you know. I saw you in New York, in this little
off-Broadway thing. You were playing a woman—" Wycherly pushed his
hair back out of his face with both hands, leaving the shirt unbuttoned.
"Don't remember the name—but you were wearing this sleeveless pink
sundress thing—"

A ridiculous urge to laugh bubbled up in Sinah's chest. There was no
point in being irritated when people recognized her—not if she'd chosen
to work in a field where notoriety was both the goal and the fate of those

who worked there. But Wycherly Musgrave was the last person she'd have pegged for a fan.

"That's Adrienne. You saw *Zero Sum Game*. I'm surprised you remember—it closed more than a year and a half ago," Sinah said kindly. "The movie's coming out this December."

"I remember you," Wycherly repeated. He looked away, as if he'd embarrassed himself. "Anyway, you said you were an actress yesterday."

"So I did," Sinah agreed blandly. "And what brings you to Morton's Fork, Mr. Musgrave?"

She already knew the answer—as well as he did, anyway, which wasn't very well at all—but it was the sort of oblivious social question that people who weren't freaks asked each other, whether they wanted to know the answers or not.

"I thought it would be quiet," he said, and beneath his words, the thought: *"I came to Casablanca for the waters."*

She smiled—at the unspoken answer, not the one she was supposed to have heard. "If you'd ended up in that river you'd have had a bit more quiet than you cared for," she said. *Not to mention water.*

Wycherly smiled a twisted smile and didn't answer. But he didn't have to. The words came to her mind as clearly as if he'd spoken them: *And how do you know I wouldn't care for it?*

"Are you sure you're all right here alone?" Sinah blurted out.

Wycherly turned in his seat and stared at her, his pale eyes a wolf-yellow in the dim light. Under the impetus of Wycherly's mind, Sinah saw herself as he saw her: potential threat. Not even prey—she could deal with that—but as something that had no particular value to his life . . . yet might still cause him trouble.

"And you are?" he said, and meant: *Who the hell do you think you are, Little Miss Movie Star? Think you're going to star in some live-action roleplaying* Beverly Hillbillies-*manqué at my expense?*

"No," Sinah protested, answering the thought and not the words. "I just . . . need help."

The words were dragged from her reluctantly, but Wycherly Musgrave would respond to—would understand—nothing other than self-interest.

"That's why I came here today."

Instantly everything changed, though Sinah wasn't entirely sure why.

Anger and impatience vanished from Wycherly's mind as thoroughly as if it were a blackboard that had been wiped clean, to be replaced by a sense of isolation so immense that it could never be challenged. She'd said something wrong—her, Sinah Dellon, the woman who always knew the right thing to say.

"What seems to be the problem?" Wycherly asked easily.

I don't know. Sinah sat down on the other chair, and found that she was wringing her hands together, gripping them so tightly that they ached. She didn't want to explain—and how could she, without opening the door to an entire farrago of nonsense?

Haunted? Telepathic? Those things belonged to big-budget summer movies, not to real life.

"Are you being stalked?" Wycherly asked, something like sympathy in his voice.

"No!" It was such an unexpected question—though obvious, all things considered—that her response was more vehement than she'd intended.

"I mean—"

"Never mind. If you actually want to make a soak you're going to have to heat water, you're going to have to fire up that stove. I can show you how," he said. Any other subject was apparently closed for the moment.

With Wycherly supervising, Sinah filled the stove from the wood box and lit the kindling. It was already stuffy in the small cabin; the added heat would make the place a sweatbox.

"I was born here," Sinah found herself saying as she worked, as casually as if she spoke to a wild animal that could not understand. "Somewhere in Morton's Fork. On the certificate it says 'Home Birth, Morton's Fork, Lyonesse County.' So I came back here when I could."

Faint flicker of interest from the mind of the man behind her.

She located a pot in the cupboard, set it on the stove, and filled it from one of the buckets of water that sat beside the stove.

"My mother was dead—she'd died when I was born. I grew up in a foster home. My foster parents weren't particularly fond of me. I don't blame them; they had their reasons. I knew where I'd come from, of course—I found this place on a survey map at the library when I was fourteen. I'd always dreamed of coming back here, finding any relatives I had left, but I wanted to do it in style. Now, well, you said you knew who I am. The whole world knows that things are going pretty well for me."

"So why the sob story?" Wycherly asked. It was brutal, but she'd expected it from him. The rich were wary of sob stories and setups, and Wycherly Musgrave, no matter how abused, was a child of privilege.

For a moment her visions and nightmares since she'd come home blazed across her thoughts like summer lightning. She shook her head, denying them. There was no smoke, no fire—no dead witch in her dreams.

"As I said, I expected to find relatives in Morton's Fork," Sinah said evenly. "You know how these mountain communities are—large families and close-knit. Even if some people move away, all of them don't. And I needed information about my bloodline. But—"

Abruptly there was a lump in her throat. She'd had several months to get used to this; she didn't expect it still to hurt as much as it did.

"There's been a problem," Sinah said in a strangled whisper. "No one here will admit my mother ever existed. As soon as they found out I was her daughter, they shut me out. Why? What have I done? What did *she* do?"

Witch—devil child—monster—

Sinah closed her mouth abruptly.

"Why don't you see if you can find the coffee?" Wycherly said, just as if she were not coming to pieces before his eyes.

As Sinah hunted through his cupboards—Wycherly had no idea where the coffee was or how to make it—he mulled over her story.

It didn't add up.

Sinah Dellon was a Broadway gypsy gone Hollywood. She wasn't pretty, with that feral fox-face meant to be seen through a camera lens or over footlights, but she was attractive in the way a clean, healthy, unpainted young woman could be, with an animal, not social, rightness. She looked—he groped for the right word—wholesome.

But this wasn't Hollywood. This wasn't Broadway. This was Morton's Fork, a location in the geographical center of absolutely nowhere. Successful actress seeks roots? Not bloody likely with only one movie in the can.

Wycherly felt a growing spark of interest, a flicker of sensation in a scarred, affectless, emotional wasteland. There was something she didn't want anyone to know—even the person she was asking for help.

He'd find out what it was.

He thought of asking Sinah to get him a beer and decided to wait a while longer. He wanted to think this through.

She probably wasn't trying to manipulate him with her cock-and-bull story. What would be the point; he didn't have anything anyone could want, and he certainly didn't look like anyone who could be pegged as the anointed heir—or even the unwanted beneficiary—of Musgrave, Ridenow, and Fields Investment Services and the sainted Musgrave dynasty.

No, she loved him for himself alone, so to speak. Wycherly smiled derisively. She'd get over that soon enough.

"So you think there's some sort of scandal in your mother's past," Wycherly said. "Was she married?" If there was one thing Wycherly understood, it was the architecture of old family scandals and never-spoken secrets.

"'Father Unknown,' says the birth certificate, but I don't think that's it. You don't—" She stopped. "You haven't tried talking to them." She shrugged wearily.

"I could."

He told himself he was only making the offer because he was bored, or because there might be some later advantage to him in it. He'd known enough actors to know their entire lives revolved around drama and self-obsession—and that projecting what they wanted you to feel was their stock in trade.

"I don't know any of the quaint native peoples well, but"—he thought of Luned—"they've shown no hesitation so far in talking to me."

Sinah turned toward him, a small jar of coffee in her hand.

"I'd be grateful," Sinah said quietly. "For anything you can do. Whether it works or not."

Her sincerity irritated him. *Don't thank me yet. I won't be any good at it.* "Don't worry," Wycherly assured her. "It won't."

Sinah located two thick, white, china mugs, and dumped instant coffee and white sugar into each. She already knew that Wycherly liked his coffee this way, but forced herself to ask anyway.

By then the water was boiling, and Sinah filled the cups from the pot. The kitchen was ovenlike and her clothes were sticky with sweat and streaked with soot. She'd gotten used to worse, though—some of those backstage dressing rooms were dirtier than this, and hotter.

She carried the half-empty bucket to the door and emptied out most of the rest of the water before carrying it back to where Wycherly sat. She mixed Epsom salts and boiling water together in the bucket until the salts had all dissolved, and tested the result with a finger. The water was steaming, but bearable.

"Here," Sinah said breathlessly. "Why don't you put your foot in this for a while and see how you feel?"

"You're joking, of course." Wycherly sounded like an affronted cat.

Without waiting for a more sensible reply, Sinah knelt down in front of him and began rolling up his pant leg.

"Watch it," Wycherly said sharply. The possibility of pain seemed to be even more disturbing to him than its actuality.

"Why don't you take a couple more of those pain pills you had yesterday? If you're out, I've got some aspirin," Sinah suggested.

"They're in my jacket. It's in the bedroom," he added hastily.

"Okay, I'll get them. Just as soon as you put your foot in that bucket."

She expected him to lash out—she felt him *want* to—but once again reality intruded: He didn't know her as well as she knew him, and more formal manners applied. There was a brief pause.

"All right." He lowered his foot into the steaming bucket, wincing as he did so. Despite his shameless overacting, Sinah felt the pain in Wycherly's ankle ease.

"You're going to need sun cream for your face, too. You look pretty horrible," she said.

"So kind," Wycherly murmured, laughing at her silently.

Sinah went into the bedroom and, after only a little investigation, found Wycherly's battered leather jacket. She searched it quickly, and found the small brown bottle. It was nearly full, and had his name and address on the label, as well as a doctor's name and the logo of the dispensing pharmacy. *For a paranoid, he's awfully trusting.* She closed her hand around it without trying to memorize the information.

"Here you are," Sinah said, coming back out. "What do you want to take them with?"

"Coffee's okay," Wycherly said shortly. He took the bottle, removed the lid, and shook several pills out onto his palm. He tossed them back and chased them with a swallow of coffee. "Of course, the coffee's actually horrible," Wycherly added, smiling slyly at her.

"I'll tell the cook when she comes in," Sinah said, sitting down in her chair and sipping at her cup. He was right; it wasn't that good. Probably the water, although it had boiled for long enough that at least the water was sterile. She drank it anyway, out of perversity, thinking vaguely about sun cream and enlarging Wycherly's wardrobe.

"Is it not passing brave to be a king, and ride in triumph through Persepolis." A half-remembered quote from his college days floated through Wycherly's head. He felt an odd, uncomfortable pang of tenderness for Sinah, similar to the feelings Luned aroused but not quite so awkward.

His foot was still in the bucket, though he could hardly feel the heat of the water now. The two of them sat in companionable silence in the sweltering room, but Sinah did not mention leaving, possibly because Wycherly could not.

Now that he had the Movie Star soggy with gratitude she'd hardly notice if he asked her to get him a six-pack of beer. He could drink as many as he liked without having to apologize. He had an excuse; he was hurt. He'd do better tomorrow, but now . . .

Aren't you even a little tired of being an object of pity?

Wycherly shook his head as if to dislodge an irritating insect, but the voice came from within, not from outside. Tired of being an object of pity? Yes, as a matter of fact, he was. And so he wouldn't have a drink— or if he did, it would be just one can, or, at most, two.

For now. For today.

But he didn't think abstinence would change anything. He thought the black beast would still be out there no matter what he did.

And so would Camilla.

He wanted to think about something, anything, else.

"Sinah?"

With an effort, he dragged his mind back to Sinah's problems. They made an interesting puzzle. What crime could Athanais Dellon have committed that her illegitimate daughter would be ostracized a good two decades later?

"Yes?" She looked up from her coffee. Wycherly tried to remember what came next in this odd meaningless social dance. After a moment he remembered.

"How old are you?"

She smiled; it gave her dimples. "Really? Or for my biographers?"

"The truth—I won't tell." The soak had helped, loath though he was to admit it, and now Wycherly felt the drugs begin to blunt the talons of pain that were clamped around his foot. They did nothing about the beast, but even so, he could afford to be charitable.

"I'll be twenty-eight this year," Sinah said. "My birthday's August 14—what's wrong?"

The mention of the date had made him turn his head, as if someone were offering to strike him. For a moment the roar of the water and the stifling reek of the river were all that was real.

"It's my birthday, too. Someone died that day," Wycherly answered raggedly.

Had it been him? It seemed weirdly possible that the last fourteen years had been a peculiar form of Hell.

"I'm sorry. But . . . you've thought of something, haven't you?" Sinah asked, watching his face.

"I think I know where you were born," Wycherly said. *August 14, 1969. The year of the calendar there on the wall.*

Here. In this house. In the bed I've been sleeping in.

"I don't know how much of this they believe themselves," Wycherly began, "but when I got here, Luned and Evan Starking, the brother and sister down at the general store, sounded as if they were pretty well convinced I was the new warlock on the block, come to take the place of the dead witch-woman."

At his insistence, Sinah had made him another cup of hideous coffee, and had poured a tall glass of tepid cider for herself.

"They wouldn't say much about her—but when I wanted to rent a place to stay, they gave me her cabin. Her name was Rahab, not Athanais, but the cabin had been deserted for something like thirty years—you can see the calendar on the wall over there—and whoever'd been there walked out—died, vanished, whatever—leaving everything behind but the bedding on the big brass bed."

Sinah stared at him uncertainly. She wanted to believe him, he could tell. But it seemed almost too pat, even to him, and it was hard to blame her for being suspicious.

"That's awfully hard to . . . Why you?" Sinah said, as if on cue.

"I told you; they figured I was her replacement. It's the hair. Red." He gestured at his shaggy, uncombed mane.

"And all witches have red hair," Sinah returned, quoting from a half-forgotten store of folklore.

"Witches, Judas Iscariot . . . all the best people. But this particular lavish country retreat is apparently reserved for all the local hoodoos, so here I am."

"And everything was still here?" Sinah asked uncertainly.

"Clothes, canned goods—everything. Most of it's still here now, or did you think I'd brought everything in that cabin with me when I came to stay?"

Wycherly stopped himself before he said anything further. There was no way this woman could know the circumstances of his arrival in Morton's Fork—or, in fact, anything about his past. And he liked it that way.

Sinah shook her head, not really listening. "All here? Nobody took anything?"

"Just like the *Marie Celeste*. And I think they were afraid to—just as they're afraid to talk to you now."

"And you haven't even met them." Sinah managed a wan ghost of a smile. "May I look around?"

"Sure. You won't find much. The clothes got cleaned out—and I think I gave one of your family heirlooms to the daily help," Wycherly added, thinking of the ornate silver box he'd given to Luned.

"I don't care. I just want to *know*," Sinah said. *I want to know the truth about myself—and what my family is.*

"Maybe you don't." Wycherly reached out and put his hand over hers, surprising both of them. "Families only make you miserable—you're lucky not to have one. And secrets are buried for a reason."

It would be too easy to be fond of Wycherly Musgrave, Sinah thought to herself. Facile charm was supposed to be *her* stock in trade, but Wycherly had it—when he chose to exercise it. *So this is where I was born,* she thought, looking around the kitchen with new curiosity. *In the cabin of the local witch-woman.*

Black magic or not, she couldn't believe that her mother's witchcraft—real or imagined—was what had turned the villagers against her. From his own words, the Starkings thought that *Wycherly* had occult powers, and all they'd done was rent him the nearest haunted house and pester him for spells.

So if they didn't object to witches, what *could* Athanais Dellon have done twenty-eight years ago to unilaterally terrify every single inhabitant of Morton's Fork? Why did they refuse to admit she'd ever existed?

Why? *Why? why?*

"As I said, feel free to look around," Wycherly said.

The inside of the tin-roofed cabin was bakingly hot, but Wycherly didn't seem to notice. Instead, he pulled his shirt tighter around him as if he were cold.

Glancing back toward him as if to confirm his permission, Sinah walked toward the bedroom and pushed open the door.

In the small bedroom, the dresser, armoire, washstand, and bedside table all vied for floor space with the ornate brass bed. There was a hand-hooked rag rug on the floor, soft and faded with time.

"Go ahead," Wycherly called encouragingly from the other room. "Nothing belongs to me except the shoulder bag and the shaving kit."

Sinah nodded, as if he were confirming her suspicions. A minute later she called back, "You didn't bring any more luggage than that?"

"This was an unexpected stop," Wycherly said. She heard water slosh as he lifted his foot out of the now-cool soak. Almost reluctantly, Sinah began opening drawers.

A bottle of patent medicine, its contents long evaporated. A sewing kit. Meaningless scraps of paper faded to blankness. A stub of pencil. The greatest find was a postcard of Wildwood Sanatorium, the hand-colored photo showing the building in all its glory, rising like Shangri-La out of the Appalachian woodland. Beyond those few scraps there was nothing—no mementos, no photos, no personal papers.

"No Bible." Sinah stood at the foot of the bed and wiped her forehead with the back of her hand. Her sleeveless linen shirt had been softened with heat and moisture until it was molded to the slender curves of her body.

"Bible?" Wycherly asked.

As she'd searched, he'd pulled his chair into the doorway to get a better view of her activities.

"Every household around here has a Bible. I was raised in Gaithersburg, and we had one. This is the homeland of Billy Sunday—they still have revivals here. Are you telling me whoever lived here—witch-woman or not—wouldn't have a family Bible?"

"Maybe it burned," Wycherly said. "Maybe Luned took it." From the sound of his voice he wasn't really interested.

"I don't think she would," Sinah said stubbornly. "But it isn't here."

"You're perfectly welcome to keep looking. Move the furniture around. Check for trapdoors and secret panels if you like," Wycherly drawled.

He was humoring her—well, she'd rather be humored than hated, if those were her choices.

"Root cellar!" Sinah exclaimed.

Luned had mentioned the root cellar the first night he'd come here—a fact Wycherly only remembered as he sat on the bed watching Sinah drag away the linoleum rug that covered most of the floor in the outer room. Beneath it, the planks of the cabin's original building showed clearly, grey with dust and grit. Once the linoleum was gone, the outline of a trap door cut into the wooden floor was easy to see.

"It's probably filled with spiders," Wycherly said helpfully.

Sinah ignored him, heaving it open. A dank, wet, earth-smell welled up out of the hole. It brought his exploration of the sanatorium vividly to mind.

"Looks dark," Sinah said. Wycherly snorted eloquently.

Holding a lighted oil lamp out in front of her, Sinah knelt beside the hole and peered down into it. "It isn't as big as the cabin. Looks like the walls are packed earth. The floor is. I bet there used to be a ladder here somewhere; they were obviously using it for storage, at least before the linoleum went down. I can see some shelves. . . . I'm going down there."

She got to her feet, setting the lamp beside the opening.

"How?" Wycherly asked. "I can't help you." He brandished the discarded Ace bandage. Meditatively, he began to wrap it around his foot. If he bound it tight enough and had something to hold on to, he thought he could probably walk, but that was a far cry from the athletics that getting into the root cellar would require. There was no ladder in the basement, and Wycherly would not have trusted one if it had been there.

"I think I can just jump down," Sinah said. "If you can come over here, you can hand me the lamp after I'm—"

As she spoke, she sat down on the edge of the trap and swung her feet over the edge. Holding tightly to the edge, she slipped down, hung from her fingers for a moment, then dropped free. Wycherly heard her grunt as she landed.

For a fleeting instant he entertained the impulse to just shut the trap again and leave her there in the dark, for no more reason than because he could. He rejected the idea with disgust as soon as it occurred to him, and dragged a chair over to the opening.

Moving carefully, Wycherly handed the lantern down into the darkness, then lowered one of the kitchen chairs into the opening. Sinah set the lantern on the chair. The root cellar was now brightly illuminated. Wycherly looked down.

As she'd said, the walls and floor were of tightly packed earth. Tiny rootlets pushed through in a dim arterial tracery, and on one wall the large serpentine bulk of the taproot from some long-felled tree bulged out of the wall like the body of some half-glimpsed sea monster.

One wall was lined with crude brick-and-board shelves, on which were stacked row after row of Mason jars. A few of those had burst, so long ago that the spillage had already rotted away into dust. What must once have been cardboard boxes, long moldered to slippery blackness in the damp darkness, were piled in the opposite corner. Whatever its original uses, it was clear that the root cellar had not been used in decades.

"I've found something." Sinah's voice was tense with excitement. "A metal box. It's heavy."

She dragged it into Wycherly's line of vision. It was a small box, about the size of a large dictionary, and its surface was a dull grey color. Sinah struggled with the blackened clasp—the box was only held by a heavy twist of brass or copper wire, but the wire was corroded into an immovable clot of metal.

"You're going to have to get it up here to open it," Wycherly said.

"I can't even lift it!" Sinah protested.

"Have you got a towrope in your car? We can use that."

Once the Jeep had been put in place she'd made several trips up and down by means of the chair and the towrope anchored to it. It was late afternoon before Sinah, backing the Jeep Cherokee carefully down the hillside away from the cabin, could use the bright yellow, plastic towrope to drag the box up out of the root cellar. Wycherly waited by the trap, sitting awkwardly on the cabin floor, to make sure the rope they'd knotted around the box didn't break, and to raise the box over the edge with the crowbar from the Jeep Cherokee.

He felt every muscle in his back and shoulders protest as he levered the box up. As soon as it was free he waved frantically at the Jeep Cherokee and heard Sinah cut the engine.

By the time she'd gotten back, he'd untied the rope and the crowbar had broken the knot of wire away from the lock.

"It's lead," Sinah said.

She was dripping with sweat and covered in cellar dust. Her hair was plastered to her forehead and neck, its honey color darkened with dampness. She looked more real than she ever had before, and Wycherly felt something kindle sluggishly inside him for a moment before it subsided.

"Lead doesn't corrode," Wycherly said. "Whoever made this box wanted what's inside to last." He pulled at the hasp, and then gently raised the lid.

Disappointingly, after all their long struggle, the box contained only a few small objects.

A knife, about six inches long. The handle was of deer horn, but the blade was stone, not steel—carefully chipped flint, sheened with oil.

A photograph in a tarnished silver frame. It was very old—the woman in the picture had the grim, pale-eyed look of the subjects of the earliest portraits, the trapped look of a wild thing caught in a cage—but the face in the picture was recognizably Sinah's own.

"I was right. It looks like this was your family's cabin," Wycherly said. And the box contained, not a solution to the mystery, but a deepening of it.

"I don't like this," Sinah said uncertainly.

"Tough," Wycherly said, slapping the photo into her hand. "You wanted to know. I told you that you wouldn't like what you found."

"You can't judge the entire world by your own experience," Sinah protested.

"Can't I?" Wycherly said. He reached for the last item in the box.

With the modern American craze for Native American spirituality, it was easy enough to identify this item as a medicine bag: the pouch—this one was beaded leather—that members of shamanic cultures all around the world wore to hold amulets and talismans, as well as other items of spirit medicine.

The medicine bag crackled between Wycherly's fingers as he held it up, the leather dried and brittle with the passing of unknown years. The leather was a deep amber color now, but he could tell that once it had been white. Sewn to the front of the bag, amid the decoration of seed beads and porcupine quills, was an unmistakably European earring, a glittering green stone in a gold-and-pearl setting.

"Where did she get it? Why did she keep it?" Indian captive? Frontier scout? Wycherly didn't expect any answer to his questions.

The story this pouch symbolized would probably never be told, but

Virginia, like all of the United States, had been Indian country once, before the rising tide of white settlers had pushed this land's first inhabitants ever westward, until at last there was no place left for them to go.

"There's something inside." The flap of the pouch was sewn shut, but
the sinew disintegrated almost as Wycherly dug his fingers under it.
There was a folded paper inside.

That's mine! Only years of an iron self-discipline meant to conceal her gift
kept Sinah from snatching the fetch-bag out of his hand. The ghost beneath her skin *knew* that object—had worn it in stubborn defiance of her
fate long after all hope was dead.

But now I have another chance. Now, at last . . .

"Give it to me," Sinah said harshly.

"It looks fragile," Wycherly commented.

"Give it to me."

Without comment, Wycherly passed the pouch to Sinah.

Sinah kept herself from crushing the pouch in her hand. Many years
had passed since she—she?—had last held it. With trembling hands she
lifted out the object, a many-folded piece of amber-colored parchment. It
came to pieces as she unfolded it, and the edges flaked away like ash. She
put the segments on the floor, assembling it rather as if it were a jigsaw
puzzle, and a sweet smell like rotting leather filled the sweltering cabin.

*Here, yes, here—so close, all the years of my life! See, blood-of-my-blood. See
what awaits you. . . .*

"It's . . . a horoscope?" Sinah said blankly.

Open, the sheet of paper was about twenty inches square, written on
in colored inks that had barely stood the test of time. The shape of the
horoscope—the nested circles divided into twelve wedges, one for each
house of the Zodiac and filled with astrological notations—was unmistakable.

"That, and something else," Wycherly said. Only half the paper was
occupied with the horoscope. The other half seemed to be a crudely distorted map of the Eastern Seaboard of the United States, with longitude
and latitude drawn in, as well as—

"Dragon's Head—and there's the Dragon's Tail," Wycherly said,
pointing. "Geomancy. I only recognize the symbols—it's some kind of
fortune-telling, I think. I'm not sure."

Sinah rocked back on her heels, frozen in the struggle within her mind, a battle against a ghostly avarice that yearned to walk in the sunlight once more. Now that she had some information at last, she felt farther away from any answers than before. A photograph and some ancient scraps of hoodoo hardly added up to a complete biography. And they didn't explain the reptilian presence slithering beneath the surface of her mind.

Nervous breakdown, Sinah told herself flatly. She was sure she could find many to agree with that diagnosis and provide appropriate treatment. Only she didn't believe it.

Reincarnation? The bag—and the artifacts found with it—seemed to imply that it belonged to an ancestor of hers. Was she doomed to have her powers turn inward, to shut out the minds of others as she'd prayed to do, only to find herself subject to a chorus of ancestral voices?

Is that how my mother died? And all the others?

Still clutching the buckskin bag, she reached out and took Wycherly's hand.

It was callused—that surprised her—and she felt the hot tender spots that meant new blisters were starting. But his raw hungers and stifled passions poured into her without any barrier, driving the other—

Marie Athanais Jocasta de Courcy de Lyon, at your service, nithling wench.

—back away from the surface of her mind to become just another of the stolen souls that lived deep within Sinah's memory.

"Well, it's old," she said uncertainly, still clinging to Wycherly's hand. "Parts of Virginia were settled in the early 1700s, but—"

"But the Founding Fathers didn't go around carrying horoscopes in Indian medicine bags, no matter what you may read about Thomas Jefferson in your revisionist schoolbooks. And while this is all very amusing, it doesn't bring you any closer to finding out what happened in 1969," Wycherly observed acidly.

Sinah folded the pieces of paper back together and tucked them into the bag again. She slipped the string over her head, and let the bag lie against her skin. Jewels worthy of a sachem's daughter, *her* daughter . . .

And this Judas-headed young drunkard, with his money and his family, I can keep him as an expensive pet. . . .

The thought carried with it a chill disinterest that made Sinah shudder. Not gone, not banished—Athanais was too powerful and cunning to be cast out by borrowed pain. Sinah fell backward when she tried to reach out and steady herself; Wycherly clutched reflexively at the hand he still held.

She stared at him, seeing her wild-eyed expression echoed in his own.

"Dizzy spell," Sinah croaked out, hearing her voice as if it were some-one else's, a stranger's—hearing, to her horror, not even the flat West Virginia drawl she'd worked so hard to eradicate from her voice, but the strange, slurred accents of long ago and far away. As if the alien impulse that had taken over her mind now was reaching out to claim her body as well.

"Some dizzy spell," Wycherly agreed neutrally, letting go of her hand. "I'm supposed to be the one who does these unscheduled brodies, remember?"

You almost drowned in the creek below the ruins. What happened to you up there, Wych? What made you fall? Sinah hesitated over the questions. To ask would give him the right to ask questions of his own, and Sinah didn't dare answer them—with lies *or* the truth.

"Okay," she said. "I'm okay."

"The rest of your answers are probably in those boxes down there," Wycherly said, "which means it's going to take Indiana Jones to make head or tail out of it—the stuff's probably already rotted to pieces."

Sinah looked so despondent that Wycherly actually wanted to say something to make her feel better. He looked around for something to distract her.

There was writing on the bottom of the inside of the lead box. The inscription was as fresh as the day it'd been made, bright silver against dark, carved into the bottom of the box by a more recent hand than that which had drawn the horoscope or beaded the bag which held it. Now that the box was empty, the marks could be seen clearly—a purposeful line of symbols, terse as a command. Symbols Wycherly had seen recently.

He felt a faint indignation—he'd managed to convince himself that everything he'd seen up at Wildwood had been a particularly vivid hallucination. To see proof—incontrovertibly displayed—that it wasn't so, struck Wycherly as a form of cheating.

"This is from—" he began falteringly. "Up at Wildwood. There's a sub-basement with some kind of altar in it. These are the same symbols."

SEVEN

LINEAMENTS
OF GRAVE DESIRE

Set me as a seal upon thine heart,
as a seal upon thine arm:
for love is strong as death;
jealousy is cruel as the grave.
—THE SONG OF SONGS

WYCHERLY LEANED BACK IN THE FULL-LENGTH SUNKEN
tub, pure sensualism driving every other thought from his mind. As with
every other room in the renovated schoolhouse, Sinah Dellon had poured
money lavishly into the bathroom's appointments. It had stained-glass
windows, hanging ferns, a sauna, heat lamps, a professional-quality wall
of lighted mirrors, and the bathtub came outfitted with a Jacuzzi and was
easily large enough for two.

A disinterestedly malicious desire to meddle had caused Wycherly to
suggest that more answers might be found up at the sanatorium, and
Sinah had agreed they should go first thing in the morning, suggesting
in turn that he might like to spend the night at her cabin further up the
mountain in order to get an early start. With a lot of strapping, ice-
packs, and a night's rest, Wycherly might actually be able to walk tomorrow.

He had to admit that this was a more pleasant place to spend the night than his own hot and airless cabin was. Roughing it was all very well if you were one of those people who believed that privation conferred purity, but Wycherly wasn't. He associated asceticism with a series of only semi-voluntary incarcerations in treatment programs, and he'd never liked it much. Sinah must have some liquor somewhere.

He broke off the automatic assessment, grinning sourly at the habitualness of it. He wasn't going to do that any more, right? A few beers— just enough to lull the black beast and keep the flying mice at bay—but no *serious* drinking.

It occurred to Wycherly for the first time that with his father dying, his days of being forced to check in to places like Fall River Sanatorium in order to retain his allowance were over. Mother would complain about his drinking, but since she'd always ascribed it to his inheritance of her own nervous sensibility, she'd never do much to interfere with it.

All the more reason not to go back to Wychwood, he decided sagely. Especially now that he'd found the woman of his dreams—one with indoor plumbing. Wycherly watched the steam rising from the water through heavy-lidded eyes.

"How are you doing?" Sinah asked from the doorway.

He could see her image reflected in the mirror, but because of the angle she couldn't see him. She'd taken a quick shower before filling the bathtub for him, and now was dressed in slim, elegant, raw linen pants, sandals, and a sleeveless, knitted-silk turtleneck in taupe. Small gold knots gleamed in her ears, and her hair was held back by a narrow suede headband. She looked . . .

She looked like a woman of his own class, a subspecies from whom Wycherly had fled his entire life.

"I'm fine," he said quickly, struggling upright and stifling a hiss of pain as his ankle banged against the side of the tub. In the mirror, he saw her wince in sympathy.

"If there's anything you need, just yell. I've brought a robe that should fit you; I keep it for . . . company. Your clothes should be out of the dryer soon. And dinner will be ready in half an hour."

She retreated.

It was all so domestic and civilized, Wycherly thought sourly as he slid back down beneath the water. He didn't want a lover, no matter how convenient. Lovers clung and tried to make you into their mirror image.

And the one thing he'd shown real aptitude for in his misspent life was killing women.

Wycherly came instantly awake, every nerve quivering. The pale, cold light of earliest dawn filtered in through the stained-glass windows on every side, turning the room into a watercolor in charcoal hues. He was sleeping on the living room couch.

He needed a drink. The need was tinged with panic, a sense that the beast that he fled from had nearly reached him. He could feel the shaking through all the deep muscles of his body, an acknowledgment of the deepest levels of his hunger.

She must keep something here. The unquestioned assumption drove him to his feet. His ankle only twinged a little. Another day or so and it ought to be good as new.

It was tucked into a corner, but Wycherly's radar found it unerringly. In his T-shirt and shorts, he padded over to the reproduction cherry-wood tea chest. It contained four bottles and as many glasses. He lifted the triangular green one out. Glenlivet. She even stocked his brand.

There was no point in bothering with a glass; it would only leave evidence of his drinking behind. Hastily, Wycherly uncapped the bottle and tilted its neck to his lips. Scotch burned his tongue and the inside of his mouth as he swallowed again and again. Fire raced down his throat, into his stomach, outlining all of his organs in flame.

Terrific. You didn't even make it to the end of the first week, he thought when he stopped for breath.

Self-loathing was as strong as the craving had been only moments ago. Carefully, Wycherly placed the bottle back inside the tea chest and closed the lid. His hands no longer shook. He felt like a new man, although the effect of such a small drink would begin to wear off almost at once.

You can afford to buy your own booze. A revulsion that had nothing to do with his drinking suffused Wycherly. He might be the lowest of the low, but he'd never stooped to stealing pennies from a blind girl's cup when his parents were available to wheedle.

And he didn't actually want to drink anyway.

So he told himself.

"Wycherly?" Sinah appeared, leaning over the rail, a ghostly form in a Mickey Mouse sleep shirt. "What's wrong?"

"Couldn't sleep," he lied glibly.

"Oh," Sinah said. "Neither could I. Are you hungry? We could make breakfast and get an early start."

It was, after all, nearly five A.M. "Sounds great," Wycherly said easily. Sinah disappeared and he limped back to the couch to retrieve the rest of his clothing.

The mist of early morning hung in the air and swirled thickly about the ground when they stepped outside. The waste heat that cities produced had long since put an end to the pea-soup fogs that they had once hosted, and now morning mist was something that only country-dwellers were familiar with. It hid most of the trees and turned the rest to grey, dew-spangled phantoms. The Jeep Cherokee was a vague, dark shape in the distance, its windows misted to opacity.

Wycherly hobbled after Sinah, using a carved walking staff she'd found among her possessions. Someone named Jason Kennedy had given it to her as a gag gift. His ankle still ached piercingly, but now he could walk on it, at least a little.

It occurred to him, as he got into the car, that he didn't really want to go back up to Wildwood Sanatorium and find out which part of what he'd seen was real and which belonged to the beast. But Sinah was set on it, and as usual, Wycherly couldn't find the strength to protest in the face of such a vital personality.

He leaned back against the seat as Sinah drove cautiously up the dirt road that was the continuation of the paved one in Morton's Fork, searching for the gates to Wildwood. She'd brought one of her trophies from yesterday with her; the postcard of Wildwood in its glory days was balanced on the dash, its tamed and tailored garden an unsettling counterpoint to the neglected wilderness outside the windows.

Wagging canes of wild rose brushed over the windows and roof of the Jeep Cherokee like goblin fingers. Sinah drove slowly through the misty dawn, the car rocking laboriously over the obstacles in the drive. Everything around them was green, a closely woven veil of life.

He wanted to rest, to sleep—and more than that he wanted the liquor that would replace those needs, wrap his consciousness in a soothing barricade that no harshness could penetrate. *What's the point of being alive, if you're just going to spend it sealed away like that?* Wycherly wondered idly, and grinned to himself. He didn't know. Why was anyone alive? It was the central riddle of existence, and Musgrave's failure son was not going to be the one who solved it.

"There they are," Sinah said.

From the insulated vantage point of a modern car, the tumbledown gates looked even more forlorn, and Wycherly suddenly remembered the bag he'd picked up from inside the pillar, the one filled with coins and beads. He'd taken it out of his pocket and put it in his shoulder bag when he'd given Sinah the pants to wash, but as he felt carefully around inside his pocket, his fingers touched a corner of it.

What was it doing here?

The half-formed question vanished as Sinah turned up the drive, heading for what had once been the terraced front entrance of the sanatorium.

"I don't think I can take the car any farther," she said a few minutes later, applying the brake and shutting down the ignition.

Wycherly looked at the eight steps and two terraces leading up to the ruined doorway. Suddenly he remembered the doorway in the deepest cellar of the mysterious ruin, the staircase leading further into the earth and the rushing water below.

"Drive around. There's a staircase leading down from the north wall," Wycherly said.

Monsters live there.

The notion was childish, unreal; chagrin stifled his impulse to warn Sinah against trespassing into the monsters' domain. He glanced toward her—she was watching him with a half-questioning expression on her elfin face, lips slightly parted.

Sinah drove carefully around the edge of the ruin. The flash of revulsion and terror she'd caught from Wycherly was still making her heart race. The image of the steps, the doorway, and the hideous river far below was vivid in her mind. Of course he wouldn't have mentioned them to her— but why hadn't he *thought* about them until now?

It was almost as if he were trying to lure her in, somehow.

Oh, knock it off, Sinah! Now who's being a moron? She pressed her hand over the bag beneath her shirt. The bag itself had been too fragile to wear, but she'd tucked it into one of those wallets-on-a-string that tourists and joggers wore around their necks. She could still feel it crackle as she pressed down on it.

She turned the key in the Jeep's ignition and pulled back the emergency brake. They were here.

"Why don't you run on ahead?" Wycherly said. "Yell if there's something interesting."

"Sure," Sinah said. She would have been more upset by his dismissive tone if she hadn't been able to clearly sense how afraid he was. His internal monologue was chaotic; the voice of someone shouting so that he could not hear another's words.

She opened the door and stepped out. After the air-conditioning in the Jeep, the morning air was wet and clammy: a stifling blanket. While she'd rambled all over these grounds in the last several weeks, she'd always stayed away from the ruins, fearful of accident. After the big quake a year or so ago out in L.A., no one who'd lived there had the least curiosity about what a ruined building looked like, and Sinah had felt no impetus to investigate.

But things were different now. And if black magic would bring her primacy inside her own mind, she would embrace it unhesitatingly. She got to the edge of the ruins and looked down, braced by Wycherly's memories for the sight of the curving staircase and the altar below.

She didn't see it.

This is ridiculous.

Sinah looked up to the sky—high, hazy, pale blue, open here where no trees grew—and back down. No altar. No black staircase, more to the point, since while she might not recognize an altar when she saw it— even from borrowed memories—everyone knew what a staircase looked like.

She turned and went back to the Jeep.

Wycherly had rolled down his window for ventilation. Though he'd seemed to be asleep, he turned and looked out at her challengingly as she approached.

"I don't see it," Sinah said. "I looked. It isn't there."

"Oh, bloody hell, girl, of course it's there—it's right in front of you."

The legacy of forgotten English nannies surfaced in Wycherly's voice as he opened the door and climbed out of the car. He dragged the encumbering walking stick after him and glared at her, as if the need to go walking was entirely her fault.

"I don't think . . ." Sinah began.

"Help me," Wycherly demanded. Reluctantly, Sinah came forward.

He put an arm over her shoulders and started for the edge of the ruin, the image of the black stairs sharp and clear in his mind.

It had to be there. He'd seen it, touched it, accepted its reality without question. *It had to be there.* He heard Sinah gasp under his weight; pain lanced through his ankle as he dragged himself up to the edge of the ruin.

He looked out over the devastation, searching. The relief he felt when he saw it was so great he could have wept.

"There." He pointed.

Sinah pushed her damp hair back from her forehead; the sunlight glinted on the small bones of her wrist, the skin made shiny with sweat. She shook her head.

"It's there," Wycherly said stubbornly, anger beginning to seep into his voice. Was she blind that she couldn't see it? Or merely playing games with him? He clenched his hand around the small linen bag in his pocket, gripping its unknown contents tightly. The disk sewn inside cut painfully into his hand.

"There . . . oh, it's farther down than I thought." Sinah's voice was flat, unreadable. "But I don't see any altar."

"You can't see it until you're there," Wycherly said. "Go on."

She looked back toward him, wide grey eyes beseeching, bargaining miracles. She wanted him to go with her. Wycherly leaned on his stave and gritted his teeth against the pain in his ankle. It hurt—but he'd follow her down in a minute if there were a bottle at the other end, he knew that. And she could offer him one.

"Will you stay here?" Sinah said quickly. "And . . . watch?"

"All right." He spoke grudgingly.

She turned away. Wycherly watched her go, vague desires for animal comforts jostling for precedence in his mind. He knew what he wanted most, but it was amusing to play the game, and imagine what else he might want instead.

Sinah began her descent, slipping a little in her haste and catching herself against the rough brick wall. When she glanced back, the sight of Wycherly was reassuring—even if he was nearly as likely to push her into the pit as provide help. Her instincts told her that he wasn't a danger to anyone but himself, but that didn't mean he was much of a help, either.

The sense that this was something familiar was frighteningly strong. As if it were water rising around her, Sinah fought against the conviction that she'd been here before—when the building was whole, when . . .

When what? You don't know what, that's what! She pushed the thought away. Down and down and down—this staircase must have been really claustrophobic when the building was whole. Sinah found herself holding her breath against the smoke of a fire that had burned to ash and cinders more than sixty years before she was born.

If you lose it here, you have no one to turn to, she told herself brutally. *No one will help you, no one will come. Wycherly's ankle is bad—even if he wanted to, he couldn't get you out of here if you fell and broke something.*

She reached the bottom level. It was chilly; a good fifteen degrees colder than it was on the surface, and Sinah shivered, even in the T-shirt and baseball jacket that had seemed too hot earlier. The air was full of the smell of things rotting and transforming beneath the earth—like the root cellar had been, but far stronger. It made no sense; there were no earthen walls or floor here to give off such a scent—in fact, this room was carved directly from the rock itself; a black, close-grained stone. Basalt? It looked something like slate, and something like black sandstone, but Sinah was no geologist. All she knew was that it seemed to be an unbroken stone face. Bedrock. The mountain's heart. She took a steadying breath. Wycherly remembered it as being covered with debris, but the floor was swept bare.

What are you suggesting: psychic groundskeepers from beyond the grave? If there is magic in the world, I'm sure it has better things to do with its time!

There was nothing down here that could hurt her—an underground stream, that was all, and Wycherly was terrified of running water. She knew that, without really understanding why; he didn't think about the reason much, if were even within reach of his conscious mind. When he'd heard the sound the first time, he'd panicked, and that was what colored her perceptions now. Detoxing alcoholics weren't all that emotionally stable, after all. *And he's going to fail again, just like all the other times. Why put himself through such hell only to make it all pointless the moment he takes his next drink?*

Because. That was the only answer to so many of the questions of human motivation. *Because.*

She tucked her hands into her armpits for warmth and looked longingly back at the sun above. Far above, the light flashed on Wycherly's copper hair as he moved. At least they could see each other. That was some consolation—though not if she were bitten by a snake. But any self-respecting snake would be out in the sunlight getting warm, not down here in this . . . pit.

Where the walls were rising up, growing higher and higher as she watched, choking her—

Sinah forced herself to inhale again deeply, to fill her lungs and empty them and fill them again, thinking of serenity, of calm oceans and sunlit glades. The oppressive sense of terror receded. She touched the bag around her neck, cautiously probing the part of her mind that seemed to have become infested with that alien consciousness. This place held no resonance for that hungry ghost, but the sense that there was something here to be learned made Sinah step warily.

Sinah had just about convinced herself that there was nothing here to fear when she saw the black altar and the gaping doorway beyond. She put her hand on the surface of the carven stone.

Hot! The stone was as hot as if it stood in direct sunlight, and vibrated faintly as though it stood directly over some sort of mighty machinery. Sinah snatched her hand back and glared at it mistrustfully. There must be some kind of trick; the basement was in shadow; the stone could not be hot.

But she didn't even stop to investigate the runes that Wycherly said this altar stone was carved with; it was the doorway that drew her. She could hear the rushing water, cold and pure and liquid, promising peace and comfort and rest. . . .

Wycherly watched Sinah negotiate the slippery steps down into what (for lack of a better term) he thought of as the temple. Now that the two of them were here, he wasn't sure what good this little side trip would do Sinah in her quest to understand her family. He hadn't been able to recognize the symbols on the altar when he'd been here before, and he wasn't really even completely sure they were the same as the ones carved into the bottom of the lead box.

There were the makings of a fine ghost story here, with mysterious legacies, mute villagers, and unexplained disappearances, but the fact of the matter was that mysteries of that sort held very little interest for Wycherly. One of his psychiatrists had told him that an interest in such things was a part of the process of self-mythologizing in which people invented inexplicable events to weave a shroud of extrordinariness around their own lives. If they could say they'd been kidnapped by space aliens or were the victims of Satanic cults, they didn't have to deal with their own emptiness and disappointments. He looked around—at the blue hills in the distance, at the verdant mountain stretching away below him. He supposed he was as bad at dealing with reality as anyone else was, but he preferred to cope by drinking himself into oblivion, not by making up fairy stories. Miracles were not part of Wycherly's worldview.

He looked back toward the sanatorium. It took him a moment to focus on the deeper darkness that was the temple, and when he did, Sinah wasn't there.

He heard her scream.

The sound was thin and wavery—the sound of despair, rather than a cry for help. It galvanized Wycherly as no entreaty could have. He went down the stairs on his rump, clutching the long walking stick in his hand to avert the possibility of falling. When he reached the bottom, he levered himself to his feet again with the physical numbness of terror and hobbled quickly forward, slipping and swearing.

He didn't see her anywhere. He rounded the altar, and his last hope died—she was not behind it. Where was she? Had she gone down the other set of stairs—into the darkness?

He looked into the opening and saw a white shape moving in the dimness. His heart was a painful airless clutch in his chest, and the edge of the altar was a hard line against his back. The shape was Sinah—it was, it *had* to be—but he wasn't sure, and in that moment Wycherly realized with a wave of despairing violence that he would do anything, *anything,* if only he could never be afraid again.

"Welcome, Seeker—at last."

The voice came from behind him. Reflexively, helplessly, Wycherly looked.

A man stood facing Wycherly across the stone of the altar. He was wearing vestments of some sort; on his head he wore a gilded helmet that was like a stylized goat's head. The horns were nielloed silver, and its eyes were yellow sapphires—they glowed as if there was a flame behind them.

They glowed almost as brightly as the man's eyes.

Wycherly tried to speak, but his mouth had gone so dry that he couldn't open it. He felt a crushing pain in his chest, a nauseated disorientation, as though he were facing a madman with a loaded gun.

He was the madman. And this was something that came from the beast—a hallucination to hold him captive while Camilla came up out of the water and destroyed him. Wycherly understood hallucinations. They had a frightening persuasiveness, but they were intrusions into the real world. The insects, the mice, the slinking dark things, even the beast itself trespassed into an otherwise familiar world.

This was different. This all-encompassing vision had the icy authenticity of genuine truth: This was not reality, and yet it was. Behind the man who had spoken were gleaming paneled walls, inset with frosted Lalique panels crafted with odd, half-familiar designs—not the bare rock of the ruined temple. Tapestries hung between the glass insets, their woven colors bright and elemental. Torches flamed upon the walls in golden holders—the floor gleamed, richly polished and covered with a faint silvery tracery.

"Go away. . . ." Wycherly croaked.

"Do you wish the power I can give you? Or . . . not?" The man smiled, revealing large, tobacco-stained teeth.

Madness, trap, threat . . .

And deep inside him, there was a part that responded with fugitive eagerness to the offer, that answered before Wycherly could censor it.

Power. Yes, power . . .

Give it to me.

"Leave me alone!" Wycherly shouted, wrenching himself away from that chill, piercing gaze. As he turned, he collided with something soft and warm. Sinah clung to him, half laughing, half sobbing in her relief.

"I thought— I thought—" she said, clutching at him as if he were a lifeline.

He tightened his arms around her—she was real, and living, and not a cold shadowy white thing waiting to drag him down to the Hell that waited for cowards and failures. He leaned his cheek against her hair, breathing in her salt and musk.

And as he did her scent kindled a fire in his blood, and a hunger—a *need*—that he had not felt in years blossomed along his nerves.

"Sinah . . ."

He forgot his fear. He forgot the apparition. His hands molded her body against his, as if he could press out the food for his hunger through the contact. She answered him with an avarice of her own, pulling his head down to hers and kissing him deeply.

Here was power. The thought flitted across the surface of his mind, taken for granted in the reality that was the elemental contract between man and woman: that one should take and one should give. He did not question the reason for any of this as he boosted Sinah up onto the altar top and clambered up after her. He sought his oblivion in her body as he had sought it in liquor—and found it.

Around him the spectral voices chanted.

". . . back, back from the darkness . . . Asmodeus, Azanoor, dark above me . . . my body to the beast and my soul to hell . . ."

Sinah came back to herself clutching Wycherly's rucked-up shirt in both hands, for a moment unable to remember where she was. Slowly her surroundings began to make sense to her. She was with Wycherly. The two of them were in the basement of Wildwood Sanatorium. The heat she'd sensed from the stone earlier was gone as if it had never been. Her T-shirt and jacket were wadded beneath her head, making a crude pillow, and her jeans still hung around one ankle.

Wycherly slept his sudden, deep, post-coital sleep against her shoulder. His copper hair spilled across her face, tickling when she breathed.

What had they done? It had been good, it had been wild—unconsciously she ran her palm down his back, smoothing the shirt and the flesh beneath—but it had been so sudden; almost mindless. They hadn't used protection. She didn't know his medical history. It was almost as if they'd been . . . compelled.

Oh, stop it! You'll be crying "rape" next!

But it hadn't been. This sort of thing wasn't her style, but she certainly hadn't been forced—or even overpersuaded. She'd flung herself into his arms, and things had gone on from there, just as if . . .

What? The thought slid away. She'd flung herself into his arms—

She'd been running away and flung herself into his arms—

She'd seen—

"So you've come back," the man said. *He wore a golden helmet, and his wintery eyes were hard as he stared at her—the eyes of a madman, a fanatic, the bogeyman that every twentieth-century woman feared. The killer.*

He stood in the middle of the temple not as it was now, but as it must once have been—outlandishly ornate, filled with symbols Sinah could not quite decipher. The scent of incense was gaggingly sweet in her nostrils, and the room had the

*warm stuffiness of a room far underground. It was like nothing in her entire ex-
perience—the spare, open rooms of her friends into channeling and crystals had
nothing in common with this . . . theological brothel.*

*"Join us, Athanais—I will not ask a third time. The Antique Rite is the true
power; you know that now. And you will belong to it—living or dead. Quentin
Blackburn swears it."*

*Cold radiated from his skin; it rolled through the stagnant air ahead of the
fingertips of the hand he reached out to her. If he touched her she would die: They
were enemies; they always had been and always would be.*

And he would not take her power from her.

She turned and ran, seeking an ally, a tool to bend to her aid.

And found him.

Sinah thrashed at the involuntary recovery of the memory, waking
Wycherly. He rolled away, barely saving himself from falling off the altar
top entirely. Sinah raised herself on her elbows, fighting to clear her head.
The flashback had nothing of the vagueness and subjectivity of the dead
woman who haunted her. This—vision—was as crisp and undeniable as
a visit to the mall.

Sinah drew a deep breath, forcing herself to focus on the temple as it
was now—stripped, ruined—and not to think of that vulpine priest in
the goat's-head helmet, like some ludicrous *Star Trek* extra. Only there'd
been nothing funny about him at the time—he'd been terrifying.

And what was almost more disturbing was that she'd had no reservations about his reality at the time. She had not even questioned how she
could be seeing what she did. And when she'd gotten free of him—when
she'd held Wycherly in her arms—she'd been so *grateful* to Wycherly just
for being real. . . .

No. Sinah shook her head. That wasn't quite right. She *had* been
grateful, but the thing that had made her couple with Wycherly like a
cat in heat was something separate from that. Something that—though
strange—seemed somehow to be less tainted than the black altar itself.

"I'm sorry." Wycherly's voice was so low she barely heard him.

He'd put his clothing back together, and was sitting on the edge of
the altar stone, his head in his hands. He did not look at her when he
spoke. Sinah came back to reality with a bump.

These days men—nice ones, anyhow—walked around with a burden
of guilt just for being men. And when something like this—something

that the previous generation would have shrugged off as the exercise of free love, and the one before it chalked up to overwhelming passion—happened, nineties men felt guilty.

"For what?" With an actress's skill, Sinah made her voice bright and carefree. "Nothing happened here that we both didn't want. No regrets, Wych."

He turned to look toward her then, his expression one of gratitude mixed with sullen disbelief. His eyes were the same pale yellow of the jewels in the goat's-head helmet, and Sinah forced herself not to recoil.

"I generally prefer beds," Wycherly said neutrally.

His thoughts were so jumbled that she could not follow any of the threads: guilt, fear, anger—and a strange sort of cringing triumph, though it did not seem to be related to her. It disoriented her just to be close to him, as though she were trying to follow a thousand conversations all going on at once.

"There's a bed back at my place," Sinah said. She hadn't meant to—just because something like this had happened didn't mean she had to make it continue—but what had happened just now had somehow bound them together as tightly as old lovers, no matter what either of them wanted.

Wycherly smiled wryly. "I was that good?"

"Good enough to warrant a second chance," Sinah said through her misgivings. She pulled on her shirt and groped for her jeans, wriggling them back up into position. "Ready to go?"

When they got back to the Jeep, Wycherly reached into his pocket for the packet he'd dug out of the pillar. It came to pieces in his hand, and all that was inside now was grey dust.

EIGHT

THE POWER OF THE GRAVE

Indeed this counsellor
Is now most still, most secret, and most grave,
Who was in life a foolish prating knave.
—WILLIAM SHAKESPEARE

WHAT A HORRIBLE . . . NIGHTMARE?

I don't think so, somehow.

Truth sat up in the Winnebago's fold-together bed, careful not to waken Dylan. A glance at her wristwatch showed her that it was a little after two o'clock in the morning; after the exhausting day they'd spent getting here, she would have thought she'd sleep longer. Stealthily, Truth slid from beneath the covers, groped for her robe, and stepped outside into the night.

The night air was surprisingly cold, and Truth was glad she'd taken the time to put on her quilted robe over her cotton pajamas. All around her was the deep blackness of the country night. The Milky Way was a bright scarf across the sky, and most of the animal sounds had quieted in this deepest part of the darkness. It was the perfect time and place to think; Truth groped her way over one of the chairs left out from last night's dinner, hesitated, and then walked on in the direction of the general store.

A few years ago Truth would have dismissed what had just happened as no more than a dream—the man, the silver serpent, the whole adventure into the Otherworld—but that was before she'd spent a season at Shadow's Gate and discovered the truth about her father and herself.

According to Thorne Blackburn, the human and divine realms had been separated by the will of the Gods in prehistoric times. The memory of the separation survived in various myths as an expulsion of the humans from Paradise, but Thorne believed that it was the Gods who had left the Garden, and not the reverse. Though communication between the Sacred and Mundane—or Natural and Supernatural—realms had continued, humans were no longer able to move freely into the world of the Gods once the two realms had been separated. Only the Gates remained.

They were most often referred to as Blackburn Gates, though Thorne Blackburn had not invented them. The Gates were passages between the pleasant world of Men and the realms of the dread lords of the Outer Spaces: the *sidhe.* They were located along the ley line convergences on the surface of the Earth, and each had once had its Guardian.

But the system of tribal Guardians that had protected these points of access to the world beyond since paleolithic times had been broken down millennia ago by the advent of the Greek states and the Roman Empire, and then smashed forever by the worldwide spread of Christianity. But at least those ancient conquerors had believed in the reality of gods and powers other than their own, and in Europe and the East the conquerors had been careful to seal the Gates beyond reopening, not merely to slay their Gatekeepers. Even Christianity had moved cautiously among the pagan kingdoms of the Western Isles, treating the native powers with caution even as it had sought to eradicate them.

But Christianity had become careless and arrogant as it consolidated its hold over Europe, and by the time it reached the New World it no longer believed in the ultimate power of any but its own White Christ. In the New World it merely slew those whom it could not convert and bereft the Gates of their Guardians, leaving the Gates in the hands of those who did not understand the nature of their trust—as Truth's own ancestors had not—or, worse, left the Gates running wild, without any controls whatever.

After great struggle, Truth had sealed the Gate belonging to her bloodline, and accepted the responsibility of who and what she was. But innate talent, no matter how great, was no match for trained skill, and so

Truth had apprenticed herself to Irene Avalon, who had been the trance medium for Thorne Blackburn's original Circle, in order to receive the training in magick and the occult sciences that she had scorned all her life.

After only a year or two of work, Truth was very far from being able to call herself Adept in the Blackburn Work, but until tonight, she'd been reasonably confident of her ability to hold her own against anything she was likely to encounter. Until she'd met . . .

Quentin Blackburn?

Can that really be his name?

She'd researched Thorne's family for her book, and he did have an uncle or great-uncle named Quentin Blackburn, who'd died about eighty years ago. He'd been a medical doctor in several sanatoriums in the East, and been known primarily for treating his patients with occult naturopathy and mineral magnetism—a little flaky, true, but light-years from what Truth had experienced tonight.

Which was what, exactly? Truth asked herself.

By now she'd reached the general store. She sat down on the bench next to the ice machine out in front and wrapped her arms around herself, feeling a little like a lost ghost, as her mind continued, hamsterlike, churning over things she already knew.

Through Irene's teaching, Truth was familiar with both the Right- and the Left-Hand Paths, the teachings that supposedly split all the world into light and dark, right and left, good and evil, and assigned every thought and action to one or the other. Truth herself was living proof that there were more ways than two: Her own path was neither black nor white, but grey—grey as mist, and often just as hard to nail down. But that didn't mean she denied the existence of evil, and what she'd experienced tonight was unequivocally that.

But was it Quentin Blackburn?

This is getting me nowhere. It doesn't matter whether I'm dealing with the "real" Quentin Blackburn or not. Any sorcerer of the Left-Hand Path would know any number of ways to anchor his spirit in the Otherworld, keeping it from moving onward in its normal progression to a new incarnation. And whether the man was Quentin Blackburn or not, he was truly evil, in the service of an abomination so foul that it made Truth slightly nauseous to remember their encounter.

She ducked her head, cringing with the anguish of the thought while there was no one here to see. She knew the source of her troubling vision: There was a *sidhe* Gate in Morton's Fork—hadn't she suspected as much when she'd seen all those disappearances?—and without its keeper it was running wild; as dangerous as a nuclear reactor careening toward meltdown.

And if that weren't bad enough, there was some unauthorized person using the blackest of sorcery to meddle with it.

"Unauthorized person." It makes it sound as if someone should be issuing ID cards.

"Truth?"

Dylan's voice jarred her out of her reverie so completely that for a moment Truth couldn't remember where she was. He sat down beside her, putting an arm around her shoulders.

"I woke up and you weren't there. Couldn't sleep?" he asked.

Truth opened her mouth to reply and found herself speechless. What could she say? Dylan was a parapsychologist, but he was *normal*—she couldn't just hit him with all the paraphernalia of a full-bore occult manifestation complete with evil wizard and expect him to take it seriously. At least, not when he was just roused from sleep.

"Dylan, have you ever heard of Quentin Blackburn? Outside of my book, I mean," she said instead.

"Why do you ask?" Dylan's voice was guarded, and Truth's suspicions instantly flared to the alert. She drew away from him.

"You *have* heard of him," she accused. She winced at the confrontational tone of her voice, but there was no way to take the words back now.

"Yes." The word came out on a sigh of . . . defeat? "I've heard of him—and so would you, if you'd read that book you picked up in the general store all the way from cover to cover. I only heard about him last year, after *Venus Afflicted* had been published. He died here, in Morton's Fork, in 1917."

"In a fire." Truth remembered the flames flickering around his ritual robes in her vision, flames as cold as death. "He died in a fire."

Dylan didn't even bother to ask how she knew.

"There was a sanatorium here in those days—one of those places specializing in diseases of the rich. Blackburn built it entirely with his own money and every penny he could beg, borrow, or steal. There was some kind of local scandal about his title to the land being not quite legal, but once the construction had started, nobody said anything—this was an impoverished area even then, and Wildwood Sanatorium meant jobs." Dylan shrugged.

"You knew." Truth was as stunned as if Dylan had hit her. "You knew about Quentin Blackburn being here—and you let me just walk right into this completely unprotected! *Why didn't you tell me he was here?*"

"Because he isn't here," Dylan answered ruthlessly. "He's dead. He died in the fire. And this is just the sort of thing I was hoping to avoid."

"What sort of thing?" Truth asked dangerously. She stood up and turned to face him. He was still sitting on the bench—he'd taken the time to pull on his jeans and loafers before he'd come after her.

"You. This. I turn around, and you're wandering down Main Street in your pajamas, talking about Quentin Blackburn as if he were about to jump out of the bushes with a knife."

He is. He's here. "So you just elected to withhold information—important information, related to my specialty—because you didn't want to *upset* me?"

"No," Dylan said brutally. "Not for that reason. Because I didn't want you chasing off after another of your occult hobby horses with nothing more backing you up than . . . the divine right of Blackburn's children, is why. Your specialty is statistical analysis, not High Magick, remember? Sweetheart—"

"Don't you *dare* call me that!" Truth heard her voice ring off the buildings, and knew that soon she and Dylan would have any number of interested listeners, but at the moment she didn't care. "First you say I'm some kind of crackpot who—"

"I did not say that!" Dylan said, raising his own voice. He got to his feet and took a step toward her. Truth backed away.

"I don't want to see you hurt—you're Thorne Blackburn's daughter—you already know what kind of sideshow the occult can turn into," Dylan said pleadingly. "When I go into the field to study personality transfers and survivals, people expect me to head for the graveyard and start digging up their Uncle Frank—and what you do is worse."

"And what do I do?" Truth asked in a low, ominous voice.

"You do magic," Dylan said flatly.

She winced away from the harsh truth—but that was what it was. Truth was a magician, just as her father and grandfather had been before her. A mage. A *sorcerer.*

Just as Quentin Blackburn was.

"And you don't think that's right?" Truth said, returning to the attack. "Professor MacLaren said that magick was *real,* that magick was possible—that drawing any line between what the human mind could and could not accomplish created a false dichotomy that prevented any possibility of a whole understanding—"

"And you're the one who refused to admit he was right—for *years!*" Dylan shot back with deadly accuracy. "Now all of a sudden you've accepted your inner occultist, but you never could do anything by halves. You *meddle,* Truth—and I didn't want you meddling here."

"In your private hunting preserve," Truth finished poisonously. "Were you afraid that I'd keep you from getting publishable results? Is that all the Unseen is to you—a chance to write another paper? What would you *do* with a ghost if you caught one, Dylan—study it?"

"Yes. Yes, I would," Dylan said evenly.

"You'd stick it in a bottle, and weigh and measure it, and never ask *why* it was there at all. You wouldn't help it to progress to a higher plane—"

"This is exactly what I'm talking about!" Dylan exploded. "If I do manage to find an intact personality transfer here in Morton's Fork, you're damn right I'm going to measure it—I'm not going to invite it home for dinner or suggest it seek counseling. Ghosts aren't *people.* Ghosts are *things*—and dangerous things, besides. I should never have brought you here."

"Because I'm psychic? I'm not psychic! Ninian and Rowan both hit a higher mark on the Rhine scale than I do!"

"Maybe," Dylan said. "But both of them know where to draw the line—and you don't."

Truth stared at Dylan, too stunned to speak. Dylan ran a hand through his hair and made an abortive gesture of reconciliation.

"Look, if it would make you feel better, we can go up to the sanatorium tomorrow morning—I mean, today. If Quentin Blackburn's haunting the place, Rowan ought to be able to smoke him out. I wanted to save Wildwood for last, but—"

"The pins on the map—they're grouped around the sanatorium, aren't they—around Quentin Blackburn? Something you knew and didn't think worth sharing with a deluded hysterical woman."

Truth felt a murderous cold rage boiling up in her, blotting out all trace of her earlier fear. In another moment, she knew she'd strike Dylan—or worse.

"Truth, honey, come back to bed. It's been a long day. I'm sorry I got us lost. Everybody's worn out and edgy. You'll feel better tomorrow, when we can both discuss this rationally."

Dylan's voice and face were pleading with her to let the argument drop. Truth had no intention of obliging him.

"We can discuss it rationally now. Are the disappearances grouped around the sanatorium or aren't they?"

"They aren't. The sanatorium wasn't built until the end of 1914. Some of those reports go back to the first settlers who came here—over 250 years. This is nothing to do with Quentin Blackburn."

Truth put her hand over her face, unwilling to let him see her expression. *The sanatorium was built in 1914—but the Gate's always been here, Dylan!*

But even as she formulated the thought, doubts struck her. What was she basing her belief in the existence of a Wildwood Gate on? A vision that was subjective at best, open to misinterpretation certainly, and that might be partially mingled with a dream?

But no matter the reality of her belief, Dylan had withheld information from her, and that Truth could not forgive.

"If you're as wrong about this little theory of yours as you are about most things, Dylan, you're sure to find out very soon," Truth said grimly.

"Come back to bed, Truth," Dylan said gently.

The last of her anger-fueled strength drained out of Truth, and she felt tired, small, and cold.

And although Truth allowed Dylan to lead her back to the Winnebago, she spent the rest of the hours till dawn curled up in the driver's seat of the camper, staring sightlessly out through the windshield, into the night.

By the time he navigated the distance between the Jeep Cherokee's passenger seat and the front door of the renovated schoolhouse, Wycherly was gritting his teeth with every step. His ankle flared whenever he inadvertently flexed it, and Sinah had nearly had to carry him into the house. Fresh beads of sweat had broken out on his skin and his shirt was soaked by the time Wycherly lowered himself heavily into a chair in Sinah's gracious, designer-perfect living room. As usual, he'd overestimated his capabilities, and he was paying for it now. At times like this he generally craved a drink more than ever, but curiously, his craving had been blotted out, probably by the pain.

It was tacitly accepted that he would sleep here tonight, and Wycherly was too tired to object much, even though the beer was back at his cabin. At least his pain pills were here.

"Let me get you some ice for that ankle," Sinah said. "It's a little late to do much good, but better late than never." She moved away.

The only ice I want has a double bourbon wrapped around it, Wycherly snarled mentally. He stared after Sinah malignantly. Sex was supposed to forge bonds of intimacy and trust—well, intimacy, anyway—but frankly, he'd liked Sinah better before he'd had her.

He glanced around the room again. Normally he would take no notice—this was the way people lived, after all—but this interior was so out of place in the village of Morton's Fork that it constantly drew his attention. Cathedral ceilings, stained glass—a country home right out of *Architectural Digest.*

As a veteran of his mother's frequent forays into home decoration, Wycherly knew this look was not lightly—or cheaply—achieved. But why do it at all? Wycherly shifted position and was rewarded with a new flare of discomfort.

She'd hoped for this moment, prayed for it, and sternly lectured herself against believing it would ever happen. Now it was—and she wished it weren't.

Her gift was leaving her.

When had it begun to fail? When she was around someone for any length of time, she learned to block out his or her thoughts and emotions, rather like turning down a too-loud television, but it was always *there* in the background, ready to be summoned to the forefront of her mind in an instant.

And now she couldn't. Not with Wycherly, anyway.

Oh, she could still feel the tidal press of his emotions, but anyone could read someone else's emotions from face or body or voice. The inner monologue of his thoughts—the endless first-person story that all people told themselves through most of their waking hours—had faded from her mind as if she'd never been able to hear it.

How could she judge him without that? People's actions, their emotions, and their words rarely bore any relation to each other, and she already knew how conflicted Wycherly was. No matter what he was feeling at the time—and usually it seemed to be irritation—there was always something else beneath the surface of his emotions, something he was hiding not only from her, but from himself.

And now she'd never be able to find out what it was.

She concentrated on her surroundings, trying to blot out the inner life with the outer. Even without her gift, she knew Wycherly must be in pain. Maybe an ice-water soak and a couple more pain pills would take the edge off it.

She remembered that he'd prefer iced tea to soda, but she wouldn't give him liquor—at least not if he didn't ask for it, and she knew his queer, twisted arrogance wouldn't let him ask. Let him steal it, then, if he had to have it—Sinah knew he knew where it was.

She opened the refrigerator and got out the tea pitcher, selecting a tall glass and filling it with chunks of lemon and lime, then pouring it full of iced tea. No sugar. Wycherly only took sugar in his coffee.

It created a false sense of intimacy to know so much about another person; a bizarre one-way relationship, like the ones fans created with soap opera stars. She didn't really know him, because he didn't know her—she was possessed of all the minutia of his life, but she was still a stranger to him, and he would treat her as such.

She could change that. Even with her gift's peculiar fading, she could make him like her. She could make him *love* her. She could be his perfect dream girl.

But it would all be an act, tailored to his expectations, and when it was done he still wouldn't know her at all. Even Jason Kennedy had never gotten quite as close as he thought he had, though their shared experience made her count him a friend.

Her relationship—love, hate, or something in between—with Wycherly didn't have to be like that. But did she have the courage to play it straight, not to trade on what her gift had gained her, to let him get to know her for what she really was—without misdirection and half-truths—and respond to that? Sinah looked down at the sweating glass in

her hands. She didn't know. How much did she need Wycherly? That
was the bottom line.

Sinah took the glass back out into the living room, to where Wycherly
was waiting.

Lunch was something clever and civilized, served with more iced tea.
Wycherly picked his way through it, feeling sleepy from the codeine he'd
taken and all the morning's exercise. The air-conditioned air was cool and
dry, and the painkillers were starting to blunt the ferocious ache in his
ankle. They spoke of safe impersonal things—not the sanatorium or what
had happened there—until the meal was over.

"I'd like to talk to you about what happened today," Sinah said. "Shall
we go into the living room?"

He shouldn't be asked to face anything like this without a drink in his
hand, Wycherly thought, but curiously, he was not even tempted to ask
her for one. The part of his mind where the black beast lived was occupied by the dark vision of a man in flames.

Who had offered him power.

Sinah fluttered around the room, unable to settle. Wycherly recognized the restless avoidance of the nondrinking alcoholic, but he knew
he'd have known by now if she was "recovering," as they called it. The
few "recovering" alcoholics he'd known missed no opportunity to flaunt
their amethyst jewelry, tell people that alcoholism was an illness, and explain for exactly how long they'd been "recovering."

It was peculiar, Wycherly thought idly, that alcoholism, like cancer,
was something they never pronounced one recovered from. For the rest of
their lives they were always recovering, never quite reaching recovery.

What did she want? Why wouldn't she come to the point after setting
him on edge the way she had?

"You wanted to talk?" Wycherly finally said.

Sinah settled into the chair placed at right angles to the couch, leaning toward him. The baggy T-shirt masked her body, but the lovely fine-
boned hollows of her gleaming throat were close enough to touch. A faint
edible fragrance rose from the surface of her skin, bringing back muted
flashes of what they'd done on the altar.

"It seems like such a stupid question," she admitted sheepishly, "but I have to . . . today—up at the ruins—did you . . . Have you ever heard of something called The Antique Church? Church of the Antique Rite? Something like that? Or Quentin Blackburn?"

It was not what he'd expected to hear. The words resonated in Wycherly's mind with an awful importance, like the pronouncement of doom. The name "Blackburn" was oddly familiar to him, and the Church of the Antique Rite had the ring of one of those semi-illicit New Age scams that the rich constantly seemed to fall for. The—vision?—had been like a brief, bright pulse of lightning, but the more he thought about it the more it seemed to unfold, as if a vast amount of information had been unloaded into his mind in a lightning stroke.

A psychic flash? In Wycherly's experience such nebulous unreliable things belonged to the realm of television fantasies, but there must be something objectively . . . strange . . . about Wildwood Sanatorium. Satanic chapels with black altars weren't a normal part of any hospital *he'd* ever been in!

"Quentin Blackburn?" Wycherly asked carefully. "Why?"

"Oh, no reason. . . ." She stopped, turning away. Either she was the worst liar of any actor he'd ever met, or she hated the thought of trying to lie to him. Wycherly found either alternative hard to credit.

"I just . . . did you . . . was there anything out of the ordinary up there today?" Sinah asked haltingly.

Sinah's question brought him a vivid flashback of that afternoon—not when he'd taken her on the altar stone. Just before that, when he'd . . .

"No. Nothing. Why do you ask?" Wycherly lied easily.

"I . . ." Her face was turned toward him, serious and sad. As if she'd expected his answer, but was still disappointed by it. A desire to change that expression made him say:

"But I've heard of The Church of the Antique Rite—or something like it, anyway."

"You have?" Her relief was a palpable thing, like sunrise.

"It's one of those neo-Satanist things: you know, sex, drugs, and orgies all dolled up as the search for higher truth. You're the one from California. Aren't New Age religions and nut-cults a dime a dozen out there?" he asked.

"Yes. . . ." Sinah said slowly, still trying to feel for the truth beneath Wycherly's emotions. She'd joined such groups more than once, but she'd always been disappointed, discovering that none of them believed the occult truths that they proclaimed so plausibly to their members.

"Hereward—an actor I dated for a while in New York—was really into that sort of thing, but I just wasn't interested," she said, groping for the words to explain.

Or to be more accurate, the images she'd seen in Hereward Farrar's mind had frightened her to death, even if she could no longer remember quite what they'd been. He'd had a deep interest in magic, as a lot of theater folk seemed to, ritual and theater being so closely intertwined. But nothing in the books Hereward had given her—or those she'd bought later—had been able to explain or control her power, and the rituals that some of them advocated seemed sort of like Zen cooking to her—an elaborate and finicky process producing no visible results.

"He loaned me a bunch of books, but I never got around to reading them," she said, cautiously shaving the truth. "I think I brought them with me when I shipped my things here from the Coast. Maybe they're still here somewhere."

"You'll probably find your church listed in the *Whole Magick Encyclopedia* or something like that," Wycherly said, sounding bored. "Fortunes bilked while you wait, that sort of thing."

"Maybe," Sinah said reluctantly. Her ability to read Wycherly's mind might have dwindled to the point where she could only feel his emotions and not hear his thoughts, but she'd still felt the flash of recognition he'd had when she mentioned The Church of the Antique Rite.

He knew what it was. And he was lying to her.

Sinah lay awake in the dark, hearing Wycherly's drugged, even breathing beside her. His mind was stilled now, the dreams moving like bright fish just out of her psychic reach. She reached out to the nightstand, where the ancient leather of the pouch crackled through the modern fabric of the neck purse as she closed her fingers on it.

It seemed to Sinah that she could feel the contents vibrating with the personality—and the will—of the woman who had first worn it. That woman would have been more than a match for the man—or ghost— who had threatened Sinah up at Wildwood today. Athanais de Lyon had never let anything stand in her way—not king, god, or devil—and Quentin Blackburn would be no different. . . .

Her easy use of her ancestress' name frightened Sinah on some deep level, as though it meant she was admitting that her self-delusion wasn't delusion at all. That Athanais de Lyon was real.

It's your mother's name; the rest of it is borrowed whole-cloth from prime-time television! she told herself bravely. But it wasn't. She already knew that. She came from a hereditary witch family, and apparently it had hereditary enemies as well. Like The Church of the Antique Rite.

But what's the point? Soon enough—the way your mind's going—YOU won't be around to care at all, her inner voice mocked.

There was too much truth to that to make the thing easy to think about. She needed help. She needed to know what Wycherly knew. Maybe she could lead the conversation around to the subject again in the morning.

No. Wryly, Sinah acknowledged that even her own sense of self-preservation couldn't make her manipulate Wycherly Musgrave that way. She needed his help—but she wouldn't trick it out of him. Maybe he'd learn to trust her.

Maybe hell will freeze over.

Another half hour of sleepless tossing and Sinah got up and went downstairs to the kitchen. On the shelf beside the teacups was the prescription for a sleep aid that she'd gotten to smooth over her jet lag when she'd been commuting from coast to coast. She shook two of the tiny white capsules—a double dose—out onto her palm and swallowed them dry. She wanted to sleep, deeply and without dreams. It was the only escape she had left.

Sinah looked around the kitchen, and out through the louvered doors into the great room beyond. *This* was supposed to have been her escape, but all it had been was another dead end.

Wycherly woke just before dawn again, as abruptly as if someone had shouted in his ear. He'd been dreaming of a vast and featureless plain and a throne made of skulls. He'd dreamed he'd grasped a serpent of white-hot metal and held it, screaming in pain, until his hands had burned away.

He couldn't let that happen. He had to . . . what?

Experimentally, Wycherly thought about the liquor cabinet on the floor below. He could have been thinking about chocolate ice cream for all the craving the thought kindled.

He didn't want a drink. *He didn't want a drink.*

Wycherly moved away from Sinah and sat up, stunned by the enormity of the thought. He'd started drinking when he was twelve—there was always liquor around Wychwood, and both parents and his older brother drank—and Wycherly could not really remember a time when he hadn't been planning what he'd do to get his next drink.

But he didn't want one now.

That felt wrong.

Moving slowly and favoring his ankle—though it was no longer very sore—Wycherly gathered up his clothes and brought them back downstairs to put them on, rewrapping the bandage around his ankle as tightly as he could. He'd loosen it as soon as he got back to his own cabin. Getting back there might not be such a bad idea, anyway. Always negotiate from a position of strength—that was what his father had always taught him.

Was the old man dead yet? Wycherly couldn't think of any way to find out without letting the family know where he was. He shrugged. First things first.

When he was dressed and about to leave, one last thought stopped him. Sinah'd mentioned having some books on magic that an old boyfriend had given her. Since she was the closest thing to a library he was likely to find in Morton's Fork, it wouldn't hurt to check them out.

There was a copy of something called *Venus Afflicted: The Short Life and Fast Times of Magister Ludens Thorne Blackburn and the New Aeon;* the name on the cover stopped him until he realized it was *Thorne* Blackburn, not Quentin, and that the man in the photograph had been born long after Wildwood Sanatorium had burned. There were books on finding your inner white light—Wycherly curled his lip in disgust—and on UFOs; there was something that looked like a general history of the occult—he set that one aside to take—but none of them was the book he was looking for.

When he picked up one of the thicker discards—*The Autobiography of the Great Beast, Written by Himself*—to reshelve it, it shifted in his hands, slithering out of the dust jacket. Wycherly caught it hastily before it hit the floor, and when he did, he realized he'd found a secret.

There was another book hidden inside the first; the back pages were cut away to make a niche for it. Something you'd never notice—unless you dropped the book, as he just had.

Wycherly pulled the hidden book out and opened it.

It was old, battered, and shabby, the gold-stamped white leather having faded to a uniform dirty grey. It was a small book—about four inches by seven, and about half an inch thick—easy enough to overlook if you grabbed the other volume. He put the dust jacket back around *The Autobiography* and placed it carefully back on the shelf before he opened the hidden volume.

The faint grey light of dawn was barely enough to let him make out what it said: *Les Cultes des Goules—The Cults of the Ghouls, Being a True Account of Certain Pre-Christian Abominations Practiced in Modern Times in the Languedoc and Navarre,* and below that *Translated from the French with Appendices and Commentary by Nathaniel Lightborn Atheling, M.D., LL.D., FRS, Oxon.* The page was printed in a mixture of black and red and said it had been printed by Charles Leggett, London, 1816.

This was the one. The same mixture of excitement and terror that Wycherly had felt at the black altar filled him now. He'd been meant to find this.

The first page was punched and embossed with an old-time library accession seal that years of dirty fingers had made easy to read. TAGHKANIC COLLEGE LIBRARY. The page was stamped: DO NOT CIRCULATE in faded red ink. Wycherly smiled to himself and read on. He wondered how Sinah had gotten her hands on it—or if she'd even known that it was there.

The first half had facing pages in English and French, both in antique type and neither easy to read. The French pages were thick with carefully drawn diagrams and illustrations, some hand-tinted painstakingly in watercolor. Wycherly paged through the book quickly, slowing only when he realized what he was seeing.

It looked like the storyboards for an antique snuff film.

He stared at the page in disbelief, then closed the book hastily, as if somehow the images printed on the paper could escape into the real world. It did no good. What he'd seen lingered in the mind's eye, poisoning the imagination.

Here was the power he had been promised.

Beyond question, he knew it was true. Didn't everything in twentieth-century culture tell him that power—respect—was bought with blood? The book and what it seemed to advocate were hideous, but maybe—if he read it carefully—it wouldn't be what it appeared to be, or at least not seem so bad.

Are you out of your mind? an inner voice demanded. Wycherly ignored it. Hastily he set the book atop the other one he wanted, and levered himself awkwardly to his feet again. Time to go.

Going from Sinah's climate-controlled refuge to the gloomy early morning was going from comfort to a clammy, faintly cool world that set Wycherly's teeth on edge. It wasn't quite rain, but heavier than humidity, and too wet to be bracingly cool. The mist deadened sound; Wycherly limped slowly through a world swathed in cotton batting, clutching his stolen books to his chest and balancing his weight on the borrowed walking staff.

His ankle hurt, but not as much as yesterday; it was more of a weight than an actual pain. The Little Heller was somewhere on his left—he could hear it, echoing off the fog—and about a mile to the right was the road that led up to Wildwood.

It seemed to Wycherly almost as if the sanatorium had weight; between his shoulderblades the skin crawled with its presence, tugging him toward it as insistently as gravity.

Hallucination.

Maybe. But the books were real. They seemed to burn with the cold destructive fire of radiation against his chest.

The river was real. He could hear the taunting chorus of drowned voices calling for him.

She isn't there. She can't be there. She's dead and buried in an expensive bronze box out on Long Island. You saw the tombstone—remember?

And since he'd been safely away at an institution whose name he no longer cared to remember, he didn't remember anything else. Trial, charges, and sentencing—if any—had been dropped into the black hole where the Musgrave family kept all its unpleasantness. He'd had to go through quite a lot of hell a couple of years later just to find out where Camilla was buried. She was really there, and he was the one who'd put her there. He'd been the one driving.

But maybe that wasn't going to matter any more.

It was six o'clock by his watch when Wycherly reached his cabin. The linoleum rug was still lying in the dooryard, curled between two trees. His weak ankle was complaining fiercely by now, and he was running low on T-3s. He pushed the thought from his mind. He'd always been good at ignoring the future.

He limped inside, leaning heavily on the stick. He'd left the windows open; it was as damp inside as out, and stuffy besides. The outline of the trapdoor was plainly visible in the floor, though at least they'd had the foresight to close it. God alone knew what else was down there, and whatever it was, he'd like it to stay there.

He closed the door of the cabin behind him and set the books he carried down on the red and white oilcloth cover of the kitchen table. *Les Cultes des Goules* seemed to glow in the dim light, drawing the attention as irresistibly as if it were a severed human hand placed there.

What an appetizing image, Wycherly thought to himself. He headed over to the refrigerator. Somehow the weird impulse of continence that had sustained him since he'd he woken up this morning was still with him, but there was nothing else to drink here but beer. Oddly enough, he'd actually have preferred water, but the thought of going near the creek still made him cautious.

He debated closing the windows and decided he wasn't up for the struggle. The place would be as dry as it was going to get in a few hours anyway. *"When it's dry, the roof don't leak, and when it rains, you cain't fix it nohow."* The tagline of an old hillbilly joke passed through his mind. True enough, and a reasonable enough way to live, if anyone was interested in Wycherly's opinion.

Only nobody was. And everyone always seemed to want to borrow trouble: his whining mother, his dull-witted brother, his overachiever sister.

And then there was his father, who until recently had lived in so perfect a world that he hadn't even understood the concept of failure.

Wycherly thought about reading through the books, but it was too dim in the cabin to read, and he didn't feel like hunting around for the lamps. Besides, now that he was back on his home turf he was starting to feel sleepy again. He'd had a restless night, and it had followed a strenuous day. Now that the sun was up, he thought he might be able to sleep for a few hours—he always slept better when the sun was up.

The bedroom was still disheveled from the day before, but he didn't care. He flung himself down on the ancient mattress, and fell fast asleep as the sun rose through the trees.

NINE

GODLY AND GRAVE

My father is gone wild into his grave.
—WILLIAM SHAKESPEARE

THIS IS ANOTHER FINE MESS YOU'VE GOTTEN YOURSELF *into*, Truth told herself with a sigh. Relations at breakfast had been strained, to say the least—Truth wondered how much Rowan and Ninian had heard of last night's quarrel and what they'd made of it.

Well, grown-ups fought. That was part of life. And it was never the end of the world, more the pity. Because Truth knew that she and Dylan would patch up their quarrel this time, only to fight again—and again. Until the fighting finally became bitter and unreconciled enough to separate them forever.

And what would she do then? She wasn't independently wealthy; she was a statistical parapsychologist, and there weren't that many job openings for one of those. The Bidney Institute was the most respected name in the field—Truth had opportunities there she just wouldn't get elsewhere.

And for that very reason, Dylan wouldn't want to leave either. Truth supposed they could just avoid contact with each other—just consider that impossible Aillard woman who ran the ghost-hunting department at the Institute. *She* was all but certifiable, and Dylan managed to work with her. Dylan, Heaven knew, was all-forgiving to the point of self-destructiveness.

With a guilty start, Truth realized how far her thoughts had wandered from the real problem—not her relations with Dylan, but her, Quentin Blackburn, and the Wildwood Gate.

If there *was* a Gate.

Between last night and this morning, Dylan had tacitly dropped his offer to begin the team's investigations with the sanatorium and that suited Truth just as well. She was more interested in what her own exploration would reveal.

Evan Starking over at the general store had been helpful, if a little confused about what she wanted. Several times he'd offered to direct her to some "real witches"—as if Truth couldn't see real Wiccans, with too much eye makeup and dripping with silver jewelry, at Tabby Whitfield's store in Glastonbury any day of the week. But finally Evan had given her some deceptively simple country directions to find the sanatorium— "just follow Watchman's Gap Trace till you come to the gates."

What he hadn't mentioned was how *far* it would be. She'd been following Watchman's Gap Trace for about two hours now—as it got steeper, narrower, and progressively more rutted, and the canteen and her bag of working tools got heavier with each step.

At last, when she'd nearly given up, Truth reached the gates of Wildwood Sanatorium.

She paused just outside the gates, feeling an odd sense of disquiet. Even through her weariness and her concentration on Earth-plane things, Truth could feel the strange wrongness here.

Something is missing.

She did not know where the conviction came from—the building had burned, the gates were in ruins; what *wasn't* missing?—but it was strong and irrefutable: Something wasn't here that ought to be here.

Truth looked around slowly, trying to cudgel her lazy mind into providing the information. After a few minutes, she acknowledged the futility of her hope with a shrug. If she wanted information, there was nothing to do but go on.

She turned up the narrow drive—it had been graveled once, and traces of the surface remained in sheltered places—and began to walk up through the long, green tunnel of roses gone wild.

The moment she passed between the gates, the sense of wrongness intensified. Truth knew it might be a case of Observer Effect, of seeing what she expected to see. She tried to discount it, but the farther Truth got from the rusted iron gateway, the slower she walked. When the rose brambles opened out enough to show her a marble bench sitting in a clearing kept close-cropped by deer, she made her way over to it and sat down, trying to sift out what she felt.

Power. To describe the reality of the Unseen World in terms of the five senses of the Earth plane could only be misleading, but Truth felt the power of the place pour over her with the driving tidal reverberation of a mighty engine running flat-out. The phantom heat of an astral blast furnace made her skin tingle.

The power was here in this physical reality that corresponded to the landscape of her dream: the forest glade, the whirlpool, the vision of Quentin Blackburn swearing he would make that power his.

But she could not just blunder forward blindly, Truth told herself sternly. Truth knew as much about the Gates as anyone alive, but she lacked her father's sanguine Summer of Love conviction that such power could be tampered with safely. Dylan had established that the "real" Quentin Blackburn had actually been here. Now Truth must determine the nature of the power here as well. Was this another Gate as her vision had suggested? She only suspected that was true—she didn't *know*.

How many unsealed Gates still existed in the world today? Thorne himself had not known, though the Blackburn Work was based on their existence. On the ability to open and close them at will, to summon the power of the *sidhe,* and, possibly, even to open a new Gate where none had been before.

Truth squared her shoulders at the magnitude of the task before her. She reached for the bag sitting upon the bench beside her and began unbuckling its closures. Time to get to work, and this place was as good as any to begin.

But half an hour later Truth had to admit that too much evidence was as baffling as too little. The first thing she'd wanted to do was identify the source and bounds of the power, but when she'd extended her pendulum, the plumb had swung out wildly, the rock-crystal weight dragging at the sterling chain until its spinning trajectory was nearly horizontal. It had wrapped itself painfully around her ribs, and after the third time she'd unwound herself, she'd given up trying to use it.

Next she'd tried the wand. One half of it was iron, its surface dark and sheened with the oil that kept it from rusting. The other half was glass, clear as water and gathering light like a lens. A thick ring of pure gold bound the two halves together. It was not really meant for dowsing—it symbolized the transformation of brute intellect through directed Will—but it would serve as a dowsing rod if the need arose.

But when she balanced it on her palms and opened her outer shields to the surrounding influences, her wand twisted wildly in her hands. Before Truth could stop it, her wand had fallen to the ground, shattering the glass portion of itself against the leg of the marble bench.

Truth stifled a cry of pure dismay at the devastating blow, and bent to pick up the pieces. She cradled the iron in her hands, for a moment uncaring of the effect the gesture would have upon the symbolic language of her inner temple. Everything would have to be reforged and rededicated.

But it is only a symbol, for convenience. Not the thing itself.

Carefully Truth wrapped the pieces of the broken wand—careful to collect all of them—first in silk, then in linen, and stowed the packet back inside her bag. She looked through the rest of the bag's contents. Some were as mundane as wooden stakes, chalk, herbs, spring water, and fishing line; some exotic—the nine-banded bracelet, flasks of Anointing Oil and Universal Condenser, knives of silver and obsidian.

It looks as if I'm either going to cook or survey, Truth observed with a wry smile. But the reality was that this was the illusive paraphernalia of High Magick, and these were the tools she must use to investigate.

Her skin itched from the outpouring of power around her, but that was a subjective, unquantifiable datum; she needed details. Truth looked through what she had left. It would have to be the mirror. As little as she liked searching this place on the Astral, it was not as if she must do it unaware and undefended. She slid the nine-banded bracelet onto her left wrist, settling it into place against her skin.

Three for iron, the bones of the Earth, which die in their season. Three for silver, the eyes of the wind, which die without care. Three for gold, the heart of the fire, which does not die, nor shall it change. . . .

Truth hesitated, gazing at the bracelet, and then for added protection, tied the phylactery low on her forehead, so that the flat stone sewn into the linen band pressed hard against the place between her brows. Occultists held that this was the location of the Third Eye, the organ whose vision was tuned to past, future, and the Unseen World. She knotted the linen band tightly at the back of her head, secure against accidental displacement, and then picked up the scrying mirror.

Her shewstone was made of jet, which, like amber, had once been a living thing, and like amber was prized by Pagans and magicians alike for its ability to hold an electric charge. The scrying mirror in her hands—or *speculum,* as the medieval magician had called it—was seven inches across, slightly concave, and polished mirror-bright. Truth gripped it firmly so that neither unseen forces nor nervous twitches could pull it from her hands, and stared down into its bright surface.

At first all she saw in it was her own image, blurred and softened by the jet and distorted by the curve of the mirror's shallow bowl. Black hair, blue eyes, unremarkable and stubborn. Her mother's daughter, with no trace of her *sidhe*-sired father in her face.

Her mind was drifting again—where was her discipline? Truth summoned her attention back to the mirror, shutting out the world. The wards that were a part of her life now would summon her back to the body if anyone approached her. All that was left was to do what she had been trained for.

Truth summoned up all her will, and thrust herself into the Otherworld. Find the Gate. Summon its Guardian. If the Gatekeeper could not be found, then she must try to close it herself.

The bland, featureless, subjective landscape was reassuringly familiar. This time Truth knew what she was looking for. If it was a Gate, its signature should be unmistakable; the power of a Blackburn Circle was as much like it as a candle was like the heart of a star.

There.

As Truth focused on it, she became aware that the architecture of this place without landmarks all bent inexorably toward it, as mindlessly obedient as the patterns made by iron filings around a magnet.

She chose not to summon her Guardians, but to go forward on foot, garbed in the red robe and white shift of a Blackburn adept. Seven silver stars burned upon her brow where the phylactery was bound on the Plane of Manifestation, and the nine-fold bracelet upon her left wrist was a cold and comforting weight. She flexed the fingers of her right hand, and her wand appeared between them, intact here in the Otherworld, though its symbol in the world below was broken.

Slowly, she approached the Wildwood Gate.

She had seen it before first as a whirlpool, then as a serpent; this time it appeared in the mutable Otherworld as a vast and cyclopean doorway: two vast pillars and a capping lintel, making a stark, hyper-real henge here in the featureless plain. It radiated power.

Once she could see the Gate, approaching it became more difficult. Though the path seemed still to be level, Truth felt as though she were trying to ascend the steepest of inclines. She made her wand into a staff and used her embodied and transformed Will to pull her forward. The closer she got, the larger the Gate seemed to loom, until—when Truth reached it after subjective hours of striving—it was so enormous that it was as if she stood at the foot of the tallest skyscraper on Earth and tried to see the top.

Cautiously she extended her fingertips to touch the stone of the doorway. It was rough and cool beneath her fingers; not an unpleasant sensation.

Truth hesitated, and as she did, she realized she was waiting for Quentin Blackburn to appear. But it was the Gatekeeper she wanted, not Quentin—even if he happened to be of the proper bloodline, he was male. Only women controlled the power of the Gates, though men could pass this legacy to their daughters.

Tell me to get back to my kitchen, will you? Uncle, you have a lot to learn!

She turned to the Gate, and spread wide her hands. Between her fingers a blue-fire lattice grew, and as if in faint reflection of that power, the ghostly image of a door appeared between the pillars of the Gate. This Gate was already open nearly far enough to allow a human to pass into the sidhe realms beyond—and while it stood unsealed, it was a portal through which the dreams and nightmares out of humankind's darkest unconscious could issue forth to be given flesh and form.

this was the reason Morton's Fork was the centerpiece of so many ghost stories and disappearances, Truth realized with a thrill of triumph. And it had to be closed.

But that must be done by its Gatekeeper. Where was she? Truth cast around for a means of calling for her, and at last summoned the least trustworthy of her Guardians.

The grey wolf slunk toward her, over a landscape that slowly had grown more craggy and boulder-strewn. Truth knelt to greet it: power, activity. She should have summoned its opposite at the same time for balance, but the wolf lost power in the presence of the black dog, and Truth needed all the power she could summon.

"Sing for me, boy," she said, ruffling the wolf's thick mane as she knelt beside him, and the grey wolf threw back its head and howled.

The lonely sound echoed from the pillars of the Gate and reverberated through the Otherworld. Truth felt the Gate stir to half-wakefulness at the call. The wolf howled again, and again. Truth waited until the last echo had died.

Waking or sleeping, Adept or innocent, alive or even newly dead, this Gate's keeper should have come in response to that summons—unless the Gate had no keeper now, and the bloodline was lost.

Truth got to her feet, sketching a symbol in the air to dismiss the grey wolf. It capered around her ankles for a few moments—its playfulness a response to the kindred power of the Gate—before loping away. Truth watched after it for a long time before she looked back at the Gate, wishing for a number of things, including that she had not just had a fight with Dylan.

The Gate must be closed. This truth was unambiguous. And its keeper had not come to her summoning. That left Truth to try to close it by herself.

She tried to feel optimistic.

She'd only done this once before, under circumstances that had left the events indelibly printed upon her mind. Truth reached out with every fibre of her being for the spellkeys that would let her lock this Gate. She reached for the fabric of the Gate itself—

And she could not grasp it. Again and again she reached for the reality behind the power cascading all around her, only to feel it slip from her grasp like smoke. It was her SELF that had been the lock of Shadow's Gate, made possible by the bond of blood, but this Gate was not hers, and Truth could neither open nor close it.

Failure.

With a full working Blackburn Circle and five years of ritual preparation, Truth would have been willing to give it another try. The Blackburn work had been designed to affect the Gates, but without a woman of the dedicated line, even Thorne Blackburn himself could not close a Gate.

She had to find its Gatekeeper. But there was no Gatekeeper.

The Astral Plane was growing dim and shadowy around her, the Gate beginning to dwindle as etheric currents swept Truth away from it. In the world below, her body was tired, and she had learned all she could here and now.

Truth let the current pull her away from the Gate, and when she was far enough from its influence, she let herself fall free, back toward her body and the tyranny of the World of Form.

*   *   *

"*Stop!*"

Heedless of his ankle, Wycherly rushed across the floor and snatched the book bound in white leather out of Luned's hands just as she was about to feed it into the wood stove fire.

He didn't know what had awakened him; he'd come up out of a deep and uneasy sleep, heart hammering in panic. And it looked like he'd woken just in time.

Quickly he riffled through the pages, making sure that the book wasn't damaged. He cursed himself for leaving it where a witless mountain girl could stumble over it.

"Don't you *ever* take anything that belongs to me—do you understand? *Ever!*" he shouted at her.

Luned regarded him miserably. "It's *evil*, Mister Wych!"

But you were the one who looked inside, weren't you, girl? a small voice inside Wycherly asked meanly.

His first panic faded and, the book safe in his hands, Wycherly looked—as always—to cover his tracks. Besides, he might need Luned's cooperation later, and right now she looked like a scared rabbit, white-faced and staring. Tears streaked her cheeks and her hands shook. She stared toward the book as if Wycherly were holding a live adder in his hands.

He almost fancied he could hear her heart beat.

"It's all right," he said, as gently as he could. "I know that it upset you. You called it evil; you're right. It is. But you have to understand, Luned, that things aren't always what they seem. Sometimes evil can be used in the service of good. I'm sorry you saw it. I wasn't expecting you back so soon. Just relax, Luned. I won't let anything hurt you."

Wycherly felt oddly guilty, as though he was now responsible for some depravity that placed him more firmly in the power of one who did not wish him well. As if what he said to Luned could actually matter.

"It's an evil thing," she repeated, less forcefully this time.

"You should get out more." He pushed his guilty agreement—it *was* a nasty little grimoire—to the back of his mind, and wondered if Luned had ever seen a horror movie—and if not, what she'd make of one.

"Don't worry about it. It's nothing to do with you."

Luned looked doubtful.

"What are you doing up here, anyway?" Wycherly said. He tucked the book into his waistband and closed his shirt over it.

She smiled with relief at the change of subject. "It's been nigh on two days since I've been here, and I expect you were perishing away here all by yourself." She turned back to the open door of the stove, picking up the poker and giving the fire a ferocious jab, as it to prove her industry.

Wycherly forced himself to smile, and sat down at the kitchen table, preparing to exercise the not-inconsiderable family charm. He wanted something, after all. And if he turned her up sweet, maybe he could get her to bring him the car's registration and plates. Then nothing would tie him to the crash, except the word of a pack of backwoodsmen who probably didn't want to testify in court.

It was a clever thought, and it warmed Wycherly. It was something his father would have thought of.

"And when Mr. Tanner came up and got the icebox to running, he got the old pump to working, but I s'pect you wouldn't know what to do about things like that, and now I can make you a nice lunch, an wash up your clothes an all, an do for you, an you could take a bath and all—"

"Look," Wycherly said hastily to stem the flow of domestic babble. "How about some breakfast? I don't know what there is, but—"

"You said you didn't eat breakfast, Mister Wych," Luned said reproachfully.

That was before I wanted something. A new cold sense of purpose guided his words, his thoughts, shaping his determination toward an as yet unknown goal. He trusted it because it was the path of least resistance, and because he couldn't see any danger in it.

At least not yet.

"Well, maybe I could manage some . . . biscuits? And coffee?" he added hopefully.

He smiled, and Luned smiled back, as if all she asked in the world was to cook him breakfast. Oddly, it made him think of Sinah, who had something of the same wistfulness in her expression but was a woman grown.

Fair game.

A few minutes later, Wycherly nursed a cup of coffee—brewed, not instant, and some of the best he'd ever had—as Luned made biscuits from scratch, fried up a skillet full of ham produced from a can, and then made red-eye gravy with coffee and flour. His ankle was better than it had been earlier this morning, but it throbbed sullenly, reminding him of its presence.

By then the inside of the cabin was like an oven; the dry heat of the stove battled the humid heat of the day to produce an overwhelming if curiously pleasant sensation. Luned pumped water when she made the coffee, and Wycherly drank two glasses full. Hydration, nutrition, exercise were the checklist for the recovering alcoholic.

He'd never felt less like an alcoholic—recovering or otherwise—in his life. Gingerly, he probed the edges of his consciousness. The black beast was gone. Camilla was gone. In their place was an undigested sense of promise, of forthcoming delights that verged on terror.

Power.

Luned produced breakfast; it was easier to choke down than Wycherly had anticipated, and easy to refuse the proffered beer. In fact, he ate with a flicker of real appetite, his mind trying ideas as though he were a mechanic sorting through a toolbox for a part that would fit.

"I twisted my ankle when I was out walking the other day," Wycherly began.

Luned, sitting opposite him, was chasing the last dregs of gravy around her blue enamel plate with a scrap of biscuit. She glanced up, her mobile face filled with worry and curiosity.

"It's fine now, more or less. It happened up at the sanatorium. What do you know about the place, incidentally?"

His unsubtle feint would not have disarmed a more sophisticated subject, but Luned readily accepted the bait. Filled with her own importance, she told him what he already knew: that it had burned in 1917.

"—and ever'body said that Attie Dellon was the one as set the fire, since it was on Dellon land but her brother never could hold his likker and he sold off ever'thing from their stead on up to the Watchtower to that flatlander man, and wasn't nobody surprised when Arioch went off down to the bottom of French Lick and busted his fool neck, but Attie couldn't get the land back nohow, even if she sacrificed her own blood sister to Mr. Splitfoot to make Quentin Blackburn fall down dead of the ague!"

"Quentin Blackburn?" The name made Wycherly sit up and take notice, but Luned didn't seem to notice his increased interest.

"That was the flatlander's name, hear tell. And the sheriff—" she pronounced it "shurf," slurring the syllables together in the clipped mountain dialect "—he come and took Attie Dellon up and didn't bring her home for a week, but couldn't nobody find hide nor hair of Miss Jael, and her brother done fell down and bust his neck while she was behind iron bars," Luned finished in an awestruck rush.

"Well," Wycherly said. "That would seem to settle it." The unsolicited corroboration of Quentin Blackburn's existence made his heart beat faster with excitement, as if it made the rest of the events more plausible. He discarded Luned's insistence on Satanic rituals, though . . . for the moment.

"Wouldn't nobody in the Fork talk to her after she'd done murdered her own kin like that, and then when Wildwood burnt and she went with it, her Mellie got took in by Reverend Goodbook, only she was wild as her ma an' took up with the conjure-man just as soon as she was a woman grown. And then her daughter Rahab become the witch-woman after Thomas Carpenter was called to glory, and *she* was Miss Attie's mother."

Wycherly reflected that any woman raised by a clergyman who named her daughter Rahab was probably making something in the nature of a personal statement.

"But Attie . . . Athanais, was it? . . . Dellon came back to Morton's Fork after the sheriff released her?" Wycherly asked, wanting to make sure of his facts.

Luned looked at him with awe. "How'd you know what her right name was, Mister Wych? Miss Attie was a witch-woman like all the Dellon girls—all their kind is wicked as sin, and we don't want none of that here in the Fork," Luned finished piously.

Wycherly hesitated between chiding Luned for believing in witches, and telling her that he'd been with Athanais' great-great-granddaughter (he guessed it would be) just last night. But neither statement would serve him—nor would questions about why the locals hadn't driven the family out a few generations earlier.

"You seem to have some use for witches here, though," he said instead.

Luned turned wide, pale blue eyes on him and laughed. "Oh, Mister Wych—*you're* not a witch. You're a conjureman. *That's* all right—we hain't had one of them for years either, but we don't mind if you've come to stay."

"I don't understand," Wycherly said, probing. "Why is it okay for me to be here and not Athanais Dellon?" *Or her descendant.*

Luned bounded to her feet as if he'd offended her. "You're just funnin' with me," she said uncertainly. "You aren't anything like her. You've got the Lord Jesus on your right hand and Old Scratch under your left foot, like the old-time prophets. But her—wherever she is a pit just naturally opens up among the kingdoms of the Earth, just like for the Scarlet Woman."

The combination of prim disapproval and Biblical language culled from Sunday sermons made Wycherly smile. The "she" Luned referred to must be Sinah—of course Luned would have met her, or at least know she was here.

He felt a faint qualm when he thought about Sinah. She'd be awake now, wondering where he was. *She'd better get used to my unreliability early,* Wycherly told himself brutally. But was that really true anymore? If the beast was gone . . .

No, he assured himself after the flash of panic. It wasn't gone. It was only dormant, plotting some fresh new horror. Things could not have changed that much. He took a deep breath, holding his right hand out in front of him.

It did not tremble.

After breakfast, Wycherly retreated to the bedroom for some privacy while Luned did what she deemed necessary to clean the cabin.

Once he'd gotten over his initial shock, *Les Cultes des Goules* was fascinating in a peculiar way. It was like a window into a world where things were somehow more real . . . were matters of life and death, in fact. Wycherly sat in a chair before the open window of his bedroom, puzzling slowly through the archaic English and the deliberately obscure French of the small white book as his mind roved randomly.

Power. He'd been offered it in a vision. But what was power? Wycherly had seen it exercised all his life, and had sought after it in vain since he'd become an adult. At its simplest, power was respect. If you had power, people listened to you. People did what you wanted. People wanted you to be pleased with them.

Wealth did not inevitably bestow power, nor did breeding or high office. Power was an intangible thing, created by the amount of belief in its reality that others had. Wycherly had watched financial kingmakers fall to earth, going from czar to clown in an afternoon, ruined by nothing more real than malicious laughter. Power resided in whatever intangible thing there was that made others bend to the will of one no better than they. Elusive as breath, enduring as the soul. That was power.

Could this book truly bestow power? A few splashy murders, some trivial community theater, the invocation of gods who were probably no more real than the God of gold and wrath worshipped in the lavish churches of his youth and certainly no more imminent—could this really be the secret? Could this be enough?

Wycherly knew in his heart that it could. The only question was, was it worth the price?

He hesitated. His father or brother would have said yes without delay; his sister would simply have laughed as if the question had no meaning. Wycherly closed the book and ran his thumb meditatively over the cover. No wonder Taghkanic College hadn't wanted this book to circulate. Parents would have withdrawn their children in droves if any of them had brought this home. He supposed it must have been stolen, concealed in the book that an old boyfriend had given to Sinah. And now he'd stolen it in turn.

But was he going to use it? And if he did use it, who should he use it on?

There was a knock at the bedroom door.

With one smooth movement, Wycherly slid *Les Cultes* beneath his pillow and grabbed for the other book (rescued from the woodbox and a future as kindling). He glanced briefly at the cover—*An Occult History of the New World*—and opened it at random.

"Come in?" Wycherly said. Luned poked her head through the door.

"I'm all done here, Mister Wych," she said, "and I'll just go on down the store and tell Evan there's a list of things you need I ought to get you."

One of the things he liked about Luned, Wycherly thought guiltily, was that she acted as if it ought to be a privilege to cater to him. Whether he deserved such treatment or not, he enjoyed it.

"I'd better give you some money, then. And the icebox—how much was that?"

"Maybe about . . . forty dollar? Mr. Tanner charged up the tanks, too." The hesitation in her voice was probably because of the price. Wycherly set *An Occult History of the New World* aside and reached for his wallet. He slipped out two twenties and added a third for good measure. He was running low. Maybe he could get Sinah to drive him down to Pharaoh; there must be a bank there.

"Here," he said. "Go wild." He held out the money.

Luned came over to him and took the bills, then hesitated. Now that he knew her better, Wycherly could see the teenaged girl in her wizened, prematurely aged child-face. He wondered if the vitamins were helping her at all. She ought to be able to get something nearly as good over the counter.

"You said," she began, and stopped.

"Yes?" Surreptitiously Wycherly glanced at his watch. Nine A.M., and it had already been a long day. And he wanted to get back to *Les Cultes*.

"You said you might want a bottle of shine—I could get it for you, to-day, maybe."

Shine. *Moon*shine. Bootleg liquor, potent and illegal.

Wycherly swallowed reflexively, remembering the dark amber liquid Evan had poured him down at the general store. It had been better than good; overproof alcohol with the dark, seductive allure of self-destruction thrown in.

"No," Wycherly said, surprising even himself. "But thank you."

The best he'd ever had, here within his grasp for the asking, and it wasn't the slightest effort to refuse it. It didn't even tempt him.

"It's good stuff," Luned assured him. "Mal's pappy was the one set up the works back in Prohibition. He don't sell it anywhere outside the Fork. Just to kinfolk."

And though the men who ran the illegal distilleries balked no more at adulterating the poisonous brew they shipped across state and county lines than big-city pushers worried about adding strychnine to their bags of heroine and cocaine, the backwoods ties of blood were strong, and Wycherly imagined that the product they sold to their neighbors would be slightly more wholesome.

"I appreciate the thought," Wycherly said. "But I don't care for any just at the moment. Maybe another time."

And as he said it, it was true. He felt no craving at all—she might as well be offering him fruitcake. He smiled at Luned, who stared at him with a puzzled expression, and got carefully to his feet.

"Thanks anyway."

"Well, if you're sure," Luned said doubtfully. She obviously didn't believe it, and Wycherly wondered how blatant his drinking had appeared to her. It didn't matter now.

Limping only slightly, Wycherly followed Luned to the cabin's front door and saw her out, an echo of a courtesy from another lifestyle. When she was gone, he hunted around until he found the bar that could be dropped into place to hold the door shut. At least he could lock the cabin while he was inside it.

He opened the refrigerator and looked inside, mostly to confirm that the beer held no fascination for him. There was a fresh pitcher of lemonade in there too; he poured himself a glass of that instead and stood drinking pensively, thinking about the book bound in white leather that waited under his pillow.

Power. Power that could be his. Guaranteed.

Wycherly Musgrave had finally discovered the one thing in the world that held more charm for him than drinking.

Once Luned was gone, Wycherly took the books out into the other room to spread them out at the kitchen table, but, oddly, the more he read, the less real his conviction became that there was power here. Despite the disgusting nature of *Les Cultes*, it was somehow difficult to take either the grimoire or the overview of the occult entirely seriously upon close examination.

What was a Planetary Hour, exactly, and why was it important? Lesser Banishing Rituals, Talismans of Mercury—it was as if the book was written in a language he only thought he knew, one that seemed explicit but was in reality opaque and incomprehensible.

But there was power in this book, just as there had been *power* up at the sanatorium. Power that, if he could manage to swear himself to it, would give him all the charisma he needed to work as much evil as he wanted; power to compel, as real as a loaded gun.

Evil? Momentarily Wycherly recoiled from the thought. He'd never wanted to be evil—he'd only wanted to be left alone.

Reflexively, he summoned the image of Camilla Redford's drowned body—the white face, the drowned eyes, looking up at him accusingly through the rippling, black-glass river. He'd already *been* evil. Even if he remembered nothing of that night, he'd killed a woman—a child, he saw now, someone barely older than Luned, who'd died with all her life unlived. That was what had led him to this unpromising place. He'd wanted to know his own desires, to measure his own need to atone.

Only there was no atonement possible, no turning back from the course his life had been set on so many years ago. He knew what he wanted now—what he'd turned away from, what he'd let slip through his fingers all the days of his life.

Power. The ability to make people do what he wanted. *That* was what he wanted. And he'd get it.

Call it a sort of belated birthday present.

TEN

THE GRAVE OF HOPE

I recoil and droop, and seek repose
In listlessness from vain perplexity,
Unprofitably travelling toward the grave.
—WILLIAM WORDSWORTH

THEIR GUIDE HAD DESERTED THEM YESTERDAY, AND BY *then the three of them—her guide, the priest, and she—had been traveling for months, having pressed always north and west, farther into the savage wilderness than any Englishman had yet penetrated.*

They'd long since left the lands belonging to the friendly Delaware who farmed and hunted alongside the members of the tiny English outpost named after Lord Baltimore. The lands they were passing through now were under the control of a tribe called the Tutelo. The guide had wanted to turn back, but Father Hansard thought they might not see any Tutelo aboriginals at all if they were fortunate.

They had not been fortunate.

They'd thought they were, for a while. She and Father Hansard had accounted themselves lucky when they'd awakened one morning to find that the guide had only taken his own horse and left them the pack mule and supplies. They were not lost. Among the supplies Athanais had kept under her personal rule was a sextant, an excellent astrolabe—and the geomantic map. All she had to do was reach the place the stars spoke of and claim the land.

* * *

The ambush, when it came, was brief and effective. A hail of arrows from cover; monstrous misshapen dark-skinned men with painted bodies, howling like demons. An arrow took Father Hansard in the throat; Athanais might have escaped herself but for that the devils killed her horse under her. It threw her as it died, and instants later she was dragged to her feet by one of the brutes.

They did not kill her, but neither did they speak any Christian tongue, and she had no other weapon with which to beguile them. She was forced along with them unwilling, her hands bound behind her back with leather thongs.

The village was a crude cluster of shacks made from tree bark and matting, more primitive conditions even than beyond the Pale in Ireland. It was filled with other savages, mostly women and children. Their only garment was a crude apron of fringed leather, and they fingered the smooth stuff of her riding dress with open interest.

Her captors shoved her ahead of them into a hut like the others. They were not gentle—Athanais went sprawling through the opening made by the rolled-up mat and fell to the floor beside the bier.

The dead woman lay upon several layers of woven mat. Her eyes were closed, and her face was sunken in the fashion of the several-days dead. She wore ornaments of shell and bone in her hair, her ears, and about her throat, and her buckskin apron was richly beaded. The she-savage's skin and hair were painted and oiled more elaborately than that of anyone Athanais had yet seen, and she was surrounded by barbaric offerings, but all the pungent spices on her and around her could not disguise the gagging odor of corruption.

At first Athanais thought they meant to make her a sacrifice, to join their pagan queen on her journey to the underworld. She fought them as they dragged her clothes from her, fought them as they cut and tore to remove garments whose fastenings they had obviously never encountered before.

When she was naked as a babe newborn, the village women came in and began to strip the dead woman as well and garb Athanais in the corpse's ornaments. When she realized they did not mean to kill her she stopped fighting them, and sat quietly through all that came after—the feast and the ceremony and the incomprehensible ritual calling upon gods older and stranger than any Athanais had ever worshipped. As the hours passed, she realized that they meant to make her one of them, and to make her take the dead woman's place as concubine to her savage mate. But Athanais was an Englishwoman—she might have been Queen of England, and she would not set aside her hopes to mingle her blood with this degenerate cattle.

She would fight them. She would escape. And if she could not prevail at first, she would not surrender. She would hate, and hate would make her strong.

She would hate.

And hate.

And hate . . .

Hate— An anger that could kill pursued Sinah into consciousness. She moved her hands weakly, completely disoriented.

"Wycherly?"

No answer.

She sat up, groaning, and looked around. It was late morning and the day outside was bright and clear.

Wycherly wasn't in the bed. His clothes were gone. She went to look over the railing. He wasn't downstairs, and though he might be in the kitchen or bathroom, Sinah somehow knew he wasn't either place.

He'd left.

She was too weak for anger; her eyes filled with painful tears and she drew a ragged breath. Well, that was Wycherly all over—didn't she know him as well as he knew himself? As David Niven once had said of another self-destructive charmer, "You can always depend on Errol, because he will always let you down."

And so had Wycherly. He knew how much she needed him—she'd been more open with him than she'd been with any human being before.

And he'd still left her.

A brisk shower and a cup of strong coffee did nothing to dispel the sense of despair she'd woken with. The dream—the vision—Athanais' memories swirled around in her mind, mixing with Sinah's sense of self the way oil would with water and leaving her with nothing but Athanais' passions, Athanais' desires.

Athanais' vendetta against Quentin Blackburn.

But that's ridiculous, Sinah told herself, striving for clarity if she could not have understanding. Athanais' memories belonged to the seventeenth century, but surely Wildwood Sanatorium and its Satanic temple was a creation of the twentieth—how could there be any connection between the two?

I don't know. Her mind felt bruised, saturated—she needed Wycherly as she needed a lifeline back to the real world. She couldn't let him put this barrier between them. Not when she needed his help so much. . . .

Not when she was truly losing her mind to a woman who might never have existed at all.

"I decided to come and see if you were dead," Sinah said, looking in through the open window. "And the door was locked."

Wycherly had been dozing through the heat of the day, his mind roving restlessly over the images he'd seen in *Les Cultes.* Now he sat up, looking toward the sound of her voice.

Sinah was standing just outside the bedroom window, the perfect embodiment of Bel Air chic. Large round sunglasses masked most of her face. She looked as if she didn't have a care in the world, but Wycherly knew it was an act, not real. He wondered if she'd noticed the missing books and had come to demand them back.

Just deny everything, Wycherly told himself. If that was Sinah's business here, he could bluff her. She wasn't, after all, a Musgrave. Only his family could see through him quite that disastrously.

"Sorry, but I got tired of half the county traipsing through at will," Wycherly said, with unconscious brutality. "But do come in; I'll go unlock the door. I'll even give you a glass of lemonade."

"And what brings you here on this bright summer's day?" Wycherly asked, holding the door open for her with feigned graciousness.

His ankle was still tender, but now it hardly twinged at all. He couldn't remember the last time he'd thought before setting his weight on it. The constant betrayals of the body seemed to have vanished. He controlled his appetites. He controlled his suffering. He had become master in his own house.

Sinah stepped inside.

"My God, it's like an oven in here. How do you stand it?"

"I am the salamander, my nature is fire," Wycherly said, only remembering afterward that it was a line from the book. "Want to step outside?" he added, trying to cover up. "It's cooler."

And it would get her away from the book.

He felt a sense of easing as soon as he'd gotten her outside. She carried out the chairs, as Wycherly filled two glasses with lemonade and brought them out to her.

At four in the afternoon at the end of July, the day was far from over, but at that hour there was a brilliant gold color to the light that made everything seem more vividly real.

"Ankle's better, too, I see," Sinah said.

"As you see," Wycherly said.

"So everything's all right now?" Sinah said. She was studying his face through the lenses of her sunglasses; he could see his face reflected in their dark mirrors.

"Except that I missed you," Wycherly lied easily. He hadn't thought about her except in relation to the book, but he knew that he didn't want her to just shut him out, decide he'd been a one-night stand. He had plans for her.

If witch blood ran in families as Luned said, what kind of blood sacrifice could hold more power than the last living survivor of a family of witches that had endured for over three hundred years?

Sinah smiled at him uncertainly. He took a step toward her; she let him put an arm around her waist. He felt the warm solidity of her ribs against his, and decided he liked the feeling.

For whatever reason.

Cautiously, Sinah leaned her head on Wycherly's shoulder, and felt his arm reflexively tighten around her waist. She felt the muted surge of his emotions—anger, excitement, an underlying animal pleasure—but his thoughts were as closed to her as if he was a thousand miles away. There was nothing here to hammer her mind, nothing that would keep Athanais from growing stronger by the hour until there was no Sinah Dellon left.

What was she going to do?

"So," Wycherly asked her after a moment, "aren't you going to ask me if I've found out anything new about the mysterious Dellon clan?"

She could hear what he was saying, but what did he *mean?* Was it just her fearful imagination, or was there a predatory undertone to his voice? It was almost as if she'd been struck suddenly blind.

"Yes, of course," Sinah said dutifully. "Have you?" She was grateful for the concealment her sunglasses offered, masking most of her face. If he couldn't see her eyes, he didn't know what she was thinking.

Was this how normal people felt?

"About what we'd expected to find," Wycherly said. "But sit down, and I'll tell you everything.

"Apparently," Wycherly began, settling into one of the straight-backed kitchen chairs, "the locals believe that your great-great-grand-mama Athanais burned down the sanatorium in 1917."

Athanais! Like the closing of a circuit, the sound of that name woke the shadow within her flesh; Sinah felt the world recede as within her, an-other being struggled for mastery.

She was Athanais—raised from her long slumber to find that the power that she had coveted was within her grasp at last. Now the sacred blood coursed through the veins of this her descendant, giving her the right to wield the power of the Wellspring, and she would come into her dominion at last.

"But why talk of that?" she said playfully. "Surely there is many an-other pleasant dalliance that we might be about this day?"

The look he gave her told her she had somehow misspoken herself—but though his hair was red, he had such an air of her bonny sweet Jamie that it led her awry. . . .

"Jamie?" Sinah echoed in confusion. *No! Not Jamie—Wycherly!*

"Dreaming of absent company? I'd leave, but this is my house," Wycherly said, and this time his playful words were edged with a de-cided coolness.

This was the worst yet. All the other times it had been as if she strug-gled for control of her body with an interloper. This time the monstrous ghost in whose reality Sinah could not quite believe had simply brushed her aside.

"I'm sorry," Sinah said in a strangled voice. She pulled off the sun-glasses and rubbed her suddenly-aching eyes. "But I think I'm going crazy."

"Well." Wycherly settled back in his chair, mollified. "I've been there a number of times—it's unpleasant, but not really dangerous. Can I help you plan your trip?"

"You don't believe me!" Sinah cried in frustration.

Somehow that was the worst. She wanted Wycherly to believe her—to trust him. But how could he if she wasn't honest with him—and how did you tell someone you were a sideshow freak from the pages of *Fate* magazine without sounding as if you were losing your mind?

And I am—only not that way. I really am a telepath—most of the time. That part isn't what's crazy. And that's what makes it harder.

"Why shouldn't I?" Wycherly said easily. "It isn't as if actors are the most stable people in the world—you're in the business; surely you've figured that out? Now tell your Uncle Wycherly what seems to be the problem, and he'll recommend a nice clinic for you."

Sinah stared at him, not sure how to interpret what she was hearing.

"Oh, come on," Wycherly said. "You've just told me you're leaving normal. It's only fair for you to tell me why."

"Well . . ." Sinah said, drawing out the word.

Wycherly always surprised her. There was kindness in him—in some ways, Sinah knew him better than he knew himself—but the combination of privilege and illness had caused him to dispense with empty conversational pleasantries a long time ago.

She hovered on the verge of telling him everything, realizing that she'd never told the whole real truth to anyone in her entire life—not even Jason or Ellis, the two men she'd felt closest to. She twisted the frames of her glasses, a tiny part of her mind hoping she wouldn't break them. That would be an embarrassing show of stress. Grace under pressure was the only dignity she had.

"Sometimes I think I'm other people." There! The statement—bald and inaccurate though it was—was made.

"Okay." Wycherly showed no surprise—nor felt any, as far as Sinah could tell. "I take it this is more than preparation for a role?"

"It's—" Sinah pressed her free hand over her heart, and felt the buckskin pouch inside its bag crackle beneath her fingers. A prized possession—but hers or Athanais'?

"I can't control it. It's like drowning."

Now she felt him recoil, though she didn't see him move. Sinah felt a rushing spectral coldness through the portal of her attenuated gift, and for a moment it was as if she was sinking into turbid water that rose higher and higher, over her chest, her *face.* . . .

"Tell me about it," Wycherly heard his own words with a strange sense of detachment, as though a strong, sure hand were placed over his own, guiding his actions through the tumult of rushing water that suddenly, vividly, filled his imagination. *To drown, to sleep . . .*

"This isn't the first time it's happened, is it?" he added.

She looked up at him with—gratitude?—and Wycherly felt something in his chest twist. He concentrated on breathing evenly, slowly, revealing nothing. *Be calm,* he told himself. *Don't even be here.*

And this time, as distinct from all the failures in his life, it worked.

"Ever since I got here—to Morton's Fork—I've been feeling . . . watched," Sinah said. "I knew Wildwood was there; I'd been on the grounds, but I'd never gone up to the sanatorium until that day I found you. And while I was there . . ."

She stopped, obviously uncertain of how to go on.

"You had a vision," Wycherly suggested. Beneath his calm, a new worry asserted itself. Did he have competition for whatever nebulous resource Wildwood Sanatorium represented?

Sinah shrugged. "I know all the arguments—self-delusion—self-hypnosis—false memories are easy enough to create under stress—because I wanted to find my family, naturally this vision would concern them. Isn't that what a trained professional would say? But it wasn't my *family* I wanted to find as much as the reason I—the reason I'm the way I am. I didn't want to be the reincarnation of Bridie Murphy!"

Wycherly had actually heard of the Bridie Murphy case, where a young woman had claimed to be the reincarnation of a murdered Irish maid from almost a hundred years before. Her testimony about her previous life was unshakable and contained things no one but the dead woman herself could possibly know. To this day the Bridie Murphy case was the one case that professional scoffers and debunkers could not find any way to dismiss.

"And who is it you think you might be?" Wycherly asked. He relaxed. Sinah was obsessed with herself, with her own problems. She hadn't mentioned Quentin Blackburn. Maybe she hadn't seen him. But there was something else she was hiding—you didn't need to be able to read minds to hear that in the hesitations in her voice.

Sinah sighed, and seemed to surrender all at once. "Marie Athanais Jocasta de Courcy de Lyon, Lady Belchamber. That's who I—she—is."

"Impressive name," Wycherly said blandly.

Sinah looked at him, smiling crookedly. "Doesn't anything bother you?"

"Are you holding a gun on me? Are you trying to get me into a strait-

jacket? No? Then I'm not sure what I've got to be upset about."
Wycherly studied her clinically. Her scarf had slipped off to form a
bright collar around her throat, and the tortoiseshell-rimmed sunglasses
were in her hands. She looked young, vulnerable, innocent—he had the
sudden suspicion that he could hurt her quite badly if she came to trust
him. The confusion the idea made him feel was disturbing.

"I guess you're what they call the original cool customer," Sinah said,
after the silence had stretched too long.

A new awareness was added to the other—that he could have her, and
that he wanted to have her.

To do with as he would.

"You've been touring in *Guys and Dolls* too long, Sinah. A simple
sense of diminished affect is my only talent, so it would flatter me if
you'd cherish it as it deserves," he answered.

Sinah smiled at him and reached out to take his hand. Wycherly
closed his own over it, wondering at how easy this was. A few kind
words, some snappy comebacks, and she was willing to be more than
kind. So she thought she was channeling a dead ancestress—so what?
The locals thought *he* was Doctor Strange.

"So tell me about Marie," Wycherly said.

Sinah got up from her chair and came to stand behind him, her hands
resting lightly on his shoulders. He didn't mind her being out of sight—
he was closer to the cabin door than she was, and the book was safely hidden. He could feel the heat of her body against his back, even through the
heat of the day. Her hands were shaking.

And Wycherly did not need a drink, did not want a drink, would not
take one if it were offered. It was so easy. All you had to do was to want
something else more.

A lot more.

"She thinks—she was called Athanais. She was involved in Monmouth's Rebellion and transported to the New World," Sinah said.

"How do you know?" Wycherly asked with interest. His school days
were far behind him, but he remembered enough to place Monmouth's
Rebellion in the England of 1685.

"I had a dream," Sinah said, and managed a shaky laugh. "Several, actually. She's like an unpleasant houseguest who just barges through the
door and settles in. I know her . . . and I don't like her very much."

"Well, that makes a change from all those airheads channelling Queen Comeasyouwere. But someone must have liked her—it looks like the name survived in the family. It was an Athanais who burned down the sanatorium."

"Was supposed to have burned it down," Sinah corrected absently. She bent, and leaned her cheek against the top of Wycherly's head in a quick caress. "What am I going to do?" she added plaintively.

"Threaten her, make her go away, the usual things. If she's a ghost, get an exorcist," Wycherly said offhandedly.

"Yes," Sinah began, on a note of relief.

She was unprepared for the toxic bolt of fury that seemed to swarm up out of her very bones, raging through her like a whipcrack of fury and loathing. The mind of Athanais, an English countess adopted into a Tutelo tribe and forced by their customs to take the place—live the *life*— of a dead woman.

Never surrender! Never surrender! Hate, and hate, and hate. . . .

"Just stay there. Don't try to move," she heard a voice say. Her body re-volted and Sinah rolled onto her stomach, bringing up the contents of her stomach in a convulsive heave and then continuing to gag, to choke, as if she were futilely attempting to purge her system of a mortal poison.

As she lay on the ground outside the cabin, too weak to move, she felt Wycherly's arm under her ribs, pulling her to her knees. With the brisk impersonal efficiency of a nurse, he swabbed her face with a wet rag and then pulled her back into a sitting position.

"I'm all right now," Sinah said unconvincingly. Her body ached with the violence of her sickness.

"Sure you are," Wycherly's tone was faintly derisive. "There's beer and there's lemonade. Which one does it for you?"

"I . . . beg your pardon?" She found the scarf around her throat and unknotted it. Miraculously, it was still clean, and she wiped her damp and sweating face. If she'd come down here to impress and beguile Wycherly Musgrave, she'd done a spectacularly poor job of it so far.

No. Not beguile. That was one of Athanais' words, the words of a woman who had sought to prevail through cleverness and trickery . . . and discovered that blind brute force would always win out in the end.

She'd ended her days as a Tutelo Indian captive, stitching her European jewels into tribal ornaments and bearing the sachem's daughters.

"I *have* lost my mind," Sinah said flatly.

"You need to get something down you to settle your stomach," Wycherly responded, as if he were answering her. "So would you rather be tipsy or jittering off on a sugar jag? Lemonade or beer?"

"Tea," Sinah said faintly, and Wycherly went inside.

Sinah got shakily to her feet, moving as far away as possible from the disgusting puddle she'd left. What must he think of her now?

What had he thought of her before? an unhelpful inner voice responded. She was Sinah Dellon, after all—the telepath, the girl who knew exactly what everyone else was thinking so well she didn't even have a life to call her own. The girl who'd never had a lasting relationship because she knew how they'd end before they started. Eavesdropper. Outsider.

Pariah.

But now that was changing, because Sinah had found the one permanent role-of-a-lifetime to play out till the end of her days.

Only it wasn't her.

Sinah gazed blearily out at the trees. Memories seeped up through the bedrock of her mind like toxic waste. Athanais de Lyon's memories—the memories of a woman who became, almost three centuries later, Athanais Dellon.

Her mother.

Sinah pulled the straight chair over closer to the door and sat down in it. The same woman? No. Just the same name, carried down through history. Different women, different lives, but always the taint, the legacy of evil that made her neighbors shun her and her descendants to the last drop of blood.

There was no hope for Sinah here in Morton's Fork, and no answers. She knew that now. She was the last of her line.

"Here you are. Tea and biscuits. Very civilized."

Wycherly came out, carrying a box of Lorna Doones and a steaming mug from which a tag fluttered. He held them out to Sinah.

"Fortunately Luned thinks I need one of everything the general store sells, or you'd be drinking bad coffee instead. You look like hell, you know," he added conversationally. "Drink your tea."

"Don't bully me." She took a careful sip and made a face. "Yuck. It's way too sweet."

"You need the sugar. You're too thin, anyway. You look like a boy."

Sinah took another sip. "The camera adds weight," she protested feebly.

"Oh come on, you don't really think you're going back to that?" Wycherly said.

Sinah stared at him in surprise. He was standing next to her, and she could feel anger and something like fear coming from him—but she could not read the internal monologue that would have explained his feelings.

Crippled. Her power lost just when she needed it most.

"Look. You just finished a big movie, and are you in La La Land doing yourself any good? No. You've run away to hide. Fine. Maybe your career arc can support an early infusion of Garbo. But in the past few days I've seen you have any number of fits, you've come down here to tell me you're possessed by your umpty-great grandmother, and while you're doing that you fall down and give a pretty good impression of somebody having a seizure. Now you tell me if that adds up to a picture of anyone who's going to be going back to work any time soon?" Wycherly asked.

"No." Sinah took a large gulp of the vile tea and forced herself to swallow.

The heat, the caffeine, and the sugar were starting to have some effect; she felt steadier, more in control. But not in control enough to try to deny the truth of Wycherly's words. She couldn't even think about working in her current condition.

How much money did she have in the bank? She'd spent most of what she had on the house, but she'd been serenely certain she could always get work, even if she had to stage a tactical retreat to New York.

Should she call her agent? She knew the answer to that, but she dreaded what she'd hear when she did. You were only as good as your next deal, and she hadn't made one.

Slowly she began to realize the scope of the trouble she was in. Her mind was going, her career was probably in ruins, and her only ally was a self-destructive alcoholic.

"Anybody home?" Wycherly said, and Sinah blinked slowly, focusing on him. The sun had sunk farther into the west and was shining right into her eyes.

"I was just thinking I probably don't have any money," she said.

"You'll survive," Wycherly said briefly. "Now, since we were wondering about which asylum to check you into, why don't you tell me what just happened?"

As she finished her tea Sinah told him the details of the vision—or memory. Wycherly didn't seem to take it seriously, but at least he was willing to talk about it.

"So instead of finding the Holy Grail she ended up a captive of these Indians who adopted her—"

"Tutelo."

"—and in a generation or two her mixed-blood Tutelo descendants married back into the European population and here you are," Wycherly finished.

"I guess so. There must be something written about them somewhere. If they're real, it would be some kind of *proof*, don't you see?" Sinah said hopefully.

"What does proof matter? Knowing whether it's objective fact or your personal fantasy isn't going to affect what's going on inside your head," Wycherly answered bluntly.

Except to tell her whether it was real or not—and she already knew it was.

"I want her to leave me alone," Sinah whispered.

"Then find out what she wants, and give it to her. Ghost, delusion, or old girlfriend, it always works," Wycherly said with cynical assurance.

But she wants my life. And she doesn't want to go away at all. And Quentin Blackburn wants . . .

Vivid as a resurfacing memory, the image of Quentin Blackburn that she'd had in the ruined sanatorium hung before her eyes. He'd wanted her to join him or die, she remembered that much—but what, exactly, did that involve?

"Look, Sinah, you really do look wasted. Maybe you ought to get inside where it's cool," Wycherly said.

Sinah cast a doubtful glance toward the cabin's open door. Wycherly grinned.

"I was thinking more of your place. Central air? Indoor plumbing? Remember?"

Sinah closed her eyes wearily. Her pretty refuge—it seemed like an isolation tank now. A straitjacket—or a prison. "I don't want to be there alone."

"Then I'll go up with you. Just let me close up the place, God knows why."

He took the mug but pointedly left her the box of cookies. A few moments later he was back, his shoulder bag slung over one shoulder and the walking stick in his other hand.

"Time for a nice walk in the fresh country air—since I don't see your Jeep," he said.

"But your ankle," Sinah protested, belatedly remembering.

"It's fine. Everything's fine," Wycherly said.

It was much later than she thought it ought to be. The sky was dark with only the last vestiges of light, and there was a wet electric feel to the air that meant there was a storm brewing.

As Truth attempted to unbend her cramped fingers from around the rim of the scrying mirror, she realized she had been gone from her body much too long—dangerously long. Every muscle protested with cold, cramp, and hunger; she felt lightheaded and shocky and hadn't had the forethought to bring so much as a candy bar with her.

By the time she managed to pack the mirror safely away into her bag, the light was nearly gone. Truth didn't relish the long walk back to the center of Morton's Fork in the dark, and among the things she'd forgotten to bring with her when she'd started out this morning was a flashlight. By the time she managed to make it back, Dylan would have—justifiably—worried himself sick.

Let him worry, a cold inhuman part of her urged. *Let him see how desperately he wants to keep you safe. It will render him much more docile afterward.*

Truth shook her head, denying that part of herself. Her right hand closed over her left, turning her pearl-and-emerald engagement ring around on her finger. She didn't want to do something like that to Dylan.

But didn't she? After what he'd said to her last night? Didn't he deserve a little payback?

Maybe so, Truth thought, but vanishing for the whole day and half the night wouldn't get *her* anything she wanted. It would just reinforce Dylan's notion that she was . . . unstable.

Unstable? Truth regarded her own word choice with horror. Was that what Dylan really thought? Was that what she was?

No. The reassuring faith in her own perceptions steadied Truth. She'd been right, hadn't she? There *was* a Gate here.

Now all I have to do to close it is find someone in the direct line and teach them how to close it. How hard can that be, really? Since there hasn't been much emigration from Morton's Fork, it should be fairly easy to find someone in the bloodline to get the Gate closed down, even if just by checking the land poll deeds to find out who owned this land before Quentin Blackburn built his sanatorium on it.

Her mental voice rambled on, soothing her with the sheer quantity of its words. All those things would be easier with Dylan's cooperation—or even his active help—and she wouldn't get them by sitting here. Telling him the truth wasn't going to be fun—but she was damned if she was going to behave like the idiot heroine in a Gothic novel and not tell him what had happened up here today.

Truth shook her head ruefully, and groaned as she got to her feet. At least it shouldn't be impossible to prove to Dylan that she was right; an uncontrolled Gate—as Truth knew from experience—acted like an enormous generator on every psychic within its range, wakening the gifts in those who had never shown them before and increasing the power of those who had them.

Truth felt a sudden, guilty, selfish thrill. Didn't that mean that Rowan and Ninian should both test significantly higher while they were here? She ought to be able to test that.

First things first, she reminded herself with a sigh. *Go and face the music, then carry on from there.*

Half an hour later, Truth would have been happy to exchange her present situation for Dylan at his most disapproving.

She was lost.

This isn't possible. All I had to do was follow the drive back to the gate and then go down the road back to the general store. Even in the dark, all I have to do is put one foot in front of the other.

But that wasn't what had happened.

The night had gotten progressively darker. It was the blanketing darkness of the country, without even a firefly to break the monotony. Crickets and frogs, made restless by the oncoming storm, called with shrill rhythm, making a cushion of insulating sound.

The first time she'd realized she was going the wrong way, she'd simply turned around and retraced her tracks. She'd passed the white marble bench on which she'd spent so many hours earlier today, its whiteness reduced to a dim grey smudge in the darkness. The bench was on the left side of the road.

Then, about ten minutes later, when she thought the gates should be appearing any moment now, she'd passed the bench again.

On the right.

Truth stopped dead, staring at it. She was certain it was the same bench—and more to the point, she'd sat down on the *first* bench she saw. There should be no other benches between her and the road.

How had she gotten turned around?

She'd tried again, placing the bench on her left hand and heading down the drive. She held her mental wards firmly against outside influence; there was a name for what was happening to her—*pook-ledden*—and if she could only hold her Will strong she ought to be able to keep from walking in circles.

But she'd passed the bench again—on the right—and that was when Truth had decided to leave the road and try to reach Morton's Fork going cross-country.

But that didn't seem to be working either. Truth was lost. And no matter how she twisted and turned, she suspected she was being drawn closer and closer to the sanatorium ruins.

But . . . why? The Wildwood Gate has rejected me, and of all the people on earth, I should be most immune to its lure. This can't be any of its doing—what's going on here?

The bag over her shoulder clinked as its contents shifted. She was hungry, and thirsty, and she could feel the tingling effects of sunburn even through the sun block she'd carefully applied this morning. Her working tools seemed to get heavier by the moment. Nothing seemed farther from actuality just now than the cold perfection of her *sidhe* heritage.

At that moment, as if Nature Herself were goading Truth, a fat, cold marble of rain spattered against the back of her neck. It was followed by another, and another, as the storm finally broke. Within moments Truth was soaked to the skin, wet and freezing. It was, somehow, the last straw.

Hardly caring what she was doing, Truth seized the power of the storm, meaning to turn it upon the force that was tormenting her. She felt the energy rise in her, crescendoing toward its climax, but before it reached its peak it was snatched away as if it had never been. As dark tidal forces sucked at Truth, she realized she'd managed to accomplish one thing here today.

She'd gotten the Gate's attention.

She struggled through the rain to the tree where the man—her lover, her father, her son—waited for her. Rain slicked back his flowing hair, plastered his shirt to his chest. He raised his eyes to hers; smiled and stretched out his hands.

She raised the hammer and the spike.

No!

Truth tried to pull herself free of the vision that was no vision—that was, in another space and time, reality. She might as well have tried to hold back the ocean. The hammered spike sheared down through flesh and tendon and bone— fire-hardened ash, it was, and he the sacrifice by oak and ash and thorn, as the ancient law demanded. She could smell the coppery-sharp scent of blood as she struck again and again, driving the spike into the wood of the living tree.

She raised her hand again, and the face beneath the blood streaming down from the laced crown of holly and thorns was her father's.

She heard his voice, telling her it was all right, that he was the sacrifice ordained, that this was his penance, but she could not bear it. Truth fought to stop herself as the second spike was hammered through his other hand, securing him to the tree.

Then she took up the knife, but it was not her hand that held it. She was the tool of a power far more terrible—it was the sidhe, *whose Gates these were, whose anger had bound Thorne Blackburn to this eternal sacrifice and service.*

Whose grant of power to their human servants demanded a teind *be paid each generation.*

"Father! Forgive me!" Truth cried, and in her hand was a knife of polished bone.

She brought it down. . . .

And the shock of its impact was the shock of her fall as Truth slammed into the ground, her foot tangled in a gorgon's-nest of branches. There was a blue-white shock of lightning overhead, and in its illumination she saw the road that led down to the general store only a few yards away.

Truth struggled to her knees, wiping her hands over and over again on her pants, but there was no blood on them, only water and mud.

What had she done?

Truth shook her head. Her sodden hair clung to her cheeks and neck. She'd done nothing—whatever had happened, it was a dream, a vision.

She had to get back. She had to talk to Dylan.

If only he'd listen.

Wycherly rolled over in the California King and checked his watch with a sigh, listening to the distant roll of thunder. All around him, Sinah's house thought its cool electric thoughts, performing all the tasks that insulated them from the outside world in a cocoon of cool dry silence . . . like a tomb.

Beside him Sinah slumbered heavily. He'd gotten her to take one of his sleeping pills, promising her sleep without dreams. Now she lay there, helpless and drugged, at the side of a man she'd known less than a week.

He could do anything he wanted to her. They'd probably never even find the body until the bones were picked clean. Who knew where she was, anyway?

The direction of his thoughts drove Wycherly from the bed, aching and nauseous. The beast was back, or something like it; a craving that Wycherly would gladly rip out his own heart to assuage. Without even bothering to dress, he blundered down the stairs, toward the one thing that had never failed him.

Less careful to conceal his traces this time, Wycherly poured a glass full with good Scotch and drank it off as if it were water. The taste made him shudder.

But five ounces of eighty-proof Glenlivet had no more effect on him than if it were water. There was no warm glow of haven in his stomach, and he realized with despair that not even alcohol would sate the beast this time. It wanted something else, and Wycherly didn't know what it was.

But it wanted it very much.

Wycherly threw the bottle across the room. It exploded on the bricks of the hearth with a satisfying impact, spraying glass and liquor over the walls and floor, but that didn't solve anything.

It wasn't what he needed.

Still naked, he padded into the kitchen, searching. The book was upstairs in his shoulder bag, beneath his clothes, but Sinah was sleeping deeply enough that he was willing to leave her alone with it for a few minutes. He turned on the lights in the kitchen, knowing he would not wake her. Now, what was here that he could use. . . .

It seemed as if the knives were whispering to him in thin steel voices. It was only when he'd opened one of the drawers and was contemplating the neatly racked rows of carving knives that he realized what he was really thinking beneath the surface of his thoughts.

He slammed the drawer with a crash. No. That was not who he was.

Wasn't it? Wouldn't this at least be a quicker death—a kinder death than the one he'd given to Camilla? The quick flash of the knife, her spilled blood the alchemical potion that would change his earthly substance from dross into to gold. Sinah would be dead, but that was the fate of everyone he'd ever loved. Who'd ever loved him.

Wycherly turned away from the drawer, gagging into the sink until he'd brought up the Scotch he'd just drank. It was mixed with blood; the dark brown bile had a foul smell. He ran water in the sink to wash it away, rinsing and spitting until the taste of his own blood was gone. When he turned off the water, he leaned back against her refrigerator, shivering with chill. He'd dodged the beast this time, but he hadn't outrun it. It was still in control.

And he was not.

But now he knew the way to gain control—one act, simple and easy to perform, that would give him what he wanted: power and peace.

The knives no longer tempted him. It was too early for the knives. What he needed was some clothesline, something long and strong, something he could use to tie Sinah to the altar, the black stone carved with the symbols from *Les Cultes des Goules*.

There he would open her body and bathe in her blood. That was it. That was all. A simple act, easy to perform. The hardest part would be getting her to go up there with him, and even that wouldn't be so difficult to accomplish. And he could put the clothesline in his shoulder bag, and the knife. He could even use the clasp-knife he carried; it would do the trick. Human bodies were so soft, so vulnerable . . .

Sinah isn't the only one who's losing her mind, Wycherly thought with cold despair.

He wrenched himself free of his own thoughts, panting as if he'd been running. Sinah Dellon was a sweet girl. He didn't know if he loved her yet, but she'd been kind to him. And now he was standing in her kitchen thinking about the best way to kill her—no, worse than that, to stake her out and butcher her like an animal, and for what?

Because he had bad dreams.

That was all they were, Wycherly told himself. Bad dreams. Not demons. The grimoire was only pretentious snuff-porn, and his visions were only an exciting new version of the d.t.'s.

But he'd really be painting himself into a corner if he murdered someone. His father would bury him in an institution somewhere until he rotted—life without parole. There'd be no reprieve for Musgrave's failure son this time.

How could he stop himself?

And how could he be sure he hadn't already done it?

Wycherly ran back up stairs, desperate to hear the sound of Sinah's breathing. When he reached the bed he crawled in beside her and took her in his arms, and though she stirred and muttered at the touch of his icy flesh against hers, she did not wake.

He held her against him until his arms ached, as though by clinging to her he could keep himself from doing anything else. And when he slid over the border of consciousness, Wycherly Musgrave didn't notice.

The Little Heller Creek was one of the many streams that fed the river Astolat. Unlike its cousin the Big Heller it was not very deep, but it was deep enough.

Wycherly crashed down the brush-covered slope that hid the creek from his cabin and took an awkward step into the stream. Only a few inches below the surface the water ran chill, forty degrees colder than the air above. He took one step out, then another.

She was waiting for him here—Camilla—Melusine—they were the same woman, the river serpent who dragged men down to drown. . . .

The water was above his thighs now, its cold something that took his breath away. Another step or two and he would reach the steep drop-off that would carry him under, into the deeps where the woman-serpent waited.

He struggled against it, standing there in the river, knowing that he was only delaying the inevitable, putting off the moment in which the white serpent would surge up out of the water to seize him. He managed to take one step back, then two, and then he stood in the shallows of another river, and watched the car headlights come inexorably on.

Even from this distance, it was obvious that the car was in trouble. It slewed from side to side until at last the curve of its arc became too extreme for the road, and it hurtled off the road and into the river. Its momentum carried it quickly through the shallow water from which escape would have been possible. For a moment the car floated, and then it sank.

From the shore Wycherly watched as the driver fought his way free from the half-submerged car. There was a moment when he could have turned back to rescue his trapped companion before the river submerged the car further, and he didn't. He floundered toward the shore, intent upon his own safety, as the car slid further beneath the water and Camilla Redford drowned.

It began to rain, though dimly Wycherly remembered that the long-ago night had been clear. He could not withdraw his attention from the scene before him enough to question the discrepancy; through the veils of rain he could see across the water to where the car's headlights were a distant, dimming beacon beneath the water. Its driver lay insensible, unconscious upon the muddy gravel of the shore. It would be a long time before another car passed.

Thunder rumbled like far-off anger, and Wycherly, waking from one dream into another, stood chest-deep in a freezing river that had never been that deep before, knowing the river's mistress was waiting for him. Rain sheeted down from the sky, making the air nearly as wet as the river, and chains of lightning danced dangerously across the heavens.

He was going to die.

He was going to drown.

She was going to drown. The woman lying in drugged sleep as the storm raged outside dreamed, not Sinah Dellon's dreams, but Athanais de Lyon's. Here was the pond, the ducking stool, the judges—godly and grave, arrayed in Puritan black—to examine her. They tied her to the stool. . . .

The shock of the water was icy, slicing through the fabric of the thin shift she wore as the water closed over her. Water was supposed to reject the witch, as she had rejected the water of her baptism, but this water closed around Athanais, filling her nose, her mouth, her eyes. . . .

And then they raised her; she stared, wild-eyed and gasping, into the eyes of her inquisitors, and heard their litany: CONFESS, WITCH, CONFESS. . . .

She shook her head, defiant, and they cast her down once more into that dark and silent world.

And they left her there.

Her lungs begged for air, a roaring grew in her ears, and Athanais came to re-

alize that there would be no further chance for repentance, no chance to escape.
They did not mean to hear her confession.

They meant to kill her.

She was Athanais de Lyon.

She was Sinah Dellon.

And she was more, a multitude stretching back across the centuries in service to
a blind need that must be slaked. This was the power that Athanais had sought.
This was the power she had bound her own bloodline to, so that her avarice and
obsession would haunt each one of her descendants. It was darkness and blood-
thirst, and it demanded service of its custodians; a child, a lover, some bloodtie—
some hearttie—to feed it.

It was Sinah's turn to feed it, now. She was bound to the burden her ancestress
had taken up; the burden whose uncompromising savagery so closely matched
Athanais' own nature. There was no escape for her, now that she had returned.
The price must be paid.

But Sinah was not the one who would pay it.

Her first perception was that she was wet. The terror of Athanais' nightmare thrust her into consciousness, but she realized that there was no water: only rain dripping onto the skylight above. A summer storm, with
its attendant thunder and lightning.

Nothing more.

Beside her Wycherly struggled, cocooned in bedsheets; his groans
were what had first wakened her. His terror was so strong that even without touching him she could feel it—a blind rejection of the stuff of his
dream landscape. She put her hands on him and shook him—hard.

His amber eyes opened instantly, but she did not feel that he saw her.
The sheets and his body beneath them were drenched in an icy sweat, and
even in the faint light coming up from the living room below she could
see that his lips were pale and bluish.

"Wych? Wycherly? It's me—Sinah."

". . . serpent . . ."

The word hissed from between his half-parted lips, as cold and con-
demning as the faces of the judges in Athanais' nightmare. Sinah recoiled
as if he'd hit her.

Wycherly struggled out of the bed, dragging the sheets from his body.

She was tainted and he knew it. The ridiculous overdramatization paralyzed Sinah for a moment. When she looked around, she could already hear the clink of glassware downstairs. She ran to the railing and looked down.

Wycherly was standing beside her liquor cabinet. He had a glass in one hand and a bottle in the other, and he was drinking as quickly and methodically as if it would save his life.

ELEVEN

GRAVE FAULTS

There's no repentance in the grave.
—ISAAC WATTS

THE RAIN HAD DECREASED TO A GENTLE PATTER AS Truth, muddy, cold, and exhausted, dragging her bag of working tools—she'd lost the canteen somewhere along the way—finally reached the place where the camper was parked. Every light was on, and she could see people moving around inside.

This is not going to be fun. But if Truth Jourdemayne had one defining characteristic, it was stubbornness. Grimly she slogged the rest of the way to the Winnebago and knocked on the door.

It was Dylan who yanked it open, staring down at her as if he'd never seen her before.

"Get in here," he said at last through gritted teeth.

Meekly Truth climbed into the RV, blinking slightly at the light. Rowan and Ninian both stared at her, faces blank with surprise.

"It's one o'clock in the morning," Dylan said. His voice shook slightly. "We've been looking for you for the last six hours."

Truth winced inwardly. She'd known this wasn't going to be easy, but she'd never seen Dylan this upset in all the years she'd known him.

"I'm sorry," she said. "It was stupid of me to go off without telling anybody where I was, but—"

"Oh, I knew where you probably were," Dylan said in a deadly flat voice. He turned to the two grad students. "Emergency over, guys. Sorry to put you through all this. Ms. Jourdemayne's fine, so why don't the two of you pack it in?"

"Um . . . yeah. Sure." Rowan glanced at Ninian, who ducked his head and mumbled something incomprehensible. Truth stepped back awkwardly as the other two made their way out the door and across the puddled gravel to their tents.

"You're soaked. You'd better get those wet clothes off before you get sick," Dylan said evenly.

"Dylan, I have to talk to you," Truth said, not moving from where she stood. Water dripped steadily from her pants and shoes to form a dirty puddle on the plastic mats that covered the rug.

"I'll make you some coffee," Dylan said.

"Dylan, I was up at the sanatorium—"

"Do you think I don't know that?" Dylan burst out, rounding on her. "You were up there chasing your obsession with Quentin Blackburn like an irresponsible child—what was I supposed to do when you didn't come back?"

"'Chasing my obsession'? There's an uncontrolled Gate up there, and its keeper is nowhere to be found—if you want manifestations, that one makes your average haunted house look as dangerous as a wet firecracker. You'll have to help me, Dylan; we've got to find out which family in the Fork is tied to the Gate, and—"

"No." Dylan's voice was very quiet. "Get into some dry things, will you, Truth? I'll drive you to the nearest airport tomorrow, but I don't want to take this thing out on these roads tonight." He reached into the Winnebago's tiny shower stall and handed her a towel.

Truth took it and wiped her face. Her hands were shaking. For a moment she wanted to go against every ounce of Irene's teaching, and use the power she could summon to lash out against Dylan, even to kill.

No. The moment of fury passed, leaving her exhausted. She began to unbutton her shirt as Dylan made tea.

"I don't want to go to the airport, Dylan," she said, peeling off the wet shirt and rubbing herself briskly with the towel. He held out her robe and she took it.

"I think you should," Dylan said. The anger he was trying to control made his voice flat and grating. "It's going to be hard enough to get anything out of these mountain people over the course of a summer without members of our group acting delusional into the bargain. I've told you before: Occult manifestations are tricky things that love to delude."

"Do you think I don't know that?" Truth demanded, sitting down to pull off her hiking boots. She set them aside, and quickly pulled off the rest of her clothes before shrugging into the welcoming terrycloth robe.

"Have you forgotten who I am?" she said, although it was a little hard to be impressive when the robe you were wearing had multicolored pastel stripes instead of badges of mystic authority.

"You're Thorne Blackburn's daughter," Dylan said, "and when I think of all the years I wished you'd come to terms with that, so that we could explore the work that Thorne did—together—"

"Oh, yeah?" Truth snarled, pushed to the end of her patience. "Then explore this: there's an uncontrolled Gate—a *sidhe* Gate, a *Blackburn* Gate—running wild up there at the site of Wildwood Sanatorium, and it's at the center of *all* the inexplicable manifestations in Morton's Fork."

"'Oh, yeah'?" Dylan echoed nastily. "Prove it." He handed her the cup of hot coffee. "I'll make you a sandwich."

"Prove it?" Truth echoed blankly. The cup burned her fingers, feeling far hotter than it was because she was so cold. "But I've just told you—"

"And I've told you time and again that your opinion—or even mine—isn't proof. Bring me something I can measure—or at least witnesses. You haven't seen yourself the way I have, Truth—ever since you turned in that biography of your father, you've just been floundering, looking for something to take the place of researching and writing it—and of hating him. Now you've found this—and you aren't even stopping to question it. You're just charging straight into it."

"But it's dangerous!" Truth said. "An uncontrolled Gate—"

"Wouldn't be that much trouble, from what you've told me about Shadow's Gate. The people in Shadowkill have lived next to one for almost three hundred years without too much trouble."

"Except for the ones who've died!" Truth burst out. "The Gate demands a blood sacrifice each generation from the keeper's own family—"

"And you've just said the family's nowhere to be found," Dylan finished for her. "So who's going to be sacrificed?"

Truth glared at him in exasperation.

"It isn't that I'm unsympathetic," Dylan said. "But if you'd just calm down and be reasonable, you'd admit what we both know—that one of the biggest dangers in this field is the chance you'll end up like Margaret Murray. She was a respected Egyptologist before she began publishing her flights of fancy about the European Witch-Cult. A reputation's an easy thing to tarnish—what about the scientists who backed Geller? Or the Frenchmen who decided they'd found the Holy Grail—and that the Plantagenets were descended from Jesus Christ? The field's full of examples like these. And so I think the best thing for you to do would be to put some distance between yourself and . . . well, let's just call it temptation."

He was going to send her away. Pure cold alarm washed away Truth's every other emotion.

Of course it wasn't as simple as that. This wasn't the Dark Ages; she wasn't even married to Dylan. While he could cut her off from any association with the Institute's project, she had as much right to be in Morton's Fork as he did. If he drove her to the nearest airport, she could rent a car and race him back here. There was nothing he could do to stop her.

But he could turn the locals against her, even get her barred from the sanatorium grounds if he tried. She could not afford to have Dylan for an enemy.

Her *sidhe*-damned arrogance had set a trap for her once again. She should have been open with Dylan long ago, and told him the whole story of her father's reappearance and strange vanishment, of her own new sense of mission. Dylan had always seemed sympathetic about the things Truth *had* spoken of, and she knew he'd studied Thorne Blackburn, but she'd never before delved into the matter of just how much of a true believer in Thorne's world Dylan was. She hadn't even told him that Thorne's claims of *sidhe* descent were the literal truth.

And now it was too late to ask. She'd misjudged Dylan's willingness to accept the Unseen significantly, and now she must do all she could to repair matters.

"You're right, of course," Truth said, forcing a smile. "I know everyone was worried about me . . ." She hesitated, choosing her words carefully. She mustn't lie, but she must tell a truth Dylan would accept from her.

"But when I was up there today, I felt . . . Well, it seemed a lot to me like what I felt at Shadow's Gate. So I was trying to pinpoint exactly what it was . . . and I lost all track of time. I never even got much past the front gate, and then I guess I might even have fallen asleep. It was starting to get dark when I started back, and then I got lost. Dylan, I would swear I passed the same bench three times without turning around once!"

Dylan smiled faintly, although he was far from mollified. "Maybe that's what you did—haunted houses are notorious for getting people turned around, as you know. And I'd be the last to dismiss out of hand the possibility that there really is a psychic locus up there in the woods—your family seems to be attracted to them.

"But that doesn't change the fact that you went over the line here today, Truth. You don't belong here. You'll only get yourself in trouble, even if you don't get hurt."

"Who are you to presume to make my decisions for me?" Truth said, very softly.

The challenge she had not meant to make hung between them in the air, vibrating with a life of its own. She could see Dylan go pale, but he did not retreat.

"I'm someone who loves you, Truth. I don't want to see you hurt," he said evenly.

Too late, Dylan; too late, my love.

"You can't keep people you love in a bell jar," Truth said slowly. "You have to let them choose their own paths, no matter how much it hurts. Do you think I *like* my sister Light—almost my only family—choosing to go off with a man who believes that everything I do is evil? I tell myself that it's her life, that Michael loves her—"

"But you don't really believe it," Dylan finished. Truth shook her head.

"But I don't want to see you hurt," Dylan repeated. "I still think it would be better if . . ."

He was wavering; Truth silenced him with a kiss. It made her feel almost as if she were betraying him. "I'm sorry," she whispered against his neck. His body trembled as he held her.

Let him take it for an apology, instead of as an admission she could not give him one. Whatever promises she'd made by implication here tonight were ones she had no intention of keeping, and Dylan would find that out, eventually.

No matter the cost to her human heart, she had to stay here in Morton's Fork, and find someone to close the Wildwood Gate.

No matter the cost.

TWELVE

THE GRAVE
BEYOND THE DOOR

Lady, you are the cruell'st she alive
If you will lead these graces to the grave,
And leave the world no copy.
—WILLIAM SHAKESPEARE

TRUTH JOURDEMAYNE TRUDGED UP THE HILL, CARE-
fully following the trail—or trace, as it was known locally. If there was a
Dellon cottage up here, she meant to find it. It was the payoff to a fort-
night's grinding work in the neighboring towns of Pharaoh and Maskelyne, where she had consulted newspaper morgues, libraries, and local
history societies. It had enabled her to exercise the research skills she'd
mastered in writing *Venus Afflicted,* and had furnished time for the breach
between her and Dylan, if not to heal, then at least to cool.

She'd made a bargain with Dylan the morning after their fight—she'd
stay away from the sanatorium unless she was with him, and confine her
meddling to backtrailing the history of Wildwood Sanatorium and locating the family that had sold Quentin Blackburn the land.

"And I'll be quiet and circumspect, and hunt up your proof, and not scare any-
body. And you'll always know where I am. Deal?"

He'd agreed. She'd known he would—he loved her, the poor fool,
and wanted to think they had a future together. He'd let himself think

that she'd realized the danger she was in and was going to follow his advice.

She'd realized the danger, all right. But Truth was a trained magician, and followed no one's will but her own. She and Dylan would inevitably fight again, but while they didn't, each day was precious to Truth, an unearned gift of normalcy and calm.

Which was about to end, now that she knew who to look for.

Like the aristocrats of another era, the names of the mountain people tended only to appear in the newspaper three times: at birth, marriage, and death. The Dellon women didn't seem to marry, but there'd been extensive coverage of the family nonetheless—in 1910, when Arioch Dellon had sold most of the family land to Quentin Blackburn for a sanatorium; in 1913, when Jael Dellon disappeared and Arioch Dellon died; in 1917 when the sanatorium burned and Athanais Dellon died. The last mention of the Dellons in *The Pharaoh Call and Record* was in 1969—the same year as the disaster at Shadow's Gate—when the birth of one Melusine Dellon was recorded.

If the Dellon family had owned the land the sanatorium was built on, it was a reasonable assumption that the Dellon family was the Gatekeeper line for the Wildwood Gate. But the moment Truth began trying to find Melusine or any of her living relatives, she'd been systematically stonewalled.

It had been Rowan who'd finally suggested that the County Historical Society would be able to at least tell Truth where in Morton's Fork the Dellons had lived. Her suggestion had sent Truth back to Maskelyne to look at page after page of deeds and land grants (some dating back to the 1700s) in a dusty upstairs room.

There Truth had found that the displacement of the Tutelo Indians who had been the area's original inhabitants seemed to have been a gentler business than it had been in other parts of the country; many of the earliest parcels in Lyonesse County were recorded as being purchased from one "James De Lyonn, a Native Sachem, or Chief, of the Tutelo Nation," and there were oblique references to intermarriage as well.

By the time De Lyonn had become Dellon, the land the Dellons owned had shrunk to an irregularly-shaped parcel that stretched in a widening V from halfway up the mountain all the way to the crest.

Truth had carefully transferred the coordinates on the grant to the copy of the ordinance map that she carried. The next day she was back in Morton's Fork. Somewhere in the area between the Little Heller and Watchman's Gap Trace there had to be . . . something.

She hadn't told Dylan she was coming here, though technically she was not breaking her implied promises: She did not expect to go as far as the sanatorium today.

But the time for breaking all her promises was near, and she would do it without hesitation if it would serve the greater oath she had sworn.

If only she could find someone of the true bloodline before it was too late.

How did you know if you were losing your mind? Not in the flashy dysfunctional way that won you a "rest cure" in any of half a dozen places Wycherly could name—and had visited—but in the quiet way that eventually made you the lead story on the six o'clock news?

It was like wondering how to become good. As far as Wycherly could tell, you never knew. There were no signs to show when you'd reached goodness. But the benchmarks for losing a soul were easy and clear.

To a certain extent, it was about the relinquishment of standards. Wycherly rubbed his unshaven chin and grimaced. He hadn't intended to grow a beard—he looked unconvincing in one, for one thing, and his father wouldn't tolerate it—but it was just too much trouble to shave, and he wasn't sure where his electric razor was, anyway. His hair was long past shaggy, as well—he looked like one of those mountain men who never saw another human being for months at a time.

But slowly you developed a new insight into necessity. Things that had seemed incontrovertible, obvious, necessary, were slowly discovered to be . . . optional. Standards of grooming, standards of behavior.

Ethics.

Sanity.

Optional.

The small, close room was lit only by the flame of five kerosene lamps, all that Wycherly had been able to find in the old cabin.

He did not want to be down here in the dark.

Though the room was naturally cool even in the sweltering early August heat, the lamp flames heated it quickly, and Wycherly was stripped to the waist, wearing cutoffs made from the slacks he'd been wearing in the crash that had brought him here. The cold of the earthen floor seeped up through the soles of his bare feet.

Over the past several days he'd painstakingly emptied the root cellar of its litter of decaying boxes and spoiled preserves.

At least, he thought he had.

The gap of missing time—of consequences that appeared suddenly in his life without antecedents—yawned beneath Wycherly's feet like the jaws of the abyss. He was sure he hadn't been drinking heavily enough to black out—but if he didn't remember this, what else was there in his recent past that he didn't remember?

Never mind. Think about now. Think about what he was going to do here.

Some of what he'd found in the boxes he could use for his own purposes. The rest he'd cobbled together from what he had on hand—*Les Cultes* seemed to assume he knew much more than he did, and the other book simply referred him to sources he didn't have.

But there'd been herbs and resins in the litter of the cardboard boxes, as well as a rusty iron dagger and a copper sickle and some bits of candle and chalk. It was enough to begin with.

Smoke hung in a flat cloud just below the low ceiling. He'd moved the kitchen table down here—the new ladder he'd bought had made that easier—and his crude implements were laid out on it. He'd drawn the elaborate figure from the book with care: The drawing covered most of the table, and the twisting, not-quite letters made his eyes hurt if he stared at them for too long. The iron knife lay in the middle of the symbol, and candles ringed its edge.

It all looked hideously real, somehow, as if this mummery was somehow more important than anything that might exist in the world beyond it.

And that was all it was, Wycherly told himself. Mummery. Theater, playacting, let's pretend. . . . It wasn't real. Not really. He was just passing the time.

Then why did he feel so revolted by what he was doing?

Stop it, Wycherly told himself firmly. *It's only a game. If you can't even do this, what good are you to anyone?*

None at all, but he'd already known that. He was a drunkard and he never intended to stop.

The thought reminded him, and he picked up the bottle of moonshine on the edge of the table. He took a dutiful swig. It tasted vile, and he shuddered. He didn't want it, and by now he hated the taste.

But he wanted even less to be tormented by visions of Sinah stretched out upon this table, and what he would do then. It seemed to Wycherly that there was no middle ground—drink, and doom himself, or embrace that strange sobriety and become something that frightened even him.

But he was hoping there was some other way, and that was why he was here—*just playing*—to explore *Les Cultes,* to prove to himself that the book's rituals had no power, that Quentin Blackburn was only a hallucination, that none of this was *real.*

That he was not compelled to do the things that made such bright pictures in his mind.

He took another drink. It was like swallowing a snake, and each swallow rekindled that burning pain in his stomach. Ulcers, he suspected, but somehow he found the pain comforting through its ordinariness. Maybe an ulcer would kill him, and take away the ability to choose.

Because Wycherly knew what he would choose when he was finally forced to make his choice. He was a weak, helpless, useless failure—a disgrace to the family name, his father said. He'd choose to save himself and let the girl die—just as he had thirteen years before. *"As it was in the beginning, it is now and ever shall be. World without end. Amen."*

The semi-blasphemy of the mock prayer made him shudder, but there was no need for that, was there? God wasn't dead, but He'd retired, and now there were new gods to take His place. Young gods, and hungry.

He set the bottle down and returned to the book.

It was a ritual of Summoning and Adoration to something Wycherly could not pronounce, but it had looked like the simplest of the rituals in the book and an easy place to start. Draw the glyph, spill the blood, read off the Names. Fortunately Atheling's translation included a phonetic rendering, or Wycherly would never have been able to manage it.

The directions for the ritual called for Wycherly to be standing in the middle of the symbol, but since the root cellar was too small for Wycherly to draw the diagram inside the nine-foot radius that was called for anyway, he thought the top of the table would have to do.

He also had no intention of providing whatever might be "a suitable Blood sacrifice for the Season and Hour." He had no idea what Season and Hour this was, and he couldn't catch any of the local wildlife anyway. And while he could probably buy a live goat or at least a chicken fairly easily, the thought of actually killing it made him recoil. Somehow the slaughter of an animal was different from the bloody fantasies of Sinah that obsessed him more each day. And if his demons wouldn't be satisfied with farm animals, why bother with them at all?

But the choreography of the rite required him to spill *something,* so he'd decided to use a few drops of his own blood and some of the whiskey. This was only a game, anyway. There was no need to make everything exact. And the book stopped short of telling him what results he ought to expect, anyway.

"Okay." The word came out in a shaky whisper, telling him how keyed up he was, how frightened.

Because he was weak. Because he was useless. Because he was a coward, a worthless accident tainting the Musgrave bloodline. His father had said so. His mother had wept.

A sullen resentful anger made Wycherly grit his teeth. He didn't deny the truth of his father's words, even to himself, but the anger within him made him want to punish Kenneth Musgrave for ever having said them.

Maybe this was the way. He picked up the box of kitchen matches that lay on the table and lit the first of the candle stubs that ringed the chalk sigil.

By the time he got to the fifth candle, he felt as if he were moving through water. His hands shook with the tingling, toxic apprehension of a man whistling his way through the graveyard, terrified of what he might awaken, but his emotions were curiously numb.

Wycherly hurried through the directions, skipping the steps he didn't understand or didn't have the equipment for. The room filled with the smoke from his makeshift brazier, making Wycherly light-headed, as if he were unconnected to both the cause and the effect of the events occurring here.

A game. Just a game . . .

As if what he did here did not matter at all, though a faint, dying part of Wycherly's soul shrilled out that it did, it did matter very much.

He picked up the knife.

Spill the blood, say the Names. . . .

He meant to prick his finger. There were a couple of ounces of shine already waiting in a battered teacup; he'd mix the blood with that and then pour it out onto the drawing.

Wycherly picked up the knife awkwardly in his left hand—that was what the book said to do and he might as well do this much of the ritual right—and laid his right hand palm-up upon the table.

At that moment, insanity uncoiled in his mind like a striking cobra: the freshly sharpened point slid off his finger, carving a deep slash across his palm and sliding up his arm. He bore down, cutting deep the way suicides did, hungry for damage.

"*Jesus H. Christ!*" Wycherly howled. The automatic oath, ripped out without thinking, was like a douche of ice water upon the coiling darkness of the room.

He was able to drop the knife.

With his bloody right hand, Wycherly swept everything off the surface of the table, knives and candles and bottle all crashing to the floor together. One of the candles lit the spilled liquor, and it burned for a few seconds with a weird blue alcoholic flame before guttering out. The careful chalk drawing was a blurred and meaningless mess, smudged with blood and bootleg whiskey.

He flexed the damaged hand. The gesture made the edges of the wound pull and gape, and Wycherly hissed with the pain. Blood flowed freely, but everything worked. *You could have severed a tendon, you stupid son of a bitch.* He held the hand up over his head, trying to stop the bleeding. Blood flowed down his arm, collecting at the elbow before dripping to the floor. His hand burned as if it was on fire.

Wycherly panted as though he'd just escaped some monstrous danger. His mind shied away from the enormity of it—even the need to punish himself did not excuse his trifling with this terrible harm. He'd never cut himself before—never even wanted to. His flirtations with self-injury had taken the form of alcohol, pills, reckless driving. Not this. Never this.

His skin was feverish. The trickling blood felt cold.

He tried to be angry, to take refuge in rage, but all he could feel was fear. Fear of losing control once and for all, of ultimate powerlessness, an inability to impose his own will even on his own body. Fear that there would finally be no place at all in which to hide.

Wycherly looked down at the table. In the light of the kerosene lanterns arrayed along the wall, the surface of the table was dim, the chalk a brighter smear. The book was the only thing still there, though he'd thought he'd swept it to the floor with everything else.

He picked it up, reaching for it automatically with his gashed right hand. His hand left a bloody smear across the grimy white leather cover, and the pain made his eyes tear, but he welcomed it. *This* was what was responsible, this perversely alluring . . . excuse. The key that unlocked all the corruption already within him.

No. It wasn't the book. It was him.

Wycherly knew about taking responsibility for his own actions, even if he'd rarely done it. He could not blame a book, an inanimate object, for the fact that he was twisted inside. Tainted. *He* was the one who'd found the obscenities in *Les Cultes des Goules* so engrossing. He was the one who'd tried acting them out just now.

He could not change. But he could at least put an end to one temptation.

I will drown my book, the magician Prospero had said. Well, Wycherly would burn his. Fire cleansed, that was the old belief.

But fire had not been enough to scour the temple in the ruins up on the mountain—only to imprison the depravity it represented.

Until he had come.

Wycherly picked up the ladder from its place on the floor and unfolded it into position. As he did, he stared at it suspiciously. He must have bought it, but he was damned if he could remember when.

Damned? Probably.

He climbed to the top of the ladder, still tightly clutching the book in his bleeding hand, and pushed open the closed trap. Smoke and heat rushed out, and the stifling air of the cabin felt chilly on his bare, sweating skin. Wycherly climbed out and dropped the trap back into place.

He felt immediately better as soon as he'd done it, as if by shutting the trapdoor he could shut his nasty experiment out of his life. It was stupid to trifle with what some of his flakier friends called deep-mind archetypes that way, and he'd been duly punished.

And now he was going to punish in his turn.

He got to his feet. He was going to need both hands to start a fire in the stove. He set the book on top of the wood stove before going to the refrigerator to get a can of beer to pour over his gashed hand and wrist. The cold and the alcohol woke the dull, sullen pain to furious life, and encouraged the wound to bleed afresh. Wycherly yanked down one of Luned's freshly laundered dish towels and wrapped his hand in it, watching the towel blossom into redness before he wrapped that in turn in the Ace bandage he'd used for his ankle. The result was bulky and unwieldy, but it ought to serve, at least for a while.

He turned back to the stove and began building a fire. When it was all ready to light, he realized that he'd left the matches down in the root cellar, and would have to go back down to get them.

"Luned—?"

The voice from the doorway made Wycherly spin around, heart hammering with startlement. He held the stove handle in his left hand like a weapon.

Evan Starking stood in the doorway of the cabin, looking nearly as surprised to see Wycherly as Wycherly was to see the young proprietor of the Morton's Fork general store.

"She isn't here." Wycherly turned back to the stove, dumping the book into the unlit stove and replacing the lid with deft economy.

"Well, I wondered if . . ." Evan's voice trailed off as he got a good look at Wycherly and the cabin: the missing table, the blood spattered on the floor.

Wycherly knew how he must appear: bloody, unshaven, red-eyed and smudged from all the smoke in the root cellar. Not reliable by any means. But if Evan didn't like his looks, that was too damned bad. Wycherly had problems of his own, and nobody had asked Evan to come up here.

"You see, Mister Wych, she's gone missing, and I wondered if you might have any idea of where she'd got herself to. She was up here yesterday," Evan said, his tone half-questioning.

Had she been? A cold knot of dismay grew in Wycherly's stomach. He couldn't remember. His last truly clear memory was of standing in Sinah's kitchen, looking at the knives while that too-vivid movie of what they could be used for played out in his head. Time since then had passed in an illusive haze, as it did when he was drinking heavily.

But he wasn't.

Was he?

Where had the moonshine come from?

"I don't think I saw her," Wycherly said, truthfully enough. And she wasn't in the root cellar, he was sure of that. The thought brought some relief.

"She didn't come home last night. We thought she might of stopped here with you, but when she didn't come home today, Pa said as how I ought to come and see you," Evan said stubbornly.

"She didn't spend the night with me," Wycherly said firmly. "But I wasn't here." He was pretty sure of that, at least, and Sinah would say it was true even if it wasn't.

"I don't know where she is," Evan said again. His voice was filled with frustration and worry.

"We'd better go out and look for her."

Some tardy impulse of guardianship—he'd tried to help Luned, even if only slightly—prompted Wycherly's offer. It was too easy to think of her floating face-down in the creek, dead. The image revolted him.

"Just let me get dressed," Wycherly added, walking off toward the bedroom.

Truth nearly walked past the cabin that stood so closely surrounded by trees that it seemed that the very forest had declared its guardianship of the time-worn structure. It looked unoccupied, but the windows were open and seemed to be unbroken.

"Hello?" Truth knocked at the front door, only to have it swing inward, leaving her staring at an empty room.

On the right was an old potbellied stove, its dogleg stovepipe piercing the wall near the ceiling. A high-backed settle flanked it. Directly ahead was a refrigerator and a sink with an old-fashioned pump beside it. There was a window over the sink, and it was open. There were three straight-back chairs, a rocker, and a stool scattered about the room, but no sign of a kitchen table. To the left, an interior door hung half-open, but she was not quite at the right angle to see through it.

"'Curiouser and curiouser,' said Alice." Truth took a cautious step backward and circled the cabin. Someone was living here—that was plain to see—but there was something not quite right about the cabin that roused Truth's suspicions.

She continued her circuit of the outside of the house. There was a stone chimney that the stovepipe fed into, and as she turned the corner she saw the open window over the sink. From this angle she could see the waste pipe poking out of the foundation; the earth beneath the waste pipe was still damp, which meant that there had been someone here as recently as a few hours ago. There was a large silver gas tank, obviously new, and a few feet further along, Truth passed through a wash of heat from the refrigerator's condenser. The refrigerator made a noise like a lawn mower, and she wondered how anyone could sleep with all that racket. Then she came to the bedroom, and saw what convinced her to enter the cabin.

The bedroom had more furniture than the outer room, containing a washstand, night table, dresser, and armoire in addition to the big brass bed. There was a braided rag rug on the floor, and freshly laundered white curtains in the open window.

And there was blood on the unmade bed.

There was a trailing spatter of dark brown spots on the incongruous pale-pastel striped sheet, and a blotch upon the pillow as though someone had wiped his hand there. It was too much for a simple scrape, but not quite enough for a gunshot.

"Hello?" Truth called again, a harder edge to her voice this time. There was still no answer.

When she went back to the front door and pushed it all the way open, she saw what she hadn't seen before—crisscrossing trails of blood drops on the floor, and a smeary puddle near the edge of the trapdoor in the center of the floor.

The devastating sense of *wrongness* caught Truth just as she stepped over the threshold; she gagged, trying not to retch, as sickened as if she had discovered herself wading through cooling blood. She reeled back, clutching at the door.

What was it?

Truth, for all her *sidhe* blood, was a magician, not a psychic. A dozen people could have been murdered in this room and she would not have sensed it. What she sensed here was *magick,* and its wrongness had an oddly familiar tang, resembling what she had sensed up at the sanatorium. She frowned in puzzlement, and steeled herself to advance into the room.

Viewed with her Otherworldly sight, the room was curiously distorted. Some aspects became larger, others vanished from sight. Solid objects disappeared; she could see the room beneath the floor as clearly as if that floor were made of glass.

After a moment's hesitation, Truth knelt and lifted the trapdoor. It came up easily.

The room below was lit by half a dozen burning oil lamps scattered haphazardly about the floor. The missing kitchen table was down there, and the smeared and bloody figure chalked upon its top glowed with dark intensity.

Truth rocked back, nostrils flaring in disgust. Though intense, the power was curiously unfinished, its intensity fading as the power of the spilled blood dissipated. Whoever had been playing around in this makeshift temple, he hadn't known quite what he was doing—able to raise the power, he could neither contain nor control it.

Having satisfied herself that there was no dead body hidden in this secret room, Truth let the trap fall shut again. As she stood, she sketched a
quick symbol in the air to hurry the fading of the dark power. Without
reinforcement, it should dissipate of its own accord within a day or so;
she'd come back to make sure.

A quick look through the bedroom was enough to assure her that no
one lurked there either, injured or otherwise. And as the first shock of the
cabin's foul magickal atmosphere faded, Truth realized she had almost
automatically moved away from the strongest source of her disquiet.

That source lay in the other room, but what—and where—was it? A
few moments later she found herself standing facing the wall to the right
of the door. Stove, settle, pie safe, wood pile; what could be here that
burned with such malign intention? Finally, in desperation, Truth opened
the door of the stove, and at last saw the thing that did not belong.

It was August, and swelteringly hot, but the stove had been prepared
for a fire: kindling scraps and tightly-wadded newspapers laid as a foundation for a few split logs. And thrust in among them was a small book.
Fresh blood still shone wetly on its binding.

Every magician knew that inanimate objects could become infused with
intention—what else, after all, was a consecration, save the infusing of its object with the intention of the magician? And even to Truth's relativistic
senses, the book radiated wrongness as if it were a living thing. Cautiously—fearful of spiders if of nothing worse—Truth reached for the book.

She pulled her hand back as if she'd been burned. Though Irene had
told Truth about pure Evil, Truth had never expected to experience it;
her few experiences with Absolute Good had shown her that both that
and True Evil existed in a continuum the practitioners of her own Balance weren't truly equipped to penetrate. Gritting her teeth and invok-
ing all her shields, Truth reached into the cold stove once again and
extracted the book.

It seemed a very small and innocuous thing to be the source of so
much psychic disturbance; roughly four inches by six and about half an
inch thick, it was almost more of a pamphlet than a book. She flipped
through it, wincing at the bloodstains: It looked like a facsimile of a
much earlier book, printed in craggy antique type. She caught sight of
some familiar symbols—Black Magick, without a doubt—but what interested her more than that at the moment was that the book had come
from Taghkanic.

Due to the convergence of a number of circumstances, not the least of
which was the presence of the Bidney Institute, Taghkanic College was
one of the largest repositories of books on magick and sorcery on the East
Coast. Only the various special collections at Miskatonic were larger, and
neither they nor the Mount Tamalpais collection in California were as accessible to scholars.

And someone found this book a little too accessible. It had obviously been
stolen—the first page was stamped plainly with the words "Do Not Circulate," and considering the contents Truth could see why.

She swaddled the book carefully in a sheet of newspaper from the stack
beside the stove and stuffed it into her purse, then went over to the sink
to wash her hands. The pump baffled her; she worked the handle desul-
torily a few times, but nothing happened.

"Who the hell are you?"

The rough male voice behind her made Truth jump. She turned
around.

The speaker was a red-haired man somewhere in his thirties. He had
pale skin that still showed the effects of a recent sunburn, and hooded,
deep-set eyes in a curious, pale shade of amber. He looked strangely familiar, though Truth could not remember having seen him before.

"I'm sorry; the door was open—" *And there was blood on the floor.*

His right hand was roughly bandaged—it was easy to spot the source
of the blood. He must be the one dabbling in Black Magick with *Les
Cultes*.

"I'm looking for a member of the Dellon family." Truth brushed her
hands together, trying to rid them of dried blood. The last thing she
wanted was for him to think she'd stolen—*re*-stolen, rather—his book.
"Would that be you?"

"Up the hill." The stranger was brusquely uninterested in small talk,
though Truth could tell from his voice that he was not local. But he knew
who she meant, and seemed to think the Dellons might still be there. Relief held Truth speechless for a moment.

As she stood there, the man walked over to the sink and worked the
pump handle briskly with his left hand until water spouted clear and
cold from the opening. He plunged his head beneath the stream, gasping
at the shock of it. Straightening again, he brushed his sopping hair back
one-handed and wiped water from his face. Apparently there was no
towel.

"Thank you," she said, putting as much warmth into it as she could. "I've been trying to track down the—"

"Why?" The question was almost a demand, brusque and abrupt.

"I need to talk to a member of the family," Truth said, trying to seem forthcoming without answering his question. "Are you a member of the family?"

"Hardly."

And whoever you are, you aren't from around here, buddy, Truth thought grimly. *Not unless you've been away at school for a long, long time.*

"I'm sorry; we haven't been introduced, have we? I'm Truth Jourdemayne; I'm here with Dr. Dylan Palmer. We're from the Bidney Institute in Glastonbury, New York."

"The one at Taghkanic College," the stranger said.

Truth was surprised. Not too many people had heard of the Bidney Institute, and still fewer knew of its scholastic affiliation. Of course, if he'd been stealing books from its library . . .

"Do you work in the field?" she asked.

"As a snake-oil salesman in a psychic sideshow? I don't think so," the man said with a sneer.

You've got a helluva lot of nerve to jeer, considering you're the one doing bargain-basement Satanism.

"Well, you're certainly entitled to your opinion," Truth said aloud.

"That's right. This is my cabin. And I don't recall inviting you in."

"As I said, I'm sorry for trespassing; but when I saw all the blood I thought someone was hurt. You'd better get your hand seen to by a doctor. You could pick up tetanus or worse out here."

She hesitated, wondering if she ought to mention the book. She didn't sense the aura of power from him that would identify him as a practitioner in the field, Black or White; perhaps he was a victim rather than a villain.

But *Les Cultes* had been in his stove; it was bloody and his hand was cut . . .

The stranger waved dismissively with the bandaged hand, and reluctantly Truth headed for the door. When she'd stepped outside, he spoke again.

"You're one of those ghost-hunters Evan was talking about, the ones running all over the place up here trying to talk to spooks," he said. The words had the faint tone of an accusation.

"That's right," Truth said. There was no point in trying to correct his misinterpretation of the facts so long as it wasn't actively libelous.

"So maybe you've seen his baby sister? She's . . ." he seemed to grope for an adequate description for a moment. "She's blonde."

"Is she missing?" Truth asked automatically.

"No; I've just been out looking for her all day for my health," the stranger snapped. "Look, if you're looking for Sinah Dellon, she's up the hill. Now leave me alone."

With a quick stride, the red-haired man crossed to where Truth was standing and slammed the door in her face.

Wycherly leaned back against the door and waited, shaking with the violence of his anger, until he was sure Miss Nosy Parker was gone. His hand throbbed malevolently, as if it were already turning septic though he'd only cut it a few hours ago—how dare the bitch who'd destroyed his family prate to him about infection like some sanctimonious district nurse?

What was Truth Jourdemayne doing here? Come to finish off the last of the Musgraves?

If only he were the last. A man could die happy, then.

His hand throbbed hotly, and Wycherly was reluctant to unwrap it to see how bad the injury really was. Why couldn't it have been his left hand? He was right-handed—what had possessed him to pick up the knife with his left? A set of stupid instructions?

Possessed. Now there's a good word for it. Wycherly shied away from the thought. No supernatural mumbo jumbo, thanks. He could get into enough trouble in the real world with only his innate defects to motivate him.

He opened the refrigerator and pulled out a beer, pulling the tab awkwardly with his left hand, and chugged it back. The sandpaper ache in the back of his throat subsided somewhat, and he opened another, wincing at the awkwardness of it. His gashed hand had soaked through the dish towel and the bandage over it, and running all over the mountainside looking for Luned hadn't improved matters.

He thought about Luned.

Perversely, Wycherly tried to conjure an image of her dead violated body, but could not. Did that mean he hadn't killed her—or that he just didn't remember it? It seemed so possible that he had killed her, with the way the pictures in the book had been taking over his thoughts.

Wycherly had never raised his hand in anger to another human being in his life. His few relationships were far too distant for Wycherly to imagine any sort of conflict arising from them, let alone the possibility they could erupt into violence.

And although he'd daydreamed about some nebulous no-fault vengeance falling upon his two siblings, it was certainly impossible to consider standing up to Kenneth Sr. in any way—even in his thoughts.

So when had women's bodies become this delectable, disassembleable toy? He could no longer imagine anything else that could be as fascinating as cutting into one, peeling back the layer of muscle and fat and revealing all the body's inner treasures like some sort of delicious surprise package.

The direction of his thoughts caught him by surprise, making Wycherly groan aloud in denial. This was beyond a joke. This was beyond self-indulgence. This was sick, monstrous.

And for once—now that it had become this bad—Wycherly knew what to do. He'd call his psychiatrist—he thought Dr. Holmen was still treating him—and he'd tell her everything. He'd tell her a girl had disappeared—she would take care of all the necessary inquiries, protect him from the police if he were a suspect.

And she'd write the order to lock him up again, somewhere safe. Somewhere he couldn't hurt anyone else.

He felt a sense of relief, as though he had run a long hard race, but the finish line was now at last in sight. There was someone he could turn to and finally lay down the burden of choice. But first he had to burn the book. Evan's arrival—and then the nosy bitch's—had driven what he'd been going to do out of his mind until now.

He could not make his phone call until he'd burned the book. Otherwise *Les Cultes* would stop him somehow—he was sure of that. Burning it would be a good-faith gesture, proving that he hadn't wanted to do what he'd done. If he'd even done it.

Although it seemed so possible that he had. . . .

The matches were still down in the root cellar, and Wycherly thought now that it would be best if the book were burned down there, too. But when he levered open the stove lid with his good hand, he discovered that all his good intentions were for nothing.

The book was gone.

THIRTEEN

AN EMPTY GRAVE

The wind doth blow to-day, my love,
And a few small drops of rain;
I never had but one true love;
In cold grave she was lain.
— ANONYMOUS

HOW FRAGILE THE BORDER WAS BETWEEN PERSONALITY and habit, Sinah thought to herself. It was habit as much as anything else that gave each person his unique portfolio of quirks and desires. It had only been habit, after all, that had made Melusine Dellon think of herself as a little twenty-something actress when all along, deep inside, she had been Marie Athanais Jocasta de Courcy de Lyon.

Athanais . . . Melusine . . . Athanais . . . the way the names recurred in the bloodline showed how superficial a thing personality was. Just a game, really, to fool all the dull blind cattle with which one must share the world—because even brute beasts could be dangerous when frightened.

She was not frightened.

Parts of her memory were maddeningly elusive; others didn't matter. It was her sense of *self* that she had recovered; the way of looking at the world that dismissed the importance of anyone who stood between her and her goal. It was a way of seeing that had been honed through the generations, and even now that the original purpose for which it had been forged was gone, the will remained.

For her, for all the bloodline, the world was divided into two classes of people: those who were Dellons, and those who were not. She was a member of the only true aristocracy there was—and as with any aristocracy, to be a member of the bloodline carried with it bitter responsibilities. Had not Athanais Dellon given up Jael, her only sister, to the Wellspring? Had not Rahab Dellon gone to it herself when her daughter—another Athanais—died in childbirth, so the covenant would be kept?

Now the time was near, and the bloodline was called to make another such sacrifice: her Wycherly, her bonny sweet Jamie, had to die. She had no other kin—it must be her lover, and pray that he had rooted a child in her belly; she was the last one left of the Dellon line that had sprung so proudly from England's dust to take root in this strange New World soil. There was no other she could send to the Wellspring, and she could not go herself as Rahab had—she was the last.

And only when Wycherly was dead would she—Athanais, Melusine, Rahab, Jael—be truly safe, for Wycherly was Quentin Blackburn's creature, and carried on the decades-old battle between the bloodline's needs and Blackburn's blind search for power.

Worn, familiar memories pulsed through Sinah's mind, as familiar as any she had ever borrowed from a passing stranger, but hers beyond doubt. As if it had happened last week she remembered her anger at her brother Arioch's foolish, feckless sale of their family land. She remembered the joy she'd felt when she'd first seen Quentin Blackburn—tall and handsome with his Eastern ways. Athanais would gladly have taken him as her consort, and spared him from the *teind* all the years of his life. He could have given her many strong children; women to serve the Wellspring and men to serve the bloodline. . . .

But Quentin had held foolish ideas about what the power that lay here in these hills could be turned to—just as Athanais de Lyon once had, centuries ago. He had laughed indulgently when she tried to explain—had offered her a share of his profit from her own stolen power, the power of the Wellspring. He had thought she was powerless against his book-magic; that she was only a woman, and weak.

Quentin had gambled against her and lost.

Or at least he would lose, and soon, Sinah thought. Quentin had gambled on his ability to seduce Wycherly and claw his way back from the gates of death by using her pretty lover. Quentin still hoped to end the bloodline forever and take the Wellspring's power for himself.

And if this white-livered descendant of the bloodline had been his only opposition, he would have succeeded. But in reaching out to Wycherly, in making his man's magick upon the Black Altar, he had given Athanais the power to return as well. And she would serve her trust just as the bloodline always had since the first spirit-warriors of the People had come to this place, following the sun.

Sinah picked up a hairbrush and began to brush her honey-colored hair with slow sensuous strokes. She felt a pang of regret that it was not longer; men loved long hair, and she would need a new lover soon, when she had given her beloved Wycherly to the Wellspring. With that gesture, she would keep the age-old covenant and consolidate her power.

And then she would remind the citizens of Morton's Fork of why they had always feared the Dellon line.

Truth walked up the hill in the late-afternoon heat and hoped that Sinah Dellon would be easier to talk to than the redheaded man had been. His face had been naggingly familiar, as if he were someone she ought to recognize, but so far, inspiration had not come.

Maybe Dylan would know who he was.

The ground rose steeply—something Truth remembered from her previous trip up Watchman's Gap Trace. Ahead, through the trees, she could see a building that might be Sinah Dellon's cabin.

It was clear that the old frame building had once been the schoolhouse for the local children, but a skilled hand had been at work on it since then—Truth could see where the roof had been raised and an addition built out through the back. The tall windows were filled with stained glass and covered with ornamental screens, and a brick apron had been laid around the foundation to showcase planters filled with artfully chosen wildflowers. There was a dark green four-wheel drive vehicle parked next to the front door, and electric lights shone through the clear glass of the fanlight over the door.

But the closer Truth got, the less this place looked as if anyone was living here at all. Weeds were taking over from wildflowers in the terra-cotta planters, and everywhere about the building there was an odd air of neglect, as though its inhabitant no longer cared about such things. Had Truth come all this way—tried everything she could think of—only to turn down one more blind alleyway?

There was only one way to find out. And if Sinah Dellon was here, all Truth had to do was convince a strange woman she had never met that she, Truth, wasn't a raving lunatic.

Truth stepped up to the door and knocked.

It wouldn't be Wycherly, Sinah thought, setting down her hairbrush and turning away from the mirror. He'd been gone this morning when she woke up—he often was, as if the devils that seized him in sleep could be outrun in waking—but when he returned, having eluded them or de-spaired of doing so, he'd use his key to gain entry. She'd become used to wakening in the middle of the night to see him standing over her bed, but she was not afraid. He was too weak, too gentle, to act with the same harsh necessity that the bloodline knew. Unless Quentin gained the power to mount him fully—and that meant blood sacrifice—he was no danger to the bloodline or the Wellspring.

She glanced out the east window in the loft, looking down on her front doorstep. There was a dark-haired woman standing on the step, hand raised to knock again. A stranger; not someone local.

Why?

Suspiciously, Sinah hastened down the steps.

"Yes?"

"*Why, she looks perfectly normal!*" Though the strange numbing of Sinah's gift persisted, granting her only the surface of the other's emo-tions, it wasn't hard to guess the woman's thoughts from the expression on her face. So the stranger had expected to see the witch-woman of Mor-ton's Fork, had she? Sinah smiled to herself. This one should be easy enough to send on her way.

"Can I help you? Are you lost?" Sinah said, schooling her voice to a youthful sweetness.

"Are you Sinah Dellon? I'm Truth Jourdemayne. Can I talk with you for a moment?"

Sinah smiled wider and opened the door.

* * *

"You have a lovely home," Truth said, looking around the great room.

"Thank you. Can I get you something cold to drink?" Sinah said. Let her lull the chit with fair speech until she'd cozened the purpose of her visit from her.

"I'd appreciate it," Truth said frankly, "it's a long walk up that hill. But let me introduce myself. I'm Truth Jourdemayne, and I'm looking for Sinah Dellon. The Dellons used to live around here; they sold the land Wildwood was built on."

"That was my brother," Sinah said without thinking. Never would she forgive Arioch for that foolish act of greed and rebellion against the bloodline; never, never, never—

"Who are you?" Truth demanded. "Are you the Guardian of the Gate?"

Sinah stared at her, grey eyes narrowing, and suddenly Truth Jourdemayne shimmered with a strange authority, a brightness that banished the bloodline's overmind as if it were only a fever-borne delusion.

"Gate? What Gate?" Sinah demanded, rattled. "Who *are* you?" She felt giddy and nauseous, and groped for the safety of a chair.

"I am Truth Jourdemayne, Gatekeeper of Shadow's Gate. I know that your great-great-grandmother once owned the land that Wildwood Sanatorium is built on. And I know there's an open Gate up at Wildwood— a gate that you need to close."

For the next hour Truth spoke as persuasively, as compellingly, as honestly as she knew how. She told Sinah all she knew about the *sidhe* Gates, holding nothing back—and realizing as she spoke that she knew far less of them than she needed to. She explained about the guardianship, the bloodlines—and the terrible power an open Gate possessed to wreak havoc on the unsuspecting lives around it.

Sinah listened with a grave, unreadable expression upon her face—as if she was listening not only to what Truth said, but to what she left unsaid as well. It was an expression Truth had seen many times—on her sister Light's face.

"You're a telepath, aren't you?" Truth said. "You can read minds."

For years Sinah had half-unconsciously awaited that accusation and had planned many times what she would say in response. Now it had come—now when her power was leaving her—and all Sinah could do was weep.

Truth held the younger woman in her arms, rocking and soothing her as if Sinah were younger still.

"How did you know?" Sinah finally asked. Truth's emotions were a faint backdrop to her own thoughts, as peaceful and even as the ocean. Sinah felt as empty and hollow as a bell without either outside thoughts or the bloodline's chorus to fill her.

"My sister is a telepath—although I suppose you might call her gift something closer to second sight. She was institutionalized for it, before I knew her. True psychics don't have an easy time of it in our culture."

It was a simple acceptance that healed a wound Sinah hadn't known she'd suffered; an acknowledgment that, however different Sinah Dellon might be, she too was human.

"I—" Sinah hovered at the edge of telling Truth everything—about the bloodline, that it had killed many times over, that she was about to kill again.

Was this woman kin to her? Was she a sacrifice that the Gate would accept? Sinah heard the faint question in the back of her own mind; the inward chorus seeping back, as inexorably as groundwater rose after rain.

"I'm not what you think," Sinah finally said. "You don't know what I—what we—have done."

"The Gate demands a human sacrifice in each generation," Truth answered. "Did you think I didn't know? But it's the Gate that kills, Sinah—not you or your family. And if you close it you can stop the deaths once and for all."

"No." Sinah spoke in a low voice, clasping her hands in her lap and staring down at them. "You don't understand. The Wellspring—what you call the Gate—takes its tithe; that's so. But it only chooses if you don't choose for it. We've always had to choose."

"And who have you chosen?" Truth asked.

Sinah hung her head, not answering.

"Sinah, it doesn't have to be this way. If you close and seal the Gate, no one else will have to die. The Gate won't be able to choose anyone, and you won't have to either. Do you *want* to kill people?" Truth asked.

"No." The bitter necessity of generations of the bloodline rose up in her to answer that. Oh, to be free of those intolerable choices, of the deaths of lover, brother, son . . . !

But if she sealed the Wellspring, her power—for good as well as for ill—would vanish. Sinah stared at Truth with wide grey eyes, feeling the painful division between her trueborn self—city girl, Broadway actress—and the bloodline through which the passions and memories of countless generations of Dellon woman had endured.

"But I can't. I don't have any control over the Wellspring," Sinah gasped wildly. *Oh, help me, help me, help me,* she cried inside. "You don't understand; I'm not really me at all. . . ."

"You can control the Gate, Sinah, I swear it. Come with me, let me show you—" Truth said.

"I thought I'd find you here. Which one of you bitches has it?"

Neither woman had heard the door open. "Ja—*Wycherly!* What happened to you?" Sinah cried.

Wycherly Musgrave stood in the open doorway, red-eyed and glaring.

Wycherly? The teasingly elusive memory rose to the surface of Truth's mind when Sinah spoke: Wycherly *Musgrave,* brother to Winter Musgrave.

A year and a half ago Wycherly's sister had come to Truth for help, and last December Truth had attended Winter's wedding, though none of Winter's own family had. Though Winter had never spoken much about them, Truth had drawn a picture of New York old money and formidable rectitude. It was hard to think of any of the Musgrave family being tangled up in sorcery, even though psychic power tended to run in families. Wycherly, however, bore such a strong resemblance to his older sister that Truth thought she would have guessed the truth eventually.

Here in the cool elegance Sinah had created, Wycherly's bloody and tattered appearance was even more disconcerting than it had been at the old Dellon cabin.

"One of you has it," he continued. "Which of you is it?"

He must mean Les Cultes. Truth twitched in guilt and felt Sinah's eyes flick to her.

"I don't know what you're talking about," Sinah said smoothly, getting to her feet. "But you certainly do seem to have a knack for getting yourself into scrapes, darling! Are you sure you've got any fingers left under that towel? Come over here and let me—"

Wycherly waved her back with his damaged hand; Sinah stopped as if he'd actually struck her.

"I suppose she's been telling you all kinds of lies about me," he said, gesturing at Truth. "Or has she just come here to make converts?"

"I've always known who you were, Wych," Sinah said, not pretending to misunderstand. "It doesn't matter to me one way or the other." She laughed, a little jaggedly. "If you only knew! But come in; forget about the book. You don't know what this means to me—Truth can help us—"

"Yes," Wycherly drawled with deadly sarcasm. "She helped my sister just fine—right into a nervous breakdown, although I'm sure that's not the way *she* tells it."

He lunged forward as Sinah retreated, and seized Truth's purse from the couch beside her. Truth barely had time to cry out in protest before he'd upended it and spilled its contents on the rug. He reached for the newspaper-wrapped bundle and missed—Truth swiped it from beneath his fingertips.

"I'll keep that, thank you very much!" Truth said briskly. "It's stolen from the Taghkanic Library anyway, and it's nothing for someone like you to be playing with."

"*Playing?*" Wycherly seemed honestly stunned. "Do you think I've been *playing,* you jumped-up yuppie bimbo? Give me the Goddamned book!"

And "damned" is just the word for it, Truth agreed silently. She took a step backward. Wycherly kicked savagely at the litter on the floor, but made no further move toward the book.

"Wycherly, please—" Sinah tried moving toward him again. "Your poor hand—"

"And you," Wycherly said, turning toward Sinah. His pale eyes seemed to burn with a wolfish intensity. "I should have known that you were too good to be true. How long have you known who I was—did you think you could get yourself knocked up and force my mother to let me marry you? I've got news for you, sister; the Musgraves are a little more progressive than that—"

"Wycherly!" Sinah's face was a study in shock—and in bewilderment—though since she was a telepath, Truth thought, surely Sinah had known from the moment she first read his mind that Wycherly was from a wealthy family, with the peculiar paranoia that engendered. "I didn't want your baby for that. . . ." she began.

As if she only heard her own words as she spoke them, Sinah stopped, an expression of confused horror on her face.

"Fine." Wycherly stood in the middle of the living room, cheeks flushed and breathing hard. Truth wondered if he'd heard or really understood anything Sinah'd said. "If you've got one, keep it. It doesn't matter now. Luned's gone, don't you see? After what I've done—"

"No!" Sinah burst out. "You never hurt anyone, Wych—I know it." She reached him and clung to his arm as if she could drag him back to the light of reason by physical strength alone.

"And what makes you think you know me so well?" Wycherly asked, with a baleful glare at Truth. "Or have you been checking up on the sainted Musgrave dynasty?"

"I can read minds, Wycherly," Sinah burst out with desperate honesty. "I can—"

He pushed her away from him, though not as hard as another man might have. "You must think I'll believe anything, don't you? You've been in Tinseltown too long, lady—I'm a drunkard, not stupid. But I see that you have company, my dear—" he added with deadly, exaggerated courtesy, "—so I'll take myself off. Don't bother to show me out—I can find my own way."

He turned away and left. His bandaged hand left a dark smear where he brushed it against the door frame. He did not shut the door behind him.

"No—wait," Sinah would have run after him, but Truth caught her back.

"You can't reason with him now, Sinah. Give him some time to cool down," Truth suggested. "He'll be more reasonable later."

Just as Dylan had been? Who was Truth to counsel Sinah when she couldn't even manage her own relationships?

But with ruthless analysis, Truth had to conclude that Wycherly wasn't a problem anymore—not the way Sinah was, at least. Without the book, Wycherly probably wouldn't be tempted to dabble further—and since he was male and not of the bloodline, it was unlikely that he could sense the Wildwood Gate, and impossible that he could manipulate it.

"Oh, why did you take his book away from him?" Sinah wailed, snatching the wrapped parcel from Truth's hands.

"Take a look and see. It's pretty raw stuff, though, I warn you—"

Sinah unwrapped Truth's hasty parcel. The newspaper stuck where the blood had dried on the cover; Sinah handled it with wary distaste.

"But—this is . . ." Sinah said. She flipped through it without interest, and wrapped it up again. "A few years ago I was dating another actor; he was into all this stuff, and tried to get me interested, but I wasn't, very. This was fitted into one of the books I borrowed by mistake; I wanted to return it to him but by then he'd moved, and I never quite knew what to do with it. But how did Wycherly get it? He's welcome to it, at any rate."

"It's still Taghkanic property," Truth said firmly, reaching for the grimoire. "And I'm going to see to it that it gets back there. If Wycherly wants to be a Black Magician, there are many safer books for him to play with."

"Oh," Sinah said automatically, "surely you don't believe in all that occult nonsense?" She put her hand up to her hair, smoothing it back in an unconscious attempt to banish the recent turmoil.

"Occult nonsense" she calls it—and yet she's willing to believe that she's possessed by her ancestors and has to make human sacrifices to a sidhe *Gate. . . .* Truth thought resignedly.

"I believe that the human mind is a very powerful tool, able to gather, focus, and direct forces that humanity, as yet, doesn't understand very well," Truth said firmly. "I believe that for years investigation of those powers was mired in superstition and religious bigotry, with the result that the so-called Occult Sciences have almost no point of communication with conventional science. But that's changing—even hospitals are experimenting with something called Therapeutic Touch, and what is that but the traditional ability to heal by the laying on of hands that religion has always claimed for itself?

"So I think it can be foolish to dismiss out of hand all magic as simple mumbo jumbo, and harmful, even dangerous, to dabble in it as if it could have no effect," Truth finished, a little sheepish at her own speech-making.

"My." Sinah held the book out to Truth.

Truth took it and stuffed it into her bag, kneeling on the floor to pick up the rest of her purse's contents.

"Sorry to preach, but you pushed one of my hot-buttons," she said. "This is my field, after all."

"You're a . . . what was it?" Sinah shook her head, as though trying to hear a very faint sound.

"I'm a statistical parapsychologist, which is a very boring, dry, and office-bound profession. If you want glamour and excitement, talk to Dylan—he's the one who hunts ghosts."

"That would be your partner?" Sinah said, trying to pull the rags of normalcy about herself. Her hands and her voice both shook, and her face was still white with shock at Wycherly's outburst.

"We're here together, yes. I told you Morton's Fork was a focus for paranormal activities—it's because of the Gate; your Wellspring."

"And if I close it, you say all my troubles will be over?" Sinah said edgily. She smoothed the front of her skirt compulsively, as though she couldn't stop.

"The ones involving drownings, unexplained disappearances, and human sacrifice," Truth answered bluntly. "Sinah, what you said earlier, about needing a child. . . . was it to give to the Wellspring? *Are* you pregnant?" Truth asked gently.

"Yes—no—I don't know! Oh, it doesn't matter now!" Sinah burst out. She began to cry in high wailing sobs, as though ridden by a shattering grief that would kill her.

Truth stayed with Sinah as long as she could, hoping to soothe her shattered emotions. Sinah had to be calm if her attempt to close the Wildwood Gate were to work. And in any event, the attempt would not be one they'd be making today. It was already late afternoon, and Truth did not want to be up at the Gate in the dark, with Sinah in an already weakened condition. It had been hard enough for Truth to close her own Gate, and that had been with Thorne Blackburn's help. She only hoped she could be as much help to Sinah when the time came.

"I'll be fine, really," Sinah said unconvincingly almost two hours later. The cubes in her tall glass of iced tea tinkled faintly with the constant nervous trembling of her hands.

"Are you sure?" Truth said dubiously.

"Of course. Look, this is my own house—I paid for the bed, I might as well lie in it. I'll see you first thing tomorrow, okay?"

"If you're sure . . ." There was no way Truth could call Sinah a liar without losing all the ground she'd gained here this afternoon.

"So it's settled," Sinah said, in a bright tone that did not quite mask the weariness underneath. "You'll be back here first thing tomorrow morning, and we'll storm the castle of the Wicked Witch of the West together."

And with that, all that was left for Truth to do was reluctantly to say her goodbyes and start back down the mountain.

* * *

Truth knew that she ought to stop to talk to Wycherly and see if there was anything she could do to help to repair the breach between him and Sinah, but when she passed the cabin again in the twilight, it was deserted and empty, and she really needed to get back to Dylan before he decided she'd broken her parole.

The flare of resentment that accompanied this practicality was something she'd learned to live with. She'd have her revenge, she promised herself, but not just yet. And Wycherly would have to wait, too.

Truth wondered what quirk of fortune had brought him to this forsaken place, and why he seemed to be so angry with the world. But whatever Wycherly's riddles were, she couldn't solve them tonight—and once the Gate was sealed, there would be time enough to look to all the rest.

"Where's Truth?" she heard an undistinguishable voice ask as she reached the door of the camper. The lights were on inside the camper; through the shaded windows, Truth could see the other three moving around inside.

"The Truth is out there!" Rowan sang back merrily, and Truth felt an instant burst of irritation—though what cause had she ever given Rowan Moorcock to think well of her?

I really hate to break this up . . . but not very much. Truth pushed open the door of the Winnebago and climbed in.

As night had fallen the weather had turned cold, wet, and overcast, and as she opened the door, the savory smell of pizza made Truth's mouth water. It looked as though Dylan had used her car to patronize one of Pharaoh's local fast-food establishments—Truth had rented it when she'd begun her research two weeks ago, since she could hardly use the camper to drive around in. She'd left the keys with Dylan this morning, knowing she would not need it today.

"Sorry I'm late," Truth said brightly. "But not too late?"

"No," Dylan said, and, spitefully, Truth didn't see welcome in his face—only relief that she hadn't humiliated him further. At that moment he was only an obstacle to her plans, and she hated him for it with a perfect passion of mind.

No. In the name of Time and the Seasons, what am I becoming? Truth drew a deep breath, and only then remembered the purse slung carelessly over her shoulder, with the copy of *Les Cultes* at the bottom of it. *That* was something that needed to be brought up soon.

And it's something even Dylan can understand—for a change. . . .

She set her purse on the counter beside the door and slid into the dinette beside Ninian. Rowan got up to get more soda out of the refrigerator, her silence more eloquent than any comment.

Did Rowan fancy herself in love with Dylan? Instant, hot jealously seized Truth—what was hers, she would keep, whether she wanted it or not.

Oh, stop it! Truth helped herself to a slice of pizza. But it would be kinder to let Dylan go to the younger woman, a part of her said soberly. Kinder to leave him to his own kind.

But I love him! Truth protested. *Don't I?*

And even if I don't, he's mine, he's mine, he's mine. . . .

"So how did it go today?" Truth said aloud, biting into a slice of pizza.

"We didn't get much done—there's a girl missing—Evan's sister; he runs the general store. Apparently she didn't come home last night," Dylan said.

"I know. Apparently a lot of people have been looking for her: no luck," Truth said, trying to gain control of her unruly emotions. Control was the first work of the Adept, and Irene had set her to it over two years ago. Slowly she felt calm radiate through her body from her Tiphareth chakra.

"Did you find any Dellons?" Rowan said. Her expression held interest in news of a mystery, nothing more. "I think it's just bizarre the way everyone keeps saying they don't exist—I was asking about them when I was asking permission to set up the monitors—you know, asking about the local witch-woman and cunning man, that sort of thing."

As Truth had learned during her own researches, folk beliefs were still a large part of mountain culture, though no one took them as seriously these days as their grandparents had. Modern mountain folk were quite capable of seeing a doctor in a nearby city and then returning home to consult with the local yarb-and-fetch woman, who was often as useful as the doctor, if not more so, in the treatment of everyday complaints.

Struggling hard, Truth strove to match Rowan's light tone.

"I found not only the cabin, but an actual Dellon. She's a local product—born here in 1969—but she was fostered out and raised in

Gaithersburg. She's an actress working in Hollywood, or so I gather, but she came back to Morton's Fork to try to find something about her past," Truth said.

She felt Dylan's eyes shift to her with strange intentness, then flick aside to Rowan, but whatever he might have intended to say, he was not fast enough to prevent Rowan's next words.

"And will she agree to come in for testing?" Rowan asked eagerly. "Did you get to take a case history?"

So he'd told them. Truth tried not to feel hurt—he'd had to tell them something, after all, and with the noise level of the argument she and Dylan'd had his students had probably overheard most of it. Still, Truth wondered how much more he'd told them—and about what.

"I doubt she could do all that on a first meeting," Dylan said pacifically. "I mentioned you were trying to track down the family that had owned the land the sanatorium was built on to see if there was some history there, since a lot of our apparition reports are concentrated in that area."

Oh, yes. There's a history there, Truth thought bitterly. Aloud she said, "Well, I've met her—unfortunately, she's getting the same pariah treatment you do when you ask about the Dellons."

"Shunned," Dylan said. "More effective than violence in an isolated community, and often just as deadly."

"They talked to me," Ninian said unexpectedly.

The other three all turned to stare at him. Ninian ducked his head. His long black hair fell forward, but failed to conceal the blush spreading over his pale skin. He looked very much as if he wished he hadn't said anything.

"Ninian?" Dylan asked.

"Before we heard about Luned Starking being gone, I was over at the Scotts' place—you know: cold spot, broken dishes, black dog—" he added, using verbal shorthand to sketch the kind of manifestations every researcher was familiar with. "They were happy to talk; Mrs. Scott's great-aunt was a spirit-caller—you know, a medium—and I told her about my gran, so we got on just fine. Anyway, after a while she went into the house to cook lunch, and I was out on the porch shelling peas with Morwen—"

"Is there a point to this, Nin?" Rowan asked, twirling her long red braid as if it were a lariat.

"I'm getting to that! Morwen's about my age; we got talking, and when I brought up the Dellons, *she* said that the whole reason the rest of the Fork wouldn't talk to them was because they're cannibals—werewolves, in fact. She said her mama'd said that if you did anything a Dellon woman didn't like she'd overlook you, drive you out of your skull, maybe turn you into a wolf yourself. She's sure that now a Dellon's shown up again, somebody in the Fork's going to die."

"And someone *has* disappeared, right on schedule," Dylan said.

"On schedule . . ." Truth said, a sudden inspiration taking possession of her. "Dylan, where's the master list, the one organized by date?"

The list was unearthed without too much trouble—it was the one that Truth had run from Dylan's database to try to chart seasonal peaks in local activity.

"Here. Look. The disappearances peak in mid-August on some kind of multi-year cycle. And I'm almost sure—" Truth jumped up again, this time for her purse, digging through it until she found her notebook.

"Yes—I was right. Most of the Dellon women have vanished within a few days either way of the fourteenth of August: the last one—two, actually—twenty-eight years ago in 1969. But why then? Lammas is the only Great Festival anywhere near here, and that's August first."

"It didn't used to be," Dylan said slowly, "or, rather, August first didn't used to be. In Pope Gregory's 1582 calendar reform, fourteen days were removed from the calendar in the conversion from the Julian to the Gregorian calendar. There were riots all over Europe, with crowds demanding 'give us back our fourteen days.' Researchers of that period still have to be careful to indicate whether they're citing New Style or Old Style dates, since both were in use for quite some time after that."

"Hard to see why anyone'd get that upset," Rowan said. "It isn't as though anybody was actually taking anything away from them." She popped a last bite of pizza crust into her mouth and chewed contentedly.

"It was before MTV, Rowan," Ninian said caustically.

"So August fourteenth is really August first?" Truth said.

"Let's say rather that the 'Feast of Sacrifice' in the old Celtic year—it was really called 'Lughnasadh'; Lammas is the Christian name for the day—falls on August fourteenth, not the first." Dylan said.

"Lew-nassat?" Rowan said.

"Farewell to the Light," Ninian translated briefly. His Scots ancestors had held onto many folk survivals of pagan practice far longer than the rest of Europe.

"And the cycle of disappearances cover roughly a month—factoring in all of them—and peak on August 14th," Dylan summarized.

"But what *really* happens to them, Dylan?" Rowan asked. "I'll buy ghosts, but not werewolves—or baby-eating wicked witches."

"Who knows?" Dylan said. "Our source data isn't exactly one hundred percent reliable—ran off, died of natural causes, even murdered—none of these things requires a supernatural explanation, though I admit it's a bit of a reach when you find most of them disappearing during the month of August. I only hope someone isn't using Ms. Dellon's reappearance as a license to, well—"

Rape and murder? Truth finished for him silently. It would almost be a more comforting answer to the problem of poor Luned Starking's disappearance than what she believed—and could not prove.

But if she and Sinah Dellon could put an end to it there wouldn't be any need to prove it. Truth tried to comfort herself with that thought.

The talk turned to the minutia of the fieldwork that was the actual reason for the presence of at least three of them in Morton's Fork. The results had been disappointing so far; for all their work, the ghost-hunters hadn't been able to record—or observe—anything out of the ordinary anywhere in the Fork. They'd been reduced to nothing more extraordinary than reconfirming the reports of Taverner and Ringrose with a new generation—necessary, but trivial in the face of what they'd hoped to accomplish.

"There's always the old graveyard down by the ruined chapel," Rowan said. "It's got a vanishing hitchhiker, ghost lights—and the chapel is supposed to be haunted."

"I'll try that if I don't find anything better," Dylan said reluctantly. "But it's really at the edge of the main concentration of events, and I'm not sure I believe in that haunted chapel. It's just too good to be true, somehow."

Rowan and Ninian exchanged glances and shrugged. "Maybe a seance?" Ninian said. "There's a Spiritualist circle that meets around here—I'm sure Mrs. Scott would let me attend."

Why hadn't they checked out Wildwood? The manifestations centered on it: It was obviously the source—the wellspring, as a matter of fact—of everything happening at Morton's Fork. It wasn't like Dylan to nibble around the edges of a thing instead of plunging right in.

Unless he was staying away from it for her sake—sort of a professional courtesy to a fellow professional. Perversely the thought irked Truth so thoroughly that she almost missed the next words spoken.

"That's reaching, Ninian; I'd rather not." Dylan shook his head. "We may not get lucky this summer—but even if we don't, this is important groundwork; don't either of you forget that."

After a last cup of tea—or, in Rowan's case, glass of Coke—both students retired to their tents, and Truth and Dylan were alone.

"Okay, now what is it?" Dylan asked, turning to her. "You've been like a cat on a hot stove all evening. You didn't, um, make a bad impression on Sinah Dellon, did you?"

His tone was wary; he looked more resigned than anything else. Truth gritted her teeth and gave Dylan her most carefree smile.

"Well, I didn't accuse her of being a werewolf, if that's what you mean," Truth answered teasingly, and was rewarded with a faint smile from Dylan. "She's a psychic, in fact."

Truth hesitated for a long moment over her next words, though honesty compelled her to tell Dylan. "We're going to go up to the sanatorium tomorrow, and, well, see what she makes of it."

Though that wasn't the extent of Truth's agenda by any means, she doubted that anything more would be visible to any observer—and in this particular Working, she was going to have to feel her way as much as any novice.

"I see. Thank you for having the courtesy to notify me in advance, at least. I hope you won't mind if I tag along?" Dylan asked levelly.

"What do you think I'm going to do—push her off a cliff?" Truth demanded, all her suspicions of Dylan freshly aroused.

"No—but since you seem to think that there's a Blackburn Gate up there that needs to be shut, I don't think that after turning the county inside out to find her, you're going to take the only member of the, er, bloodline up there just to show her the view." Dylan was trying to be reasonable, but the anger that had been simmering for the last two weeks was an undertone in his voice. "Did you tell her about the Gate? Does she even know why the two of you are going up there?"

"Yes," Truth said, not looking at him.

She was caught between wanting to lash out at him for speaking to her this way—and grieving for the love that was slipping through their fingers as neither of them acted to save it. Why couldn't he see the world the way she did?

Dylan wanted proof, but nobody required independent verification of the weather—when someone said it had rained yesterday, people accepted his testimony without a thought. Anything someone else could confirm that easily with his own five senses didn't need to be proven.

And now—when Truth had discovered the use of more senses than five—she did not need to test, and prove, and test again, like a blind man moving through a minefield. She simply *knew*, and she was impatient with those who insisted that she blind herself again. What part could Dylan play in her future if that was the world she lived in? In the bad old days it had always been the woman's place to submit without a murmur of protest, to give up herself for her marriage. Everyone said things had changed, but attitudes fostered by social privilege died hard. She could not go back to being blind, or even pretending to be, and it was time to admit to herself that she would not be the one making the accommodation in their relationship; it would be Dylan. How could she ask that he make every concession on behalf of a relationship Truth wasn't even sure she wanted anymore?

"And do you have any idea of how to shut your Wildwood Gate?" Dylan asked gently.

Truth glanced at him then, startled by his insight. The question was more of a concession than she'd expected from him—a willingness to meet her on her own ground, if only theoretically. Perhaps Dylan, too, mourned for what they were losing.

"No," Truth admitted, though the honesty cost her. "I don't. But going up there with Sinah Dellon is the first step to finding out. You can't build theories without facts, remember?"

"Fair enough," Dylan said. "And in that case, you'll want an impartial observer with you. You know that I want more proof before going along with your particular theory—but I'm willing to take a look."

Truth bit back her immediate response.

Dylan's presence was the last thing in the world that Truth wanted: a non-Adept—someone who could be manipulated by the power of the Wildwood Gate in just the way that he thought Truth would be by a simple haunting. But Dylan was still thinking like a scientist, intent upon verification and proof.

Still? Dylan was a scientist—he always would be. When had *she* stopped requiring objective proof for the things she saw?

When I realized they were real.

Truth bowed her head, as if in defeat.

"Truth?" Dylan said.

"What?" She'd been swept away by her own melancholy thoughts, and came back to the moment with a jolt. "I guess you're going to come along then," she said slowly. *And may all your gods help you, Dylan, when I'm the one proven right.*

"But that isn't all I did today," Truth went on hastily, to change the subject before she heard Dylan's reply. There was something she'd almost forgotten to mention to Dylan. *Something he might actually be useful for,* a small part of her mind sniped spitefully. She drew a deep breath. "I came across something rather curious—and rather nasty. I'd like your opinion on it."

She dug through her purse until she found the book again—it was at the bottom of her bag, since she'd thrown it in first—and drew it out. The blood-stained newsprint wrapping it was crumpled and rather ragged by now, but it covered the book well enough.

"Tell me what you think of this," she said neutrally, setting the bundle down on the table between them.

Dylan unwrapped it, as carefully as if he thought it might bite. "Yuck," he said, when he saw the blood-soaked cover. "Is all this blood?"

"I don't know," Truth said. "It might be. Wycherly had cut his hand pretty badly when I saw him. It's probably that."

"Wycherly?" Dylan said, flipping quickly through the book.

"Wycherly *Musgrave*—Winter's brother."

"Oh. The adult-onset RSPK you worked with last year," Dylan said, placing the reference. "And he had this? What's he doing out here?"

"Well, he's living in the old Dellon cabin—not the place Sinah has—and trying to practice Black Magick, at least from what I could tell," Truth said. The memory of the nastiness she'd encountered in that cabin made her pull a wry face.

"Sinah says the book is hers, but as far as I could tell, she didn't have much interest in it. Wycherly was obsessed by it, though; when he found out I'd taken it, he was almost raving."

"I see you managed to fend him off, though," Dylan said absently. "I'm glad you brought this back—it disappeared from the Special Collection about five years ago. The Atheling translation isn't all that rare, but it's damned expensive to replace—and it isn't the sort of thing I'd want running around loose, either."

"What is it?" Truth asked. "Some kind of grimoire, I'd guess?"

Dylan grinned at her. "Do you want the Cook's Tour, darling? I warn you, it could be rather lengthy."

Truth smiled back, warmed as much as saddened by the fragile camaraderie. Once she and Dylan had been able to talk about almost anything—when had she started to weigh her words with him?

"Tell me everything," Truth said honestly. "I'm fascinated."

"All right." Dylan smiled at her and then drew his face into an expression of professorial dignity.

"Late in the sixteen hundreds a young relative of King Louis of France became obsessed with finding the survivals of pre-Christian worship that he was sure must exist among the peasants on his own lands.

"To begin with, you must understand that the lands he held were in the Languedoc, which has been Christian longer than most of the rest of Europe, although it's generally also been known as a hotbed of Christian heresy for most of that time. In any event, whatever it was that the Comte d'Erlette found when he went looking, what he eventually circulated in manuscript as a faithful report of his peasants' activities was a peculiar mixture of blasphemy and demonolatry."

"Demonolatry—worshipping demons, not evoking them?" Truth asked. Despite her mandate as Gatekeeper and Grey Angel, the occult was not her field of study, and she frankly found classic ritual magick's endless obsession with the names of demons pretty boring.

"Got it in one," Dylan said. "Whether the Comte stumbled onto one of the Black Virgin cults common in Western Europe and completely misunderstood what he saw, whether he made it all up out of dopedreams, or whether some of what he saw was actually there is something we'll never know. A few years after he started circulating the manuscript, d'Erlette vanished. The manuscript survived, as those things tend to, which brings us to The Church of the Antique Rite."

"Antique Rite? *Which* Antique Rite?" Truth asked. As names went, that one was about as generic as they came.

"The ones in *Les Cultes des Goules,* apparently, which is what our unfortunate French Comte titled his manuscript," Dylan said. "The Church of the Antique Rite's practices are probably based on the descriptions in *Les Cultes des Goules*—although we can't be absolutely sure. What we do know is that at least some of the cultists migrated to the New World and managed to flourish here and there around New England, as much as that sort of thing ever does. You'll find mentions of them now and again in local histories, mostly hopelessly garbled.

"I imagine most of the congregations stuck to drugs and orgies, and didn't go in for the Comte's vision of wholesale human sacrifice—that's a lot less common both through history and today than TV news would like to think. The rest of the Church's development and history is really only of interest to a specialist, but I could go into it, if you'd like."

"No, thanks," Truth said frankly. "Call it vanity if you have to, but the Blackburn Work and what it stands for seems light-years away from . . . that." The memory of Wycherly's red-rimmed glaring eyes was suddenly vivid. "Does anyone actually do this sort of thing today?" Truth asked, poking at the blood-stained book with a wary finger.

Dylan shrugged. "I doubt it—but we wouldn't know if they did, because damn near everything the cult prescribes is utterly illegal. I think Hunter Greyson did a paper on the history of the cult while he was at Taghkanic—you might want to give him a call."

"Hmm," Truth said, not wanting to commit herself to any particular course of action. And *Les Cultes* was less her business than the Wildwood Gate was, anyway, though the book seemed to be bad medicine indeed for a vulnerable and unbalanced personality like Wycherly's.

"Let's see how tomorrow goes," Truth suggested. She would have liked to be more grateful for even this small recovery of the harmony she'd once taken for granted, but she knew that tomorrow's events would probably smash it into a thousand pieces.

You ought to have asked that woman to come to dinner and bring her friends, Sinah thought, but even so simple an expression of hospitality seemed to be beyond her strength. Once Truth had left she'd retreated to her bed—as if she were a wounded animal retreating to its burrow—and now hovered between waking and sleeping. The scene with Wycherly had left her aching with grief, and all Truth Jourdemayne's talk about ley lines, ancient power spots, and opened and closed Gates made a threatening and incomprehensible muddle in her mind.

Sinah thrashed fretfully, tangling the covers around her in an uncomfortable knot, sliding through dreams where she awaited judgment by an English court that had been dust for three hundred years into a waking where she knew she had gambled her heart and her sanity on an attempt to discover who she really was . . . and lost them both. Now the curse that defined her life faded away into the memories of all those other lives, as Sinah's fierce sense of self dissolved, leaving her to become only the latest child of the bloodline, Guardian of the Wellspring.

She didn't even have the energy to condemn the idea of her transformation as foolish nonsense. The one thought that rode uppermost in her thoughts was that the Wellspring—Truth called it Wildwood Gate—must be guarded, protected. And Truth threatened that, both with her knowledge of the bloodline's secrets and her desire to meddle.

But if she closed the Gate—sealed the Wellspring away from human contact—wouldn't that make it safe, too? And then no one else would have to die. . . .

Soft—weak—spineless — The first Athanais' scorn scoured her, making Sinah writhe in anguish on her restless bed. Abruptly she sat upright, unsure what had pulled her to the surface of sleep. Some noise outside—raccoons or foxes? The phone? The phone was her link to the outside world, the world of sanity and common sense. She should use it; pick up the phone, call someone.

Sinah ran her hand fretfully through her hair. Call who? And what could she tell them—that she'd discovered she was some sort of hereditary druid who'd gotten back to her ancestral home just in time to sacrifice a fresh crop of virgins? That there wasn't any Sinah Dellon—or if there was, she was only an empty vessel, to be filled by the memories of generations of guardians?

Why was I born, if it was for this? She rested her head in her hands, only to be roused from her misery by the sound of a car's engine starting up.

Not even stopping to grab her robe, Sinah ran downstairs and flung open the door. She was just in time to see the Jeep Cherokee's taillights receding into the darkness as it drove away.

"Wycherly!" Sinah shouted uselessly.

It was him—she knew that even if she could not see or feel him. Who else could it have been?

When she turned back into the house she saw her disheveled purse lying open on the couch. Wycherly must have come in while she drowsed fitfully upstairs, found her purse, and taken the Jeep Cherokee's keys.

She sat down and slowly began to put her purse back in order. Wycherly's actions baffled rather than angered her. She would have loaned him the Jeep Cherokee if he'd asked—or driven him anywhere he wanted to go, since she wasn't sure Wycherly was really a safe driver these days. Surely he knew he had only to ask.

Unless he no longer trusted her.

Sinah didn't have to see into Wycherly's mind to know what lay there: He thought she'd lied to him, and her pitifully inept—too little, too late—confession of how she knew what she did had been misunderstood, only serving to implicate her even further in his eyes. He was convinced that he was responsible for the Starking girl's disappearance—

And he wasn't. It was her—the bloodline—the Wellspring. The time for the Great Sacrifice of one of the bloodline grew near, and she'd done nothing to protect the people from the influence of the power. She who could raise up the dead, heal the sick, call spirits, and quicken wombs by the power of that portal into the spirit realms, had failed in this simplest of her tasks.

With a moan, Sinah buried her face in her hands. She could no longer distinguish between fact and wild imagination. She was losing her mind. She didn't know what was real any more. She wasn't psychic—she probably couldn't even read people's minds.

And there wasn't a wizard's cave up on the mountain that demanded human sacrifices every summer when the moon was full.

But there was.

She knew there was. And until she gave it its due sacrifice, no one was safe.

No one was safe at all.

"I had a bad night," Sinah said, in answer to Truth's look of shock at her appearance. She knew she looked terrible—the chameleon who'd dazzled producers and audiences with her charisma was revealed at last as a wan little hedge-wren, all her illicit fairy glamour stripped away. A few hours ago she'd managed to pull on last night's discarded clothes, but they hung on her, slovenly and unkempt, as though she'd somehow lost a dozen pounds between yesterday and today. She hadn't even been able to manage perfunctory makeup.

"Come in," Sinah said dutifully, though every word was an effort.

"Sinah, I'd like to introduce my colleague, Dr. Dylan Palmer. Dylan's going to accompany us up to the sanatorium this morning, strictly as an observer," Truth said.

"Sure." She was too tired to argue; too tired even to be surprised that she had not known he was there. Her Gift was gone. Wearily she turned away from them and headed in the direction of the kitchen. Maybe a good cup of strong coffee would lend her the energy she lacked.

Behind her, Truth and Dylan stared at each other blankly for a moment, then Truth stepped into the house and Dylan followed, shutting the door behind him.

"Was she like this when you left last night?" Dylan asked.

"No," Truth said, frowning in the direction of the noises coming from the kitchen. "Upset, certainly—that was an ugly scene with Wycherly—but calm."

"Did he come back last night, I wonder?" Dylan asked.

There was a crash from the kitchen.

When they got there, it was to find Sinah kneeling on the floor, weeping hopelessly. The shattered remains of the glass coffeepot she'd filled—then dropped—were spattered across the brick floor.

Truth and Dylan exchanged a quick look of agreement, then Truth guided Sinah back out into the living room while Dylan cleaned up the mess in the kitchen.

"What is it?" Truth asked, kneeling in front of Sinah and looking up into her face.

Sinah's skin was nearly the color of the pale-oyster leather couch on which she sat. All the color, the vibrancy, which Truth had seen in her yesterday was gone, and she seemed to have aged ten years overnight.

"Is it Wycherly? Did he come back? Did he hurt you?" But Truth's own wards gave no hint of any active magical tampering around Sinah—only the faint aura of linked power that marked her as one of the Gatekeepers.

"No. I haven't . . . seen Wycherly." The words were dragging, weary, and when Truth took Sinah's hands in hers the fingers were icy cold.

"Are you all right?" Truth asked again. Sinah seemed almost as if she was in shock, yet without the overlay of emotional agitation that Truth would expect.

"I know he thinks he killed that girl, Luned," Sinah said in a low voice. "But he didn't kill her—I did. Because I didn't do what I was supposed to do—I killed her. Me." And no matter how many deaths there were, they would not be enough if the Great Sacrifice was not made: one of the bloodline, one of her kin . . .

Truth put her arms around Sinah. The room was not overcooled, but Sinah's body was chill, and she shuddered as if she were in the grip of a fever.

"I'm so tired," Sinah whispered against Truth's cheek. "I just want to die. . . ."

Truth held her tightly, knowing there was nothing she could say that would ease Sinah's black depression. It was the Gate, she told herself. Things would be better once they'd faced it.

"I made coffee," Dylan said, coming into the living room with a mug in each hand. He looked from Truth to Sinah and raised his eyebrows inquiringly. Truth shrugged, minutely.

"And if you're willing to turn me loose in your kitchen, I can guarantee an extravagant breakfast," Dylan added. "You look like you could use a good meal." He held out the mug invitingly.

With an effort painful to see, Sinah drew herself together and smiled at him. "What's that they say, Dr. Palmer? You can never be too rich or too thin?"

She took the mug, and drank down the steaming liquid as though it were tap water.

"Ugh," she said, setting the empty cup on the coffee table. "What's *in* that?" But a little color had come back to her cheeks, and she looked more substantial.

"Strong coffee, lots of sugar, and a splash of cream. Good for what ails you," Dylan said cheerfully. "Feeling a little better?"

Sinah made a face. "Yes. I think so. And I think I'll take you up on that offer of breakfast, Dr. Palmer."

"Please. Call me Dylan."

While Dylan cooked, Sinah disappeared to shower and change, reappearing just as Dylan slid the first omelet out of the pan. She'd changed to natural cotton jeans and a sleeveless coral linen blouse and her hair was held back by a matching coral silk scarf. She'd also added a deft touch of makeup. Yet underneath that careful camouflage, Truth could see that nothing had really changed at all. Sinah Dellon was a woman nearly at the end of her tether.

Truth had set the table while Dylan cooked, finding the dishes and utensils in the neat kitchen without trouble. Now she and Sinah settled into their places while Dylan served.

"Omelets—and fresh biscuits—and coffee not mucked up with all that sugar; you'll make some woman a perfect husband some day," Sinah joked, raising the mug to her lips.

"I already have, I hope. Truth and I are engaged; we'll be getting married in December."

Will we? Truth carefully did not look toward him, knowing her face would betray things she did not want him to see. She forced a smile and concentrated on her eggs.

"That's wonderful," Sinah said dutifully. She'd taken a biscuit, and was methodically crumbling it onto her plate, without eating it.

Breakfast went quickly—Dylan really was a good cook—and between them, the two researchers managed to bully Sinah into eating at least half her omelet. Truth cleared away the dishes—Dylan had cooked, after all—and was just returning from stacking them in the dishwasher when she heard him say:

"Do you have any questions or reservations about what we're going to do here today? You don't have to do this, you know."

He was sitting next to Sinah, his hand over hers.

"But I thought . . ." Sinah sounded bewildered.

"Yes, she does," Truth said, her voice hard. She strode toward the table.

Both of them turned toward her. Truth held back her fury with an effort—though if she summoned the lightning to strike Dylan dead this instant, it would not only serve him out for his meddling, but give Sinah proof that the Unseen World was real.

"I thought we'd agreed that you were here as an observer, Dylan," Truth said. "Sinah has already agreed that what she needs to do is go up to Wildwood with me to try to close the Gate."

"Has she?" Dylan asked. "I'd like to hear that from her."

I will never forgive you this, Dylan, Truth thought with icy anger. She had never tampered with his work, and now he was meddling in this most dangerous, most vital task of hers.

But Sinah was looking at Dylan with a strange smile on her face, an expression that transformed it until Sinah appeared almost to be another woman entirely.

"You think it isn't there, don't you? You think your leman is chasing shadows, don't you, city boy? You're wrong. It's there. Come and see it."

It was as if someone else had stepped in to Sinah's body. Her voice held a mocking lilt, and the vowels were blurred and stretched into a kind of English accent Truth had never heard before.

"Come and see," Sinah said, and laughed.

Disassociation. Multiple personalities, Truth thought automatically. But hearing her, Truth felt a small thrill of fear. She'd taken it utterly for granted that Sinah would be her ally the next time she faced the power of the Gate.

But what if Sinah had something different in mind?

FOURTEEN

THE NATURE OF THE GRAVE

In ev'ry grave make room, make room!
The world's at an end, and we come, we come.
—SIR WILLIAM DAVENANT

THERE'D BEEN A FOUR-WHEEL-DRIVE VEHICLE PARKED
in Sinah's driveway last night, but Truth saw no evidence of it this morning. It meant that they were forced to use Truth's rented sedan for the
drive up to the ruined sanatorium. When they reached the battered iron
gates, Truth switched off the ignition.

"This is as far as we go by car. The road gets pretty rough from here
on. I don't think the car can make it."

Dylan and Sinah got out of the car without comment. Truth went
around to the trunk to retrieve her bag of working tools. She wasn't sure
what help they'd be, but she felt better for having them with her.

"Look, Truth—" While Sinah loitered near the ruined pillars, Dylan
had come around the back of the sedan to join Truth.

"Get away from me." Truth's tone was deadly. She did not even glance
toward him. "You're here to observe? Observe. And keep your mouth
shut."

Out of the corner of her eye she saw Dylan recoil, saw the tardy awareness of the irrevocable insult he'd dealt her appear in his eyes. His mouth
went hard, bracketed by white lines of tension, but he said nothing more.
Truth walked past him as if he didn't exist.

"It's a nice day for a walk, isn't it?" Truth asked Sinah when she
reached her.

Though it was still morning, the air was luminous with mist, promising a high, hazy, August scorcher to come. The colors were much
brighter than they had been on the rainy evening Truth had visited
here—today the green of the surrounding undergrowth seemed especially brilliant, almost electric. Each breath brought the mingled sensuous smells of decay and growth, of fresh earth and growing things.

"I guess so. I just want to . . ." Sinah shrugged.

"Come on then," Truth said, taking her arm. The two women began
to walk up the overgrown drive, toward the sanatorium itself.

The trees that had grown up—volunteered, in the local vernacular—
among what had once been rolling lawns were fewer than Truth would
have expected. She saw the white marble bench that she'd become so familiar with on her last visit sitting alone in a ring of deer-cropped grass;
beyond it was a sundial, tipped on its side. Ahead she could see the gap
in the trees that indicated the sanatorium building itself.

As she and Sinah came closer, first grass, then trees, then underbrush
dwindled away, until they walked over a flagstoned drive laid in the
midst of sterile brown earth covered only by drifts of fallen leaves and the
dried twigs and fallen branches left by winter storms. Truth stopped and
looked around.

"It's as if it were . . . blighted, somehow," Dylan said softly.

And that wasn't right, Truth thought, puzzled. The Gates were the
Gates of Life Itself—they should be surrounded by abundance, not steril-
ity.

Ahead, the few remaining pieces of the bearing walls reared up into
the sky. Eighty years of wind and rain had done their work upon the
stone, but there was none of the softening and erosion that plant life
would have caused. The site stood as stark and sterile as if it were a palace
on the moon. Gingerly, Truth ascended the broad steps to the archway in
which had once hung an ornate door.

"Careful," Sinah warned her.

Truth gazed out over the enormous ruin. The scope of the destruction was breathtaking; the sanatorium looked as though it had been bombed, not burned. In its heyday, it must have been magnificent.

"Quentin said he was going to make it the grandest spa there ever had been," Sinah said in an odd remote voice, this time with the flattened accent of the hills.

Truth glanced toward her. Sinah's mouth was drawn, her face almost masklike. Truth wondered what the other woman was experiencing, but kept her own shields firmly in place. She did not want to confront the power of the Wildwood Gate until the moment she meant to challenge it, lest she be drained by fending off its strength.

"Where do we go from here?" Truth asked. To her left she could see Dylan working his way around the edge of the ruin, as if he were looking for something. So long as he stayed away from her, she didn't care what he did, Truth told herself. She turned back to Sinah.

"Down. We have to go down inside—to the Black Altar."

Truth followed Sinah as the younger woman picked her way carefully around the exposed edge of the basement's crumbling ruin to the black marble stairway that led down into the hidden sub-basement. She was aware that Dylan followed them, but did not let the knowledge penetrate her concentration. There was no room for ego here in the presence of such power.

Truth's psychic walls had never been meant to stand against the power of the Gate itself, a force so much a part of her that to deny it was like denying her own nature. By the time she and Sinah reached the deepest level of the ruins, Truth felt as if she were moving underwater, as giddy and detached as if she'd been sniffing nitrous oxide.

She reached out and took Sinah's hand, and felt Sinah's fingers cold and trembling within her clasp. Though Truth knew from experience that telepaths did not like to be touched, Sinah's hand tightened over hers, as though any human presence was a comfort in this place.

It was cool and dark here so far below the surface, where the warmth and light of the sun so rarely penetrated. The leaves of fourscore autumns had been ground to a soft, pale dust beneath their feet, and lay like strangely colored snowdrifts in every corner. The exposed brick and pipe on the walls above their heads gave both women the curious feeling of being behind the scenes, as though some great and secret show were taking place just out of sight.

Sinah did not need to tell her where to go. Truth could feel the Gate, as though the two of them walked on very thin ice indeed across the surface of a maelstrom of enormous power.

"It's there," Sinah said. She pointed.

In the dimness it was hard to make out any details, but for Truth it was as if her astral sight overlay the real world, outlining everything in sharp silver fire. She could see the altar Sinah had spoken of, and behind it the cave opening, and the steps leading down to the spring in the rock below. The entire sanatorium had been built directly over this spot.

Just as Shadow's Gate was. Did Quentin Blackburn have any more idea than Thorne did of what he faced here?

She heard the sound of a footstep scraping over the powdered leaves, and knew that Dylan had joined them.

"What do I have to do?" Sinah said. Her voice sounded young and frightened.

"You'll need to open yourself to the Gate," Truth said. It seemed that a wind only she could feel was rising, catching both of them up in it. "Just relax. I'll be right with you. There are some words that you should say, but your intent will be the most important thing."

Truth kept her voice soothing, lulling, and saw the other woman begin to relax. "It isn't for us to tamper with the Wellspring," Sinah said breathlessly.

"But you won't be," Truth said, encouragingly. "You've always asked it for favors, haven't you? Now you're just asking it to close. Don't think you're here to force it against its nature. No one has that kind of strength."

"All right." Sinah reached out her hands, and now she and Truth stood facing each other, holding hands directly above the Wellspring. Truth reached out with her mind, matching her energy field with Sinah's and using it to gently pull Sinah with her into the Otherworld.

"What is this place?" Sinah stared around herself.

She was alone. The sky was grey, the ground was grey, everything was grey and lightless, except that she could still see.

She wasn't sure what she'd expected—all she had to go on were her ancestral memories, but whatever they had led her to expect, it wasn't . . . this.

She was standing in the middle of a graveyard. Shattered and broken tombstones, laid out in no recognizable pattern, stretched as far as the eye could see. The stones seemed to rise up toward the top of a hill, and on its summit was a lifeless, twisted oak tree, its trunk only a darker shade of grey than the surroundings. Its branches reached toward the sky like the broken hands of torture victims.

"Truth?" Sinah whispered. "Dylan?"

No response came. She looked down at her hands—she was as grey as this eerie landscape, as colorless, and as doomed.

Her nerve broke. Her ancestresses had believed devoutly in the pains of Hell, and now Sinah ran as if the jaws of Hell pursued her—as if this nightmare had a finite area, something she could outrun.

The ground was soft and unpleasantly springy beneath her feet. There was no movement to the air, as though this place, for all its seeming vastness, was actually locked somewhere inside a very small box, away from light and life and air. The tombstones made an obstacle course to her flight; she collided with them and bounced off them, the pain of the impact telling her that this was no dream or hallucination, that this was somehow a real place that she had come to.

At last, winded and staggering, Sinah tripped over a tree root—how could she have? there were no trees save the one in this awful place—and fell sprawling. When she looked up, she found herself upon the steps of a vast and ruined cathedral she had not seen before.

"Truth?" Sinah whimpered again. Truth, please come help me, I'm all alone here and I'm so frightened. . . .

At last it occurred to her to reach out for the power of the Wellspring, to draw upon it to defend herself just as generations of Dellons always had. But it didn't work—instead of the pure cold light, inhuman in its power, what she touched was foul, unclean, as noxious as a piece of maggoty meat.

"Welcome, Child of the Sacred Spring."

Sinah turned toward the voice, welcoming the sound—any sound—in this dead silent place . . . until she saw what had made it.

The doors of the cursed cathedral were open, and in its dim recesses she could see a crude altar formed from a shapeless lump of stone. Upon it crouched the thing that had spoken—huge and horned and goatlike, yet horrible in the way no animal could be. She felt its hunger like an assault, and scrabbled backward on hands and knees. Where was the Gate Truth had said she must lock? Where was the Wellspring she must guard?

"So you see, Athanais, I have won at last."

She turned, and almost sobbed with relief. No monster this, but a man in long clerical robes. He held out a hand to help her to her feet.

"Quentin."

The bloodline knew what this place was. This was the blasphemous Church Quentin Blackburn had sworn he would build in her sacred place, trapping the Wellspring beneath his cursed altar and making her power his own.

"You have not won," she said, scrabbling back from him and pulling herself upright along a tombstone. Its surface crumbled away beneath her hands as if it were ancient bone.

His smile widened, impossibly wide, and now Melusine saw that Quentin Blackburn had only looked human in contrast to the thing that awaited within the ruined church.

"Have I not? I am the Gateway to your precious Wellspring, now, Athanais."

Her mental image of the man she had loved and killed so long ago wavered and vanished. All that was left was this monster with its mindless hunger for power and revenge.

"And what has all your power gotten you?" she said sadly. *"Oh, Quentin—can't you see that you've gained nothing—not in this world or the next? Let me help you; together we can—"*

"I gave you your chance to join me. Now join my master."

She had thought she was safely removed from Quentin, but time and distance meant nothing in this place. His hand closed upon her wrist, and Sinah found herself on the threshold of the cathedral, being pulled inside. On the altar, the thing waited for her, a hideous mockery of the god of lust and fear that the bloodline had paid homage to on soft summer nights.

If Quentin got his way here, she would die the death from which there was no redemption, and the Wellspring would be unprotected forever. She struggled against him with a strength that transcended reason or understanding, the ultimate effort that the human spirit can only muster in the face of something more terrible than death.

And in the distance, she heard a howling.

At first she thought it came from more of Quentin's servants, but the frenzy with which he redoubled his efforts to drag her to the Black Altar told her it did not. Struggling toward the graveyard, her face turned away from his, it was Sinah who saw the great grey brute appear out of the mist. It gathered itself and lunged at Quentin Blackburn, snapping and snarling. He put up both hands to defend himself, and Sinah was free.

"SINAH!"

She ran toward the cry. Truth was seated upon the back of a white horse—it danced and skittered, as if it did not want its feet to touch the ground—holding a hand out to her.

"Hurry—I can't —" Truth gasped.

The grey wolf flashed by them, fleeing, and Sinah grabbed Truth's wrist with all her strength. Truth did not even wait for her to mount, but urged the mare into flight, her hand clasped on Sinah's arm in a punishing grip. Sinah ran beside her, willing to be dragged, anything, to escape this terrible place.

Exhaustion made her blind; an eternity later, Truth stopped long enough to pull Sinah up behind her, and then the mare ran on, on and on and on. . . .

"Sinah."

No. She was cold, frozen to the bone. Someone shook her, and she reluctantly opened her eyes.

She'd been so certain, somehow, that she was indoors, perhaps in a hospital, that the open air of the hidden temple came as a jarring shock. She was lying on smooth cold stone; sound and sensation came back to her along with sight. She pushed Truth away and sat up.

"Are you all right?" Truth's voice was insistent.

"I'm . . . Sinah." That was the most important thing. She shook her head, trying to clear it. She was Sinah—but for how long?

"What happened?"

Sinah saw Truth flinch in irritation at Dylan's question, but the dark-haired woman said nothing.

"It's Quentin Blackburn. He wants to kill me," Sinah said.

Somehow it didn't seem enough.

"It's only fair," she amplified, still feeling dazed. "After all, I've already killed him."

They got back to the car—Dylan drove—and soon Sinah and Truth were sitting in the breakfast nook once more while Dylan puttered around in the kitchen. In a few moments he came out with two steaming mugs.

"Mulled wine," he said, setting one cup down in front of each of the women. "I know it's out of season, but Truth will tell you it's the best thing in situations like this."

Truth sipped at her mug. "At least it tastes better than the stuff I buy," she commented. "How are you feeling, Sinah?"

"I don't know," Sinah said. "Tired, I guess."

Both of the others looked at her as if she'd said something peculiar.

"What?" Sinah asked.

Dylan looked toward Truth, acknowledging her right to lead the questioning.

"I'll want you to tell me in detail what you experienced up there at the sanatorium, Sinah, so we can compare notes, but first—Dylan, what did *you* see?"

Dylan frowned, concentrating scrupulously.

"The event took about five minutes. When I arrived on the ground level, you and Sinah were already standing in front of the altar-like stone, holding hands. You seemed to be in an altered state, so I didn't disturb you. I'd just seen that it *was* an altar, with carving along the side facing me, and was moving over toward it to get a closer look, when the temperature seemed to drop abruptly, and I felt . . . a chill would be the best way to describe it. Sort of apprehensive, the way you do when you've wandered into a not-very-good neighborhood." Dylan paused. His voice was neutral, carefully distancing himself from the phenomena he was reporting, as a good researcher must.

It was that objectivity that Truth had lost. Her path might lie balanced between White and Black, but her judgment could not lie balanced between belief and skepticism. Truth believed.

Dylan glanced at her—questioningly—and went on. "At the same time I became aware of the sound of running water—not loud, but seemingly coming from all directions—and Sinah fell to her knees. You released her hands and started trying to rouse her. I checked my watch, then moved to help you. When I next noticed it, the temperature had to normal, and I didn't seem to hear the sound of the water."

Truth considered.

"And you, Sinah?" Truth asked.

"You're going to think this is crazy," Sinah began hesitantly, but soon was telling them the whole story of the grey place, the graveyard, the Black Altar and its monstrous god—

"—and it was so real—like virtual reality, except I could feel, and touch, and smell. It seemed to go on for hours—I'd swear it wasn't just five minutes." She shuddered, reaching for her mug again and draining it. "I don't ever want to have another nightmare that real! And he—

Quentin—was dragging me inside, when you showed up, Truth. On a white horse, just like a cowboy hero." She laughed, shakily.

"And I had a hard time doing it," Truth said. "I'll get to my part of the story in a moment, but—you said Quentin Blackburn was trying to kill you? And that you've already killed him?"

"In 1917," Sinah said. "He died in the fire that I—that my great-great-grandmother Athanais set. She—I—she—oh, it's so confused! I don't believe in reincarnation—I don't!" Sinah wailed in protest.

"That doesn't matter, if reincarnation believes in you," Dylan joked. Then, seeing how distressed Sinah was, said, "You don't have to believe in a full-fledged transmigration of souls to believe that some people are capable of remembering things that happened before they were born— sometimes in great detail. The capacities and capabilities of the human brain are vast, and scientists now believe that there is more natural inter-connectedness between human minds than was ever before thought pos-sible. Possibly memory is even programmed into the mitochondrial DNA, passed down from mother to daughter across the generations."

"Maybe," Sinah said, sounding relieved to have a scientific-sounding explanation. "You know what they say: 'Dammit, Jim, I'm a telepath, not a trance medium.'" She smiled at her own feeble joke.

"But tell us about Quentin Blackburn," Truth urged.

Sinah frowned, running a hand through her hair. "I sure fancied him," she said, her voice slowing and deepening and taking on a pronounced mountain accent. "He come up here with some cityfolk paper saying as he had fair title to everything from Mauch Chunk Trace to Watchman's Gap—Ari'd done sold it off for two thousand paper dollars and a bottle of store-bought whiskey.

"I tried not to mind Quentin none—wasn't nothing I could do about him, but I figured if he took up with me I'd get the land back somehow, even if he had to die sudden. But he built his hospital right over my Wellspring, and then he started doing . . . things."

Sinah stared right at Truth, but it was no longer Sinah who looked out of her eyes. It was Athanais Dellon, the last true guardian of the Wildwood Gate, who had died in 1917 protecting her charge the only way she could.

"I couldn't stop him, Miss Truth. He was riling up what isn't good for man nor woman to meddle with; I go my ways, Lord knows, but this was hurtful when it didn't need to be, and, well, it drove off the hunting and blighted the forest. It wasn't natural. I told him and told him I couldn't let him be; that it wasn't right for him to meddle like he was. But he just put his nose deeper into that book of his and went on about how they understood this sort of thing over in Europe. I loved him more'n I ever did any natural man, but he studied to shut me out, Miss Truth, and I couldn't let him do that. I warned him, I did. . . ." Tears slid unnoticed down Sinah's cheeks.

"Sinah?" Truth said.

"Yes, I . . . well, that's how it was," Sinah finished lamely, obviously not quite sure of what she'd been saying.

"Quentin Blackburn was a member of The Church of the Antique Rite," Dylan summarized, "who came to Morton's Fork wanting to tap the power of the psychic locus—the Gate—here, just as his great-nephew would years later at Shadow's Gate."

"But Thorne Blackburn wasn't evil," Truth objected.

"Granted," Dylan said, "Thorne was a cockeyed idealist, but his great-uncle seems to have been in it for temporal power, just as some of the European magickal orders were at the same period. So his lover, Athanais Dellon, burned the sanatorium down with Quentin inside, killing both of them and destroying his access to the Gate."

"But not very well," Truth pointed out dryly. "Because Quentin's still here."

She stood and stretched, turning away from the table and looking out across the living room. The sun was high and the stained-glass windows were brilliantly lit, throwing their multicolored shadows of light across the pale walls and furniture. It should have been a beautiful and peaceful place.

"I've seen him before," Truth began, slowly, "both times I've visited the Wellspring on the Astral. Whether it's him—a discarnate spirit retaining ties to the Earth plane—or just some sort of psychic echo, it means his Church managed to taint access to Sinah's Wellspring pretty thoroughly. Today, the harder I tried to reach the Gate, the more I got bogged down, in, well, *nothing*."

Truth paused, searching for words that both Dylan and Sinah would understand. "Travel to what we call the Astral, the Otherworld—where you were, Sinah—is a subjective experience, different each time. The Otherworld is usually defined by the expectations of the beholder, unless someone else's expectations override his. I'll be the first to admit it's a very strange place, but it's a natural one. Except this time. I felt as if I were on the wrong frequency. I couldn't get out, I couldn't go on . . . but it was, oh, like I was trying to run a Mac program on an IBM computer; just a mess. I knew you must be there somewhere, Sinah, so I kept trying to reach you, but it was—it was like moving through phantom oatmeal."

"I'll have to remember that description for my next lecture," Dylan said, but his tone was sympathetic. "As for Quentin Blackburn . . . I'm sorry darling. I didn't take you seriously, but you were right—even if he isn't there, his threat has to be taken seriously. You provided concrete proof of that—I should have believed you and investigated for myself immediately."

"Proof?" Truth said blankly. Dylan's handsome apology seemed somehow inadequate; a formality instead of a true healing. She felt untouched by it inside, as if there were still arguments between them to resolve.

"Nobody who wasn't dabbling in very nasty things indeed would have anything like that altar," Dylan explained. "The fire may have destroyed everything else, but the altar's chiseled right out of the bedrock. It's carved with symbols from the Antique Rite, and it's obviously part of the sanatorium construction. As for the rest. . . ."

"We still need to seal that Gate," Truth said, over Sinah's automatic wince of protest. "But it looks like we need to get Quentin Blackburn out of there first, and that's something I can't do."

There was nothing more that any of them could do that day, and anyway, before proceeding, Truth wanted more information on what they faced. Dylan left very soon; he had his own work to do, besides rejoining the search for the still-missing Starking girl. Truth stayed with Sinah, who seemed to welcome her company.

When Dylan was gone, Truth reheated the rest of the mulled wine and got Sinah to drink it. Under the influence of the alcohol and sugar, Sinah agreed to lie down and get some rest—so long as Truth promised to stay with her, and wake her if she started to dream.

"You'll stay, won't you? You won't leave me."

"Of course I won't leave you." Truth smoothed Sinah's hair back, and the younger woman relaxed again on the freshly made bed. Truth felt a sudden flash of tenderness—though she'd known Sinah only a day, the woman was already closer to her than a sister. Than her own sister.

Truth sat beside Sinah until she saw that the woman had entered the

gates of sleep and was resting quietly, and then went back downstairs to
the phone. She was just as glad to have privacy for what she was going to
do next.

"Hi, Truth!" Grey's voice carried sunnily through the connection, and
despite her worries, Truth smiled.

Hunter Greyson was a practitioner of the Blackburn Work, though he
had come to it from the Right-Hand Path whose precepts he had followed in more lifetimes than this. He was more advanced in the Work
than Truth herself, since she had only recently returned to the Path after
a long absence.

"Of course you know that I'm not calling just to chat, but—how is
Winter?" she asked, thinking of Wycherly and cradling the phone
against her ear. The afternoon sun slanting through the stained-glass
windows made the room a kaleidoscope, staining everything it touched
with its random hues.

"Doing fine. She's gotten a job at the Arts Council, helping them with
grants and fund-raising, and she's started painting again. She says she'll
scale back her activities once the baby comes, but I don't know." Grey's
voice was fond. "You'll have to find time to come out and see us again,
Truth."

"I will," Truth promised, hoping it was one she could keep. She
thought of mentioning that Wycherly was here in Morton's Fork, but
something made her hesitate. Winter and Wycherly had not parted on
good terms, though Truth knew that Winter, at least, would welcome a
reconciliation.

But if Wycherly were turning to the Left-Hand Path?

"But the reason I called is—Grey, what do you know about The
Church of the Antique Rite?" Truth said quickly.

There was a moment of silence. "You haven't run into anyone saying
he's a member, have you?" Grey asked warily.

"No, but I think I've found one of their old temples." Truth paused,
not certain of how to explain what had happened today. She didn't want
to tell Grey about the Wildwood Gate—though, like all Blackburn Ini-
tiates, he knew about the Gates in theory.

But theory isn't practice—I'm living proof of that.

"Did you try to banish it?" Grey asked, skipping over several inter-
mediate steps in the conversation. Anyone coming across such a tainted

site—except, possibly, another disciple of the Left-Hand Path—would certainly try to cleanse the negative energies that would inevitably linger in the area.

"I did my best, but my best doesn't seem to be much good," Truth admitted. "It's, um . . . determined," was the word she finally settled for, knowing that Grey would be able to decode what she really meant.

It was good to be able to talk to one of her own kind, even though Hunter Greyson was not quite what she was. His power was the result of years of study, not inherited psychic gifts or *sidhe* bloodline. Hunter Greyson was human.

Grey chuckled, in acknowledgement of the effort Truth must have made and the resigned frustration in her voice. "You'll need a specialist, then. Do you or Dylan know any White Magicians?"

Grey was not referring to race, but to belief—White Magicians were members of the White Lodges, followers of the Right-Hand Path. In its simplest form, Christianity was White Magick, as opposed to Truth's own path as its profane mirror-image, Black Magick, was.

Michael Archangel. Truth thought of the man her sister, Light, had chosen—the warrior of the Light who felt that Truth's own path was a grievous error that would lead only to sorrow and pain. Michael Archangel was a White Magician.

"Yes. I think I know someone I can call." She hesitated again about mentioning Wycherly and once more decided against it. "Keep well, Grey."

"And you, too, Truth. Go with the Wheel," Grey said, bidding her farewell.

When Truth hung up the phone, it was a long time before she could bring herself to make the next call.

She'd invited Sinah to come and join Dylan and the others for dinner; Truth hoped to persuade the others into a jaunt into Pharaoh as a break from the tensions of the day.

Sinah had simply laughed at the invitation, though she'd been anxious enough for Truth to come back to spend the night that Truth was fairly sure it was the prospect of going to Pharaoh and not a desire to be alone that had prompted Sinah's refusal.

One more mystery to solve when she had the time.

But it was probably just as well that Sinah had refused, since that left

Truth free to stop at Wycherly's cabin on her way down the mountain several hours later. But Wycherly was not there, and only the faintest trace of magick remained, cold and neutral as an unused hearth.

"You did *what?*" Dylan demanded.

Luned Starking had not been found, and by now everyone assumed the worst. Caleb Starking, Luned's father, had even—though with reluctance—filed a missing persons report with the sheriff's department, and tomorrow most of the area between the general store and Watchman's Gap would be searched with dogs.

With everyone so discouraged, Truth's suggestion of dinner in Pharaoh had been a welcome break from the tension of the last two days. The researchers had managed to find a nice restaurant—nice for Lyonesse County, anyway—and have a civilized, sit-down dinner in a setting a little more spacious than the camper's kitchenette. It was even air-conditioned, which, after three weeks in Morton's Fork, seemed like the height of luxury. Rowan and Ninian had rushed through their dinners and gone off to see what other delights Pharaoh might provide, leaving Truth and Dylan alone. Truth had been relieved; she'd thought it would be nice to have a little more privacy than usual when she brought up the subject of additional magickal activity up at the sanatorium.

"I called a friend of mine to see if he'd be willing to come and cast out the doppelganger of Quentin Blackburn from the Church of the Antique Rite," Truth repeated.

"Of all the—" Dylan said. He stopped speaking suddenly, but Truth could see the dark flush of anger across his cheeks.

"Dylan!" Truth said. "You saw yourself what was up there—you said yourself it was haunted."

"I said it was haunted," Dylan agreed shortly. "If it's haunted, that means we study it," he added, as if he were speaking to a very simpleminded child. "We don't blot it out of existence."

But what about the Gate? Truth had known she was overstepping the bounds of Dylan's fragile tolerance when she'd made her call to Michael, but not by how much.

Truth had thought he'd be more sympathetic after this morning—even if he hadn't experienced what she and Sinah had, he'd seemed to believe what they'd told him about it afterward. But how much did Dylan really believe, and how much of his true opinions were masked by the professional courtesy of the researcher who does not wish to alienate his test subjects?

A test subject . . . is that what I am to him?

"That temple is too dangerous to just leave as it is," Truth said. "Please, Dylan—I don't want to see you hurt."

"You've stepped way over the line on this one, Truth," Dylan said, and now his voice held an uneasy mixture of sorrow and regret. "I agree with you that there's something nasty in the wood pile up at Wildwood, and The Church of the Antique Rite is nothing you want to mess around with. But the site, the congregation, and Quentin Blackburn all burned in 1917, and ghosts don't kill. The locals avoid the site—"

"Then what about Luned Starking? Where is she?" Truth demanded.

She kept her voice down with an effort, not wanting to disturb the other diners. The Lyonesse Pantry was a simple, plain, mom-and-pop establishment that would certainly not thank them for causing a flashy scene.

"Maybe she and Wycherly Musgrave eloped together," Dylan suggested briefly. "That is not the point. The point is that Morton's Fork is my research project, and you're riding your hobbyhorse right through the middle of it. How dare you make a decision like this without consulting me—especially after how you slapped me down this morning?"

So he was still sulking about that, was he? *I do it because I have to. It's my job.* The realization that this was no more than the truth—and that Dylan could not be expected to accept it—grieved her. It had not seemed like such a momentous decision when she'd first made it, but day by day, hour by hour, Truth's decision to follow her father's path was separating her from the realities of mundane existence.

And from those she loved.

"I'm sorry, Dylan," Truth said evenly, though her heart wept. "I feel that the place as it stands is more of a danger than you seem to think— to Sinah, certainly, since whatever's up there has a personal interest in her—and also to Wycherly, if he's gotten tangled up with The Church of the Antique Rite as he seems to have. You know that impressions linger in a place—you've told me that's what a lot of hauntings are, just the playback by a susceptible mind of recorded images—and I think Wycherly's unstable. I think that place could reinforce unstable elements in his own personality."

"Do you think he's killed Luned?" Dylan said. His voice was still hard with anger; he had not forgiven her.

"I know that Sinah doesn't think so," Truth said slowly, thinking back to that last scene at Sinah's house. "I . . . don't know. Luned wasn't at Wycherly's when I stopped there yesterday, and he said he'd gone out searching for her. He didn't . . . *feel* . . . as if he'd killed someone recently," she added.

If Wycherly had killed Luned, traces of her life force—her purely animal part, not her soul—would still have been clinging to him hours later, perceptible to anyone with Astral Sight. But the Astral Sight began first and foremost with the willingness to see, and without that Dylan had no way to experience any of the things Truth spoke to him of. She began to wonder—as she had so many times over the last weeks—how much of what she'd told Dylan about her Overworld experiences he believed, and how much he had only refrained from openly disputing.

"Well, that's reassuring," Dylan said sarcastically. He threw his napkin on the table. "His aura says he didn't kill anybody, so it has to be a Gate that nobody can find but you. I guess dinner's over. Let's go find the kids."

Why are you being so unreasonable? Yes, maybe I should have talked this over with you first—but then you should have said yes, you know you should; we both know that uncontrolled psychic loci are dangerous. . . . Is it because you're as afraid as I am—and not of this? Dylan . . .

Before she could speak, Dylan got to his feet, summoning the waiter. As the waiter left with Dylan's charge card and the check, he turned back to Truth.

"Did your exorcist give you any idea of when he was going to show up?"

"The day after tomorrow," Truth said crisply. "He'll be flying into Bridgeport and driving out the morning of the fourteenth." *August 14th. Lammas, Old Style, and the Wildwood Gate must be fed with the blood of the Gatekeepers. . . .* "I'll be staying at Sinah's tonight, in case she has any more problems."

"I see," Dylan said.

The charge-slip was brought and he signed it, then gestured for Truth to precede him from the restaurant.

Wycherly stood beside Sinah's Jeep Cherokee, looking across the street to a little *boîte de nuit* calling itself the Lyonesse Pantry. Kitchen smells of roasting and baking hung on the hot night air that molded Wycherly's shirt against his skin.

Through the large lighted open windows, he could see fake oak panelling, scattered square tables draped in tired white linen, the worn red carpet and the straight-backed wooden chairs. There were plastic flowers on the tables, and votive candles in tall soot-smeared chimneys, making this easily the most upscale eatery within sixty-five miles.

The thought brought a sneering smile to his face. This was how the other half lived—fat contented sheep, slumbering their way toward Armageddon.

He wasn't one of them. Not him. He'd seen Hell already.

His right hand throbbed, awkward in the light rigid cast that was supposed to keep him from tearing the forty-eight stitches taken in his palm and wrist. It had taken him most of a day to make up his mind to go to a doctor—but even after he'd rebandaged the wound with supplies bought from the Walgreen's in Pharaoh, it had throbbed sullenly, and the thought of infection had frightened him. Finally he'd driven all the way to Elkins and gone to an emergency room, suitably fortified for the drive by several beers and a fifth of Scotch.

As long as he could reach for a bottle, it kept him from reaching for a knife.

It was a good thing he'd held onto his AmEx, because it had cost him over four hundred dollars to get his hand cleaned and sewn up, and himself inoculated with antibiotics against infection. The intern had scolded him for letting his injury go untreated for so long before bringing it in, but Wycherly hadn't listened. He'd had other things to do, but first he'd needed to find a hotel room, and a bank.

He'd found the room, though the bank would have to wait until tomorrow. He'd thought he might like food, but gazing at the trite domestic scene made him realize that he wouldn't. There was a bottle back in his room—and, frankly, whether his stomach or his liver or anything else would hold out much longer was finally a non-issue. He'd come to these hills to find out the truth, and he'd found it—or enough of it. The subtleties of good might be beyond his reach, but his unruly stubbornness rebelled from being anyone's—any *thing's*—helpful servant.

For a while he'd thought that loving Sinah might save him, but she was just like all the rest—she saw the money and the family name and nothing more. Why else would she have indulged him so much with her body and her attentions?

And if that wasn't the way things really were, he didn't have time to find out what the truth was. Wycherly had things to do—the things he could do best: ruining people's plans, disappointing those who depended on him, failing those who trusted him, and breaking things. He was weak, he was useless—everyone had always said so. And if he'd discovered anything in the last few weeks, it was that he didn't *want* to be of use to anyone.

He was weak. Now someone would discover just how dangerous a weak man could be.

"Happy birthday," Wycherly sang tonelessly under his breath. "Happy birthday to me. . . ."

The long drive back to Morton's Fork was unnaturally quiet, with everyone in the car afraid of saying the wrong thing; apparently Rowan and Ninian had argued as well, for they stared fixedly out of opposite windows and didn't even try to break the silence.

The car passed through the main street of Morton's Fork—closed and dark at nine o'clock—and past the pale bulk of the camper; a modern American luxury abandoned in a place that was anything but. Dylan swept the sedan up Watchman's Gap Trace toward Sinah's house without even asking Rowan and Ninian if they wanted to be dropped off first.

Sinah's house was a beacon. Every light in the place was on, and inside, Truth could see Sinah moving around. The stained glass windows gave the house the look of a Christmas tree ornament as they pulled up out front. The Jeep Cherokee was still missing, and Truth knew that she had to ask Sinah where Wycherly had gone; now the stakes were too high for her to just let something like that slide.

"Thanks for a lovely evening," Truth said when the car stopped, struggling to keep the sarcasm out of her voice. As she opened the car door and stepped out, she realized that she'd meant to stop at the camper for her toiletries and a change of clothes. Well, maybe Sinah could loan her something.

"Goodnight, Truth," Ninian said, and Rowan waved. She saw Dylan take his hand off the wheel to rub his eyes, and knew he felt as tired and frustrated as she did. She waved—to the students—and turned away, reaching in her purse for Sinah's keys. Behind her she heard the sound of the car backing down into the road.

Sinah had dressed and made herself up carefully, but the makeup stood out chalky and clownlike on her pale, pointed face. She tried to smile at Truth, but she could not hold the expression. It came and went, flickering across her face.

"Everything okay?" Truth asked.

"If you mean, 'am I still here and haven't had any nightmares on-or-off Elm Street,' yes. But what comes now? I know you've called in some kind of specialist witch-doctor, but I can't do what you want, Truth—I can't!"

Truth had to be careful not to push Sinah too far—she'd already had a glimpse of how ruthless the personality overlay of the bloodline could be in reacting to a threat. She thought that danger would end when the Gate was closed, cutting Sinah off from its power and from those archived memories. It was an unsettling experience for anyone when the Unseen came looking for them, and for a Gatekeeper, heir to enormous power yet raised without an inkling of its existence . . .

"Relax, Sinah," Truth soothed. "Nobody's asking you to do anything tonight, and I'm sure we can deal with anything that might turn up tomorrow. Do you think you can sleep now? Or shall I turn my skills to beating you at poker?"

Again the on-off flicker of a smile from Sinah. "Wycherly—" she stopped and grimaced. "Wycherly was giving me his sleeping pills—Seconal—he had a prescription for them."

"Borrowing prescriptions isn't a good idea," Truth said automatically. But the barbiturate would interrupt Sinah's Stage Three sleep—the dreaming stage—which should protect her from nightmares—or worse. "Is the prescription still here?" she asked reluctantly.

Sinah went into the kitchen to see. Truth knew that some of the younger woman's oddly docile behavior came from shock—Truth had hit her with a lot over the last twenty-four hours, and she'd been under a tremendous strain for a long time before that. It was no wonder that when someone with a decisive personality crossed her path—and Truth felt that decisive was a reasonable description of someone who had also been called "meddling," "bossy," and "managing"—Sinah was willing to obey her in an almost childlike fashion.

"Here they are." Sinah came back from the bathroom carrying a brown-and-white bottle. "They were in his shaving kit. He just left everything."

"Did he take your Jeep?" Truth asked, and Sinah nodded reluctantly.

"The day you first came up here. Later that night."

"Have you seen him since then?" Truth asked. "I went by his cabin tonight on my way back to town, but it didn't look as if he'd been back there."

Sinah shook her head. "He . . . he'll be back when he gets ready," she said, her voice shaking with the effort it took for the words to seem casual. Truth didn't have the heart to press her further.

Seconal was a pretty strong narcotic, but one night's use—or two, or three—shouldn't kill or addict Sinah, and if a pill could make the difference between dreamless sleep and a night spent tormented by jangled nerves . . .

"Why don't you go ahead and take one?" Truth suggested. "Whether you get much rest or not, it'll put you out for eight hours."

"That's what Wycherly said," Sinah said, sounding more adult now. She took the bottle into the kitchen to get a glass of water.

Truth watched her go, wondering if it was Sinah she'd been talking to, or . . . something else. Truth only had experience of the negative aspects of the Gates, but somewhere in the tangled web of Sinah's inherited memories must be the remembrance of a time when the Gate's guardian wielded its power consciously, for hele and ill. The Gates were supposed to control the Earth's fruitfulness—And if Sinah could control such power, what else could she do?

Truth thought back to the sterile, blighted area surrounding the burned sanatorium and felt a vague disquiet. Despite what Thorne had once believed, the worlds of gods and men were *not* meant to be merged, and average people could get into enough trouble here in the World of Form without adding in divine or supernatural abilities.

"Well, goodnight," Sinah said, coming back from the kitchen. "I'll go on up to bed now. Are you sure you have everything you need? The loveseats both fold out—there are sheets in the linen closet—or you could just bunk in with me. It's a California King, so heaven knows there's room enough, and I plan to be dead to the world."

She heard what she'd said, and winced. "Unfortunate choice. Let's say, 'sleeping soundly,' okay?"

"Goodnight, Sinah. I'm sure I'll be fine," Truth said.

And no matter how primitive the accommodations, they'd be better than lying beside Dylan in the camper, feigning sleep and wondering if he were doing the same thing.

Perhaps it was the stresses of the day or just being in an unfamiliar place, but Truth didn't feel the least inclination to sleep. She read—Sinah had a jackdaw-eclectic collection of books, including Truth's biography of Thorne Blackburn—and eventually she admitted that she didn't intend to go to bed at all.

What am I waiting for? she asked herself.

She was hardly expecting another magickal assault—the effects of the tainted Gate seemed to be place-bound, and she'd had little indication that Quentin Blackburn was likely to seek them out. But just in case, Truth went around the house once more, blessing and sealing the place at every door and window with the star-in-circle that the followers of her tradition saw as a symbol of Man in the midst of the natural world. When she was done she looked in on Sinah, who was sleeping peacefully. The younger woman had fallen asleep with the bedside light on, an open book in her hand. Smiling to herself, Truth turned out the light and closed the book.

But snug below again with a cup of coffee and a book, Truth had to admit that she felt no more settled than before, even though she was absolutely certain that no malignant forces could enter here.

But just because she and Sinah were safe, did that mean she could say the same for the other residents of Morton's Fork? Today was the 11th of August—the 12th, rather, since it was after midnight—and August 14th was the peak date for the disappearances in Morton's Fork.

Truth wasn't sure what had happened to Luned Starking—though she suspected that Sinah was right, and the girl had gone to the Gate—but she did know that Morton's Fork was the sort of place from which people tended to . . . disappear—through the Gate, or otherwise.

And there's nothing you can do about it, Truth told herself firmly. The Wildwood Gate was not hers to control, and she could hardly mount a one-woman foot patrol of the area to discourage trespassers.

But on sober reflection, there was one thing she *could* do.

Listening very carefully for sounds that would mean Sinah was awakening, Truth opened the front door and stepped outside. The heat and humidity of the August night made it feel as if she were stepping into veils of wet silk. Truth's blouse and slacks immediately wilted and began to cling.

The air was electric—there would certainly be a storm here within a day or so, a week at the most.

Why not now? Weather was the first magick, easiest to control: fire and storm, wind and wave, the deep heartbeat of the dreaming earth. . . .

She felt the power begin to gather in a tingle at the base of her skull, in the location of the oldest part of the brain. It spread, sketching the pathways of the nerves, until Truth had become a vast creature of light and energy, a creature so ethereal that the very air was solid enough to touch. With wings of energy borrowed from the veils of Earth Herself Truth reached out, touched high-riding clouds, created voids in the sky to harry them on. . . .

Soon the waxing moon was hidden by clouds, and the wind was rising.

That should take care of that, Truth thought to herself half an hour later, as she listened to the rain drum steadily upon the roof of Sinah's house. Anyone answering the lure of the Wildwood Gate would be much less likely to venture out on a night like this than on a clear one. The Gate's medium was suggestion: if it truly had the power to yank its sacrificial choices from their miles-distant beds and drag them into its presence, Truth had not seen any evidence of it. And though the human mind was remarkably suggestible, it was likely to think a soaking rain a good solid reason for staying home.

Truth, curled up with her book, did not even think to wonder about how easy, how obvious, that solution had been, nor how uncanny she would once have thought it to summon storms with a wave of her hand.

FIFTEEN

THE GAP IS THE GRAVE

And my large kingdom for a little grave,
A little little grave, an obscure grave;
—WILLIAM SHAKESPEARE

I GUESS I MANAGED TO SLEEP A LITTLE AFTER ALL.

Truth uncoiled herself from her cramped position on the loveseat. From the light shining in through the fanlight over the door, it was around five in the morning—maybe even earlier.

Truth got to her feet, doing shoulder-rolls to work out the last of the stiffness. Still not sure what had awakened her, she went upstairs to look in on Sinah. She found the younger woman sound asleep lying in a position that suggested she'd fallen from an airplane. The blankets were on the floor.

Truth smiled as she covered her up again. No, Sinah's sleep remained undisturbed. So what could it have been?

Still wondering, she walked to the octagonal clear-glass window at the eastern end of the loft and looked out.

After the storm of the night before, the sky above was colorless and clear. The second floor of the building was roughly at treetop level; she could see the entryway of the house below, its brick courtyard empty. Mist from the river formed a solid bank of white in the distance, and mist hung in the air, blending and softening the shapes and colors. Truth pushed open the window, wanting a breath of the coolness that would so quickly be gone in the fullness of the day. She leaned her head out and took a deep breath. Everything seemed remade, just for this moment.

She heard the sound of an automobile engine.

Wycherly, coming back? It didn't sound like the Jeep Cherokee's engine, but she couldn't be sure. Quickly closing the window, Truth hurried downstairs.

She opened the front door and stepped outside. For a moment she thought the sound was gone, but then she heard it again. It didn't sound like the powerful engine of a four-wheel-drive vehicle, but whatever it was it had to be using Watchman's Gap Trace—there was no other road near enough to hear. The sound faded into the distance again, moving on. Whoever was using Watchman's Gap Trace, the old schoolhouse was not their destination.

Suddenly an unwelcome suspicion took possession of her. She didn't want to think it, but somehow it seemed so likely.

And it won't hurt you to check, Truth told herself, as she ducked back inside to leave a note for Sinah.

"Are we there yet?" Rowan Moorcock asked. Despite her question, the redheaded psychic strode up the overgrown drive of the sanatorium ahead of the two men, unimpeded by the weight of her heavy backpack.

"What do you expect to find, Dr. Palmer?" Ninian Blake asked. Though it was still relatively cool, his long black hair was held back with a rolled bandanna tied around his head, and his face was beaded with sweat. He wore a backpack as heavy as Rowan's, but despite his obvious discomfort, he made no complaints.

"I'm not completely sure, Nin," Dylan replied. "When I was up there yesterday with Truth, I got a very strong sense that there was *something* there—and there's definitely a stone altar that's been the focus of some sort of cult activity. I want to take a look and see what else we might have missed, get pictures of what's there, that sort of thing."

"Which cult?" Ninian asked, smiling faintly at his own might-be pun.

"Something not all that common," Dylan said, "but let's see what the evidence suggests. I'll save the lecture until we get up there—and down."

* * *

Warned by his previous experience, Dylan led them north, on a more-or-less direct route to the black staircase that led down into the depths of the ruins.

"Whoa," Rowan said, looking down.

It was a little after six in the morning, and the day's air of peace and serenity gave the lie to the experiences Dylan had borne witness to yesterday morning. But he knew better than to trust any subjective impression in dealing with a haunting or potential haunting.

That was what worried him about Truth.

For a woman who had spent most of her adult life emotionally isolated—and Dylan had known her ever since she'd first come to Taghkanic as a lonely and defensive young graduate fiercely determined to quantify the Unseen World and reduce its phenomena to columns of numbers in a printout—Truth was much too quick to trust now that she'd reached an accommodation with her past and her magus-father's legacy. She believed in the presence of a Blackburn Gate—in Quentin Blackburn's continued presence—and in her mission to seal the Gate, no matter the cost.

It never occurred to her that the site might be haunted by something else entirely—something that played on her deepest desires and hopes and fears, twisting them to its ends.

Dylan sighed. He didn't want to see her hurt—physically, mentally, or professionally. There'd been a certain amount of talk about her after she'd published *Venus Afflicted,* even though the book had been scrupulously accurate, containing only the verifiable facts about Thorne's life and none of the lurid speculation. But the fact that she'd chosen to write about a magician at all inevitably attracted to her some of the aura of the lunatic fringe that she'd spent her entire adult life lashing out against—and parapsychologists, like Caesar's wife, needed to be not only above reproach, but above suspicion.

Their field was littered with the histories of those who had crossed the line, believing their subjects instead of studying them objectively. His stubborn, reckless darling could end up among their number all too easily.

And worse, she could end up dead.

"The most dangerous place in all the world for an unprotected medium is a haunted house." Professor MacLaren's oft-repeated aphorism echoed in Dy-

lan's ears. Despite Truth's insistence that her abilities came from training and not inbred psychic gifts, Dylan suspected that Truth possessed the same psychic gifts that her mother and her half-sister did. In which case—if Wildwood Sanatorium were a true haunting—Truth was the last person Dylan would want anywhere near it.

"It seems odd that the building would burn so thoroughly," Ninian said, breaking into Dylan's thoughts. "Wouldn't it have been built out of brick and stone and stuff? Where are they? And if it did burn, where's the wreckage? It would have fallen in."

Ninian was still breathing quickly, and he'd taken the opportunity of the halt to slide the backpack containing the recording equipment from his shoulders and lower it gently to the ground.

"For that matter," he added, sounding indignant, "where's the water? It rained katzenjammers last night; you'd expect a hole in the ground to be full of water."

"It looks like a bomb site," Rowan said. "Like something at the bottom blew up and disintegrated everything else. Brrr." She hugged herself and shivered. "Cold up here."

Dylan glanced at her sharply. He didn't feel any chill, and Rowan's constitution was normally as robust as an ox's. But Rowan Moorcock was also an experienced psychic—Dylan had used her mediumistic abilities on more than one of his ghost-hunting expeditions.

"Anything?" he asked quickly.

"No . . ." she said doubtfully, and then shook her head. "Nothing."

"Ninian? Any twinges?" Dylan asked then. After criticizing Truth so thoroughly for leaping headlong into psychic danger, he wasn't about to drag his young students into an identical mess.

"You know me, Dr. Palmer; deaf as a post," Ninian said with a slight smile.

While that wasn't entirely true—Ninian scored particularly well on tests for psychometry and precognition—it was true that his abilities were far less dependable than Rowan's. Since Ninian was that rarity—an adult, healthy, sane, male psychic—neither he nor Dylan complained too much about the comparative weakness of his gift.

"Okay. Let's go down, then. Mind the cameras—they cost more than you do," Dylan said.

"Not since my last tuition bill," Rowan mourned, leading the way.

* * *

Truth watched the three figures disappear over the edge of the ruins from the concealment of a stand of trees just south of the site. She'd come here overland from Sinah's cabin, unable to lose her way now that she was keyed—however roughly—to the local Gate.

So Dylan was stealing a march on her—throwing a little party here to which she was not invited? Truth smiled mockingly. She could not quite suppress the unworthy thought that it would be nice if something he couldn't handle came and smacked him down—that would teach him to dismiss her warnings out of hand like the ravings of a spoiled child!

A moment later she sternly rebuked herself for even thinking such things. Hand anyone over to the evil of the grey place from which she'd rescued Sinah? Never!

Truth frowned. Neither the Gate nor Quentin Blackburn seemed to have any Material Plane power that did not stem from indirect sugges-tion—and Dylan was always going on and on and *on* about the precau-tions he took when investigating a haunted house. The place was dangerous, but Dylan was a professional trained to investigate such things. He shouldn't be in any danger.

But she'd still feel better if she stayed around and kept an eye on mat-ters, not that Dylan would thank her for it. Cautiously Truth stepped from behind the tree and started up the rise to the ruin.

It took the three researchers about half an hour to make it all the way down to the sub-basement and unpack their equipment.

The temple area was reasonably large—although there was no real way of telling what size it might actually have appeared to be when it was fully paneled and furnished. Though the floor was covered with pow-dery leaves from seasons past, so many other things that ought to have been here were not—melted ritual implements, for example. Of course, they could have been looted sometime in the last eighty years, yet every-one the three of them had spoken to in their weeks in Morton's Fork had said that the sanatorium was a shunned place, a place that none of the na-tives would go near.

Whether or not anyone had stolen from the burnt ruins, all that re-mained were the steps leading down into the sub-basement and some sort of opening in the east wall—a tunnel or an alcove. The opening was the sort of thing that you'd expect anyone to investigate, but yesterday neither Truth nor Sinah had given it a second glance, as though they couldn't see it.

Or as if they already knew what was there.

"Nin, have you got one of the high-powered lamps out yet? I want to take a look at something," Dylan said.

"Steps," Rowan said comprehensively.

"Old steps," Ninian added. "At least we know where the water goes now. The floor must be slanted."

Dylan's lamp shone on a rough-hewn rock wall. Beneath his feet were steps—smooth and shallow and worn, with treads of irregular depth, but obviously man-made. The opening exhaled dampness even in this humid air: the scent of wet rock and fresh water.

"Can you see the bottom?" Rowan said, arching over Dylan's shoulder and trying to get a better view.

"No," Dylan said. "The staircase curves around at an acute angle. Let me see if I can—"

He took a step forward, off the temple floor, and immediately felt a flash of warning strike through him. If the lamp should fail, if there was something down there . . .

"Let's leave this for last," Dylan said, taking a step back and switching off the lamp.

Both Rowan and Ninian had worked with Dylan before, and fell into their routines with the familiarity of previous experience. The first priority was to document the ritual purpose of the site: Ninian held the light while Dylan photographed the altar from various angles and Rowan did reference sketches showing the layout of the entire area.

"Whoa, an actual Satanic ritual altar," she joked.

"Not really," Dylan said, gently correcting her. "Satanism is a Christian blasphemy—The Church of the Antique Rite claims to be pre-Christian in its basis and aims."

"The Church of the Antique Rite?" Ninian said. "What would *that* be doing this far west and in somebody's basement? Didn't they insist on meeting in blasted churches anyway?"

"And if they did, what would a non-Christian sect be doing meeting on Christian holy ground anyway?" Rowan added. "It doesn't make any sense!"

"Ah, that would be the Templar influence . . ." Dylan said, falling easily into lecture mode.

As he continued going over the walls and floor carefully for any signs that might be left from The Church of the Antique Rite's visitation, and photographing some areas for later study, Dylan briefly outlined the history of the cult much as he had to Truth, reminding both of the young parapsychologists that many of the spontaneous phenomena associated with hauntings and visitations could be produced both by conscious intent—as with the group of researchers in Toronto who had created their own ghost entirely out of whole cloth—and by an extended period of religious worship.

"—but unfortunately any researcher who asks to set up his cameras in Canterbury Cathedral during the Mass is going to be thrown out on his ear," Dylan finished dolefully. "It's unfortunate that religion is the one area in modern life that's still 'hands off' to science."

Dylan was so occupied by the demanding work of searching the walls for marks and inscriptions that he did not realize what was happening to Rowan until she tossed her sketchbook aside and stood up.

"Got a . . . headache," she mumbled, fumbling in her pocket.

"Ro!"

Dylan was startled by the urgency in Ninian's voice—not the younger man's style at all—until he glanced down at Rowan's cast-off sketchbook. The tangled pages were not covered with sketches, but with symbols—elaborate symbols that Dylan recognized, but Rowan shouldn't know.

Ninian dropped the battery lamp and grabbed her hand. Her fingers flew open, and a small glittering object hit the stone floor with a click.

Rowan's eyes flew open wide. "What the *hell* are you doing?" she cried in a normal voice. "I was reaching for a pill!"

She pulled out the bright plastic box of Excedrin and brandished it at Ninian like an excuse. But the thing that had been in her hand hadn't been the small box of painkillers.

Ninian picked up the penknife and handed it back to her. "Sorry I startled you," he said, his tone saying clearly that he felt he'd overreacted.

"Moron," Rowan muttered. "And you broke the battery lamp, too, I bet, dropping it like that."

"It's all right," Dylan said absently, "I'm finished with the walls, more or less." He picked up her sketchbook and flipped through it, holding it so she could not see the pages. "Rowan, what were you doing just now?"

"Copying the engravings along the bottom of the altar," she answered promptly. "You know, sometimes they just don't show up on film, and . . . Jesus," she said, as Dylan turned the open sketchbook toward her. "I didn't do *those.*"

"Yes, you did," Dylan said. "You'd better go back up to the car and wait for us there. Nin and I can finish up."

"But I'm okay now, really," Rowan said. "It was just—"

"Go back to the car *now.*" His frustration—and his desire to say much the same thing to Truth, who wasn't even here—made him speak more harshly than he might have otherwise. Rowan shrugged weakly and began to make her way back up the steps.

"Everything all right down there?" Truth asked.

The basement was almost fifty feet below the surface; Truth was a tiny figure as she stood perilously close to the edge and looked down. She was still wearing the same clothes she'd been in last night at the restaurant, and Dylan wondered if she'd walked all the way up here in loafers.

"Dylan?" Truth asked. "Rowan?"

"Just your average sort of psychic attack," Rowan called back gamely as she started up the steps. Truth waited until Rowan reached her, and helped the young psychic up the last few steps before starting down herself.

"Anything I can do?" she called from the landing. She neither apologized for her presence nor volunteered an explanation.

"Yes," Dylan finally said. "Come and take notes—we're going to measure temperature variation now."

The morning sun—the basements were still in shadow, but in a few hours that would change—and the warm outdoor air made any really conclusive evidence of cold spots or fluctuation impossible to obtain, but Dylan wanted a baseline series, and the complex ambient thermometer was at least a little more portable than some of their other equipment.

The smaller of the two seismographs sat on the altar stone, its needle lying flat against the stop. The larger one would give them more information, but it would be a matter of great difficulty to get it down into the temple area, and some of the motion sensors and infrared cameras probably couldn't be brought up to the sanatorium at all.

Despite their recent conflicts, Truth and Dylan worked closely together now, with Truth taking written notes to supplement Dylan's dictaphone report, since all forms of recording equipment were likely to spontaneously malfunction at the site of a psychic locus.

Dylan watched her closely at first—he knew she was sensitive to the sanatorium's emanations, and he wasn't really sure she'd told him everything about her experiences here. But as far as he knew, all of Truth's interactions with the locus had been deliberate, and she'd be on her guard now.

And what about Rowan? Had he been over-hasty in sending her back to the car? She might simply have pulled the penknife out of her pocket to make it easier to find the aspirin. But when he thought of her sketchbook Dylan shuddered inwardly. No, Rowan had definitely been under some sort of influence from whatever inhabited this place. They'd better all be on their guard—even him.

Ninian had been using a tape measure and a level, determining the exact dimensions of the room and searching out any concealed gradients. Now he leaned back against the Black Altar, rubbing his eyes.

"Nin?" Dylan said.

"I'm . . . okay," Ninian said. "It's just . . . I feel so cold."

Dylan glanced at Truth, and a moment of perfect sympathy and agreement passed between them. "Time to go," Truth said, smiling faintly. She began bundling Dylan's equipment—including the ruined lamp—back into the knapsacks.

"Come on, Ninian," Dylan said, clapping the younger man on the back. "Time to go. Can you manage one of the packs?"

"Sure," Ninian said. "I just . . . this place gives me the creeps."

Dylan glanced at Truth.

"Not me," she said. "Nothing that should constitute a danger, anyway. But I'm not psychic, I'll remind you, and Ninian is. Besides, I'm shielded. Here's your hat, what's your hurry, as the saying goes," she added, passing the packed knapsack to Ninian.

Shrugging it onto one shoulder, Ninian started up the steps. Dylan turned back to Truth.

"You don't feel anything . . . special about this place?" he asked, part of him morbidly curious to see what she said.

Truth had been about to reach for the portable seismograph; she turned back to him, and Dylan could sense her weighing how frank to be with him. How could they have drifted this far apart? Once he would have said he was her closest confidant in the world.

"No," Truth finally said. "The Gate is here, of course; I can feel that. But I'm not all that likely to notice anything else, unless I'm on the Astral and the source is, too; that's the difference between a magician and a psychic. I'd offer to look around for you, but after the way this place took down both your psychics, I'd say you don't need any more evidence that there's something here." She turned back to the seismograph.

As neat an evasion as I've heard lately, Dylan thought unhappily, carefully fitting the plumber's level into his rucksack and swinging it onto his back. Truth backed up to the backpack balanced on the altar and stooped to bring her arms level with the shoulder straps, shrugging them into position and then standing to take the weight.

"Let's go, then, and . . . thanks for stopping by. I guess you may be right about giving this place a good solid banishing," Dylan said reluctantly.

Truth smiled slightly; it encouraged him to continue.

"Oh, and by the way, do you happen to know where that fissure over there goes?" Dylan asked casually. "It's too bad there's no way of telling whether it was a part of the ritual space that was used when The Church of the Antique Rite was down here."

Now Truth stared at him as if he'd lost his mind.

"The Gate itself is down there. Sinah's Wellspring. If you go down there, you'll die. Would you like to test *that* theory, Dylan?"

The climb back to the surface passed in silence. Truth was surprised to see that it was still morning. She glanced at her watch. It was almost nine A.M. on a bright, beautiful August morning, but when she'd been down there in that sub-basement, it could have been any hour, or none. The sooner they shut the place down—Gate and blasphemous Church both—Truth told herself, the better.

Dylan climbed up past her and headed for the drive, his face closed. They reached the car without incident; Rowan and Ninian were both standing beside it, their expressions saying plainly that they could not understand why they'd been sent away from where the action was.

But they went, which is more than I've ever done, Truth acknowledged ruefully.

Aloud she said: "Could you drop me back at Sinah's place, Dylan? I really need to get back there." *Maybe she'll still be asleep.*

"Okay," Dylan said, "but don't you think you might be carrying this protection thing a little too far? I mean—"

The guilt she felt at leaving Sinah as she slept made Truth speak more sharply than she'd intended.

"You can still say that, after *this?* I promised to protect her, Dylan."

She watched his expression relapse into stubborn unhappiness—so much for their fragile truce!—and when Dylan turned away toward the car, Truth couldn't think of anything to say. It was true that there was probably little real danger to Sinah just now—but she'd given her word. Why was Dylan deliberately provoking her?

Unless he felt as trapped as she did.

A short time later the car pulled up in front of Sinah's house.

"See you folks later?" Truth said hopefully.

"Maybe," Dylan said. "It depends."

But he didn't tell her what it depended on, and she stood on the steps forlornly watching the car drive away. When it was out of sight, she went inside.

She closed the door and stood very still, listening. All quiet. She went upstairs. Sinah was just beginning to stir, and Truth pounced on her own written note and crumpled it.

"Good morning," Sinah said sleepily, then: "You're already dressed."

"I never got undressed," Truth said. "How did you sleep?"

"I don't remember," Sinah said, but her eyes didn't meet Truth's. "Well, what shall we do today?" She stretched.

Oh, I don't know . . . go back up to the Gate so you can push me in? Truth warned herself that she must never forget that Sinah could be as much of a danger to her as anything else in Morton's Fork. At any moment she might decide, with the simple necessity that had ruled the Dellon women for generations, that Truth was a threat . . . or a suitable sacrifice.

And just try explaining *that* to Dylan! Truth sighed. She was going to have to try to do a lot of explaining to Dylan . . . and soon.

Explain why I can't marry him. Explain why love isn't enough. Explain that I have . . . things to do with my life that he doesn't want to even be a part of. Explain that I don't want him to meet me halfway—I want his complete surrender.

"It's up to you," Truth said. "Michael should be here tomorrow to sweep Quentin Blackburn out of our lives, and then you and I can take on the Gate again."

"Tomorrow's the fourteenth," Sinah said, and shivered. "It's my birthday."

"Then we ought to celebrate it," Truth said firmly. "Tell you what:

why don't you get dressed, and we can go down to the general store and pick up my car. Maybe Dylan will give us breakfast." *Maybe Hell will freeze solid.*

"Are you sure?" Sinah said hesitantly. "I don't want to—"

"Dylan's a nice guy." *To everyone but me.* "I'm sure he'd love to see you. You can't spend the rest of your life barricaded in here—luxurious as it is."

"All right." Sinah tried a smile, and then swung her legs over the edge of the bed. "And I can extend a rather belated invitation for all of you to make full use of the facilities here. I lived in a camper like that once—the water pressure is *not* what I would call four-star!"

She couldn't go on working at the Institute. Truth dawdled over a morning cup of coffee in Sinah's dining room, listening to the sound of her hostess in the shower. The discovery was a bitter one, and Truth resented it. For one thing, how would she earn her living if she quit her job?

It was true that Thorne Blackburn had left a sizeable estate—and it had increased through the years, with the royalties from his books—but his fortune was mired in litigation. And it might never benefit her anyway—Truth's parents had not been married, and it might be devilishly hard to prove what everyone knew—that she was Thorne Blackburn's daughter.

But her future course was clear, and after this morning with Dylan, Truth knew she could no longer put off making her decision explicit. Since the day she had discovered her heritage, Truth had been pulled in this direction, and she didn't see how she could combine a life of freelance occult do-gooding with her work at the Institute. Being a do-gooder took too much time, for one thing, and the hours were terribly irregular.

But if it's what I need to be doing, I'll find some way of managing it, Truth assured herself. At least she wouldn't need to relocate; as Dylan had told her many times, she could find trouble wherever she went.

Dylan. Telling him that she'd decided to quit her job and join the Occult Police would probably be the last straw.

As Truth and Sinah reached the place where the dirt road turned to blacktop, they could see two sheriff's cars and a large van with official markings drawn up near the general store. In front of the building she could see Caleb and Evan Starking talking to a man in a broad-brimmed hat.

"What's going on?" Sinah asked, coming to a stop. She looked as if she might bolt at any moment.

"The sheriff's department must be coming out with dogs to see if they can find Luned Starking," Truth said.

Still Sinah hung back. "Come on," Truth said with a touch of impatience. "There's nothing to be afraid of."

"I don't . . ." Sinah began. "I thought I could handle it, but it's been such a long time since I've met a bunch of people all at once like this, that I—"

Of course. She's a telepath. In the onrush of events and the press of her own problems, Truth had nearly forgotten that Sinah had this particular ability.

"We could go back," Truth suggested, but Dylan had already risen from the table set up in front of the camper and begun walking toward them.

"How nice to see you again, Ms. Dellon. Can I introduce you to my young colleagues? I know they'll be delighted to have the opportunity to meet an actual movie star," Dylan Palmer said.

"Rowan Moorcock, Ninian Blake." Each stood as Dylan made the introductions: a tall, strapping-looking young woman with long cinnamon hair; a slender brunet of the sort her foster mother would have categorized as "interesting." They must be the other ghost-hunters that Truth had mentioned.

Ninian extended a hand. Because it was the expected thing, Sinah grasped it, bracing herself. But there was no way to prepare herself for what occurred. She recoiled, jerking her hand free from Ninian's clasp.

She was blind. No, not blind exactly—she could still see colors, movements, shapes. But her gift, her ability to hear what others did not say, had vanished at last. She could no longer feel the press of others' emotions—even if she touched them.

She looked at the others, bewildered. She'd met Dylan only briefly when she could still sense emotions, and the other two she'd never met before at all. She had no idea of what they were thinking, or what they might be like inside. At last she was alone in her mind, alone with only the voices of ancestral ghosts and the consciousness of the Sacred Water Place like the light of a sullen invisible sun.

"Sinah?" Truth said.

"Just a twinge," Sinah muttered. "Pleased to meet you, Ninian." She took his hand again and squeezed it firmly.

The young man smiled uncertainly and sat back down in his chair. Dylan held his own chair for Sinah, who slid gratefully into it, before going to find seats for Truth and himself.

A lifetime's habit of concealing her difference from other people made Sinah conceal her normalcy now. What could she say? That she could no longer eavesdrop on people and use what she knew to manipulate them like puppets? A fat lot of sympathy *that* would get her!

But there are other ways to spellbind a man. Older, surer, and more secret. . . . The internal voice was as compelling, as insistent, as any external voice had ever been. Sinah tried to shut it out, praying that it would not simply rise up and engulf her.

"Some coffee, Ms. Dellon?" Dylan said.

"Please," Sinah said. "Call me Sinah. And is there any possibility of tea?" she asked, noticing the tag hanging out of Rowan's cup. "I hate to be a snob, but . . ."

"Tea's better for you anyway," Rowan said promptly. "I'll make it." She bounced to her feet and ran into the camper, letting the screen door slam behind her.

"How is Rowan feeling?" Truth asked Dylan in formal tones.

"No lingering effects; not even a headache," Dylan said. "But it's just proof that haunted houses aren't something to be taken lightly."

"Or haunted un-houses," Truth added, more to herself than to him. She wondered how she could make the time to talk to Dylan privately. Sinah looked as if she'd seen a ghost; Truth wondered what had happened.

"Something wrong?" Sinah asked.

"She had a bad spell this morning," Ninian said, grinning faintly at his own pun. He saw Sinah's look of puzzlement and amplified. "We were up at the Wildwood, and, well." He shrugged. "I shouldn't make fun of her. Ro's a medium, and that place is enough to give The Amazing Randi the whim-whams."

"You were up there?" Sinah said. "At the sanatorium?" Inside her she felt the rest of the bloodline rally together, searching frantically for a way to drive out these interlopers, these *outsiders*. "You shouldn't go up there. It's dangerous." Her voice roughened.

"We're taking every precaution," Dylan said soothingly. "And Truth has even taken some extra ones on our behalf. I hate to break this to you folks," Dylan said, raising his voice slightly to include Rowan, who was stepping carefully down out of the camper with a mug in one hand and a pastry box in the other, "but the site probably won't be available after tomorrow."

Well. I guess Dylan thinks the best defense is a good offense.

"Urban renewal?" Rowan wondered aloud, setting the mug down in front of Sinah. "Milk or sugar? We've got both; I just couldn't carry them all at once."

"Plain is fine," Sinah said, taking the cup.

"I called a friend of mine to come and banish the . . . residue . . . of The Church of the Antique Rite," Truth said evenly. "So if that's what you're studying, with luck it'll be gone by tomorrow afternoon."

Rowan looked from Truth to Dylan, her jaw hanging slightly open in shock. It didn't take a telepath to pick up on the young woman's sense of frustrated indignation. "But . . . you just *called* some *faith healer?*" Rowan sputtered.

"No," Truth said. "Michael is . . . the sort of person who can deal with places like that. You've all been up there. There's very little doubt that The Church of the Antique Rite was meeting in the sub-basement of Quentin Blackburn's sanatorium. It's a nasty little cult, and nasty little cults leave psychic residue. I wouldn't be any more comfortable leaving that lying there than I would be leaving around an unexploded bomb. And neither should you be."

Sinah glanced from face to face. Rowan still looked indignant, but subsided when Dylan did not protest. Dylan looked thoughtful.

"Probably the best thing," Ninian said soberly. "We never did get any documented history on the sanatorium itself for the database—not even a ghost."

"Oh, pooh, Nin, where's your sense of adventure?" Rowan teased. "I think we should have turned it inside out ourselves. If you don't bet, you can't win."

Ninian just snorted. Truth envied Rowan her lighthearted sense of adventure—whatever paranormal events Rowan Moorcock had been witness to in her life, they had not dimmed her inexhaustible appetite to experience more. Perhaps she simply didn't know how high the stakes could get.

"Pardon me," a new voice said. "Is one of you folks a Doctor Palmer, from Taha—Tagga—well, from some university in New York?" the man finished with a grin.

It was one of the sheriff's deputies.

"Taghkanic, actually," Dylan said, getting to his feet. "It pronounces easier than it looks. I'm Dylan Palmer, this is Rowan Moorcock, Ninian Blake, Truth Jourdemayne, Sinah Dellon. What can I do for you, officer?"

"I'm Sergeant Wachman of the Lyonesse County S.D. Caleb over to the general store said you folks were . . . hunting ghosts?"

Sergeant Wachman's accent was broad and flat, with vowels that had changed little in the last four hundred years. He was a tall man with the fair coloring so common in these hills. The broad brim of his navy-felt sheriff's hat cast his eyes into shadow, but Truth could feel him watching Sinah.

"Well, Morton's Fork is supposed to host the largest number of paranormal occurrences in the local area," Dylan said. "We're parapsychologists from the Margaret Beresford Bidney Memorial Psychic Science Research Laboratory, which is affiliated with Taghkanic College in New York. We've been here for almost three weeks now. I met Luned Starking a couple of times when I was in the store. Do you think you'll find her?" Dylan asked.

"Well, it's going to take divine intervention, after the rain we had the other day," Sergeant Wachman said. His eyes were still on Sinah. "You said *Psychic* Science?" he added. "You mean, tarot cards and things like that? Like they have on the television?"

"More or less, Sergeant. Would you like a cup of coffee? It's fresh." Dylan's easy smile didn't waver, but Truth could sense the tension in him, left over from their own fight, that might easily spill over into this new outlet. And like it or not, Lyonesse County certainly qualified as the backwoods, and for many people, there was little distinction to be drawn between "psychic" and "Satanist."

"I wouldn't turn it down," Wachman said. He scratched his head, pushing his hat to the back of his head. His skin was fair, red, and freckled, giving him the bland, stolid, bovine look.

"My turn," Ninian said. He got up and headed for the camper. At Dylan's gestured invitation, Sergeant Wachman took Ninian's seat.

"Dellon . . ." he said. "You any kin to old Miss Rahab Dellon who used to live up in the hills here with her daughter?"

Sinah flashed a look of mingled panic and shock at Truth. "I'm her granddaughter," Sinah said. "At least, that's what my birth certificate said."

"Why, sure you are." Wachman's face held nothing but an expression of pleasure. "My daddy used to talk about you; you're the little foundling baby he drove on down to the hospital in Elkins about thirty year gone this month." Abruptly realizing what he'd said, he stopped, flushing pinkly. "I mean to say—I'm sorry, ma'am, I didn't mean to go telling your age out of turn."

Sinah smiled. "I don't mind at all, Sergeant, especially since you're the first person who's looked pleased to see me since I got here."

Now Sergeant Wachman looked embarrassed. "Well, folks down here in the Fork take some time to warm up to strangers. Not that you're quite a stranger, Miss Dellon."

Ninian came back with paper cups, sugar, and the carton of milk all awkwardly tucked under one arm while he carried the half-full coffeepot in his free hand. Though he moved with the dramatic awkwardness of a young heron, Truth had never actually seen Ninian drop anything.

"Sorry we're out of real cups," he said, setting his burden down on the table. "But there's plenty of coffee."

Rowan pushed the pastry carton toward him. "And plenty of calories."

"Just what I don't need," Wachman said with a wistful sigh. "The wife's always after me to take off a few pounds. . . ." Despite which, he helped himself to a slab of crumb cake from the bakery in Pharaoh.

"Ambrose, we're ready to go with the dogs. Got some of the girl's clothes for a good scent trace. You want us to start up at the old Dellon place?" The speaker—another uniformed deputy—was whip-thin and intense, but despite that, he bore a strong family resemblance to Ambrose Wachman.

"That'll be a good start. Remember, your radio isn't going to work worth diddly around here, so you be sure to bring it on back here around noon and let me know what you're up to, Davey-boy."

The younger deputy saluted and went back to the others. In a moment, two green and white Lyonesse County four-wheel-drive vehicles rolled slowly past the Winnebago, and disappeared up Watchman's Gap Trace Road.

"You living at the Dellon place, Miss Dellon? It's pretty raw."

Sergeant Wachman sipped his coffee. A faint dusting of powdered sugar starred his tie and his short-sleeved navy shirt.

Ninian picked up his cup and went over to stand behind Dylan.

"No. I bought the old schoolhouse further up the road and renovated it before I moved in."

Sinah's voice—like her face—was small and pinched, and Truth wondered what thoughts were uppermost in the sergeant's mind. Did Wachman suspect *Sinah* of killing Luned? Was this all some long *Columbo*-style charade to get her to confess? Even if Truth didn't know what was going on in Wachman's mind, surely Sinah must. Was it that frightening?

"That's right. You did one hey of a lot up there; put in a phone and a septic system and all. You plannin' to move back here? Or you got other places to be?"

"I—yes—no—I don't know." Sinah jumped to her feet, knocking the rickety chair backwards as she rose. Covering her face with her hands, she ran for the only possible refuge—the Winnebago.

"Miss Dellon!" Sergeant Wachman also stood. "I didn't mean—"

"Maybe if you'd tell us what you needed, we could be of more help," Dylan Palmer said. His words were cordial, but his tone was not. "We'll be happy to be of assistance, but I think you'd better leave Sinah alone."

"It isn't a good idea to threaten an officer of the law in these parts, Sunny Jim," Wachman said. The placidity was gone; now his broad, fair face looked like that of an animal about to charge.

"It's just that all the recording equipment is in there," Rowan said, seemingly oblivious to the tension in the air, "And if any of it breaks, it comes out of Dylan's salary. Besides, Sinah's been through a lot lately, with nobody here but us willing to talk to her or anything." Rowan flashed Wachman her sunniest smile, obviously intent on using her femininity as a weapon.

And, thought Truth wryly, Rowan's tactics seemed to work just fine. Wachman relaxed, though he didn't resume his seat.

"So you use machines—not psychics?" He sounded oddly disappointed. "Isn't Miss Dellon working for you?"

"Maybe you'd better tell me why you're asking all these questions," Dylan said. "And what you came here for. I'm sure it wasn't to pass the time of day."

For heaven's sake, Dylan—lighten up! You're the one who always says how important it is to get along with the locals!

Though she wanted to run after Sinah and see if she was all right, Truth didn't dare move and disrupt the delicate balance of the scene. The last thing any of them needed was to spend tonight in jail.

"I came," Sergeant Wachman said heavily, "to see if one of you *parapsychologists* had enough witch blood in him to hoodoo me up some place to start on that Starking girl, 'cause this mountain's a big place, and she could lie where she is till she rots if we've got nothing to go on and a trail seventy-two hours cold." His face flushed red with embarrassment and anger.

There was a stunned silence from the other four. Whatever any of them had expected from a county sheriff in rural West Virginia, it hadn't been something like this.

"Well, for heaven's sake, Sergeant Wachman, you don't want Sinah for that," Rowan said matter-of-factly. "You want me." She looked pleased and relieved to have solved the problem so easily.

Truth was almost sure Rowan's obliviousness was an act, and a good one. But with Wachman's attention fixed firmly on Rowan, Truth was finally able to get up and slip away.

"Sinah, are you all right?"

Sinah whirled around with a gasp when she saw her.

"It's gone, Truth—it's all gone. I'm all alone!"

There was little that Truth could do for her—though Sinah had apparently never wanted her power, she was understandably upset now that it had vanished. At least Truth was able to reassure Sinah that Sergeant Wachman's interest in her was professional, nothing more.

"He just wants a psychic to help him look for Luned, that's all. I think Rowan's agreed to help him."

"A psychic?" Sinah said blankly. "Like on TV?"

"Everything all right in here?" Dylan asked, opening the door.

"Just nerves," Sinah said quickly. "He wants a psychic?" she repeated, so Dylan could hear.

"He's grasping at straws," Dylan said in a mild voice. "And it can hardly hurt for Rowan to try a little remote-location work for him with the map. If it works, fine. If it doesn't, he's no worse off than he is now."

"Many police departments will consult psychics as a last resort," Truth said for Sinah's benefit. "It's a pity that the psychics usually aren't that reliable."

"If the Institute gets its Central Registry program off the ground, that could change. It would be a place where people could not only find a referral to a professional psychic, but consult their track record as well," Dylan said, speaking to Sinah.

"Sort of a Ghostbusters Blue Book," Sinah said with a wan smile. "Well, I don't deserve a listing in it."

"But Rowan does." Dylan stepped inside and squeezed past them, opening one of the boxes full of odds and ends and rummaging through. "Truth, do you remember where we packed the test kit?"

The camper rocked again as Rowan climbed in. "Hi. Sergeant Wachman's gone to get a big topo map of the area for me to work off, so I thought I'd come get my music. I brought the Walkman in here—now where did I leave it?" Rowan began opening drawers and poking through them.

Had Rowan spent last night here? A stunning flash of jealousy flared through Truth. How dare she? Truth turned to go, but there was someone else now in the camper's narrow doorway.

"This looks like the stateroom from *A Night At The Opera,*" Ninian said. "But since everyone else is here, I thought I'd come in, too. That guy worries me."

"Oh, he's nice!" Rowan protested. "He's just a cop." She finally located the bright yellow Walkman and its headphones, and began untangling the cord. "And a cop's gotta do what a cop's gotta do."

Ninian made a grumbling sound but said nothing else, slithering past the others to sit down in the driver's seat.

"Now—where are the tapes? We crammed everything in here so fast last night when the storm hit—it was that or get washed away, and you should have seen the three of us here wondering if the Winnebago was going to be the next thing to go," Rowan rambled on obliviously.

Truth felt the tension in her chest ease, and smiled sourly. It was a more reasonable explanation than the one she'd come up with—even if Dylan did want to cheat on her, he'd hardly do it with one of his student advisees.

What was happening to her? Truth wondered worriedly. She wasn't acting—she was *reacting*—dancing like a puppet to some invisible pull on her strings.

But who was the puppeteer?

"Wups!—there he is! Gotta go," Rowan said, and bounced out the door again, both hands full.

"Rowan!" Dylan shouted, too late to catch her. "Dammit, I can't find the kit!"

"It's in here." Truth stooped and pulled out a built-in drawer under the couch in the back. "Remember? You put it there so you could find it easily." She dropped a small cardboard box into his hands.

"Oh. Right." Dylan had the grace to look sheepish. He opened the box. The pendulum—a lathe-turned, brass plumb-bob on a length of heavy fishing line with a ring at the end—was right on top. He scooped it up. "Thanks, Tru."

Truth smiled at the odd, light shortening of her name. When Dylan left the camper, Ninian followed him.

"Do you want to lie down for a while, Sinah?" Truth said. "You can use the couch here; it's no trouble."

"No," Sinah said, squaring her shoulders as if in defiance of her inner demons. "I'd like to watch. I've never seen a psychic work before."

"Now, this might not work," Rowan was saying in a didactic voice.

The small card table in front of the camper had been cleared, and the enormous topographical map that covered the local area was laid out.

"I *know* it won't work," growled Wachman.

"—because forensic psychometry is a specialized field, and since I don't know anything about police work, I could misinterpret what information I *do* get, or it could be too vague to do you any good. I might tell you to look by running water, for instance, and what good does something like that do you? But let's see what I get. Have you got a photo? Something she wears frequently?"

"This is the best we've got. It's a couple of years old."

Wachman was plainly impressed by Rowan's brisk matter-of-fact dismissal of her possible accuracy. He produced a picture; obviously a school photo. In it Luned stood, scrubbed and grave, wearing a yellow dress and staring fixedly into the camera. Rowan took the picture between her fingertips and laid it down on top of the map.

"Okay." She took a deep breath, and Truth realized that for all her breezy demeanor, Rowan was nervous.

"Got the pendulum? Oh, and somebody needs to mark the hits."

"I've got a pencil," Dylan said, dropping the pendulum into her hand. Rowan's fingers closed over it as if it were a lifeline—but only for a moment. She began shaking out the line. When she had it unkinked, she lay it top of the map and reached for her headphones. She slipped on her earphones and settled the Walkman in her lap. There was a pile of tapes on the corner of the table.

"What are you going to do?" Wachman asked, a little uneasily.

"I'm going to rock," Rowan said absently, and pushed the button on her tape player. Instantly the driving sound of guitars could be heard seeping around her earphones as the music took up in midphrase. Ninian—out of Rowan's sight-line—winced, and Truth sympathized. How could anyone bear to listen to that stuff when it was as loud as that?

Incredibly, Rowan turned it up even louder. Truth heard a howling that was probably the lead singer but sounded like the Wild Hunt in full flight. Despite the pounding rhythm, Rowan did not move to the music. Instead, she sat perfectly still, her left hand in her lap, and slipped the first finger of her right hand through the ring at the end of the pendulum's cord. She held her arm straight out above the map, so that the weight at the other end of the cord hung free directly over the center of the map.

"Rowan and I work together frequently," Dylan told Wachman. He spoke in a normal voice; there was no way Rowan could possibly hear him over the hammering of the music. "She uses music to shut down outside stimulus and trigger an altered state. Every psychic practitioner has his or her own method; I'm afraid that parapsychology isn't a very exact science as yet."

"And you think this is going to work," Wachman asked dubiously. Whatever he'd come to them expecting, this obviously wasn't it.

"That depends on what you mean by work," Dylan said smoothly. "Rowan is certainly going to enter a trance. She may or may not be able to pinpoint some search locations on the map for you. And whether what she finds turns out to be accurate or not is something I can't tell you in advance."

"Fair enough," Wachman said, mollified.

The pendulum began to move almost immediately, at first swinging back and forth, and then settling into a circling motion familiar to Truth.

"Hit it," Rowan said, when the pendulum stopped.

Dylan made an X on the map and stepped back again. The pendulum began circling again almost at once.

"And she isn't moving it?" The question this time came from Sinah. Dylan turned to her and smiled.

"Of course she's moving it, but at a preconscious level, in response to stimuli uncensored by her conscious mind. At its most basic, the trance state is the splitting of the conscious and unconscious minds so that a dialogue can be enacted between them. Rowan's clairvoyant—what that means in essence is that she's receiving information outside of normal perceptual channels. Most people do, to some extent—what else is a hunch, after all, but acting on information you didn't know you had?— but either the clairvoyant receives more information, or has better access; we're not quite sure which."

"You don't seem to know a heck of a lot, do you?" Wachman grumbled.

"Maybe not," Dylan said agreeably. "But at least we know we don't know it."

"Hit it," Rowan Moorcock said again.

"Well, according to my calculations, you found the general store, the Starking house, and the old Dellon cabin—all places she's been before, but where we already know she isn't now. But these other two are worth checking out." He rolled up the map. "I'll just drive on up and see what kind of mischief Davey's gotten himself into. Thanks for your time—and the coffee."

Wachman strode off purposefully to the green and white sedan still parked out in front of the general store and got in.

"Did you get anything else?" Dylan asked Rowan quietly.

Rowan was rubbing her temples, and it was one of the few times Truth had seen the girl looking anything less than ebullient.

"Yes, Dylan. I didn't want to say anything, but—I think she's already dead. I think she's drowned."

SIXTEEN

GRAVE WORDS

There is a silence where hath been no sound,
There is a silence where no sound may be,
In the cold grave—under the deep deep sea,
Or in the wide desert where no life is found.
—THOMAS HOOD

"I CAN'T BEAR THE THOUGHT OF JUST STANDING around here waiting," Sinah said with a shudder, as the others prepared to resume their daily tasks. "And I suppose I have a few phone calls to make—to my business manager, for one thing," she added reluctantly. "But maybe you could swing by in a few hours, Truth, and we could run down to the IGA in Pharaoh? I'm sort of stranded without the Jeep—Wycherly borrowed it, and he hasn't brought it back yet," she added for Dylan's benefit.

"That will be fine—around three, then?" Truth was reluctant to let Sinah out of her sight, but what harm could it do, really? If Sinah meant to sacrifice herself to the Gate there was little Truth could do to stop her when it came right down to it.

"Perfect. And why don't all four of you come to dinner tonight?" Sinah added. "It won't be fancy, but you can at least get your laundry done and take a few showers without rationing every drop."

"That would be great," Dylan said. "I'm afraid my plans for today are to drive the camper to someplace called—I swear this is true—Bear Heaven, to get the tanks flushed and topped up. Having the camper's a damn sight better than sleeping on the ground, but for every advantage, there are equal and opposite drawbacks. That's Palmer's Law."

"See you tonight then," Sinah said, smiling. She waved and started off up the road.

"And where do *you* suppose Wycherly Musgrave is?" Dylan asked Truth, when Sinah was out of earshot and Rowan and Ninian had left for their check-sites. It was the closest thing to a civil conversation they'd had in days, and Truth was absurdly grateful for it.

"Probably back in Long Island by now—that is, if he hasn't wrapped Sinah's car around a tree somewhere. Three guesses who the wrecked Ferrari over there in the junkyard belongs to," Truth said absently.

Dylan glanced briefly in that direction, where a flash of the car's blood-red paint job was still visible among the rusted wreckage of older cars.

"And what are your plans for the afternoon?" he asked, leaning back against the side of the camper.

"Well, I was going to write up my notes, but if you're going to be driving my office . . ." Truth said, striving for a light tone.

"You could come with me."

Once she would have accepted such an offer without question; now, recent events made her wary, searching the innocent statement for hidden traps and tests. She sighed.

"Dylan, we need to talk," Truth said.

"I know," Dylan said. He sat down at the table. Truth followed suit, bracing herself to be honest—and to accept honesty in return.

"Lately it seems as if we've been going off half-cocked in opposite directions. Why didn't you tell me you were going up to the sanatorium this morning?" she asked.

Dylan considered the question, giving it full weight before he spoke.

"Frankly, I didn't want . . . I don't know what I didn't want. But the way you've been acting since you got here . . . well, it isn't like you, Truth."

"I'm afraid it is like me," Truth said soberly. "People change, Dylan. Mostly in their teens and early twenties, of course, when everything else is changing so much that it just sort of fits in. But I guess I'm sort of a case of arrested development, Dyl. I held the line against everything for so long that when I gave up doing it I guess I changed more than either of us was expecting."

"Maybe you did. But I love you, darling, no matter what crack-brained notions you have. I just don't want to see you hurt. You're so reckless. . . ." Dylan said, his voice trailing off as he envisioned the scope of Truth's recklessness.

His expression made her laugh. "Me? Oh, no, Dylan; if you want reck-lessness, take Rowan! I swear it made my blood run cold to listen to her offer to tweak the tail of that psychic locus just to hear it squeak. I know what I'm doing, Dylan, even if it doesn't look like it. I'm as careful as I can be."

Dylan got to his feet as if he could no longer contain himself. He stood, half turned away from her, one hand pressed against the back of his neck as if unconsciously he were trying to make himself submit to some-thing.

"Look. All kidding aside, I know you . . . believe in magick. But in our little corner of the world you can easily get a distorted view of how accepted it is. You've studied Thorne's life—in fact, you wrote the book. Are you ready to expose yourself to that much . . . ridicule?" he finished in a strained voice.

This was hard. She'd expected it to be, but its difficulty had already exceeded her expectations. It would have been simpler if Truth had sim-ply told Dylan that she didn't love him, didn't care, wanted nothing more to do with him.

That wasn't true. But unfortunately Truth wanted him on terms of complete honesty, complete openness—and she didn't think that was possible.

"If I have to become a laughingstock I will—for what's right. It isn't that I believe in magick, Dylan; magick believes in me. And . . . I sup-pose I haven't told you everything about what I learned over the last few years. I suppose if I'm going to be . . . open about my beliefs, we need to discuss that most of all."

Now it would come—the open break between them.

"All right," Dylan said, as warily as any man would under the cir-cumstances.

Truth took a deep breath and willed down the rising tide of her stormy emotions. She had only one chance at getting this right, but the words must be said.

"You know that Thorne claimed he'd been fathered by a Bright Lord of the *sidhe*—a nonhuman force. Well, it's the truth. He was. I have as much proof of that as I'll ever need. And I'm his daughter. I'm . . . not quite human, Dylan."

Her throat was raw with the effort it had taken to force out the words, bald and unpersuasive though they were. Dylan did not laugh—but would any man laugh when the woman he loved confessed to being delusional? If he did not trust and believe in her, her confession could seem like nothing else to him.

Dylan ran a hand over his forehead. He was sweating.

"I know that Blackburn . . ." he began. His voice died. "You'll have to give me time, Truth. I'm sorry. This is a lot to take in."

And there's more. There's my life's work—and it isn't sitting in a sterile cubicle at the Institute juggling numbers!

"Yes. I know. I'm sorry." Trite, meaningless words—but what else could she say? *I'm sorry, Dylan, love. I'm sorry.*

"Why didn't you bring this up before?" The desperation in his voice made her heart ache.

Because I thought I could ignore it, pretend it didn't matter. We weren't planning on children, after all. Because I thought I could pretend to be a normal human being.

"I'm sorry, Dylan," Truth said again.

They sat there in silence for a long time, not looking at each other, until Truth finally got up and walked off in the direction of the general store. While she was inside buying supplies to make up for a missed breakfast, she heard the camper's engine start up and saw it move slowly up the street.

She'd never felt more desolate in her life, but Truth told herself stubbornly that it wasn't yet time to despair. If Dylan could accept what she'd told him this morning, they would have a basis for discussion of all the rest.

If he could not, Truth would leave as soon as the Gate was sealed, and do her best not to see Dylan Palmer ever again.

* * *

"This is a wicked place," Michael Archangel said simply, gazing down at the Black Altar.

To earthly eyes, Michael Archangel was a tall man of indeterminate age, with the black hair and eyes and olive skin that bespoke a Mediterranean heritage. He wore a dark suit that was peculiarly out of place here in the rambling, overgrown ruins of the burnt sanatorium, and looked like any mundane businessman.

But Truth knew he was more than that—much more. She kept her second sight well barricaded whenever she looked toward him, but the presence of what he was beat against her shields like constant sunlight. Someday, inevitably, there would be war between them, as Michael followed the Right-Hand Path, the path of Light—and Truth did not.

If there had not been that unspoken thing between them, Truth could have liked Michael. He was the one whom Light Winwood, Truth's sister, had chosen for her life partner. And though he could never be her ally, Truth trusted Michael to be true to his own nature. Michael Archangel was the closest thing to a White Magician that Truth knew.

It was early on the morning of August 14—and the sub-basement temple at Wildwood Sanatorium was cold and threatening. Today there was not even the sight of blue sky and sunlight in the world above to warm them: The day was misty and overcast, unusually cool for August, and the stone walls seemed to radiate cold. Truth, Michael, Dylan, and Sinah stood once more before the altar stone that symbolized Quentin Blackburn's power.

Truth's problems with Dylan were worse than ever—they had both carefully avoided each other last night at Sinah's. Later there would be time for Truth to talk to Dylan, to make a clean end to things as she knew she must. But now Truth must set her private griefs aside in the face of the responsibility she bore.

Beside Truth, Sinah twisted nervously.

Truth had not wanted Sinah to be here for this, but she hadn't really been able to think of any good argument to keep Sinah away. Sinah was terrified of Quentin Blackburn and the grey place she had been trapped in on the Astral Plane, even more than she was afraid of the bloodline and her duties as Gatekeeper. When Truth had told Sinah that Michael would be coming to put an end to all that remained in this world of Quentin Blackburn, Sinah had demanded to be present, and Truth still needed her cooperation—or the cooperation of whatever ancestral memories dwelt behind Sinah Dellon's grey eyes—to seal the Wildwood Gate. So Sinah had come with them when Michael had picked Truth up at Sinah's house this morning.

When Michael had arrived at Sinah's, Dylan had been with him. Truth could not imagine how they'd connected, or what they'd found to talk about. Or what Dylan had told Rowan and Ninian—left behind in town—for that matter.

"Have you heard anything from Wycherly?" Truth asked, to distract Sinah from what Michael was doing. "He's probably going to need to make a statement to the sheriff's department. He was probably the last person to see Luned alive, if she kept house for him."

By now the consensus in the Fork was that Luned Starking was dead. Soon the rumors would begin that Sinah had caused the death. Truth hoped she'd have the sense to be far from here by then—once the Gate was sealed.

Sinah shook her head. "He didn't kill her," she said, her voice shaking with the effort it took to force the words out.

Michael stepped forward and brushed his fingers lightly across the top of the Black Altar, his mobile features twisting in distaste at what he felt there. After a few moments he straightened from his examination of the altar and turned to the three who were waiting.

"There is sufficient evil here that I may act. Are any of you believers?" he asked in his deep voice. "I know that *she* is not," he added, indicating Truth.

Sinah shook her head uncertainly, while Dylan's answer, to Truth's surprise, was a strong "Yes."

"Very well." Michael's eyes met Truth's briefly, and she experienced a searing shock of recognition, of a sense that she knew his true name—

Then it was gone.

"I will ask you, Truth, and Ms. Dellon merely to keep still minds, and to place your trust in the power of the Light. The Darkness finds its power in your weakness; if you have faith, you will come to no harm."

Truth could not quite believe that—it was a fundamental dispute about the use of Man's capacity to know and do that was at the root of Truth and Michael's conflict—but this was not the time to argue. Let Sinah trust in Michael, if she could; Truth would trust her own strength to protect her, and do nothing to hinder what Michael intended to do.

Michael extended his hand to Dylan, who stepped forward. Then Michael turned to the case he had brought with him and began to remove its contents, setting them upon a small folding table which he had also carried here.

Most of what she saw was familiar to Truth—the apparatus of High Magick was nearly universal—but some of them were unique to Michael's path: the monstrance containing the consecrated wafer which Michael held to be the actual body of his god; the vial of viaticum; a long, narrow strip of violet silk, embroidered with the symbols of his faith. When he had everything he would need set out, he draped the *stola* about his neck, kissing the ends of it before and after he did so.

Michael lit the candle and lifted it to ignite the censer of incense that stood beside it. Then, as the thick, white smoke curled upward—its fragrance nearly lost in the open air—he took one last item from his bag— a book—and began to read.

"'Blessed is the man that walketh not in the counsel of the ungodly, nor standeth in the way of sinners, nor sitteth in the seat of the scornful—'"

It was not the Catholic Church's Ritual of Exorcism—Truth had read that once—though the words sounded vaguely biblical. Exorcism or not, she felt their power like a rising wind—and felt, too, the power of that which rose to contend with them.

"'His delight is in the law of the Lord; and in his law doth he meditate day and night.'"

Now it was Dylan who held the book and read, his face grave and his voice quietly steady. Sinah stepped closer to Truth, pressing against her, and the younger woman's fingers were icy in Truth's own.

Holding the monstrance in both hands, Michael raised it high over his head. The gold and crystal disk caught the rays of the morning sun and flashed like a mirror.

Then he brought the monstrance down upon the altar.

There was a lightless flash; a wordless soundless shout of rage, as though someone—some *thing*—had been burned. Truth saw a bright flash of red as fresh blood welled up around the wafer in its crystal case, and the stone surface of the altar directly beneath it began to smoke, giving off a horrible stench of burning and rot.

"'And he shall be like a tree planted by the rivers of water—'" Now Michael and Dylan spoke together—Dylan reading, a little raggedly, Michael rolling forth the sonorous syllables without need of the book.

Next Michael took up the censer and swung it over the altar; the sweet smoke of burning frankincense veiled the repulsive scent of the burning stone, making it possible to breathe once more.

But this was only the beginning. Truth struggled to draw a breath, and could not make her lungs serve her. Her heart lugged heavily in her chest; she felt a sense of pressure, an uncomfortable weight on her sinuses, her lungs, her eyes, as though she had been placed into a pressure chamber and was being slowly and painfully oppressed by the weight of a thousand atmospheres. Dylan and Sinah felt it, too—Dylan was sweating and pale, and Sinah looked as though she might faint at any moment.

Michael laid the fingertips of his right hand on the altar beside the smoking monstrance. There was a sudden release of the pressure.

"'—the tree that bringeth forth his fruit in his season; his leaf also shall not wither; and . . .'"

For the first time Truth heard Michael falter. He reached out his left hand to Dylan; Dylan took it, quickly, and Truth heard Dylan gasp.

"'. . . his leaf also shall not wither . . .'"

The light in the sub-basement dwindled, as if a shadow had come between the sun and the earth. But the darkening continued. It was sunset—twilight—night. The light was gone.

Truth took Sinah in her arms and held her tightly.

A great wave—a sorrow, a death, a mortality for which Truth had no name broke over her like a crushing wave. This was nothing she knew how to fight, this mindless, endless hunger to destroy, to ruin, and to leave no new thing behind itself.

For a moment she felt the flames rise around her and seemed to feel Quentin Blackburn's last mortal thoughts—rage and arrogance and cheated fury.

"*Athanais!*" his voice shouted.

For one instant Truth saw Quentin Blackburn clearly. He had Thorne's eyes, Thorne's reckless charm—but his face was carved deep with lines of anger and dissatisfaction that had never been any part of Thorne Blackburn's heritage. He wore unfamiliar ornate robes, and a horned crown in eerie echo of the *thing* upon the altar in the Grey Place was bound about his brow.

And as Truth watched, he was dissolving away, being sucked down into a vortex of flame that purled as if it were water, into a void that was not even darkness, but absence of all color and image.

"*No!*" As the astral temple that Quentin Blackburn had constructed began to dissolve under Michael's onslaught—carrying away all that remained of Quentin's personality, and, perhaps, his soul—Sinah screamed and twisted in Truth's arms, and suddenly Truth felt the power of the Gate itself, a cold pure heartless fire, as Sinah reached out to it to save her lover.

"*Be still, woman!*" Michael roared. Beads of blood stood out along his forehead like a row of thorns. He pointed his finger at Sinah with a gesture that had the impact of a whiplash, and she slumped unconscious in Truth's arms.

Truth lowered Sinah gently to the floor. Sinah wasn't hurt, but she had certainly been . . . silenced.

With Sinah unconscious the siren lure of the Gate faded, but the distraction had cost Michael dearly. The tide of darkness began to rise up again, as painful in its way to Truth as Michael's light had been. Truth knew already that any power she might be able to summon and wield could have no effect here—both the Right- and Left-Hand Paths were closed to her by her own vow. She had survived her own encounter with the power of The Church of the Antique Rite because of that very fact—but Michael was a Servant of the Light, his own power set in direct opposition to that which the Antique Rite represented. And Michael's strength was failing.

"'I shall not be afraid for the terror by night.'"

Dylan's voice, calm and certain, sounded through the suffocating essence of this blighted place like the tolling of a bell.

His voice went on, reciting the beautiful words of the litany; the defiance of a small weak thing, a thing that could not prevail against the vast forces arrayed against it, a thing that could easily be hurt, shattered, destroyed—but could never be made to submit against its true will.

Dylan's words resounded to their end, and now Michael's voice rose above Dylan's once more, calling upon the power that was his to command with renewed strength.

"'His leaf also shall not wither, and whatsoever he doeth shall prosper.'"

The darkness lifted as if Truth had suddenly been given sight. As she crouched over Sinah's unconscious form, she saw Michael reach for the small bottle of oil on the table and begin to anoint the altar with it, as carefully as if the inanimate stone were the body of a dying loved one. In the center of the smooth black stone, the monstrance still smoked.

"'The ungodly are not so: but are like the chaff which the wind driveth away,'" Michael said firmly. "'Lift up your heads, O ye gates and be ye lifted up, ye everlasting doors—'"

He capped the vial of oil once more and set it aside, and picked up the large iron bell that awaited him.

Or was it a sword? Truth blinked and looked away. Her eyes insisted that it was both—and neither. She closed them, shutting out the lying images, and the bell—it must be a bell—began to ring in vigorous double peals.

The sound of the ringing drowned out Michael's next words—though Truth, looking toward him again, could see that his lips were still moving—and each peal struck through her with a separate shock, as if something of her own substance were being cast out with the very sound. But distressing as it was for her, the effect on the temple was far worse.

It was as if the image before her eyes now was a reflection in a pool, a reflection that shimmered into nothingness with each stroke of the bell. Each time it reformed itself again, but each time the image seemed somehow lighter—*weaker*—than before.

The thirteenth double stroke sounded, and Michael set the bell aside. As the fading echoes cleared, Truth could see that everything was just as it had been before—but somehow it was more ethereal, cleaner, new. Whatever had been here was gone, and the physical reality that she saw had been reborn.

Sinah stirred in her arms, and Truth rocked back on her heels to give Sinah air. The sun had broken through the clouds now, and the light was almost too bright, though it was nothing more than ordinary sunlight. Truth squinted as she looked toward Dylan. He was leaning back against the side of the altar, and she could see dark rings of sweat staining the fabric of his shirt. He looked like a man who had been flogged.

The altar stone seemed somehow to be less black—although that could be a trick of the light—and the band of symbols that had been carved upon its side was gone as if it had been rubbed away. Truth straightened wearily out of her crouch, and as she did she saw that the monstrance that Michael had placed upon the altar's surface was also gone. All that remained behind was a shallow depression in the stone— but Truth could not reasonably say that it was something that hadn't been here before.

It was over.

Then Michael sketched the Sign of the Cross in the air, and she realized he was not finished. He meant to go on—to seal this place against any possibility of Quentin's return—but if he did, he would seal it against Truth and Sinah as well.

"Michael—*no!*" Truth said. She straightened up and staggered toward him on unsteady legs.

He finished the Sign and turned to look at her. It hung invisibly behind him, burning into Truth's senses like a rebuke.

"Would you have me cast out this evil and not set up wards against its return?" Michael said. He looked tired—bone weary, as though this excruciating task were one he had done too many times before, and already knew that he had to do over and over again.

"I won't have you locking me out," Truth said bluntly, not caring what either Dylan or Sinah made of her words. "I need you to leave this place open."

Michael gazed down at her, stern pity in his dark eyes. Behind him, Dylan stirred uneasily.

"If I were to do that, it would in time call worshippers to it once more. There is one already . . . though for him there is still time. I cannot allow such a thing to be—you who will not believe in the truth, believe at least that I believe it. To omit to protect is as great an evil as to do harm. How many innocents will you sacrifice to your pride?" Michael asked austerely.

"None, if I can do what I mean to do here," Truth said.

"But can you? If you fail, who will pay? Once I could have saved you from your heritage, Truth—beware of where your pride will lead you."

"It's already led me there," Truth said. "And while I know you don't approve, it was my choice. Just leave it, Michael. There's a lot less to worry about with the Antique Rite gone."

"Yet your Gate remains. What of the lives and souls it will yet claim?" Michael persisted.

"That's my responsibility," Truth said briefly.

"And the souls of those who will die here are mine," Michael returned, and raised his hands again.

"*Black spirits and white, red spirits and grey . . . come horse, come hound, come stag and wolf—*" Truth gathered her own power.

"I said no." Her voice was hard.

"Truth, look—" Dylan said, and Truth silenced him with a gesture much like the one that Michael had used upon Sinah, though Truth's had no force of compulsion behind it. She did not take her eyes from the man before her.

"Don't fight me, Michael. I value you for making my sister happy, and you've done something here today that I couldn't have done. But I mean to have this my way. I swear to you it will be all right."

The moment she said the words, Truth knew that somehow they had been a mistake—that somehow she had been tricked into doing something that Michael desired.

"Very well—upon your own head and by your hand are all deaths of this place from this moment. They are yours to expiate—and the right to choose penance is mine," Michael pronounced.

Truth's Way was that of the Balance, but she had been trapped by the very taint in her blood that he had reminded her of. Michael had exacted her oath to atone for those as-yet-unlost lives, to exalt Life above Death and unbalance the Wheel which held there was a time for everything to happen.

Yet if she did not let him do it—with her own vow serving as the power to bind her—she would have fight Michael Archangel here and now.

How dare he speak to me like that—child—chattel—his kind were servants crawling in the mud when I—when we— Truth felt the echo of *sidhe* rage like a pale whipcrack across her mind.

"Very well. I agree." Truth's eyes flashed dangerously, daring Michael to rejoice in his victory.

"And should harm come to any here through your inaction, I will know—and avenge." His eyes burned into hers for a long painful moment, and then Michael turned away to pack his tools.

With an effort, Truth banished the mocking whisper of fury from her mind. She'd won the day—gotten what she wanted. This was no time and place to yearn over what might have been.

She turned away, and Sinah was sitting up, a dazed, unfocused expression on her face.

"What happened?" Sinah asked. Her voice was faintly slurred. "Did I faint?"

Dylan walked past Truth to where Sinah sat, and helped her stand, staggering a bit himself.

"It looked like it," he said. "Stress . . . shock. Nothing to worry about."

Truth could see Sinah and Dylan already beginning to forget, to tell themselves that what had happened here was only suggestion and metaphor. Soon they would be able to convince themselves that all they'd seen had been some bloodless rite of blessing, that Michael Archangel was only some kindly well-meaning ecclesiastic who'd done a friend a favor.

And that they'd never been in any real danger at all.

"So what happens now?" Truth asked Michael, setting aside their eternal confrontation. "You look all in—I'm sure we can find you a place to get your head down somewhere."

"Another time, perhaps." Michael looked at his watch. "But I need to get back to the airport. Light is waiting for me at the hotel there—we were heading for Japan when you called, Truth, so I thought I might just as well bring her with me. But I don't like to leave her alone—and if I make good time back there perhaps we can get an earlier flight to California."

He closed his eyes for a moment, and suddenly Truth saw how very tired he was—and Clarksburg was a good two hours away by the map.

"Are you sure you're in any shape to drive?" Dylan asked, just as Truth was about to say something. "Why don't you have Truth drive you back—if Light's with you, I know she'd love to see her."

"Oh, yes, that would be great!" said Michael with guilty relief.

"You can just rent another car for the drive back," Dylan said to Truth. "There must be somewhere closer than Clarksburg to turn it in."

"Elkins or La Gouloue, I think, but Rowan can drive, if Michael wants a shotgun. I've got work to do here," Truth said brusquely. She saw Sinah's eyes flash with pure panic at her words, confirming the rightness of Truth's decision. As much as Truth wanted to see Light, the Gate was more important now. And she didn't really relish spending any more time than she must in the company of Michael's disapproval.

Steeling herself against Dylan's objections, Truth walked over to where Sinah was leaning against the Black Altar—now a harmless normal block of stone.

"Sinah?" Truth said. "Sinah, you have to help me now. Michael has cleared the way, but it's time to close the Gate."

Cautiously, Truth reached out with her *sidhe* senses. She could detect no sign of Quentin Blackburn's tainted Church, but that wasn't proof it was gone. The iron test would come when she and Sinah tried to close the Gate again.

Close it, seal it, close it. . . . The words ran through Truth's mind over and over again. They'd had to delay too long—first with the endless obstacles Quentin had placed in their way, then with waiting for Michael to arrive. It was the middle of August—either the *teind* to the Wildwood Gate must be paid in the Gatekeeper's blood, or Sinah must lock and seal it forever. There was no third choice.

Sinah stared at Truth, her eyes dilated in utter panic.

"I—I—I—" she said.

"Truth." Dylan touched her arm hesitantly, as though he were afraid she'd turn on him.

"Truth, can't you see she's all in? All of us are. I know this is important to you, but she can't possibly be of any help to you in her current condition. Give her some time," he said mildly.

"There isn't any time," Truth said tightly. *Didn't you hear what Michael did to me? The next person who dies here is my fault—*MINE*—trapping me and binding me to the Wheel forever. . . .*

"There has to be time," Dylan said soothingly. "Sure, the disappearances peak in August. But does it really matter if you do your thing now, in a few hours, or even tomorrow? After the sheriff's men searching all through the woods yesterday, nobody's going to go wandering off up here."

Dylan's was the voice of reason, Truth admitted bitterly, whether he believed in the reality of the Wildwood Gate or was simply saying whatever he thought she'd be likeliest to believe. And unfortunately, it was good advice. Sinah was already exhausted and upset. It would take time to re-persuade her to close the Gate.

"I feel really silly dragging you out like this just because I have ghosts in my backyard," Sinah said to Michael as she got out of the car.

Truth climbed out after her, and as she did, she saw Michael smile. "It was no trouble, Ms. Dellon. It is an—avocation of mine," he finished with curious precision.

"Well, I still feel awful, making you come all this way. The least I can do is feed you breakfast."

"Thank you, but I must be on my way. Perhaps there will be another time," he said.

"Sure," Sinah said, in a tone that indicated she'd be just as happy if that time never came.

"I'll see if Ninian or Rowan can drive Michael back," Dylan said. He hesitated, as though there were many things he'd like to say, but could not in front of the others.

"Well, see you later," Dylan said at last. Truth watched as the sedan drove off down the dusty road. When she turned back, Sinah had gone, and Truth followed her inside.

"Sinah?" Truth followed the sounds to the kitchen, and found Sinah standing over the sink, washing her hands.

"I thought breakfast would be a good idea," Sinah said brightly. But Truth could see her eyes, and they were flat, scared, and evasive.

"Why don't you let me do that?" Truth said. "I'm not much of a cook, but I can manage eggs. A solid meal, a few hours rest, and then we can go back up to the sanatorium again and seal the Gate."

Sinah didn't answer directly, simply going to the refrigerator and starting to lay things out on her cutting board. "I thought your friend took care of all that," she said offhandedly.

"Don't go into denial on me now," Truth said, trying for a note of humor.

"I'm not." Sinah looked directly at her, and her grey eyes were as opaque as painted contact lenses. "I just think I've humored you long enough, Truth. Fun is fun, but it's a long walk on a hot day and I'm tired of playing."

"Humored me?" Truth could not have been more stunned if Sinah had slapped her. "Is that what you think you've been doing?"

"What else?" Sinah's tone was coolly bored. "But playtime's over."

Truth had expected evasions, refusals—anything but this outright denial. "I can't believe you're saying this," Truth said honestly. "When I came up here for the first time three days ago, you were almost hysterical—you knew about the Gate—you told *me* about it! What about Athanais de Lyon?"

"What about her?" Sinah answered with the same maddening serenity. "Grow up, Truth."

It seemed as if everyone had been saying that to Truth all summer: grow up, stop playing around—as if the dangerous intangibles that were her life's work were only toys.

"Tell me," Truth said urgently. "You read my mind, when I came here—do you think I'm playing? Even if your gift has vanished—"

Sinah regarded her blankly, a faint superior smile on her face. "You weren't really taken in, were you? Party tricks. I swear, Truth—it was a game."

Such was Sinah's serene conviction that for a wavering instant Truth doubted herself. But no. Sinah had not been playing when she'd begged Truth to save her from her nightmares, nor had Truth imagined any of the rest. *It's as if she's been hypnotized, or simply . . . forgotten most of her life.*

But if this were some new trick of the Gate, or even of Sinah's own human mind, there was little Truth could do to change it with a frontal assault.

"If it was, it was a cruel one," Truth said coolly. "And I hardly think you were being fair to Wycherly. Remember him?"

"Of course I remember Wycherly," Sinah said after a pause. The statement was far from convincing. "Why don't you go wait in the living room, and I'll make us a nice omelet?"

And I can just hope she doesn't try to poison me, Truth thought darkly.

Kill her, Jamie's lady said implacably. *I can't,* Sinah Dellon answered, as her hands moved with clever independence among the bowls and jars: chopping, testing, mixing.

And not even because she had any intrinsic objection to killing. She should, she ought to have, normal people did, but all she felt was an amoral interest in whether it would serve her purpose.

And it wouldn't. It wouldn't protect the Wellspring. Kill Truth, and the others would still know the Wellspring was there. Kill them all, and their disappearance would be noticed. People would come and she'd be locked up for ever, away from the Wellspring, without any of the bloodline to follow her.

The world had changed so much. Sinah looked back wistfully across a three-century span with as much nostalgia as though she'd lived through each year. If she had not, others had, and she remembered them.

Was it because of Athanais, who used the power of the Gate to grasp at life through her descendants? The first European member of the bloodline had never found what she sought after here in the wild Virginia wilderness all those centuries ago. Only imprisonment of another sort, as terrible as that she had fled, to live and die among members of an alien race. Her daughters and granddaughters and great-granddaughters had

kept the trust that the Tutelo sachem's blood had laid on them: to guard
and serve the Wellspring.

But the bloodline had been defeated at last by the one enemy cleverness and trickery couldn't foil—time. The twentieth century—with its
computers and records, its police and everyone demanding to know
where someone was *every single minute*—was what would cause the bloodline to break its trust at last. The Wellspring would be known, plun-
dered, left unguarded. She had been too weak. . . .

Sinah whisked eggs and cream together with automatic gestures, and
slid the mixture into a waiting pan. When the surface had hardened, she
eased in the rest of the ingredients—cheese, onions, mushrooms, pep-
pers—and folded the omelet over with an adroit gesture. A little big, but
suitable for two.

Time. I need time. She tossed bread into the toaster, and reached up into
the cupboard to take down jam to go with it.

As she did, she saw the bottle of sleeping pills.

Wycherly's pills. Strong ones, too. He'd left them here. Just one the
other night had made her sleep without dreams for hours. What would
more do?

And how can I get Truth to take them?

Within the depths of her mind, Sinah felt Athanais stir, and laugh.
This was something Jamie's lady knew how to do.

Sinah took down a teacup from the cabinet and set it on the counter.
She shook several capsules from the jar and began opening them, spilling
the white powder inside into the cup.

Truth paced around Sinah's living room, wishing irrationally that Dylan
were here. Dylan was the one with the charm to soothe the tantrums of
balky psychics, not her.

But how much help would Dylan be without belief? *None,* Truth admitted ruefully. She listened to Sinah clattering around in the kitchen
making brunch, and wondered what arguments she could use to get past
that stubborn barrier that Sinah had so easily flung up between them.
Truth had a terrible sense that time was running out, that there was not
much more time left in which to save Sinah.

Save Sinah? Truth was puzzled at the direction of her own thoughts.
Surely she had already saved Sinah when Michael had driven away all that

was left of the ego, the personality, of Quentin Blackburn. All that was left was for Truth to gain Sinah's cooperation to close the Wildwood Gate.

Truth could have pulled Sinah into the Otherworld by brute force at any time—all it would take was a touch, skin to skin, to bring her there for at least an instant—but would that work, or just make things worse? The Light could not compel, relying for its power on moral suasion. The Dark compelled, claiming the right of those with power to do anything they could. Truth's way was a more difficult one—it was true that she could force others to work her will, but in doing so she assumed responsibility for the action and any harm it might cause. The Grey Path: a wavering middle ground, which could easily slide toward impotence . . . or evil.

"Brunch is ready!" Sinah called cheerfully.

There was a fresh-cooked omelet, strong tea, fresh orange juice, and thick-sliced toast slathered with preserves from a jar with a designer label. Fancier wasn't always better, Truth decided, taking a bite; the jam was far too sweet. But she was hungry, and ate the toast anyway. And everything else was perfect.

But she was no closer to finding a way to persuade Sinah to close the Wildwood Gate. She stifled a yawn, and realized her mind had been wandering.

"Sorry," Truth said apologetically. "It's been a big day already. Can I help you clear away? And then—I hope I can persuade you to come back up to Wildwood. If you'll just think matters over . . ."

"Oh, I have," Sinah said with a bitter smile. "But why don't you go into the living room and rest? I can handle things here."

Without waiting for a reply, Sinah began stacking plates. She picked up the pile and headed off to the kitchen.

Truth stifled another yawn, then gave in to it. Why was she so sleepy? She got to her feet. The room reeled around her and she staggered, off-balance.

Drugged. I've been drugged. But . . . why?

Sinah had drugged her. But how? They'd shared every dish on the table.

The jam. It had already been on the toast when Sinah had brought it out from the kitchen, and Truth had accepted it innocently.

"Sinah . . . why?" Truth said, holding onto the table and keeping her eyes open with an effort.

"Oh, are you still up?" Sinah came back into the room and saw her. She smiled coldly. "Come on, Truth. Lie down, and sleep for a long, long, time. . . ."

Sinah came forward and took Truth's arm, walking Truth into the living room and pushing her down without effort onto one of the oyster leather loveseats. Truth's head lolled back, and she could feel herself sinking, fading away.

"Why?" Truth mumbled.

"I needed time, dear sister," Sinah said in an oddly formal voice. "And I would not have thee prating at me as if I were a congregation! Now sleep, and dream, and all will be taken care of whilst thee dost slumber."

I . . . can't, Truth thought.

But she could, and she did.

SEVENTEEN

PATHS TO THE GRAVE

I'll do as much for my true-love
As any young man may;
I'll sit and mourn all at her grave
For a twelvemonth and a day.
          —ANONYMOUS

IN THE LAST RAYS OF THE SETTING SUN, THE LAND-
scape looked as if it had been dipped in blood. Wycherly Musgrave sur-
veyed his kingdom, curiously at peace. For the first time in his life he had
found something he really wanted to do—and he was doing it.

He wondered where Sinah was. The memory of her betrayal still
hurt—she'd known who he was all along, and had been kind only out of
some self-interested sort of mercy—but he still wanted to see her one last
time. To tell her off, maybe, or to gloat over the fact that she wasn't going to get what she was so obviously after.

Nobody would, after tonight.

The hardest part of the whole affair had been locating what he wanted.
After that, obtaining it had not really been any more difficult than obtaining a cash advance on his AmEx. But the crates were heavy, and his
injured hand was still giving him trouble. He couldn't remember if he'd
forgotten to fill the prescription for antibiotics that the doctor in the
emergency room had given him, or if it had run out. All he knew was

that he didn't have any, and that beneath the bandages his hand was red and sore and throbbed in time with his heartbeat.

Not that anything like that would matter soon.

He probably ought to at least return Sinah's car, Wycherly thought. She hadn't called it in as a stolen vehicle—they'd have snagged it one of the times he'd left it parked on the street if she had—and he ought to be grateful to her for that.

But she'd find it eventually—or what was left of it.

And he was running out of light. He'd come back to the Fork this morning, in search of the last thing he needed to carry out his plan. He'd thought he'd have to rely on stupidity and human greed, but instead he'd gotten lucky. He turned to his companion.

"C'mon, Seth old buddy. Head 'em on up, move 'em on out."

Seth Merryman, who had been born with Down's Syndrome and all the sweetness and trust that implied, smiled. He was happy to come and do a favor for the nice man who'd come up to him on the porch of his Ma's house and offered him a chance to earn a crisp twenty-dollar bill for a little hard work. Nothing to be afraid of in a little hard work. And he got to ride in a shiny new Jeep Cherokee, too, just like he'd seen in the movies.

At first Truth was content to let someone else answer the door.

But no one came, and the noise turned from an insistent ringing to a relentless pounding to a slower—but louder—thumping. Truth tried to sit up, to move, but nothing happened.

That frightened her—enough to make her force her eyes open. She was lying on the floor in a dark room, and someone was pounding on the door.

Dylan. She rolled onto her face, with every drugged and sleeping muscle protesting, and dragged herself on hands and knees to the door. She pressed her cheek against it. It was vibrating with the impact of the kicks.

"Dylan?" she whispered. Why was he making all this fuss? What was wrong? Summoning all her strength, she reached up and twisted the knob.

The door slammed inward with painful force, shoving her backward. The pain helped to clear her head; Truth struggled backward as Dylan squeezed through the gap.

"Truth!"

The lights came on with a painful intensity as he flipped the switch. While she was still trying to shield her eyes from the light Dylan knelt beside her and pulled her into a sitting position.

"Truth! God in Heaven—what's happened to you?"

Funny, Truth thought fuzzily, *that's the first time I've ever heard Dylan really swear.*

"Drugged," Truth mumbled. "Sleeping pills."

But it was starting to wear off—how long ago had she gotten the dose?—and she was able to get to her feet with Dylan's help. He mixed her a glass of strong salt water, and then held her head while she voided all that was left in her stomach. There probably wasn't much—if any—of the drug left there, but she wasn't willing to take any chances.

Truth staggered to her feet again and washed her mouth out vigorously, then drank from the bathroom tap thirstily. Her mouth felt dry and swollen. Yogis and great adepts could control the machinery of their own bodies to such an extent that one of them could have flushed the toxins from his blood by the force of directed will alone, but Truth had a long way to go before she reached that level of competence.

"Where's . . . Sinah?" Truth asked. Her speech was still slurred, and the light made her eyes ache. "What . . . time?"

"Almost six. I don't think she's here, but I'll check. And make you some coffee. Will you be all right here alone?"

"Yes," Truth said. She felt Dylan move away from her, and gripped the edge of the counter for support, breathing deeply. *Think, dammit!* She had to get moving, get her body and mind under control.

Remembering her earliest lessons, Truth inhaled a deep breath of air, pushing it down deep into her lungs. Then she exhaled and pulled in more air, visualizing her body using the oxygen to speed her heart, her blood, flushing the toxins from her body. Slowly her head began to clear.

"She isn't here," Dylan said. "Coffee's on its way."

"I need some fresh air," Truth said slowly, and Dylan guided her as she moved on unsteady steps to the front door.

He opened it, supporting her carefully, and Truth drew in healing lungfuls of warm fresh air. The sky was a deep blue, and the light was as thick and golden as buckwheat honey. Six o'clock, Dylan had said. She'd slept the day away.

Because Sinah had drugged her. . . .

"How did you find me?" Truth said groggily. She didn't think she was tracking 100 percent yet, but she had to be, and soon.

"Oh, I just looked through a clear pane in one of the windows and there you were, lying on the floor. I thought you'd come down to the fork, but then I found out that nobody had seen you all day, and I thought there might have been some kind of accident, and then Mrs. Merryman showed up at the general store, so I came looking for you. I thought you were dead," he added, and hugged her fiercely. "Are you *sure* you're all right?"

"I will be," Truth said. "Wycherly left his sleeping pills here, and I guess Sinah fed them to me. But why?"

There was a silence from beside her.

"Dylan?" Truth said.

"I don't know," he said grimly. "But I'm willing to guess. The reason Mrs. Merryman was so upset was because her son has disappeared—a boy with Down's Syndrome. His name is Seth."

Seth did most of the work, and soon the two crates in the back of the Jeep Cherokee had been opened and their contents carried to the deepest basement in the burnt sanatorium. Wycherly stayed on the surface, watching Seth work. He shivered in his leather jacket. It might be August, but he was damn cold—and there was no need to invoke the supernatural to come up with an explanation for that one.

Fever.

The infection in his hand was spreading. The three fingers of his right hand were pale and swollen where they poked out of the makeshift bandage. He'd just kept winding it with more and more gauze as it had gotten dirty—he hadn't dared look at it for longer than he could remember. He knew that the infection could become gangrene, and the route to a slow agonizing death.

But that didn't matter now.

Wycherly looked down into the depths. He didn't want to go down there at all. He was afraid of the place. But Seth apparently wasn't, working quickly and tirelessly until everything was finished.

"All done, Mister Wych!" Seth said on his last trip up.

Wycherly glanced at the sun. He didn't think he could spare the time to drive the boy back to where he'd found him and still have the light. And while the flashlight clipped to his belt would be of some help, he didn't think he could manage the stairs into the sub-basement one-handed in the dark.

"I tell you what, Seth: I'll give you another twenty dollars—that's forty all together—if you can walk all the way back to the general store by yourself. What do you think of that?"

"Forty dollars?" Seth sounded puzzled.

Wycherly pulled out his wallet—awkward, doing everything left-handed—and removed two twenties. The boy held them—one in each hand—and stared at them, enchanted.

"Come on," Wycherly said. "I'll walk you part way."

He walked Seth back to where the Jeep was parked, its right headlight shattered from his collision with the front gate earlier in the day. He glanced at Seth, and then, surrendering to impulse, drove him out through the gates and a little way down the main road toward the general store.

"There you are," Wycherly said. "Are you sure you can find your way?"

"Stay on the road. That's what my daddy told me. He said, 'Seth, always stay on the road and you won't get lost.'"

Better advice than my daddy ever gave me, Wycherly thought bleakly. "Go on, then," he said aloud.

He watched Seth out of sight with an odd, vaguely paternal pain, as though there were some sort of answer here. There was a bottle in the glove compartment, but Wycherly didn't reach for it. He wouldn't need it to get through the next hour, and then he wouldn't need it ever again.

When he turned back toward the sanatorium gates, it was dark enough that he almost missed them. He turned hastily, unable to control the Jeep properly with only one hand, and this time he hit the left half of the iron gates. It made a horrible grating sound as it slid along the side of the Jeep before settling to the ground. The Jeep wove forward at a crawl as Wycherly scrabbled for the headlights and finally got the remaining headlight turned on. He wished he could think of some way to shine it down into the pit, but even the four-by-four's designers hadn't figured out a way to drive it down stairs like these. He pulled up as close to the edge of the staircase as he dared and left the headlights on anyway, hoping they'd give some light.

The blasting caps and pencil fuses were right where he'd left them. He picked them up in his good hand, hefting their weight experimentally.

Everything you saw in Saturday morning cartoons about lighting the fuse on a stick of dynamite was wrong; all dynamite would do left to it-self was burn. You needed blasting caps to explode it, and fuses to ex-plode the caps.

Wycherly had been involved in enough questionable deals in his ca-reer to know that the easiest way to get his hands on some explosives was to find someplace they were being used, go to the bar nearest to the site, and bide his time. The man who had stolen the dynamite for him—and for a lot of money—had explained how to use them very carefully to Wycherly—twice—to be sure he understood, and he did. He was confi-dent of his ability to detonate sixty pounds of TNT and blow this hell-hole in the ground sky-high. All he had to do was get down there and light the fuse.

He didn't want to go down there. He didn't want to go down there in a *really* big way. But even less did he want to find himself cutting up girls—or more girls—girls with hot warm living flesh, whose sleeping weight had been a sweet presence next to his.

Sinah. Or Luned, or Camilla. There were few things in life that Wycherly Musgrave had ever found so completely soul-shatteringly *re-pugnant* as the delight he had slowly come to take in thoughts of cruelty and torture. Whether Quentin had forced it on him, or whether it was something that sprung from within him, Wycherly abhorred it utterly. The drink kept it at bay, but it couldn't banish it entirely; he'd been damned from the moment he'd said "yes" to Quentin Blackburn in this very place, from the moment he'd opened that book, and damnation was a patient thing.

The white book and the Black Altar, like lock and key, and together they were poison. He'd wanted to destroy the book—he'd had that much health in him after all. But the bitch had made that impossible.

That left him only one thing to destroy.

And in the final analysis it didn't really matter whether the book could really make him do things like that, or if the Black Altar really had unnatural power. That was the beauty of his plan. As long as he followed it to the letter, nothing else mattered. For the first time in almost two decades, it didn't even matter whether he had been behind the wheel of that car back in 1984. Camilla Redford would be avenged, her murder expiated.

Whether he'd committed it or not.

He'd reached his destination; the pit gaped before him. His volatile package tucked under his arm, Wycherly began to make his way, swearing and cursing, down into the dark.

It took Truth half an hour to shake off most of the effects of the sleeping pills, and she still couldn't really understand why Sinah had drugged her.

You pushed too hard, that's all. You're lucky it wasn't rat poison in the jam instead of Seconal.

"Where's my car, Dylan?" Her working tools were locked in the trunk—not the best place for them, but the best of the available alternatives. She'd have to get them out. She was going to need them.

"Out in front. Mrs. Merryman was down at the general store when I left—she's saying some pretty wild things."

"She's saying that Old Miss Dellon's come back and sacrificed Seth to the Gate," Truth said absently. "I'm afraid she did. And this time, it's my fault." Her mind was elsewhere: on finding Sinah and making her do what she wanted, whatever the cost.

"You can't believe that," Dylan said automatically.

Truth rounded on him in exasperation. "Of course I can—because it's *true!* Weren't you listening to Michael this morning? Or did you think what he did up there was all a dumbshow for the rubes? I wouldn't let him replace Quentin Blackburn's magick with his—so the place becomes *my* responsibility—and so does every death that happens there."

Dylan tried to look sympathetic, but what came across was only frustration. "So what are you going to do now?"

Truth suppressed another flare of anger. Dylan had rescued her. She owed him something for that. But oh, she grieved for what they could have been together!

"I need to go back up to the sanatorium. If Seth's still alive, that's where he is, anyway. Will you drive me?"

"Are you sure you're up for this? Truth, you're all in, and we know that place is dangerous." Dylan, the treacherous voice of reason.

"It's dangerous," Truth agreed wearily. "That's why I have to go, Dylan. Because it's dangerous, and it's my job."

"All right, then. Come on."

"Stop! *Dylan!*" Truth croaked.

"I see him." Dylan slowed the car to a stop and rolled down the window. "Seth? Seth Merryman?"

The young man came to a stop, thrusting both hands behind him guiltily.

"I'm Dylan Palmer. I met you and your mother last week, remember?"

"I didn't break no dishes," Seth said hastily.

Dylan forced a smile, though he wasn't as reassured by seeing Seth alive and well as he had expected to be.

"I know you didn't break anything," Dylan told Seth soothingly. "But everyone's worried about you. Where've you been?"

"With a man," Seth said evasively.

Beside him on the seat, Dylan felt Truth stir impatiently.

"What man, Seth?"

Seth giggled. "With the conjureman. He said he'd give me a whole twenty dollar if I'd carry stuff for him. I'm strong—I can carry," he added proudly.

"Where?" Dylan said.

And Seth answered: "Up at the burned place."

Dylan glanced at Truth. She opened the passenger door and got out, slinging her bag of working tools over her shoulder. "Come on, Seth—Dylan's going to drive you back to your family."

"Truth!" Dylan said in an urgent under-voice.

"Drive him back, Dylan; I'm going to keep going. You can join me afterward. Or . . . not," she added, with a faint sorrow in her voice. "But you know where I'll be."

He wanted to argue with her—Hell, he wanted to *throttle* her. But what he did was smile at Seth as the boy got into the passenger seat.

Up at the burned place with the conjureman, carrying things. Dylan couldn't even begin to decode that. Maybe Truth knew. He watched her determinedly walking up the road in the direction of the sanatorium for a long moment before he wrenched the wheel of the car savagely around, turning it back toward the general store.

Driving—and trying not to think about what Truth was doing—gave Dylan plenty of time to brood. He'd been a fan of Thorne Blackburn back when Truth had still been engaged in her postmortem parental feud. Thorne had never made any secret of his belief in his nonhuman parentage—but then, most of Thorne's statements had been, by his own admission, lies told to inoculate his followers against blind belief. Dylan had never taken his claims seriously.

But Truth did—which meant she'd received something which passed, at least in her own mind, for proof. And, if Dylan were willing to trust the evidence of his senses, he'd seen her perform enough miracles in the last two years to constitute proof—of *something*—for nearly anybody.

The trouble was, Dylan *didn't* trust the evidence of his senses. Every ounce of training he had warned him not to do so. *"Your eyes can deceive you—don't trust them,"* said the wizard in *Star Wars,* and even if it came out of a pop movie, it was still good advice. People trusting the evidence of their own eyes reported that Venus was a UFO and Elvis walked the earth today. There was nothing as untrustworthy as the human senses.

But they're all we have, Dylan thought, wrenching his mind back to the present as he came in sight of the general store.

It seemed as if she'd been walking forever. Like a sad ghost, Sinah wandered along trails that had become familiar over the months she'd spent here. She was not alone in her mind. She never had been, not from the day she'd been born, and even if the presences now weren't the minds of others, but only the scraps of ancestral memories and the more demanding presence of Athanais de Lyon, they were comforting in a weird way. Her own thoughts—her own mind—wavered in and out like a weak radio signal, and they held no more answers than the thoughts of others did.

You should have killed her, Athanais whispered, serpent-soft, in her mind.

"It wouldn't solve anything," Sinah answered aloud. But surely the act would be an end in itself—when she'd seen Truth finally pass out under the influence of the powdered pills she'd mixed with the jam, she'd felt a reflux of a purer joy than any she'd ever known, a pure delight in cruelty.

"No," she said, this time answering unspoken urgings. That was not the person she wanted to be.

But what could she do? *Guard the Gate—Pay the* teind*—Guard the Gate* . . . whispered the chorus of ancestral voices, but she could not guard it from the twentieth century, and in the quarter of a century since she'd been born, the twentieth century had finally arrived in Morton's Fork.

Dr. Palmer and his team had come, for one thing, and now others would, too, just as Quentin Blackburn had eighty years before. Her great-great-grandmother Athanais had not stopped Quentin. She had only killed him, and with her own death, broken the bloodline so that her daughter received nothing but the obligation without knowledge.

Was that what had turned the fear of the locals first to anger, and, finally, to hate? That the Dellons no longer had the power to answer their pleas for help, though the sacrifices must go on? Sinah sat down on a fallen tree, for once indifferent to all the bugs that must be swarming beneath its rotting bark. It made so much sense. They hated the Dellons because the Wellspring had failed them. Since Athanais Dellon had died in 1917, the Wellspring only took, not gave—the sterile area around the sanatorium was proof of that. And the memories that clogged Sinah's mind were not true memories at all—only the echoes of all of the bloodline who had gone to the Gate in their turn: her mother, her grandmother . . . everyone that she could have loved.

And Wycherly?

No. He was far away from here by now. He'd gotten away. He was not going to be the bloodline's Great Sacrifice to the Wellspring.

Are you sure? the voice of Athanais de Lyon asked with feline cruelty.

And Sinah wasn't. All she was sure of was that she, Sinah Dellon, who'd had a charmed life and a charmed career, was going to be the last of the bloodline.

The one who failed once and for all time.

Despite the fact that in the world above it was still afternoon, by the time Wycherly made it to the bottom of the black staircase it was already night beside the Black Altar.

Wycherly moved forward cautiously toward the altar stone. If he fell holding the parcel he'd probably merely kill himself without doing any other damage. The flashlight didn't give him quite enough light to see his way, but for wholly mundane reasons. The taint that Wycherly had expected to face here had gone.

Disbelievingly, he put his left hand palm-flat on the altar top. He felt nothing—Quentin was gone.

It didn't really matter. Whatever monstrousness had infected Quentin Blackburn and kept him pinned here for generations had passed to Wycherly now. Quentin's book and Quentin's evil, and Wycherly to expiate the corruption as best he could.

Would blowing up the altar stone destroy . . . whatever it was? He wasn't sure, but it was the best he could do. Shrugging off his confusion, Wycherly knelt beside the altar and opened the package, working awkwardly with only his left hand to rely on. The blasting caps lay in neat rows on their cardboard backing, and the fuse was an innocuous coil of string.

As he worked, he became conscious of the sound of running water. It was an annoying sound, making him think of deep black rivers and drowned women swimming through their depths. It threaded its way into his thoughts, breaking his concentration and forcing him to go back over the same motions over and over again.

Abruptly he was certain he knew where the sound came from. The cave, whose doorway he'd shied away from before, must lead down to an underground river, not to a spring as he'd first thought. It was the only explanation. And now the river was rising for some reason—hadn't there been a storm here a night or two ago?—and soon the water would come rushing out of the cave's mouth, sweeping him and all his work away.

Wycherly got to his feet, thinking vaguely of sandbags. The sound was so clear that he was surprised to see that the floor of the chamber was still dry, so maybe the water wasn't rising.

But why was it so loud?

Cautiously Wycherly got to his feet and began to move toward the opening in the rock wall beyond the altar. Slowly. As if he were stalking something.

She'd always been too impatient for her own good, Truth thought irritably, and today was the final proof. The bag over her shoulder was a dragging weight, and she wasn't entirely sure why she'd brought it with her. Habit, she supposed. The leftover toxins from her drugging weighed down her muscles, making every step an effort. Sweat trickled down her face and neck, making her clothing a soggy, chafing weight. She was probably going to fall on her face right here.

The sensible course of action would have been to go with Dylan to drop Seth back at his mother's house and then go on up to the sanatorium—or even have Dylan drop her there first. But to be perfectly frank, she didn't trust Dylan not to come up with some new delaying action—all perfectly reasonable, of course . . .

Stop it. Dylan isn't your enemy.

And at least Seth hadn't been the Gate's latest victim. Her honor was still clear. There was still time.

Truth gave up and stopped for a rest, pulling her shirttail out of her slacks to scrub her face dry. That was the trouble—there were no villains here, only victims. Even Sinah who'd all-but-poisoned her, even Michael. Even Wycherly . . . wherever he was.

And I hope that wherever it is, it's a long way from here. His sister's a psychic, and those things always run in families—always! Whether he thinks he has any trace of talent or not, just his showing up at the Gate could trigger an event.

Truth tried to put those thoughts out of her mind. There was little she could do if he *was* there. He wasn't all that fond of her to begin with—Truth winced mentally as she recalled their last meeting—and it was unlikely he'd do anything she asked.

But would Sinah?

Oh, yes, Truth promised herself, a wolfish grin pulling her mouth back in a lupine smile. *She fed me a Mickey Finn. I'm entitled to a bit of my own back for that. This time, she'll do what I want.*

By the time she reached the turnoff to the sanatorium it was twilight. Truth checked her watch: half an hour since she and Dylan had parted. It would have been only a matter of minutes for him to reach the general store again; if he were coming back at all, he would be here at any time.

She didn't know whether she wanted him to come back or not.

She stopped to rest again, gazing absently at the sanatorium gates. Her reactions were slowed with exhaustion; it took her a long moment to recognize what she was seeing.

Half of the sanatorium's iron gate had been ripped away.

Truth blinked, but what she saw didn't change. The inward-sagging gates, rusted into immobility with the passing of eighty years, were no longer in the same position they had been the last time she'd seen them. One was knocked farther open—she saw the fresh parenthesis in the gravel where the gate had gouged a track—and the other had been moved several feet down the drive and was lying in the ditch. Fresh wheel ruts in the gravel—exposing the still-damp earth beneath—showed where the vehicle that had done the damage had stuck and strained. Slivers of broken headlight glittered like shards of ice among the stones.

Who had been here since this morning?

She tried to cast her mind back to when she had come up here with Michael, Sinah, and Dylan. It seemed a thousand years ago, but Truth was sure the gate hadn't been broken then.

Had Dylan brought the camper up here for some reason afterward?

Her fogged mind refused to present her with any opinions. *This won't do,* Truth thought. She had to snap out of this daze somehow. *Keep moving. Maybe that will help.*

Up the drive, retracing the path she seemed to have walked a hundred times by now. She wished she'd never seen this place, she wished she'd never come to West Virginia. And slowly, as she walked, Truth became aware that she was being watched.

It was a consciousness as elemental as the relationship between hunter and prey. There was something out there—something utterly tangible and real—and it was watching her.

Truth stopped, looking around, but all she could see was the disorderly hedges of wild rose, brilliant in the late-afternoon light. She tried to drag her mind back to the mundane realm; what could it be? A bear? Someone searching for Seth?

"Hello?" Truth said. A startled rustle of the bushes. Silence. Visions of rural marauders took unwelcome possession of her imagination.

In the distance, faint as the buzzing of a dragonfly, Truth could hear the distant sound of a car engine. So Dylan had come back. The thought gave her spirits a faint but real lift, but habit propelled her to push onward without waiting for him.

Now she could see the white marble bench again, serene in the middle of its shabby meadow. Whoever was watching her was in that direction.

Though she'd never wanted to see that bench again after her first visit here, Truth left the drive and walked toward it into the undergrowth. She could hear the car engine getting louder, and now she could see a shadowy shape crouching behind a stand of forsythia.

"Hey!" Truth shouted hoarsely.

There was a blur of movement as the figure bolted—a screech of brakes—and the automatic blare of a horn. Truth heard a woman scream.

Sinah stood framed in Dylan's headlights like a jacklit doe. She stared at him, eyes wide, and Dylan fancied he could almost see the pulse fluttering in her throat. A moment later Truth floundered out of the brush behind Sinah and grabbed her arm.

Dylan got out of the car and walked toward them.

He was surprised by the pure, elemental fury that he felt. The dose of pills that Truth had ingested could easily have been fatal—and Sinah had given it to her, motivated by what madness or whim he did not know. He grabbed Sinah by the other arm.

"What did you think you were doing?" he shouted, trying to yank her away from Truth.

Sinah burst into tears and clung to Truth. Dylan stared at Sinah in angry confusion. Truth reached out her free hand and patted Dylan's arm.

"It's all right now. Hush, Sinah, love, nobody's angry with you." Her voice was gentle and fond, but Dylan could see Truth's face—serene, remote . . . inhuman.

Oh, stop trying to scare yourself! Dylan thought crossly. Truth was no more a member of the Fairy Race than Thorne was. There were no such things as—

. . . *ghosts?* Dylan finished with wry self-mockery. *"There are more things in heaven and earth, Horatio, than are dreamt of in your philosophy."* Words he'd always lived by.

"Thanks for coming back," Truth said to Dylan.

"I think I can be counted for that much support in a crisis," Dylan said raggedly. "I dropped Seth in front of the general store and came back as quickly as I could. I expected to find you passed out in the middle of the road, so I was going slow. Lucky for her. When she darted out in front of me I thought she was a deer; I almost didn't brake in time."

"She was running away from me. Sinah—*Sinah.* Can you hear me? Nobody's going to hurt you. Can you tell me what's wrong?" Truth coaxed.

After a moment Sinah answered. "I'm the last," she said in a ragged whisper. "I'm the last. I failed. They'll come, they'll find it. . . ." Her head drooped with weariness and despair.

"No, they won't." Truth spoke with compelling urgency. "Close it with me, and you protect it forever. You have to close it, Sinah—no one can find it then. I know it's hard, but you've always known it had to be done. The Wellspring doesn't belong in the modern world. People will only get hurt if it stays. You know what you have to do—"

She went on, her voice lulling, until at last Sinah raised her head and answered, her voice as heavy and drugged as Truth's had been when Dylan had found her.

"Yes. All right. I'll do what you want."

Dylan would have protested—would at least have done something to rouse Sinah from this trance—but at that moment he saw something gleaming in the distance.

"Look," he said, his voice low. "There's a light up at the sanatorium."

Down to a sunless sea. The phrase circled around inside Wycherly's brain as if it were the answer to all Life's riddles. *Down to a sunless sea . . .* It was a line from a poem, but he no longer remembered which one.

He hadn't brought the flashlight, but that didn't matter. His left hand trailed along the curving rock wall, and Wycherly moved slowly, inexorably, down the stairs. *Down to a sunless sea.*

All he could hear was water: trickling, roaring, gushing, purling on from nowhere to nowhere, down here in the dark. Tickling scraps of spiderwebs brushed his face, and he batted them away absently. *Down to a sunless sea.* He did not have to ask where he was going—he knew.

He was going back. To the river edge, to that August night a dozen years ago. To where he should have died.

He reached the last step. He was surrounded by a darkness more absolute than blindness, but it didn't matter. He knew where he was going.

"That's my car," Sinah said, sounding faintly indignant.

The Jeep Cherokee stood parked at the edge of the ruined foundations, its single, dimming headlight shining futilely out across the hole.

"There's a light down inside there," Dylan said. "But I don't see anyone."

"Wycherly," Truth said. "He's Seth's witch-man."

Dylan cupped his hands to shout, but Truth stopped him.

"No. We'd better go down," she said. *And pray that he's still there, that I can hold Sinah's will long enough to do what needs to be done, and that Dylan doesn't turn out to be my worst enemy.*

"I don't like this," Dylan Palmer said mildly.

The tiny pencil flashlight in his hand flicked its thin beam back and forth over the piled bundles of slim cylinders wrapped in reddish paper that were stacked about the base of the smooth loaf of stone that had once been the carven Black Altar. They looked like parcels of emergency flares.

"Isn't that dynamite?" Truth asked weakly.

A fading flashlight resting atop the altar gave a faint amber light. The lozenge of sky above their heads was a deep indigo, and the normal heat of an August night was replaced, here, with a damp chill that seemed to well up out of the secret places of the earth.

"Yes," Dylan said tightly. "It looks like somebody was getting ready to set that off. Look, Truth, can you and Sinah tune in to the locus from—"

"Wycherly!" Sinah cried suddenly.

She'd been standing quietly next to Truth. Now she went flying past, toward the darker shadow that was the gateway to the underground spring.

"Sinah!" Truth shouted. She grabbed for Sinah—physically and psychically both—and missed. Sinah disappeared through the opening, vanished as surely as if she had teleported.

"Damn . . . *damn,*" Truth muttered. Adrenaline had finally washed the last of the sleeping pills from her system. She looked back at Dylan—helplessly, apologetically.

"I've got to go down there," she said.

"Wait a minute—wait!" Dylan grabbed Truth roughly and all but shook her. "Can you see in the dark? Wait until I get a flashlight—some flares—something."

Truth opened her mouth to refuse, and Dylan shook her again. "What if they're hurt? What if there's more dynamite? Wait right here—and if you stir so much as one step I'll break your little neck!"

"Yes, Dylan," Truth said meekly.

But as soon as Dylan reached the surface and disappeared, she turned away, taking the flashlight from the deconsecrated altar stone and following Sinah down the worn and curving ancient stairs to the Wellspring.

Truth turned off the flashlight as she entered the cleft—far better not to waste it. The darkness closed around her almost instantly, but she did not need to see to discern her surroundings. Cautiously she reached out: The untainted power of the Gate, familiar and soothing, beat against her *sidhe* perceptions.

"Sinah?" she called, hesitantly. She could not find Sinah or Wycherly against the backwash of the Gate's power. *Please, let her answer, let her still be alive. . . .*

"Here," Sinah said. "Truth? I've found him. Hurry, please!"

Truth flicked on the flashlight again, and in its dim illumination she could see Sinah, standing beside a kneeling figure. Wycherly.

"Is he . . . ?" *Lords of the Wheel, don't let him be dead!*

"He's alive. But I can't wake him up—and I think there's someone else down here, too." Sinah's voice shook; she sounded scared and alone.

Truth flicked the dying flashlight around the space. She was inside a cave carved from the same black stuff as the chamber above. It seemed to be about sixty feet across, and she could not see its roof when she turned the flashlight upward. In the center of the chamber was the Wellspring, welling up out of a natural caldera in the rock. Truth could feel the wintry chill emanating from the water even from where she stood; the cold of clear, fresh water from the heart of the Earth. From where she stood, Truth could see no outlet for the waters; the floor of the cavern was the same smooth, close-grained stone as the rest.

She flicked the light quickly around the rest of the cavern. Toward its edges, the floor was covered with debris: colored bottles, wrapped bundles, baskets . . . and bones. Some were brown with age and decayed nearly to unrecognizability, some were fresh and new.

Some very new.

Sinah moaned at the sight of the scattered skulls, but at least she hadn't seen what Truth had. There was a body that lay face down at the very edge of the Wellspring, one arm trailing in the water. The body wore a yellow T-shirt and jeans, and Truth was afraid she knew who it was.

"Stay there, Sinah, I'm going to take a look at something."

Truth set the flashlight down, its beam pointing the other way, and went over to the body. She gingerly turned it over. Luned Starking.

The arm that had been in the water was white and cold as ice cream. But Luned was not dead. Truth pulled her away from the lip of the Wellspring and hoped the action did not trigger retribution from the powers of this place.

Sinah picked up the flashlight and turned it on Truth. By now its light was a faint red beam.

"What—who—" Sinah sounded rattled, on the edge of hysterics.

Truth only prayed that Sinah could hold herself together for a little while longer. She didn't want to find herself facing any of the previous Gatekeepers—or Athanais de Lyon.

"It's Luned Starking. She's still alive."

"Where?" Sinah sounded baffled and frightened. "Truth, I can't make him wake up. Wycherly!"

Truth turned toward Sinah and couldn't see her. The flashlight lens was now a copper disk in the darkness—Truth could clearly see the filaments in the bulb as they faded into darkness.

"Truth!"

It was Dylan's voice this time, distorted almost to unrecognizability by the cave. Sinah squeaked and even Truth jumped when she saw the flicker of white light on the wall.

"Dylan?" Truth said. "Point that somewhere else, will you?"

"Are you all right?" he demanded. In the refracted glow of the powerful hand torch, Dylan appeared like a rather distraught ministering angel. When Truth spoke, he flicked the beam away from her, and Truth saw his face grow intent as he saw the accumulated bones.

"So far," Truth said. "Sinah and Wycherly are here, and Luned. She's alive."

"But what . . . ? This is amazing," Dylan said.

"Truth!" Sinah called insistently.

Truth got to her feet—there was nothing she could do for Luned at the moment, except lay her down carefully—and went back to Sinah. Dylan was still standing at the foot of the steps, slowly playing his light over the whole chamber.

"Shine that over here, would you, Dyl?" Truth said. She knelt beside Wycherly and Sinah and felt the arctic cold of the stone bite through the fabric of her thin summer slacks. She'd been down here less than five minutes and she was already shivering; this place was like an icebox.

Dylan obliged. Wycherly was kneeling at the very edge of the Wellspring, head bent as if he'd been gazing into its depths. His hands were balanced on his knees; the right one was swathed in dirty gauze, and the fingers Truth could see poking out of the bandages were badly swollen.

"I can't wake him up, I can't move him," Sinah said, tearfully.

Truth tried, but Wycherly's muscles were tensed and he held his position with robotic stubbornness. His eyes were open, but he neither saw nor heard them. It was as if he were . . . elsewhere.

"He's gone through the Gate," Truth said. Or had he? Wycherly could not have been here more than an hour at most—the Jeep's headlight had still been shining full-strength. Was there still time to summon him back?

Dylan came over to them. "I'm taking Luned up to the Jeep," he said. "It'll be warm inside, and warmth is what she needs most right now. Does Wycherly have the keys? Otherwise I'll smash a window."

Truth rummaged through the pockets of Wycherly's leather jacket. "Here they are." She held the keys out.

Dylan dropped the key ring into his pocket, and held out a bundle of slender cylinders to Truth. "Hazard flares. It's the only other thing I could find on short notice that makes light."

Truth took one and struck it alight, holding it at arm's length. The sulphurous smoke made her cough, and she tossed the flare away from her, only realizing after it had left her hand that she might be tossing it into a pile of flammable material.

Fortunately it landed in an area that was free of the litter of centuries, and burned against the bare stone with a hellish, cherry-colored light. A few feet away, she saw Dylan stoop to lift Luned. The beam from the lamp in his hand jiggled wildly as he stood once more and began to carry her toward the stairs.

"It won't help," Sinah said softly. In the uncertain light of the hazard flare, her face was older, sad and knowing. "She's a-gone. The Power's done took her. It don't matter where her natural body is."

We'll see about that! Truth vowed silently. She closed her eyes, willing herself to see her surroundings with Otherworld sight. Here, right on top of the open Gate, she should not require the elaborate centering and meditation techniques she usually used.

She didn't. It was as if the power that held this place had only been waiting for her consent before replacing her version of reality with its own. The darkness vanished, and the real world was gone.

This was a place she had not seen on her last two attempts to reach the Gate. She stood upon a high cliff, with the sea crashing and foaming on the rocks below. The wind of a gathering storm scudded toward her, and far out to sea Truth could see the shimmering form of an elaborate Gateway.

Quentin Blackburn's influence was gone; his attempts to twist and taint the power of the Gate unsuccessful. This was the thing itself: The Gate Between The Worlds. The place where the intricate network of ley lines that covered the Earth's surface crossed, allowing the Gatekeeper access to the power of the Earth Herself.

"Wycherly!" Truth shouted against the howl of the wind. In this ghostly land it seemed that she could see the shape of a shining path upon the wind—a path more ghostly still, made of wind and sea foam, leading out to the sidhe Gate.

Did she dare to take that path—pass through that portal to confront her inhuman cousins in the land beyond?

Truth hesitated, gazing around her. If that was where Wycherly and Luned had gone, she must follow, and try to ransom them back somehow. Otherwise she would have lost—her vow would be broken, and her penance Michael Archangel's to mete out.

As she strained her eyes toward the unreal ocean Truth saw a tiny figure already on the path, grey and luminous and far distant.

Wycherly?

Truth nerved herself to take the first step into nothingness.

"NO!"

A force crashed into her from behind, jostling her forward and yanking her back almost in one gesture. She swung around, staring into Wycherly's face.

He was red-eyed, gaunt, and unshaven—a faithful reflection of his physical body in the material world—but here he grasped her shoulders with two good hands, glaring at her wildly as his mouth struggled to form words.

And above and behind him, hovering like smoke, was a shadowy nimbus that seemed to be the darkly lucent form of the golden-eyed Goat, the shambling inhuman creature that Quentin Blackburn's deepest sorceries paid homage to.

But though Wycherly resonated with Quentin's black energy, the unwitting pact between them had not yet been sealed in blood. There was still something of Wycherly that Truth could touch. She reached out for him, preparing to fight with all her might—

—and as her fingertips grazed his stubbly cheek there was a flash of darkness, a jarring discontinuity.

Truth opened her eyes to darkness, with the stinging sensation of a slap still on her cheek. Dylan was standing over her, empty-handed. The lamp lay on the floor, casting its beam out across the dark surface of the Wellspring.

"Don't you ever do that again," Truth told him in a low angry voice.

"He didn't—I did," Sinah said, in a more normal voice. "I thought you were going to be lost forever—like Wycherly."

Quickly Truth reached out and grabbed Wycherly by the arm, willing him to follow her back to the Material Plane while the trail of her own passage was still fresh. She felt the energy flash between them, painful as a spark of static electricity, and then Wycherly began to stir.

As the three of them stared at him, he turned toward Sinah, blinking in the light. Truth looked back at Dylan in baffled apology.

"Grant me a little common sense," Dylan said. The affectionate—

though worried—tone of his voice took the sting out of his words. "I know better than to jar a psychic out of a trance."

Or a magician out of a spirit-walk, Truth corrected mentally.

Dylan looked at Sinah, real anger in his expression. "But I wasn't expecting her to move so fast."

"Sorry," Truth mumbled. She wished she hadn't accused Dylan, but still felt groggy and disoriented. If this was Wycherly, then the other figure Truth had seen in her brief vision must be Luned Starking, closer than Wycherly to passing into the realm of the Bright Lords, but still on the human side of the Gate. She ran a hand through her short, dark hair and looked back toward Sinah.

Sinah was cradling Wycherly in her arms with an expression in which fright and maternal tenderness were equally mixed. He did not seem as alert as he had seconds ago, and even from this distance, Truth could see that his body was wracked with shudders.

"He's burning up with fever," Sinah said. "But he was ice-cold a minute ago."

He wasn't HERE *a minute ago,* Truth corrected silently. *And he could slip back into the Otherworld at any moment, this close to the Gate.* She took a deep breath and tried to marshal her scattered thoughts. There was something about this place that was so peaceful it made thinking difficult.

Too peaceful, in fact. The peace of the grave.

"Close the Gate, Sinah," Truth said. "You have to. If you don't, he'll just go right back there."

The look Sinah shot her was one of pure annoyance. "At a time like this? We've got to get Wych and Luned out of here, to a doctor—"

She's stalling.

"You tried to kill me today," Truth said brutally. "And I think you owe me five minutes of your time for that. You're the only one who can shut this thing down. Now, it's true that it might not have to be you; I can go dig up a distant relative—you must have one somewhere—but while I'm doing that, Wycherly, Luned, and probably a couple of other people *will die.* Maybe even you. And that would really irritate me. So are you going to do what I want, or do I get to slap you silly?"

Sinah stared at her, stunned.

"For the record, I endorse the sentiments, if not the expression," Dylan said from behind Truth. "She's right. You can't let this go any farther, Sinah. Not if you have the power to stop it."

Truth felt a pang of gratitude at Dylan's support, but suppressed it quickly. Now was no time to be tangled in her emotions.

"Oh, all right!" Sinah—and it did seem to be Sinah, at least this time—said. "What do I have to do?"

"Just give me your hand," Truth said. Reluctantly, Sinah raised one hand and placed it into Truth's.

And Truth drew Sinah into reality.

The two of them stood on the edge of the sea-swept cliff, and Truth could see Luned's tiny figure toiling toward the half-open Gate. Truth looked behind her, to landward, where the astral landscape dissolved into a curtain of grey mist, and thought she could discern, far away, a faint speck that might be an approaching figure. Wycherly, coming toward the Gate once more.

"Okay," Sinah said. "Now what?" She looked seaward, in the direction of the Gate, but plainly she was not drawn to it as Truth was.

This time there was no Thorne to show Truth what to do; no grimoire to serve as a touchstone. The memory of what she had done before would have to be enough.

Truth took a deep breath.

"Say what I say:

"I am a hawk/Above the cliff—" Truth began, the words of the spell that had sealed the portal at Shadow's Gate. But this time the words were only words, without inner meaning.

Truth stopped. Sinah looked at her, sullenness fading into real fear.

"It isn't going to work, is it?" she said. "I'm sorry, Truth—I'd help you if I could. But I don't know what to do!"

"It's all right," Truth said soothingly. "We just have to find the right way."

As she spoke, her mind worked frantically. She'd studied her father's grimoire and knew the liturgy meant to end in the opening of the Gates. Could she simply invert the ritual? At least it would give them a pattern to follow. And in the Otherworld, the symbol of the thing was the thing itself.

But the two of them couldn't do something like that alone. The ritual was meant for a full working Circle, and a full Blackburn Circle numbered sixteen people: The Gatekeeper and three other Guardians, the Hierophex and Hierolator, the Hierophant and Hierodule, and eight members of lesser grade—a balance of male and female energies. Without that to draw on, it didn't matter who Sinah was—or who Truth was, for that matter.

The Otherworld wavered around them like a candle flame.

"Sinah, don't fight me," Truth said. "Just relax and accept what is. Just—"

Once more the world wavered, and darkness spilled into it like ink into fresh water.

The cold of the cavern was a fresh shock each time she became aware of it, Truth thought. She blinked, trying to bring things into focus.

Dylan had shut off his flashlight to conserve the batteries. While their attention had been elsewhere, he'd struck another flare to replace the one Truth had lit when he'd taken Luned up to the car. It was just guttering out now—they'd been down here fifteen minutes.

"It isn't going to work," Sinah said flatly.

"Yes it is," Truth said firmly. "At least, I think it will. I've got an idea."

She'd carried her bag of working tools down with her: It was the work of only a few minutes to scribe out a nine-foot circle in chalk and sketch the basic "north-gate" glyph inside it. The needle of the compass she always carried reeled drunkenly about its dial, useless; Truth located the cardinal points almost by guess and set the dish of incense in the North. Opposite it—nine feet away, across the diameter of the circle—she set the one candle she had with her. She filled her small crystal bowl with water from the Wellspring itself and placed it in the West, where it shone like a crystalline lens, and then unwrapped her flint-and-horn knife and placed it meticulously in the East.

"Okay. It's ready. Dylan, can you help me carry Wycherly into the middle of the circle? Without smudging the figure too much, if possible, but having drawn it is the most important thing."

Truth's voice shook slightly as she spoke—she hoped it was with cold, not fear. Fear was death to an Adept.

"What is it you have in mind?" Dylan asked, neutrally.

"We're going to do a full Blackburn Working, the nine powers and the four summonings, all the way up to the Opening of the Way, and reverse it. It's the only thing I can think of," Truth said baldly.

"Aren't you twelve people and two weeks short?" Dylan asked. So he did know the Work as well as she thought.

"Yes. I think I have a way around that." *I only hope it works.*

"Okay, let's take it slowly this time," Truth said, keeping her voice level and encouraging.

The four of them were huddled together in the center of the chalk figure on the floor, sitting so close that their knees touched. Wycherly was propped up between Truth and Sinah—Truth would not have chosen to use a sick man unable to give his consent, but she had no choice. They were out of time.

Time . . . it was a meaningless construct in the Otherworld. Minutes here could seem to be hours there. Or . . . days. In the Otherworld, there was all the time they needed to learn what they must.

"Dylan, Sinah, I want you both to try to breathe together. Sinah, you've done this before—don't fight it this time. Let it pass over you as if it were a dream. Dylan, I don't know what you'll see; you might just fall asleep. You can think of this as lucid dreaming, if that helps you work with it."

"Okay," Dylan said calmly. "I'll do my best to hit an alpha state, but it's not easy when you're freezing to death."

"Just do your best," Truth told him. Gratitude welled up in her for his gift of calm trust when she needed it most. "Sinah?"

"I'm ready," the actress said. "Break a leg, Truth."

Truth smiled. "We'll start with something very mundane: a simple hypnotic induction. I'm going to count backward from one hundred, and I want both of you to count with me. Visualize a staircase that you're descending."

"Not hard, all things considered. I think I'm going to be seeing those stairs in my sleep," Dylan said.

"Fine. When you get to the bottom, you'll be at the Gate. One hundred. Ninety-nine. Ninety-eight . . ."

And in a world where reality was a by-product of the Will, surely Truth could will the Circle, the Sign, and all the rest into being with her desire alone?

Because she *had* to.

EIGHTEEN

BEYOND THE GRAVE

Under the wide and starry sky
Dig the grave and let me lie.
Glad did I live and gladly die,
And I laid me down with a will.
—ROBERT LOUIS STEVENSON

"I CALL UPON YOU, BROTHERS AND SISTERS OF THE ART, BY *the blood we share—lend me your power in my father's name!"*

There was a flickering moment when Truth was sure that it had worked, when she could feel the braided energies of the other three mingled with her own and with something far greater, all directed by her will. Then they were gone, slithering out of her psychic grasp and leaving her . . .

Alone.

Try again, *Truth thought, and willed her consciousness back to the physical world.*

It didn't work.

Her eyes still opened on a landscape of pale mist, sea and sky. . . .

And another presence. An inhuman one.

Truth could not gaze at it directly. It was a flicker of light, a discontinuity in the world, as far outside Truth's conception of the natural realm as the Otherworld itself was outside the average person's. Yet it was sentient, self-willed and purposeful.

"*You seek the key,*" *the shining figure said.* "*Have you the courage to step through the door and take it?*"

There was no door—yes, there was. As the wordless question formed in Truth's mind, she was aware of a threefold echo—the others. But she must concentrate on what was before her: trap, or opportunity?

Truth looked through the door. Beyond, on a plinth of black stone, lay a silver key as long as her arm.

"*Yes.*"

Truth stepped forward, and passed through the door.

He was dreaming, Dylan assured himself, dreaming lightly, so that the awareness of the dream-state was superimposed on the images he saw. Was this what Truth meant when she spoke of traveling to the Otherworld, the Astral Plane that so many psychics talked about? If it was, the Astral Plane—like so many realities—was disappointing after the grandiloquent images conjured up by its description.

Dylan stood in the corridor outside his office at the Bidney Institute, and Miles Godwin, the current Director, was standing in front of his door.

"*You seek the key,*" *Miles said.* "*Have you the courage to step through the door and take it?*"

Yes, he was dreaming, and this wasn't getting them anywhere. He must be heading for Stage Three sleep, but Dylan supposed he should wait for Truth to wake him up. He'd agreed to go along with her playacting, even if it was ridiculous.

The cruel honesty of his thoughts shocked Dylan, though not enough to rouse him to the surface of wakefulness. He'd always respected Truth, even at her most maddening—when had he started dismissing her perceptions as those of a deluded child? He'd seen things for which there was no rational explanation—couldn't this be one?

"*Have you the courage?*" *Miles said again.*

Oh, what the hell, Dylan thought, *about to walk into his office. Sure I do.*

But did he? He didn't have the courage to tell his fiancée she'd become a babbling lunatic, did he? And she'd warned him, promised him, pleaded with him . . .

And that made him a coward. He wasn't brave at all. He was a coward. His little box of scientific open-mindedness was another safe way of not thinking about anything outside it. He'd just drawn the boundaries a little wider than most people's, that was all.

So.

He might owe this attempt to Truth, but Dylan owed it more to himself—to the memory of the brave and open-minded man he'd once thought he was.

In the way of dreams, all this introspection had taken only a moment. The man still stood, facing Dylan in front of his office door. The figure didn't look like Miles now—like someone, but who?

"I don't have the courage," Dylan said. "But I have the will. And I want the key."

Now Dylan was standing alone in front of the open door to his office. Inside, on a desk that was simultaneously his own familiar desk and a black double cube, lay a bright copper key as long as his arm.

Dylan stepped forward.

He was moving. Wycherly lay, eyes closed, drifting at the behest of whatever power pulled him forward. Only the sudden tardy realization that the droning was a car engine—he was asleep at the wheel!—made him open his eyes.

But he wasn't in the front seat—he was curled up sideways on the tiny back seat. It was night, and the headlights of oncoming cars turned the raindrops on the windshield to spangles of light.

This was his car. It had been a birthday present and a bribe—he'd just completed six months of sobriety in the course of his third clinic in the last three years.

He was nineteen.

"No," Wycherly said, struggling to sit up in the Fiat's cramped confines. Had everything else been a dream?

"You awake, Wych?" Camilla Redford said, turning around in the front passenger seat to look at him. Her voice was slurred—she'd been drinking, he'd been drinking, they'd all been drinking. There'd been a party at Randy Benson's house: Wycherly didn't remember all the details.

Who was driving the car? Wycherly sat up, pushing Camilla down in her seat, painfully aware that the Fiat was going much too fast, starting to drift sideways. He caught a glimpse of a blond head—the driver behind the wheel—just as the car hit the edge of the embankment with a sharp shock and went careening down the side.

There was a brief, breathless moment when it seemed that everything would be all right, before any of the passengers realized where they were. Then the car began to fill with water.

Wycherly was terrified. This was the crash that had killed Cammie, and this time he *was the one who was going to drown. Wycherly struggled to be somewhere,* anywhere *but here—and suddenly it was as if he slid like smoke through the car's roof, hovering above the scene.*

The moon had been full that night. Now Wycherly's mind allowed him to place the scene properly in the past, and the moon illuminated the scene with a ghostly azure radiance, spectrally bright. It had rained earlier, a brief August shower, but the sky was clear now. Wycherly could see the white Fiat below, its roof just above the surface of the water. Soon it would slip sideways into deeper water, rolling onto its side.

The driver's-side door thrust open, and Wycherly saw the blond who had been driving struggle out of the car, dragging the back seat passenger with him as he struggled toward the shore. Dragging Wycherly.

The shock of recognition jarred Wycherly loose from his peaceful vantage point, and all at once he was lying on gravel staring up at the stars. Randy Benson was standing over him, crying.

"I can't be here. I can't. My dad has plans for me," Randy moaned.

Randy and Wycherly hadn't seen much of each other before tonight, but Wycherly had heard about him—the golden boy: athlete, straight-A student, scion of a family that could number senators and signers of the Declaration of Independence among its ancestors. A son, Wycherly's father had told him, that any father would be proud to have. A son like Kenny Jr. should have been.

Like Wycherly should have been.

The Fiat slid further beneath the surface. Camilla was still inside. She'd stay there until the wrecker arrived and pulled the car out of the river.

"She's dead. Oh, God—she's dead. I can't be here," Randy said again. Tears still ran down his face, but sheer terror had stopped his crying. "She's dead—but you? You're a drunk, a loser. Nobody cares about you. And your dad can buy you off."

Randy stepped back into the water—clever, clever, not to leave any tracks for the police in case Wycherly remembered something later. In a moment he was gone from sight, and Wycherly lay, looking up at the stars, waiting for the sirens to start.

Randy was the driver. RANDY. *Wycherly hadn't even been at the wheel.*

The realization worked slowly through him like the dose of a drug. Wycherly hadn't been driving that night. It had been Randy, not Wycherly, who had killed Camilla Redford.

He was innocent. He'd always been innocent.

"Do you want the key, Wycherly?" his father said.

Wycherly sat up. It was cold here on the gravel and he shivered. Kenneth Musgrave, Sr. was standing beside him, gazing down at Wycherly with his usual expression of impatience and distaste—as though Wycherly wasn't good enough.

But he never would be, would he? Nothing Wycherly could do would be enough for his father. And the golden god that had been held up to him as the measure of perfection was just as far from perfection as Wycherly himself—flawed, fallible . . . murderer.

"You want the key," his father said. "Have you the courage to step through the door and take it?"

The key. He'd been searching for the key all his life.

Kenneth Musgrave pointed out over the water.

Wycherly looked. He'd thought it had already sunk, but he'd been wrong. The Fiat was still riding fairly high. Cammie's head must still be above water. And on the driver's seat somehow he could see the gleam of a gold key as long as his arm.

Wycherly hesitated, pure panic gripping him. He could save her. He could get the key. But to do it meant going out into the water where the monsters were. As he faltered, he saw a thick ripple in the surface of the river.

There was something out there.

It didn't work. Sinah had been whipsawed by too many strong emotions in the last twenty-four hours to feel anything more than weariness. She got stiffly to her feet, wincing as cramped muscles protested. She'd almost thought the elaborate theatrics Truth had gone through this time had a chance of working, but here they were: same damp cave, same running water, same flickering candlelight.

"Ah. And do you find our cribbage to your liking, pretty maid?" a voice said.

Sinah spun around—and stared into the eyes of Athanais de Lyon.

She was standing in a cell. There were wisps of straw on the floor. Sinah drew a panicked breath, and almost choked on the smells of rot and sewage. She prayed to wake up, knowing as she did that this could not be a dream. Surely—if this were a dream—surely she would not be able to smell *things?*

"Do you seek the key?" Athanais asked. She threw back her head and laughed.

This is too real, *Sinah thought, clawing desperately for her sanity. Athanais was wearing a seventeenth-century gown that looked like something out of Richard Lester's* Three Musketeers. *The dress was made of bright yellow satin, and when it had been clean and new it must have accented Athanais' red-haired, green-eyed beauty to perfection.*

But now the gown was tattered and soiled, its hem black and draggled. Rats scuttled in the corners of the cell; a stinking tallow candle dripped fatly down into the receiver of a battered pewter candlestick. There was a rhythmic thudding going on outside the cell, and against her will and her better judgment, Sinah went toward the window.

" '*Tis the gallows they build,* madame—*a fit end for those who have not the courage to seek the key!*" *Athanais cawed.*

It was true. Sinah stood on a chair and looked through the small barred window. In the square below, their work lit by torches, men worked to build a gibbet large enough to hang half a dozen people at once.

A fit end to a witch—and wasn't that what Sinah was? A woman who used her special powers to her own advantage, living in a world of privilege while those around her struggled through obstacles and imperfection? Who rejoiced in others' failures, knowing that she'd had a hand in them, standing aloof while others floundered.

"*What . . . key?*" *Sinah said slowly, stepping down from the chair. She was trapped in this* Nightmare on Elm Street *dream sequence, and she couldn't see any way out. If she died here, did she die in reality?*

Athanais was standing beside the door to the cell.

"*You seek the key,*" *she said.* "*Have you the courage to step through the door and take it?*"

Through the grille set into the door's upper portion, Sinah could see the key, hanging on the wall beyond. It was iron and as long as her arm. She could already feel it in her hands—cold, and heavy, and her passport out of here.

"*Yes,*" *Sinah said, but she wondered if that was true. What if there was a whole world out there that went with the cell? A world in which she would be a hunted alien, never really belonging, forced to survive by her wits and what powers she could summon?*

Sinah cast an anguished look toward Athanais: the ghost beneath the skin, the thing she'd always feared most—insanity and death. She could despise Athanais de Lyon all she wished, but how much real difference was there between Athanais de Lyon and Sinah Dellon? Sinah had been willing to condemn Wycherly to death for her own convenience—had accepted the bloodline's imperatives without really trying to fight back—had nearly poisoned a woman who had only been trying to help her.

The temptation to stay where she was—to refuse to try for the key and thus ensure she'd never taste the bitter failure that had brought Athanais to this cell—was a sweet lure. Maybe she should just take the time to think the whole thing over carefully, maybe take a nap here on this bunk.

No. You've got to escape. You've got to get back to the others. Truth's right; if I can't make up for the past I can at least take responsibility for the future—good or bad!

Sinah gritted her teeth, squared her shoulders against everything she'd ever feared, and stepped forward.

She passed through the door.

This was real.

Dylan stood in the doorway of his office, seeing the copper key gleaming on the desk/double cube only a few feet away. He could already sense how it would feel in his hands, chill and smooth and heavy.

This was no dream, no reverie, no stress-triggered hallucination. This was re-ality—Truth's reality.

This was what she'd been trying to tell him. She did not live by fantasy or acts of faith; she saw reality—her reality—and acted accordingly.

For a moment Dylan wavered. He could close his eyes, turn back, slam the door. Not come down four-square on the side of—of sorcery, for God's sake; not an allegory, not a metaphor—real magick. Something far removed from religion or even prayer; a willful reaching into some invisible realm to . . .

To make a laughingstock of yourself insisting that things exist which aren't even important to most people.

But the key was here. And if it was real, so was all the rest. If he had the courage to believe in it.

"Observer-created reality." A catchphrase the boys in the physics department liked to bandy about flitted through Dylan's head. So be it. This was the reality he created, and God have mercy on his soul.

"In the beginning. . . . "

Dylan reached for the key.

Wycherly stood on the edge of the river for one agonizing moment. He knew that in one sense this was not real—that no matter what he did in the next few moments, Camilla would still be dead a dozen years ago.

He looked back at his father—at the image of his father. It was not really Kenneth Sr.—even if Wycherly threw himself into the river now, he would not change his father's opinion of him. Even if he went home, confronted the Honorable Randolph J. Benson with the truth, got him to confess that he'd been the one driving that night—it would not matter. In his father's eyes—in the world's eyes—Wycherly would always be a failure.

It was easier to be a failure.

It was safe.

There was something out there in that river—if not Cammie, then the ghosts of everyone else he'd hurt or betrayed throughout his life. They were waiting for him, waiting to drag Wycherly down to lingering, agonizing death. He could see the white gleam of their serpent-bodies beneath the black glass of the water. They were out there. They were as real as the car, the key, Camilla. . . .

With a sob, Wycherly stumbled into the water, shambling clumsily out until it was deep enough to swim.

The water was icy, numbing his body until he could not tell whether serpent hands caressed him or not. He reached the Fiat, clinging to the door to keep from being swept away by the current while he worked to open it. When it finally yielded, the shock made the car slip beneath the surface.

Only seconds.

Wycherly reached for Camilla, and felt the clasp of ophidian fingers, burning and implacable, closing about his ankle. Tears of terror ran down his face as he ignored them, dragging Camilla out of the car, up to the surface. He felt her body shudder as she dragged life-giving air into her lungs, and knew that this moment was the end of every certainty in his life.

He reached past her for the gleam of gold still inside the car.

"Go through that door," the bright presence said. "Or . . . stay here with us."

Truth looked around herself, and all of a sudden her perspective shifted. THIS was the Bright Realm. She had already passed through the Gate. Beyond the door lay only the Otherworld that led to human realms.

She could stay here and leave the confusion of soft emotions behind, flee a world that thought of her as a cross between a sideshow and an outpatient. Return to a world that was Truth's own far more than Earth could ever be. Dylan didn't want her—he didn't believe in her; he'd never be her proper mate.

She could stay here. She could even close the door from this side, a parting gift to the foolish Earth-children who'd presumed to treat her as an equal. This would be the only chance she would ever get. Stay.

And be as much an outsider here?

Truth looked at the shining being. Cold, perfect, pure . . .

And heartless. Stay, and the part of herself that loved would have no place.

"No," Truth said sadly, and stepped through the door.

She reached for the silver key. It was cold and smooth and heavy in her hands.

"I am the key for every lock. . . ."

* * *

No one was perfect. No one person could be enough. But this time it was human weakness, not human strength, that the spell was woven of, the lacks in mind and heart and hand and will that all of them fought and lived with every day—those everyday battles became the substance of the battle they fought now.

And Sinah chose good—

And Dylan chose freedom—

And Wycherly chose love—

And Truth chose service—

Not aiming for miracles, not aiming for perfection, but trusting that human strength and human goodwill would be enough.

And in the end it was. The fourfold being took the key forged from all of them, courage and honesty and persistence and patience, and set it into the lock.

As if the will and the gesture had been enough, the Gate swung shut, pulling the key from their hands, and then the key, the lock, the Gate, the hill—all were gone.

Truth opened her eyes.

The hazard flare still burned.

"When do we . . . oh," Sinah said, meeting Truth's eyes with sudden comprehension.

"'Oh,' indeed," Dylan said, opening his eyes. He took a deep breath. "Darling, I think it's time for a long talk—a real one, this time." He smiled.

"It worked," Truth said, shutting her eyes tightly against the stinging of sudden tears. *Never to go home, never, never, never . . .* a part of her mourned. But she'd made her choice.

They all had.

Wycherly groaned, opening his eyes and reaching out groggily. His bandaged hand brushed Sinah's knee and he recoiled with a mew of pain.

"Oh . . . God," Wycherly moaned faintly, lying back against Sinah and closing his eyes in exhaustion.

Truth scurried to rescue her working tools, looking to Dylan before she snuffed the candle. She packed them away carefully.

"Wycherly—no!" Sinah cried in protest.

* * *

The bandage had darkened where Wycherly had bumped it; Sinah had unwrapped it, thinking of bleeding and burst stitches, but what she found instead caused her to cry out in dismay. If there had ever been stitches they'd been torn out long since by the swelling, and the raw, blood-red edges of the cut gaped wide.

The foul smell of infection rose from the wound. A jellylike, greenish-white pus oozed from pockets on the palm and the wrist, and the skin around the incision was the deep purple-black of emperor grapes. Angry red lines ran up his arm, as bright as if they were painted on. Gangrene.

"This doesn't look good," Dylan said, shining the torch down at Wycherly's hand. The white light made all the colors more vivid, brilliantly ugly.

"We've got to get him to a doctor—him and Luned both," Truth said. "Dylan, can you spare a T-shirt to get that wrapped up again?"

"No. Let me," Sinah said suddenly.

She lay Wycherly down on the scuffed chalk sigil. His eyes glittered feverishly with the pain, fixed on her face as if the sight of her could save him.

So each of them had looked who had come to her for healing.

The bloodline's knowledge was fading from Sinah's mind—the knowledge, the power, her own fey gifts, all fading away now that the Wellspring was sealed. But for a few minutes more some scrap of power remained.

She knelt beside Wycherly, and clasped his swollen, seeping hand between both of her own, summoning the spirit of the Athanais Dellon who had been the bloodline's greatest healer.

There were two patterns here—the thing as it was, and the thing as it ought to be, whole and healed. Slowly Sinah/Athanais erased the discrepancies between them, and as she did, she felt the power that she wove with slip away, fading as a stove's heat does once the cooking is done.

Until at last the power was gone, the last echoes of it stilled.

And the hand between her own bled freely—clean, honest blood with no taint of rot in it.

The last echoes faded, and Sinah was alone.

Wycherly opened his eyes and sighed. "I had the strangest dream," he whispered to her, reaching for her with his free hand.

No. Not alone.

* * *

"Come on," Dylan said, holding out a hand.

"Dylan—look!" Truth said.

All three of them turned to where Truth was pointing.

The surface of the Wellspring was sinking, as though, with the passing of the power, the water, too, was vanishing into the living rock once more. In moments, all that was left was a small pool cradled in the bottom of the bare rock basin, and then that too was gone.

Truth shrugged wryly and hefted her tool bag onto her shoulder. Dylan turned back to Wycherly.

"Can you stand?"

"On my own two feet," Wycherly said, as Dylan and Sinah helped him upright. "And doesn't that sound damned significant?"

NINETEEN

THE PEACE OF THE GRAVE

But an old age, serene and bright,
And lovely as a Lapland night,
Shall lead thee to thy grave.
—WILLIAM WORDSWORTH

IT WAS AUGUST 17, AND TRUTH WAS BIDDING FAREWELL to two of the three people she was now closer to than anyone else on earth. After all that had happened, there didn't seem to be a lot of reason for the party from the Bidney Institute to stay in Morton's Fork any longer. Rowan had already driven the rental car back to Elkins, and the other three would pick her up there in the camper before beginning the long drive back to New York.

Wycherly's hand was in bandages, though this time the cut was healing normally. Luned Starking was still in the hospital in Elkins, being treated for shock, exposure, and her long-term immersion in the icy waters of the spring. Wycherly had taken cheerful responsibility for the hospital bill, and according to the doctors, her arm had escaped permanent damage. Luned should recover from her ordeal without any ill effects.

"Are you two sure you're going to be all right?" Truth asked again.

"For the tenth time—yes," Sinah said, laughing. Wycherly tightened his good arm around her waist.

Truth doubted that either Wycherly or Sinah had the least desire for any more involvement with the Unseen World, but she didn't have to choose her friends on the basis of their magickal power.

She supposed she ought to phone and tell Michael the Gate was sealed. He could come back sometime and consecrate the site of Quentin's temple to his heart's content. At least, he could consecrate whatever he could find after the explosion. None of the four of them had seen any reason the site should remain at all, and they had needed to dispose of the dynamite, if not of quite so much of it as Wycherly had originally carted down there.

"You'll visit?" Truth asked. "You'll write? You both have to come to the wedding—oh, Wycherly; your sister will be there—" she said contritely.

"That's all right," Wycherly said grandly. "I suppose I ought to get a look at the fortune-hunting gigolo she married," he added banteringly.

"And I guess I'd better actually make those phone calls and see if I have a career left," Sinah said. "Or if I even want one. I may not even be any good any more," she said halfheartedly.

"You can find that out when the time comes," Dylan said. "And if there's anything I can do to help . . . ?"

"Do you really mean that?" Sinah said, only half joking. "It's going to be harder than I ever imagined—guessing what people mean instead of knowing. I'll make so many mistakes!"

"Everyone does," Truth said. For a moment her eyes were remote, but the shadow passed. "And you, Wycherly?"

"I'm going home to say goodbye," Wycherly said. "My father's dying. I suppose I owe him a last chance to tell me I'm worthless." He smiled—only a little bitterly—at Sinah. "Want to come with me? It's a great place to practice guessing the truth, and Mother will have a fit."

"Let her," Sinah said. "I have ancestors that fought on *both* sides in the Civil War and met the Mayflower, besides. And Morton's Fork isn't really home for me—it never was. Maybe we can find home together."

To which Truth, her arm around Dylan's waist, could only add "Amen."

> *A kiss is but a kiss now! and no wave*
> *Of a great flood that whirls me to the sea.*
> *But, as you will! we'll sit contentedly,*
> *And eat our pot of honey on the grave.*
> —GEORGE MEREDITH
> *"Modern Love"*